CW01456475

THE
WOMAN
IN
DARKNESS

Books by Charlie Donlea

SUMMIT LAKE

THE GIRL WHO WAS TAKEN

DON'T BELIEVE IT

THE WOMAN IN DARKNESS

THE WOMAN IN DARKNESS

Charlie Donlea

BANTAM
SYDNEY AUCKLAND TORONTO NEW YORK LONDON

BANTAM

UK | USA | Canada | Ireland | Australia
India | New Zealand | South Africa | China

Penguin
Random House
Australia

Addresses for the Penguin Random House group of companies can be found at
global.penguinrandomhouse.com/offices.

First published in the United States by Kensington Publishing Corp. in 2019
First published in Australia by Bantam, an imprint of Penguin Random House
Australia Pty Ltd, in 2019

Copyright © Charlie Donlea 2019

The moral right of the author has been asserted.

All rights reserved. No part of this publication may be reproduced,
published, performed in public or communicated to the public in
any form or by any means without prior written permission from
Penguin Random House Australia Pty Ltd or its authorised licensees.

Cover design by James Rendall © Penguin Random House Australia Pty Ltd
Cover photograph © Getty Images/Dmitry Ageev
Printed and bound in Australia by Griffin Press, an accredited ISO AS/NZS 14001
Environmental Management Systems printer

A catalogue record for this
book is available from the
National Library of Australia

NATIONAL
LIBRARY
OF AUSTRALIA

ISBN 978 0 14379 515 5

penguin.com.au

MIX
Paper from
responsible sources
FSC
www.fsc.org   FSC® C009448

For Cecilia A. Donat
Great-aunt, old lady, friend

I fear I am writing a requiem for myself.
—Mozart

THE RUSH
Chicago, August 9, 1979

*T*HE NOOSE TIGHTENED AROUND HIS NECK, AND THE OXYGEN DEPRI-vation spun his head into a splendid mix of euphoria and panic. He allowed the nylon to take the full weight of his body as he eased off the stool. Those who did not understand "The Rush" would consider his pulley system barbaric, and no one but him fully knew its power. The Rush was a sensation more formidable than any narcotic. There was no other vector of life that could provide an equal experience. Quite simply, it was all he lived for.

As he lowered himself off the stool, the rope to which the nylon noose was tethered creaked with the strain of his body as it slithered through the grooved rim of the pulley while he sunk toward the floor. The rope curved over the winch, ran down to a second pulley, then back up and around the third and final crank to form an M.

Attached to the other end of the rope was another strap of soft nylon, which was wrapped around his victim's neck. Every time he lowered himself from the safety of the stool, the nylon around his neck took her weight as she levitated like magic off the ground six feet in front of him.

Her panic was finally gone. There was no more kicking or flailing. When she rose now, it was dreamlike. The Rush saturated his soul, and the image of her floating in midair enraptured his mind. He took her weight as long as he could bear, bringing himself to the brink of unconsciousness and to the edge of ecstasy. He closed his eyes briefly. So tempting was the lure to continue toward the high, but he knew the dangers of allowing himself to wander too far down that lurid path. To travel too long on its trail would prevent return. Still, he couldn't resist.

With the nylon tight against his throat, he focused his half-closed eyes on his victim hovering across from him. The noose tightened its grip, pinched his carotid, and formed spots in his vision. He let go momentarily, closing his eyes and giving in to the darkness. Just for a bit. Just for a second more.

THE AFTERMATH
Chicago, August 9, 1979

WHEN HE CAME BACK TO THE PRESENT, HE GASPED FOR AIR, BUT none would come. In a panic, he searched with his foot for the edge of the stool until his toes found the flat wooden surface. He stepped onto it and relieved the pressure from his neck, taking huge swallows of air as his victim sunk to the floor in front of him. Her legs no longer supported her when she reached the concrete. Instead, she crumpled in a heap, the weight of her body pulling his end of the rope until the thick safety knot lodged on his side of the pulley, keeping the noose slack around his neck.

He pulled the soft nylon over his head and allowed time for the redness to leave his skin. He knew he'd gone too far tonight. Despite the protective foam collar he wore, he'd have to find a way to hide the deep purple bruising on his neck. He needed to be more careful now than he'd ever been before. The public had started to catch on. Newspaper articles began to crop up. The authorities had put out warnings, and fear was rising above the warmth of summer. With the public's heightened awareness, he had begun to stalk more carefully, plan more deliberately, and cover his tracks more thoroughly. The bodies he could hide, he had found the perfect location. The Rush was more difficult to contain, and he worried that the veil covering his secret life would be pulled away by his own inability to conceal the elation he carried in the days after his sessions. He would be smart to shut things down. Lie low and wait for the panic to calm. But The Rush was too much to ignore. His existence depended on it.

Sitting on the stool, he turned his back to his victim. He took a moment to bring his emotions under control. When he was ready, he turned to the body to begin the clean up and preparation for transport the next day. When he was finished, he locked the place up and climbed into his vehicle. The ride home did little to tame the residual effects of The Rush. When he pulled to the front curb, he saw the lights of the house extinguished. It was a good thing tonight. His body was still trembling, and he could not have managed normal conversation. Inside, he dropped his clothes in the washing machine, took a quick shower, and climbed into bed.

She stirred as he pulled the covers over himself.

"What time is it?" she asked with her eyes closed, head sunk into the pillow.

"Late." He kissed her cheek. "Go back to sleep."

She slid her leg over his body and draped her arm across his chest. He lay on his back, staring up at the ceiling. It usually took hours for him to settle down after he returned. He closed his eyes and tried to control the adrenaline that coursed through his veins. His mind replayed the past few hours. He was never able to remember it all, not clearly and not so soon after. In the weeks ahead, the details would come back to him. But tonight, behind closed lids, his eyes fluttered in wild saccades as the memory center in his mind offered brief sparks of the evening. His victim's face. The terror in her eyes. The nylon noose at a sharp angle around her neck.

The images and sounds swirled through his mind in a fast flurry, and as he further played out the fantasy, the sheets stirred next to him as she woke. She curled farther into his side. With The Rush pounding in his veins, the flushing of endorphins through the dilated blood vessels audible in his ears, he allowed her to kiss his neck, then his shoulder. He permitted her hand to sink to the waist of his boxer shorts. The Rush overtook him, and he rolled on top of her. He kept his eyes closed as she let out soft moans, which he blocked from his mind.

He thought of his workspace. Of the darkness. Of the way he could lay himself bare when he was in that place. He took on an easy rhythm and focused on the woman he had brought there earlier in the night. The woman who had levitated like a ghost in front of him.

4

THE SWEET SCENT OF ROSES

*T*HE WOMAN REACHED INTO THE GARDEN, PINCHED THE CLIPPERS TO THE *base of the rose, and severed its stem. She repeated the process until she had six long-stemmed red roses in her hand. She climbed the stairs to her back porch, placed the roses on the table, and sat down in the rocking chair. Staring out over the field, she watched the young girl approach, climb the stairs, and walk up to her.*

Her voice was high-pitched and innocent, the way all children's voices should be.

"Why do you always take roses from the garden?" the young girl asked.

"Because they're beautiful. And if they're left on the vine, they'll eventually wither and go to waste. If I prune them, I can put them to better use."

"Do you want me to tie them?" the girl asked.

She was ten years old and the sweetest thing to ever come into the woman's life. From her apron, the woman removed a twist tie, handed it to the girl, and watched as she carefully picked up the roses. Avoiding the thorns, the girl wrapped the tie around the stems, twisting until it bound the bouquet in a tight bundle.

"What do you do with the flowers?" the girl asked.

The woman took the perfect bundle from her. "Go inside and clean up for dinner."

"I see you pick them every day, and I tie them for you. But I never see the flowers again."

The woman smiled. "We've got work to do after dinner. I'll let you do the painting tonight, if you think your hand is steady enough."

The woman hoped the bait was enough to veer the conversation.

The girl smiled. *"You'll let me paint all by myself?"*

"Yes. It's time you learn."

"I'll do a good job, I promise," she said before running into the house.

The woman waited just a moment, until she heard dishes clinking inside as the girl set the dinner table. Then she stood from the rocker, carefully arranged the newly bundled roses, and walked down the porch steps and out across the field behind the house. The sun was setting and the shadows of birch trees cut across her path.

As she walked, she lifted the flowers to her nose and inhaled the sweet scent of roses.

PART I

THE THIEF

CHAPTER 1
Chicago, September 30, 2019

*T*HE CHEST PAINS HAD STARTED THE YEAR BEFORE.

There was never a question about their source. They were stress-induced, and the doctors promised they would never kill him. Tonight's episode was particularly distressing, though, waking him from sleep with a cool chill of night sweats. He tried to suck for air, but it was like breathing through a cocktail straw. The harder he worked to inhale, the more distraught he became. He sat up in bed and fought the fear of suffocation. History told him the episode would pass. He reached for the bottle of aspirin he kept in the nightstand drawer and placed one, along with a nitroglycerine tablet, under his tongue. After ten minutes, the muscles of his chest relaxed and his lungs were able to expand.

It was no coincidence that this most recent bout of angina coincided with the arrival of the parole board letter, which sat on his nightstand. He had spent time reading the letter before he fell to sleep. Accompanying the letter was the judge's summons for a meeting. He grabbed the document now as he climbed from bed, his sweat-soaked shirt cold against his skin as he walked down the stairs and headed to his office. He twisted the combination lock on the safe under his desk and pulled open the door. Inside was a stack of old parole board letters, to which he added the latest.

The first parole hearing correspondence had arrived a decade before. Twice a year, the board met with his client, denying him his freedom and explaining their decision in a properly worded essay that would stand up against appeals and protests. But last year, a different document arrived. It was a lengthy review by the board chairperson, who described in rich detail how impressed the board was with his client's progress over the years, and how his client was the very definition of "rehabilitation." It was after reading the final sentence of that letter, which indicated the parole board's enthusiasm for their next review and the suggestion that great opportunities lay ahead for his client, when the chest pains had begun.

This latest correspondence marked the arrival of a slow-moving train that carried as its freight pain and misery, secrets and lies. That proverbial train had always been just a speck on the horizon, never making progress. But now it was a full barreling freighter growing larger by the day, impossible to stop, despite his many efforts. Sitting behind his desk, he stared at the middle shelf of the safe. A file folder was stuffed fat with pages from his investigation. An exploration that, during times of sorrow and angst like tonight, he wished he'd never embarked upon. The ramifications of his findings, however, were so profound and life-altering that he knew he would be empty had he not. And the idea that his own lies and deceptions might soon crawl from the shadows under which they had rested for years was enough to cause his heart to, literally, ache.

He wiped the layer of perspiration from his forehead and worked hard to fill his lungs with breath. His biggest fear was that his client would soon be free to continue the search. The investigation, which had been declared fruitless, would enjoy a resurgence once his client walked from prison. This, he knew, could not happen. Everything in his power must be done to prevent it.

Alone in his study, he felt a new chill come upon his body as his saturated shirt pressed to his shoulders. He closed the safe and spun the dial. The chest pains returned, his lungs tightened, and he leaned back in his chair to fight again the panic of suffocation. It would pass. It always did.

CHAPTER 2
Chicago, October 1, 2019

*R*ORY MOORE INSERTED HER CONTACT LENSES, ROLLED HER EYES, and blinked to bring the world into focus. She despised the vision her Coke-bottle glasses offered—a bowed and distorted world when compared to the crispness of her contacts—but she loved the shelter her thick-rimmed frames provided. So, a compromise. After her contact lenses settled, she slipped non-prescription glasses onto her face and hid behind the plastic casings like a warrior ducking behind a shield. To Rory, each day was a battle.

They agreed to meet at the Harold Washington Library Center on State Street, and thirty minutes after Rory had dressed in her protective armor—thick-framed glasses, beanie hat pulled low, coat buttoned to her chin with the collar up—she climbed from her car and walked into the library. Initial meetings with clients always took place in public locations. Of course, most collectors had trouble with this arrangement because it meant hauling their precious trophies out into the daylight. But if they wanted Rory Moore and her restoration skills, they'd follow her rules.

Today's meeting called for more attention than normal, since it had been arranged as a favor for Detective Ron Davidson, who was not only a trusted friend but also her boss. Since this was her side job, or what others annoyingly called her "hobby," some part of her was honored that Davidson had reached out. Not everyone understood the complicated personality of Rory Moore, but over the years, Ron Davidson had broken through to win her admiration. When he asked for a favor, Rory never gave it a second thought.

As she walked through the library doors, Rory immediately recognized the Kestner doll that was housed in a long, thin box and resting in the arms of the man waiting in the lobby. The blink of an eye and a quick glance at the gentleman holding the box was all it took for Rory to run through her appraisal of him, her thoughts flashing like lightning through her mind: midfifties, wealthy, a professional of some sort—business, medicine, or law—cleanly shaven, polished shoes, sport coat, no tie. She quickly backtracked and rejected the initial thought of a doctor or lawyer. He was a small-business owner. Insurance or similar.

She took a deep breath, arranged her glasses squarely on her face, and walked up to him.

"Mr. Byrd?"

"Yes," the man said. "Rory?"

The man, a full twelve inches taller than Rory's five-two stature, looked down on her petite frame and waited for confirmation. Rory offered none.

"Let's see what you've got," she said, pointing at the porcelain doll that was carefully packaged in the box, before walking into the main section of the library.

Mr. Byrd followed her to a table in the corner. The library was only scantly populated in the middle of the afternoon. Rory patted the table and Mr. Byrd laid the box down.

"What's the issue?" Rory asked.

"This is my daughter's Kestner doll. It was a gift for her fifth birthday, and has been kept in pristine condition."

Rory leaned over the table to get a better look at the doll through the plastic window in the box. The porcelain face was badly split down the middle, the crack starting somewhere beyond the doll's hairline, running through the left eye socket and down the cheek.

"I dropped it," Mr. Byrd said. "I'm beside myself that I was so careless."

Rory nodded. "Let me have a look?"

He pushed the box toward her and Rory carefully unlocked the latch and lifted the lid. She inspected the damaged doll like a surgeon's initial assessment of an anesthetized patient lying on the operating table.

"Cracked or shattered?" she asked.

Mr. Byrd reached into his pocket and produced a ziplock bag that contained small pieces of porcelain. Rory noticed his thyroid cartilage rise and fall as he swallowed hard to control his emotions.

"These were everything I could find. I dropped it on hardwood, so I think I located all the pieces."

Rory took the bag and analyzed the shards. She went back to the doll and gently ran her fingers over the fractured porcelain. The split was well opposed and should come together nicely. The restoration of the cheek and forehead could be made to look flawless. The eye socket was another issue. It would take all her skill to restore, and she'd likely need help from the one person who was better than Rory at restoring dolls. The shattered portion, Rory was sure, would be found on the back of the head. The repair there, too, would be challenging due to the hair and the small bits of porcelain she held in the ziplock bag. She didn't want to remove the doll from the box until she was in her workshop for fear that more porcelain might fall from the shattered area.

She nodded slowly, keeping her gaze on the doll.

"I can fix this."

"Thank God," Mr. Byrd said.

"Two weeks. A month, maybe."

"As long as it takes."

"I'll let you know the pricing after I get started."

"I don't care what it costs. As long as you can fix it."

Rory nodded again. She placed the ziplock bag containing the shattered pieces into the box, closed the lid, and relatched the lock.

"I'll need a phone number where I can reach you," she said.

Mr. Byrd fished a business card from his wallet and handed it to her. Rory glanced at it before sticking it into her pocket: BYRD INSURANCE GROUP. WALTER BYRD, OWNER.

Rory attempted to lift the box and leave when Mr. Byrd put his hand on hers. A stranger's touch had never been well tolerated, and Rory was about to recoil when he spoke.

"The doll belonged to my daughter," he said in a soft voice.

The past tense caught Rory's attention. It was meant to. Rory looked at the man's hand on her own, and then met his eyes.

"She died last year," Mr. Byrd said.

Rory slowly sat down. A normal response might have been *I'm sorry for your loss.* Or, *I see why this doll means so much to you.* But Rory Moore was anything but normal.

"What happened to her?" Rory asked.

"She was killed," Mr. Byrd said, taking his hand off Rory's and sitting down across from her. "Strangled, they think. Her body was left in Grant Park last January, half-frozen by the time she was found."

Rory looked back at the Kestner doll resting in the box, the right eye shut peacefully, the left eye open and askew with a deep fissure running through the orbit. She understood what was happening, and knew why Detective Davidson had been so adamant that she take this meeting. It was a classic bait and switch that Davidson knew Rory would be helpless to resist.

"They never found him?" Rory asked.

Mr. Byrd shook his head, dropping his gaze to his dead daughter's doll. "Never had so much as a lead. None of the detectives return my calls anymore. It feels like they've simply moved on."

Rory's presence in the library that morning proved Mr. Byrd's statement false, since it was Ron Davidson who had convinced her to come.

Mr. Byrd brought his gaze back to her.

"Listen, this is not a setup. I reached for Camille's doll the other day because I was badly missing my daughter and needed to hold something that reminded me of her. I dropped the goddamn thing and shattered it. I couldn't bring myself to tell my wife because I feel so guilty, and I know it would send her into a fit of depression. This doll was my daughter's favorite possession through her childhood. So please believe me that I want you to restore it. But Detective Davidson told me that your work as a forensic reconstructionist is heralded in the City of Chicago, and beyond. I'm prepared to pay you anything it takes for you to reconstruct the crime and find the man who wrapped his hands around my daughter's neck and choked the life from her."

Mr. Byrd's stare became too much for Rory to handle, penetrating the protective shield of her non-prescription glasses. She finally stood, lifted the Kestner doll box off the table, and secured it under her arm.

14

"The doll will take a month. Your daughter, much longer. Let me make some calls and I'll be in touch."

Rory walked out of the library and into the fall morning. She felt it as soon as Camille Byrd's father had used the past tense to describe his daughter, that subtle tingling in her mind. That nearly imperceptible, but now ever-present, whisper in her ears. A murmur her boss knew goddamn well she wouldn't be able to ignore.

"You're a real son of a bitch, Ron," Rory said as she exited the library. She had been on hiatus from her job as a forensic reconstructionist, a scheduled break she forced herself to take every so often to avoid burnout and depression. This most recent pause had been longer than any of her others, and was starting to piss off her boss.

As she walked along State Street and back to her car, with Camille Byrd's shattered doll under her arm, Rory knew the vacation was over.

CHAPTER 3
Chicago, October 2, 2019

*H*ER PHONE BUZZED FOR THE FIFTH TIME THAT MORNING, WHICH she again ignored. Rory stared at her reflection in the mirror as she pulled her dark brown hair back and tied it off. She was not a morning person and on principle did not answer her phone before noon. Her boss knew this, so Rory felt no remorse for ignoring him.

"Who is incessantly calling you?" a voice asked from the bedroom.

"I'm meeting Davidson."

"I didn't know you decided to go back to work," the man said.

Rory walked from the bathroom and slipped her watch onto her wrist. "Am I going to see you tonight?" she asked.

"Okay, we won't talk about it."

Rory came over and kissed him on the mouth. Lane Phillips had been her, what? Rory wasn't traditional enough to label him a "boyfriend," and this far into her thirties, she thought the description sounded juvenile. She'd never considered marrying him, despite that they'd slept together for the better part of the last decade. But he was much more than her lover. He was the only man on this planet, aside from her father, who understood her. Lane was . . . hers, that was the best Rory could do in her own mind, and they were both okay with that.

"I'll tell you about it when I have something to tell. Right now, I don't know what I'm getting myself into."

"Fair enough," Lane said, sitting up in bed. "I've been asked to appear as an expert witness on a homicide trial. I'll be testifying in a couple of weeks, so I'm meeting with the DA today. Then I'm teaching until nine tonight."

When Rory tried to back away, he grabbed her hips.

"Are you sure you won't give me any clues about what Davidson lured you back with?"

"Stop by tonight after your class and I'll catch you up."

Rory gave him another kiss, batted away his roaming hands, and walked out of the bedroom. A minute later, the front door opened and closed.

Her phone rang two more times as she sat in morning traffic on the Kennedy Expressway. She exited on Ohio Street and snaked through the grid-pattern streets of Chicago. She pushed through the congestion until she reached Grant Park, circled the side streets for fifteen minutes until she found a parking spot too small for even her tiny Honda. Somehow she managed a brave parallel parking maneuver, unsure if she'd be able to escape the twisting and turning and bumper kissing when it was time to leave.

She walked through the tunnel that cut under Lake Shore Drive and along the picturesque path until she came to the cusp of the park. Grant Park was a magnificent piece of real estate that separated the high-rise buildings of The Loop from the lakefront. The park was always a popular destination with tourists, and this morning was no exception. Rory walked through the crowds until she spotted Ron Davidson sitting on a bench near Buckingham Fountain.

Despite that her coat was already buttoned to her neck, she pulled it tight, lifted her collar, and pushed her glasses up the bridge of her nose. It was a mild October morning and others around her wore shorts and sweatshirts, enjoying the lake breeze and bright sunshine. Rory was dressed for a brisk fall day: gray coat secured top to bottom, collar up, gray jeans, and lace-up Madden Girl Eloisee combat boots, which she wore everywhere, including during the dog days of summer. As Rory approached the detective, she pulled her slouchy fleece beanie down on her forehead. The edge of the hat touched the top of her glasses. She felt protected.

Without introduction, she sat down next to him.

"Well, Christ be the king, it's the lady in gray," Davidson said.

The two had worked enough cases together for Davidson to know all of Rory's quirks. She shook hands with no one, something Davidson had learned after a few attempts where his hand floated in the air while Rory averted her eyes. She hated meeting with department personnel other than Ron, and she had little tolerance for red tape. She had never accepted a deadline on a job, and worked strictly solo on her cases. She returned calls at her leisure, and sometimes not at all. She hated politics, and if anyone—from an alderman to the mayor—tried to pull Rory into the spotlight, she disappeared for weeks. If her skills as a forensic reconstructionist weren't so outstanding, Ron Davidson would never tolerate the headaches she caused.

"You've been off the grid, Gray."

Rory allowed the corners of her mouth to curl slightly while she stared at Buckingham Fountain. No one but Davidson called her "Gray," and over the years Rory had warmed to the nickname—a combination of her attire and her detached outward persona.

"Busy with life."

"How's Lane?"

"Fine."

"Is he a better boss than me?"

"He's not my boss."

"Yet you spend all your time working for him."

"Working *with* him."

Ron Davidson paused for a moment. "You haven't returned a call for six months."

"I told you I was on hiatus."

"There were a few cases I could have used your help on."

"I was getting burned out. I needed a break. Why do you think most of the detectives who work for you aren't worth a shit?"

"Ah, I missed your candor, Gray."

They sat in peaceful silence for a few minutes people-watching the tourists who passed through the park.

"Will you help me?" Davidson finally asked.

"You're a real bastard for doing it that way," Rory said.

"You hadn't returned a call for half a year. You've been too preoccupied with Lane Phillips and his Murder Accountability Project. So, I got creative. I thought you'd appreciate it."

More silence.

"Well?" Davidson asked again when enough time had passed.

"I'm here, aren't I?" Rory kept her focus on the fountain. "Tell me about her."

"Camille Byrd. Twenty-two-year-old gal who was strangled. Body was dumped in the park here."

"When?"

"Last year, January. Twenty-one months," Davidson said.

"And you guys have nothing?"

"I made some threats and banged some pots, but my guys are stumped on this one, Rory."

"I'll need the files on the case," Rory said, still looking at the fountain, but noticing the bend in Davidson's neck as the head of Chicago Homicide looked up subtly and exhaled in relief.

"Thank you," he said.

"Who is Walter Byrd?"

"Wealthy businessman and a personal friend of the mayor's, so there's been some urgency on the squad to put this one to rest."

"Because he's rich and connected?" Rory asked. "There should be urgency for any parent whose child is killed. Where was her body found?"

Davidson pointed. "East side of the park. I'll show you."

Rory stood and allowed Davidson to take the lead as they walked. They made it through the park until they came to a grassy knoll off the walking path. A row of birch trees flanked each side of the area, and Rory's mind calculated the ways someone could transport a body to this location.

Davidson walked onto the grass. "Her body was found here."

"Strangled?"

Davidson nodded.

"Rape?"

"No."

Rory walked to the location where Camille Byrd's body had been found, and turned in a slow circle, taking in the lakefront and the boats resting on the water. She continued to turn and saw the Chicago

19

skyline. Fat white clouds hovered like overinflated balloons in the otherwise-blue sky. She imagined the girl's body found in the dead of winter, bloated and lifeless and frozen through. She imagined the bare trees of January, the foliage stripped by cold.

"Dump her here. Why?" she said. "It's such a risk with no protection from the trees. Whoever did this wanted her to be found."

"Unless he killed her here. Something got out of control. A heated argument. He kills her and runs."

"That's a lovers' quarrel," Rory said. "And I'm assuming your guys exhausted that angle. Talked to all her boyfriends, current and past? Workmates, old flames."

Davidson nodded. "Covered and cleared, all of them."

"Then it wasn't someone she knew. She was killed elsewhere and brought here. Why?"

"My guys don't know."

"I need everything, Ron. Files, autopsy, interviews. Everything."

"I can get you all of it, but I've got to put you back on the payroll to do it. Make it official that you're working again. Then I can get you anything you need."

Rory went silent again as her eyes took in the scene. So many things were firing in her brain. She knew herself well enough not to attempt to tame the influx of information. She wasn't aware of everything she was learning. She knew only to take it all in, and then, in the days and weeks ahead, her brain would sort out the things it was calculating and inventory the images it was capturing. Slowly Rory would organize it all. She'd study the case file. She'd get to know Camille Byrd. She'd put a name and narrative to this poor girl who had been strangled to death. She'd see things the detectives had missed. Rory's uncanny mind would piece together bits of a puzzle everyone else had deemed unsolvable until she had reconstructed the crime in its entirety.

Her phone rang, pulling Rory back from the inner workings of her mind. It was her father calling. She thought about letting it go to voice mail, but decided to answer it.

"Dad, I'm in the middle of something. Can I call you back?"

"Rory?"

She didn't recognize the voice on the other end of the call, only that it was female and panicked.

"Yes?" She took a few steps away from Davidson.

"Rory, it's Celia Banner. Your father's assistant."

"What's wrong? My dad's number came up on my phone."

"I'm calling from his house. Something's wrong, Rory. He had a heart attack."

"What?"

"We were supposed to meet for breakfast, he never showed. It's bad, Rory."

"How bad?"

The silence was like a vacuum that sucked the words from Rory's mouth. "Celia! How bad?"

"He's gone, Rory."

CHAPTER 4
Chicago, October 14, 2019

*I*T TOOK A FULL WEEK AFTER THE FUNERAL BEFORE RORY FOUND THE time, and the gumption, to enter her father's office. Technically, it was her office as well, but since she hadn't handled a formal case in more than a decade, Rory's involvement in the Moore Law Group was not immediately evident. Her name was on the letterhead, and she drew a 1099 every year for the limited work she did for her father—mostly research and trial prep—but as her role at the Chicago Police Department and Lane's Murder Accountability Project demanded more of her attention over the years, the work she did for the firm became less obvious.

Besides Rory's occasional employment, the Moore Law Group was a one-man firm with two employees—a paralegal and an office administrator. With an anorexic staff and a manageable roster of clients, Rory assumed the dissolution of her father's law practice would require a bit of time and expertise, but would, ultimately, be conquerable in a couple of weeks of concentrated work. Rory's law degree, something she earned more than a decade ago, but had never truly put to use, made her the perfect and only candidate to take care of her father's business affairs. Her mother had passed years before and Rory had no siblings.

Rory entered the building on North Clark Street and rode the elevator to the third floor. She keyed the door and pushed it open. The reception area consisted of a desk in front of tan metal file cabinets straight out of the seventies, and was flanked by two offices. The one on the left was her father's; the other belonged to the paralegal.

She dropped a week's worth of mail onto the front desk and headed into her father's office. Her first order of business would be to shuffle the active cases to other law firms. Once the firm's docket was cleared, there would be the matter of paying bills and settling payroll for the staff with whatever funds were stashed away. Then Rory could close the lease on the building and shut the place down.

Celia, the office administrator and the one who had discovered her father dead in his home, had agreed to meet at noon to go through the files and help with reassignment. Rory settled her purse on the ground, popped open a Diet Coke, and got started. By noon, a mountain of paperwork surrounded her as she sat at her father's desk. She had emptied the file cabinets from the reception area, and the contents were now organized into three stacks—pending, active, and retired.

She heard the front door open. Celia, a woman she'd met a handful of times over the years, appeared in the doorway to her father's office. Rory stood.

"Oh, Rory," Celia said, rushing past the stacks of files to embrace her in a tight hug.

Rory kept her arms straight at her sides and blinked several times behind her thick-rimmed glasses while the strange woman invaded her personal space in ways most of Rory's acquaintances knew not to.

"I'm so sorry about your father," Celia said into her ear.

Celia had, of course, uttered the same sentence at the funeral a few days before. Rory had been just as stoic in the dimly lit funeral hall, standing next to the coffin that held the wax sculpture of her father. When she felt the warmth of Celia's breath in her ear now, and sensed what she guessed were the woman's tears spilling onto her neck, Rory finally put her hands on Celia's shoulders and broke free from her grip. She took a gathering breath and exhaled away the anxiety that was rising from her sternum.

"I've been through the file cabinets," Rory finally said.

A confused look came over Celia's face as she looked around the office and recognized the amount of work Rory had done. Celia patted the front of her jacket to collect herself, wiped her tears. "I thought . . . Have you been working on this all week?"

"No, just this morning. I got here a couple of hours ago."

Rory had long ago stopped attempting to explain her ability to conquer tasks like this one in a fraction of the time it took others. One reason she never practiced law was because it bored her to death. She remembered classmates spending hours studying textbooks that she memorized in a single skimming. And others taking months-long review courses to prepare for the bar exam, which Rory passed on her first attempt without opening a book to prepare. Another reason she avoided lawyering was because she had a strong aversion to people. The idea of haggling with another attorney over the jail sentence of some two-bit criminal made her skin crawl, and the thought of standing before a judge to plead her case caused her to wheeze with angst. She was better suited working solo to reconstruct crime scenes, her final opinions coming in the form of a written report that ended up on a detective's desk.

Rory Moore's world was a walled-off sanctuary she allowed few to enter, and even fewer to understand. Which was why this morning's discoveries were particularly disturbing. She learned that her father had several active cases heading to trial in the coming months that would need immediate assistance. Rory had already considered the likelihood that she'd be forced to dust off her diploma, swallow down the bile, and actually make her first appearance in court to explain to a judge that the lead counsel had died and the case would need an extension at best, a mistrial at worst, and that she'd require some guidance from Your Honor to figure out what the hell to do from there.

"A couple of hours?" Celia asked, tugging Rory back from the recesses of her mind. "How is that possible? This looks like every case we've ever taken on."

"It is. Everything I could find in the file cabinets. I wasn't able to check the computers."

This was a lie. Rory had no trouble logging on to her father's database. It was password protected, but barely, and Rory had quickly hurdled the minor security precautions to cross-reference the cases in the file cabinets with those on the hard drive. Despite that she

24

had every right to access the computer files, being so far removed from the daily workings of the firm made it feel like trespassing.

"If it's in the cabinet, it's in the computer," Celia said.

"Good, then this is everything." Rory pointed to the desk and the first stack of folders. "These are pending cases. Should be simple enough to call these clients and explain the situation. The firm won't be taking them on and they'll have to look elsewhere for representation. I think it would be professional to make a list of other firms that handle these types of cases, so our clients have somewhere to start."

"Of course," Celia said. "Your father would want that."

"The second stack is the retired files. A simple form letter explaining that Frank Moore has died should suffice. I'll leave those two piles for you to handle?"

"Not a problem," Celia said. "I'll take care of it. What about those?"

Rory looked at the final hoard of records she had set on her father's desk. The sight started her hyperventilating. She felt the walls of her carefully constructed and meticulously cinder-blocked existence vibrating with unwanted trespassers from beyond.

"These are all my dad's open cases. I teased them out into three categories." Rory placed her hand on the first pile. "Currently negotiating plea deals—twelve." With her spoken words, she felt her underarms warm with perspiration as she touched the second group of files. "Awaiting court appearances—sixteen." A bead of sweat rolled down her spine to dampen the small of her back. "And finally"—she moved her hand to the last pile—"preparing for trial—three." Her throat caught when she said "three" and she coughed to hide her fear. The three cases going to trial would need immediate assistance.

A fearful look came over Celia when she saw the blood drain from Rory's face, as if the heart disease that claimed her father surely ran in the family and might strike twice in the same month. "Are you okay?"

Rory coughed again and regained her composure.

"I'm fine. I'll find a way to deal with the active cases if you could handle the rest."

Celia nodded as she picked up the mound of pending cases. "I'll start contacting these clients right away." She carried the stack to her desk in the reception area and went to work.

With her father's office door closed, Rory fell into his chair and stared at the files and the four empty Diet Cokes that had fueled her morning work. She clicked the computer to life and searched for criminal defense attorneys in Chicago who would be willing to take the cases.

CHAPTER 5

Stateville Correctional Center, October 15, 2019

*F*ORSICKS WAS HIS ALTER EGO. HE HAD ANSWERED TO THE MONIKER FOR so long now that he wasn't sure he would respond any longer to his real name. The nickname originated from the number that had been assigned to him the first night he arrived, stamped onto the back of his jumpsuit in large block font: **12276594–6.**

Before prison guards knew an inmate's name or the crime for which he had been convicted, they knew his number. His had been shortened to the final two digits in the series—"four-six"—which had morphed over the years into what most inmates and some uninformed guards believed to be his last name—"Forsicks."

He walked into the prison library and clicked on the lights. It was his home within the walls of the penitentiary. He had run the place for decades. Lifting weights and ballooning his body had never interested him, and joining the animals in the prison yard to colonize into sects of gangs was equally unappealing. Instead, he found the library, befriended the elderly lifer who ran the place, and bided his time. The lifer started wheezing during the winter of 1989 and never saw the last decade of the twentieth century. A guard rapped on the bars of Forsicks's cell the next morning to tell him the old man was gone, paroled to the heavens. The library was Forsicks's to run. *Don't screw it up.* He wouldn't.

For thirty years, the library had been under his control. In total, he had logged four decades on the inside without a single incident. The stellar track record had turned him nearly invisible, like the superheroes he read about in comic books he managed to score every month. He despised comics and graphic novels, but made sure to read them just the same. They gave him a softer persona and helped hide the longings that still loomed in his soul.

Prior to jail, he had set his life around The Rush—the feeling that washed over him after he spent time with his victims. The Rush had controlled his mind and shaped his existence. It was something from which he could never escape. After he was caught, though, he had no choice but to conform to life in prison. Withdrawal had been agonizing. He longed so badly for the feeling of power and dominance The Rush had once provided, for the incongruous sense of righteousness he enjoyed when he slipped the nylon noose around his neck and offered himself up to the lure of euphoria that only his victims could provide.

But after the dizzying withdrawal had subsided and he settled into the years in front of him, he looked to something else to fill the void. It quickly became obvious what it would be. The secret that had destroyed his life lay buried somewhere outside the walls of this prison, and he decided to spend the final chapter of his life unearthing it.

He sat at his desk in the front of the library. Only in America could a man who murdered so many be given such freedom—a desk and an entire prison library over which to rule. But after so many decades in this place, only a scant few on the inside knew his story. Even fewer cared. His anonymity was another reason he never corrected anyone who called him Forsicks. It added to his cover. The world had turned the lights out on him years ago. Only recently had the halogen of the past started to flicker back to life. Alone in his library, he unfolded the *Chicago Tribune* and found the headline on page two: 40 YEARS AFTER THE SUMMER OF 1979, THE THIEF SET TO WALK FREE.

His gaze passed over his old nickname, "The Thief." He couldn't ignore what the title did to him, the subtle stream of adrenaline it provided. But he was also aware of the downside to such a perfect signature—it was sure to draw attention and stir up memories. As headlines started popping up and talking heads began discussing the summer of '79, he would need to find a way to avoid the protestors and escape those who planned to haunt and torture him. He needed just a small window of anonymity after his release to complete his final journey, the planning of which he had dedicated his life in prison. It was a voyage he'd waited decades to embark upon, and had foolishly believed others could accomplish for him. But The Thief was the only one who could unearth the thing that haunted him, the secret that had ruined him.

This many years after his reign of terror, his victims were faceless and anonymous. Even when he visited the darkest parts of his mind and tried to conjure some of The Rush that used to fuel him, he could only scantly remember any of the women. They were all dead and gone, erased from his memory by time and indifference.

Only one remained vibrant in his memory, clear and present as if forty years were merely a blink of the eye, a single beat of his heart. She was the lone standout he could never forget. She ran through his thoughts during the quiet days in the library, and haunted his dreams when he slept. She was the only one he remembered, and his looming freedom presented a long-overdue opportunity to sew up loose ends with her.

CHICAGO
August 1979

ANGELA MITCHELL STARED AT THE TELEVISION. SHE STOOD WITH HER friend Catherine Blackwell and watched the news report. On the screen, a reporter stood in front of a darkened alley as the sun set on the summer night. Trashcans rested against chain-link fences, and weeds pushed through the cracks of the uneven pavement.

"Another woman," the reporter said, "has been confirmed missing. Samantha Rodgers, a twenty-two-year-old from Lincoln Park, was reported missing on Tuesday after she failed to show up for work. Authorities believe she is the fifth victim in a string of unexplained disappearances that started in the first week of May."

The reporter walked along the boulevard. A few pedestrians passed behind her and stared into the camera with stupid grins, unaware of the tragedy being reported.

"The disappearances started May second with the abduction of Clarissa Manning. Since then, three other women have gone missing from the streets of Chicago. None have been found, and it is suspected that their disappearances are all related. Now, Samantha Rodgers is feared to be the latest victim of a predator the authorities are calling The Thief. The Chicago Police Department continues to warn young women not to walk the streets alone. The authorities are asking for any leads in the whereabouts of the missing women, and have set up a tip line."

"Five women in three months," Catherine said. "How have the police not been able to find this guy?"

"They have to know something," Angela said in a quiet and reserved voice. "They're probably keeping the details away from the public so as not to tip this guy off to what they know."

Angela's husband walked into the room and clicked off the television. He kissed her lightly on the forehead. "Come on. Dinner's ready."

"It's just terrible," Angela said.

Angela's husband ran his hand over her shoulder and pulled her close for a quick hug. He cocked his head toward the kitchen, making eye contact with Catherine as he left the room.

Angela continued to stare at the blank television screen. The reporter's profile was burned into her mind, an afterimage that allowed Angela to recall every detail of the woman's face, the alley, the green street signs in the background, and even the dumb looks on the faces of the passersby who had walked through the frame. It was a gift and a curse to remember everything she saw. She finally blinked the reporter's image away, allowing it to fade from her visual cortex just as Catherine tugged lightly at Angela's elbow, pulling her toward the dinner table.

CHICAGO
August 1979

FOUR OF THEM—ANGELA AND CATHERINE, ALONG WITH THEIR HUS-bands—sat around the dinner table. Thomas, Angela's husband, had finished grilling chicken and vegetables, and they settled for the air-conditioned safety of their dining room rather than the original plan of eating on the back patio. The summer heat was stifling, the humidity thick, and the mosquitoes unrelenting.

"Sorry to spend another summer night inside," Thomas said. "We wait all year for winter to leave, and still find ourselves stuck inside."

"I've been spending all my days outside lately," Bill Blackwell, Catherine's husband, said. "One of our foremen quit a couple of weeks ago. I've been running his crews, so a break from the heat is fine with me."

"We haven't hired anyone to replace him yet?" Thomas asked.

Thomas and Bill were partners in their concrete business, pouring foundations for new homes, paving industrial parking lots and indoor garages. Their business, started when they were both twenty years old, had grown to a midsized company with a unionized labor force.

"I've got a request in to Local 255. They're working on it, but until we hire someone I'm running the crews, which means I'm outside all day. And with temperatures in the midnineties, I'm very happy to be sitting inside tonight."

"If it helps," Thomas said, "I had to work the Bobcat when one of our guys was sick this week."

"That doesn't help," Bill said. "Driving a Cat is not the same as running the crews. If I get any more mosquito bites, I'll contract malaria."

"Should we be more sympathetic toward our hardworking men, Angela?" Catherine asked.

Angela stared at her plate, a detached look on her face.

"Angela," Thomas said.

When she didn't respond, he reached out and touched her shoulder, startling her. Angela looked up suddenly. The expression on her face made it seem like she was surprised to see others in the room.

"Bill was just saying how bad the mosquitoes are," Thomas said in an encouraging voice. "And that he's working harder than I am down at the shop. I need my wife to defend me here."

Angela tried to smile, but ended up simply nodding at Thomas.

"Anyway," Catherine said, pointing at her husband's neck, "if you get any more bug bites, you'll not have to worry about malaria as much as needing a blood transfusion. It looks like Dracula got to you."

Bill put his hand to his neck. "I had an allergic reaction to the bug spray," he said.

Thomas kept his hand on Angela's shoulder, an attempt to coax her into the conversation. She put her hand on top of his, and offered another false smile.

"I'm not sure insect repellent works on vampires," Angela said.

This brought chuckles from the group. Angela tried to engage in the dinner conversation, but all she could see was the afterimage of the television reporter still burned in her mind, and all she could concentrate on were the women who had gone missing this summer.

CHICAGO
August 1979

W HEN THEIR GUESTS WERE GONE, ANGELA CINCHED THE TOP OF THE garbage bag and tied it off. Her husband wiped his brow with his forearm as he stood in front of the sink and cleaned dishes. Entertaining was a new experience for her, and something to which Angela was still adapting. Before meeting Thomas, she had never enjoyed the experience of close friends, or any friends at all, for that matter. She had spent her life on the outskirts of societal norms. Vivid memories from Angela's youth reminded her why traditional friendships were impossible.

When Angela was age five, a girl had approached her in the kindergarten classroom to offer a Betsy McCall doll and the invitation to play together. To this day, Angela could feel the overwhelming sense of discomfort from someone standing so close to her, and the revulsion that came at the thought of touching a doll so many other children had handled. Even before kindergarten, Angela had taken to carrying her possessions in plastic sandwich bags to keep them safe from germs and filth. Her parents had learned that Angela's tantrums—complete sensory detachments—were quelled only when her belongings were safe inside the plastic bags. The habit continued through grade school, and kept her sealed off from friendships as tightly as her possessions were protected from the world.

So, hosting Catherine and Bill Blackwell for dinner had taken Angela as far out of her comfort zone as she'd been in months. But it was a good thing. It was making her life more normal. She had Thomas to thank for her transformation. Angela would forever be aware of the sideways glances she encountered from most of the world, but she took solace in the fact that Thomas accepted her, despite her many idiosyncrasies. Through her marriage, a new world had opened up. Catherine was the first person she called a friend. Around others Angela managed to control many of the unique habits that plagued the rest of her time. Catherine had seen some of these idiosyncrasies, and had accepted them. Like Angela's aversion of physical contact by anyone other than Thomas, and her affliction to loud noises, and the way she could become transfixed by something her mind wouldn't stop working on—as had occurred tonight when she watched the reporter explaining that another woman had gone missing. She had been unable to concentrate on anything else for the rest of the evening.

Despite her friendship with Catherine, Angela had never warmed to Catherine's husband, who was one of Thomas's closest friends. But this, too, seemed to be a nonissue for Catherine. They met frequently for lunch while their husbands worked.

"That was fun," Thomas said.

"Yeah."

"You and Catherine are becoming good friends?"

"We are. And her husband is nice, too."

Thomas came over to her. "Catherine's husband has a name, you know."

Angela averted her eyes, staring at her feet.

"I know tonight was hard for you. But you did great. I also know Catherine provides a level of comfort for you, but you can't only talk to her and me. You have to talk to everyone who's in the house. It's just polite."

She nodded.

"And you have to call people by their names. Bill, right? Catherine's husband's name is Bill."

"I know," Angela said. "He just . . . I'm not used to him, that's all."

"He's my business partner, and he's a good friend, so we're going to see him a lot."

"I'll work on it."

He kissed her forehead again, like he had when she watched the reporter covering the latest disappearance, and went back to the dishes.

"I'm dropping this outside," Angela said, lifting the tied-off garbage bag.

She headed out the kitchen door, which led to the backyard. She walked across the small plot of grass, and noticed the utility door to the garage was open. It was dark now and light spilled from the garage and through the door frame to form a trapezoid on the grass outside the door. When Thomas was grilling the chicken, Angela remembered Catherine's husband—*Bill*, as Thomas had just reminded her—walking freely in and out of the garage. It was another part of the night that made her uneasy, knowing the garage was a mess of clutter and junk. Angela had a hard time with things that were not strictly organized, and she was so embarrassed by the appearance of the garage that she had considered closing the door at one point during the evening as a nonverbal way of asking Catherine's husband to stay on the patio.

Angela shut the utility door now and pushed past the chain-link fence to enter the darkened alley. Lifting the top of the trashcan, she placed the garbage bag into the empty bin. A cat hissed and darted from behind the cans. Startled, she dropped the trashcan top, causing a loud metallic ruckus to echo through the alley while she let out a scream. Dogs barked from adjacent lots.

Angela took a deep breath and looked down the alley. A streetlight glowed at the far end of the block, casting swaying shadows of tree limbs onto the ground. In her mind Angela pictured a satellite image of the city limits, and referenced her location now as she stood in the shadowed alley on the far fringes of the city. Angela's thoughts turned to the diagram she had meticulously created, in which she placed red dots to mark the suspected location of each abducted woman. She had highlighted in bright yellow the area that joined them all. Her neighborhood was far outside the colored pentagon.

With a rumble in her chest and a tremor in her hands, Angela retrieved the top of the trashcan and haphazardly threw it back in place before running through the yard and into her kitchen. Thomas had finished the dishes and she heard the Cubs game playing in the living room. When she peeked in on him, Thomas was in a deep recline in the La-Z-Boy, which meant he'd soon be snoring. With her fingertips alive with adrenaline, she snuck into her bedroom and knelt at the foot of the bed. Opening the trunk, she found the stack of newspaper clippings and her map of the city.

She'd spent the entire evening suppressing her obsessive-compulsive needs. Angela's freshly learned self-restraint had done her well. It opened up a new world with Thomas, and had allowed her to forge a friendship with Catherine. But Angela knew she could not completely ignore the needs of her mind and the demands of her central nervous system, which screamed for her to organize and list and break down the things that made no sense. She saw things as either straight and ordered with sharp, ninety-degree angles, or in complete disarray. The calls of her mind to piece together in rigid order anything that did not line up smoothly had always been loud and impossible to ignore. But lately, those screams had been deafening. The idea that there was a man who had eluded the police, and who had thrown the city into a state of paralysis, was the very definition of chaos. And ever since Angela had allowed her fierce and unrelenting psyche to consider this man, whom authorities called The Thief, she had been able to think of nothing else.

She brought her stack of newspaper articles to the small desk in her bedroom, clicked on the light, and spread them out in front of her. Angela read them all for the hundredth time, determined to find what everyone else had missed.

CHICAGO
August 1979

ANGELA SPENT THE FOLLOWING MORNING AT HER KITCHEN TABLE surrounded by the previous week's newspaper clippings about The Thief. She had read them late into the night as Thomas slept on the La-Z-Boy. Now he had left for work and Angela was back at it. Both the *Tribune* and the *Sun-Times* lay before her as she meticulously worked the scissors around the corners of each article. She'd even managed to score a *New York Times* that had a brief write-up about the events in Chicago, the article drawing parallels to the "Son of Sam" killings from three years earlier. Angela read and re-read the news pieces, concentrating on the five women who had gone missing, and cataloguing everything that had been reported about each victim. She collected photos and created her own biographies. She knew so much about each woman that she felt connected to them.

Angela worked hard to hide from Thomas the full scale of her affliction. There had been stretches in the past when her obsessive-compulsive disorder had consumed her, overwhelming her mind in ways that prevented routine rituals of daily life. During the darkest times, the illness tethered Angela to the completion of redundant tasks her brain insisted were necessary. And the more she tried to break free from those tumultuous duties, the more paranoid she became that something terrible would happen if she interrupted the cycle of meaningless assignments. The loop of paranoia fed itself until Angela was lost to its power.

She felt that pull happening again now, and knew she needed to tame this current bout of obsession if she hoped to avoid a relapse. But she felt helpless when her mind focused on the missing women and the anonymous man who was taking them. Angela believed she could find a link between the victims. What she would do with her discovery, Angela hadn't decided. Perhaps she would share her findings with the authorities. But Angela was careful not to get too far ahead of herself. Thinking too far into the future opened her mind to wild speculation that caused angst and fear. If Thomas noticed her missing lashes and thinning eyebrows again, he'd worry about a relapse. This would send her back to her therapist's office, which would spell the end to her research. She couldn't let that happen. The women who stared back from the newspaper clippings deserved her attention, and Angela was powerless to ignore them.

After the press clippings were catalogued and ordered, she packed up her files and placed them back in the chest at the foot of her bed. It was 10:00 A.M. when she brought her coffee out to the garage. She carried with her two homemade breakfast sandwiches wrapped in foil. The garage was a detached two-car unit behind their bungalow-style home. A cement walkway led from the patio off the kitchen and ran to the utility door at the back of the garage, the front of which opened into the alley. The previous night, Angela had allowed her imagination to create irrational nightmares of what waited in the dark shadows after the cat ran from behind the trashcans. This morning, the sun was bright and her fear was gone.

She walked through the utility door and hit the opener on the wall, causing the large garage door to rattle upward, and allowing the morning's sun to brighten the area. Because she rarely ventured into the garage, it was incongruent to the home she kept. If the space were hers and not Thomas's, Angela would have it ordered and meticulous the way everything else in her life needed to be. Instead, it was a mess of cluttered shelving filled with tattered books and dusty storage containers; there were paint cans coated with the drippings of a home project from when she and Thomas had painted the bedroom; there was car repair equipment, which

Thomas had stacked in the corner, and an old couch they had meant to sell, but had never gotten around to. The couch was now filthy from dust and dirt, and covered by old magazines and newspapers. It was her morning project.

Wednesday was garbage day, and Angela's task was to drag the old couch into the alley for the garbagemen to haul away. The breakfast sandwiches were her bribe to the guys for hauling away such a large piece of trash. Before she could get to the couch, though, Angela started with the magazines and newspapers that covered it, dumping them in the trash. After ten minutes, the couch was empty of the clutter that had covered it. Positioning herself near the entrance of the garage, she grasped the arm of the couch and pulled. It was weighty and her progress was slow, but after ten minutes, Angela managed to drag the couch into the alley. She needed to move it another twenty feet to the garbage area, but she had spent her strength hauling the heavy piece of furniture this far. She walked into the garage to catch her breath and regain her energy.

As she took deep, recovering breaths, she looked anxiously at the cluttered shelves, knowing that Thomas would be upset if she took her obsessiveness for order to the rest of the garage when she had told him she planned only to move the couch out to the garbage. But her fingers tingled as she looked at the chaotic shelving. Inspecting the items, she found things she had forgotten existed—old glassware from before she had married, and holiday decorations she and Thomas had never used.

On another set of shelves, Angela stumbled over old wedding gifts that were both impractical and unwanted. She found a picnic basket flanked on each side with compartments for wine bottles. Never in her life had she been on a picnic, and the idea of sipping wine while sitting among insect-infested grass caused her skin to crawl. She lifted the top of the basket. Something inside caught her eye. A closer inspection revealed a thin jewelry box.

She looked around the garage, and then out into the alley, as if she had just discovered a hidden treasure and worried about another learning her secret. She pulled the box from the depths of the basket and opened it. A sliver of morning sunlight slanted through the side window of the garage and struck the diamonds of the necklace, brilliantly highlighting the green peridot they encircled. It wasn't unusual for Thomas to make extravagant purchases. He'd done so in the past and Angela's birthday was just a week away. She immediately felt guilty for having spoiled his surprise.

"Can I offer you a hand?"

The deep, unfamiliar voice caused Angela to jump. She dropped the necklace back into the basket and spun around, finding herself face-to-face with a man she did not know. Her lungs expanded in an unintentional gasp, and a whine escaped into the air. The man stood in the alley by the couch, but his presence felt much closer. He had deep-set eyes darkened by the morning light, which shined down from behind him and silhouetted his form. The black presence of his shadow crept across the garage floor, coming so close to Angela that her skin tingled with goose bumps.

"Looks like you're stalled."

"No, no," Angela said without thought. She was backing away toward the utility door behind her, her feet staggering. As a general rule, Angela Mitchell avoided eye contact whenever possible. But the charcoal holes in the man's face were too cryptic to ignore.

"I'll just give it a push with you," the man said. "Help you get it over to the trashcans. You're throwing it away, yes?"

Angela shook her head. Her mind flashed to the biographies she had amassed on the missing women. The newspaper articles she had scanned and studied. The map of the city she had marked with the locations of the disappearances, and the bright yellow pentagon she had highlighted to demark the area of the city to avoid. She was filled now with the same sense of dread as when the stray cat had hissed from behind the trashcans. Last night, she had sensed another's presence, and she had run back into the house before her mind could dwell too heavily on the feeling. And since then, Angela had worked hard to compartmentalize the thought, to suppress the idea that someone had been present with her in the alley, watching from the shadows. To allow her mind to concentrate on that fear, to permit her psyche to continuously strike the flint that might throw sparks onto the tinder of her anxiety, had the power to drive her mad. Once that thought was ignited, she would be unable to stifle the flames.

Years before, a vagrant thought like that could send her into a weeks-long state of paranoia and obsessiveness where she'd lock herself in her home, checking and double checking the door locks, climbing from bed in the dark of night to make sure every window was secure, lifting the phone one hundred times in a row to make sure a dial tone was present to prove it was functional. Angela had worked too hard over the last few years to allow her new life to be ruined by the inner workings of her convoluted mind. But now, as she stared at the man in the alley, she wished she'd paid closer attention to the warnings her brain had sent last night.

"My husband will be right out," she managed to say. "He'll help me the rest of the way."

The man looked beyond Angela, through the frame of the open utility door behind her, and to the back of the bungalow. He pointed at the house. "Your husband is home?"

"Yes," Angela said too quickly.

The man took a step forward to the precipice of the garage, bringing his murky shadow closer until it bent off the floor and climbed up her legs. Angela could almost feel it.

"You sure I can't help?"

Angela backed farther away; she turned and hurried through the utility door and into the backyard. She ran to the kitchen door and fumbled with the handle until she pulled the door open and stepped into the safety of her home, immediately locking the door behind her. She peeled the curtains to the side to peek outside. The man stood next to the abandoned couch, staring through the open garage door at the back of Angela's house. Over the pounding in her ears, the squeaking brakes of the garbage truck broke through as it turned into the alley. The stranger looked behind him and hurried away as the truck approached.

Angela's hands were shaking. She couldn't bring herself to go back outside to talk with the garbagemen, to deliver the sandwiches in exchange for them taking the couch. Instead, she ran to the bathroom, lifted the lid to the toilet, and vomited until her eyes teared and her sternum ached.

42

CHAPTER 6
Chicago, October 16, 2019

RORY MOORE PULLED UP NEXT TO THE UNMARKED SQUAD CAR, driver's side to driver's side. She rolled down her window and pushed her nonprescription glasses up the bridge of her nose. It was dark and shadowed inside her car. She was sure Detective Davidson couldn't see her eyes, always a plus.

The detective handed her a manila envelope through the window.

"Autopsy and tox results," he said. "Plus all the notes and interviews taken on the case."

Rory took the package, saw Camille Byrd's name printed on the bottom of the folder, and thought of the girl's shattered Kestner doll and her father's pleas for help. Rory dropped the file on the passenger seat.

"You're officially on the case," Ron said. "I filled out the paperwork this morning."

"When was the last time any of your guys looked at any of this?" Rory asked.

Davidson ballooned his cheeks as he exhaled a defeated breath. Rory knew he was embarrassed by the answer he was about to offer.

"It's over a year old, with nothing new in months and over five hundred new homicides so far this year. It's cold."

Rory's mind flashed back to the morning in Grant Park when Ron had shown her where Camille's frozen body had been found. Rory's heart ached, the way it did for the victim of every case she took on. It was why she was so selective. Within the tiny world of forensic reconstruction, no one could do what Rory Moore routinely accomplished. She had breathed fresh life into cases that were colder than a Chicago winter. It was simply in her genes. Her DNA was programmed to see things others missed, to connect dots that looked scattered and incongruent to everyone else. She left the straightforward reconstructions—the car wrecks and suicides—to others in her profession who were better suited to handle such trivial cases, the ones detectives could figure out on their own with a little effort and a lucky break. Those clinical cases never challenged Rory. She reconstructed cold case homicides, cases others had abandoned and given up on. But she accomplished this by developing a deep and personal connection with the victim. She accomplished this by learning their story, discovering first who they were. Why they were killed always followed. It was a taxing technique that drained her emotionally and often brought her closer to the victim for whom she was seeking justice than she was to anyone else in her life. But it was the only way Rory knew how to do her job.

Rory knew that Ron Davidson, who ran the Homicide Division inside the Chicago Police Department, was under pressure from every direction, political and social, to pull Chicago's unsolved murder rate out of the toilet. The city had one of the nation's lowest homicide solve rates; so when Rory agreed to take on Camille Byrd's icy cold, unsolved homicide, it represented an opportunity for Ron to knock a case off his docket without expending many resources. Rory reconstructed crimes on her own, rebuffing assistance from any of the Homicide detectives. For years, the force had kept Rory on retainer, and if she weren't so selective about the cases she took on, she'd have a new one every week.

"I'll take a look and let you know what I find," Rory finally said.

"Keep me posted."

Rory's window began its ascent.

"Hey, Gray," Davidson said.

Rory stopped the window halfway up, looked through the glass at him.

"Sorry about your dad."

Rory nodded and started the window back up before the two cars drove off in opposite directions.

CHAPTER 7
Chicago, October 16, 2019

*R*ORY WALKED INTO THE NURSING HOME AND ENTERED ROOM 121. The lights were dim, and the television cast the room in a blue glow. A woman lay still in the bed, her eyes open but not acknowledging Rory's presence. Rory approached the hospital bed, which sported tall guardrails on either side to protect its occupant. She sat in the adjacent chair and looked at the woman, who continued to stare at the television as if Rory were invisible.

She reached out and took the woman's hand.

"Aunt Greta. It's me, Rory."

Her great-aunt inverted her lips, sucking them into her mouth the way she did after the nurses had removed her dentures.

"Greta," Rory said in a whispered voice. "Can you hear me?"

"I tried to save you," the old woman said. "I tried, but there was too much blood."

"Okay," Rory said. "It's okay."

"You were bleeding." Her great-aunt looked at Rory. "There was too much blood."

A nurse walked into the room. "Sorry, I tried to catch you before you came in. She's having a bad day."

The nurse adjusted the pillows behind Greta's head, placed a white Styrofoam cup with a straw extending out of it on the over-bed table.

"Here's your water, hon. And there's no blood around here. I hate blood, that's why I work in this place."

"How long has she been like this?"

The nurse looked at Rory. "Most of the day. She was fine yesterday. But, as you know, dementia takes them back to another part of their life. Sometimes just briefly, other times for much longer. It'll pass."

Rory nodded, pointed at the Styrofoam. "I'll get her to drink."

The nurse smiled. "Call me if you need anything."

As soon as the nurse was gone, Rory's great-aunt looked at her again.

"I tried to save you. There was too much blood."

Greta had been a nurse, and though it had been many years since she practiced, the dementia, which was ravaging her mind, pulled her back to the darkest moments of her profession.

Greta went silent and looked back at the television. Rory knew it would be one of those visits. Her great-aunt was ninety-two years old, and her mental capacity varied widely. Sometimes she was as sharp as ever. Other times, like tonight and over the past two weeks since Greta had learned about the passing of Rory's father, she was lost in the past. In a world that Rory could not penetrate. The best chance over the last several years to catch her in a coherent state came at night. Sometimes Rory came and went in a matter of minutes. Other times, when Aunt Greta was alert and talkative, Rory stayed into the early hours of morning, talking and laughing like she remembered doing as a child. Few people fully understood Rory Moore. Her great-aunt Greta was one of them.

"Greta, do you remember what I told you about Dad? About Frank, your nephew?"

Greta chewed some more on her capsized lips.

"The funeral was last week. I tried to bring you, but you weren't feeling well."

Rory saw her great-aunt's chewing grow faster.

"You didn't miss anything. Except me squirming in the corner trying to avoid everyone. I could have used you for cover, old lady."

This brought a quick glance from Greta and the subtle twitch of a smile. Rory knew she had broken through on a night that had offered little opportunity.

"What better way to deflect attention from myself than to wheel in a little old lady everyone loves?"

46

Rory felt her great-aunt squeeze her hand. A tear formed on Greta's eyelid and then rolled down her cheek. Rory stood and quickly pulled a tissue from the box to wipe Greta's face.

"Hey," she said, trying for the eye contact she normally worked to avoid. "I've got a tough one I need your help with. It's a Kestner doll with a bad fracture through the left eye socket. I can fix the break, but I might need some help with the coloring. The porcelain is faded and I'll need to color over the epoxy. You want to lend a hand?"

Greta looked at Rory. She stopped chewing her lips. Then she nodded with a subtle bob of her head.

"Good," Rory said. "You're the best. And you taught me everything I know. I'll bring your colors and brushes next time I visit and you can take a look."

Rory sat back down in the bedside chair, reached for Greta's hand again, and spent an hour watching the muted television screen until she was sure her great-aunt had drifted off to sleep.

CHAPTER 8
Chicago, October 16, 2019

S HE PULLED UP TO THE FRONT OF HER BUNGALOW AND PARKED on the street, which was lined with her neighbors' cars. It was just past eleven o'clock, and Rory felt good about her visit with Greta. She didn't always feel that way when she left her great-aunt's side. Alzheimer's and dementia had stolen most of her personality, turning her at times into a nasty old woman who could spit insults like a drunken sailor one moment, and babble incoherently the next. Despite the ferocity of the abuse, the vile version of Aunt Greta was preferred to the vacant-eyed, hollow soul Rory often found when she visited. Each of Greta's personalities was tolerated because occasionally, like tonight, there was a glimpse of the woman Rory had loved her whole life. It had been a good night.

The dog across the street barked as Rory walked up her steps and keyed the front door, grabbing the mail on her way in. She dumped the stack of envelopes, along with Camille Byrd's autopsy report, onto her kitchen table and pulled a glass from the cabinet. The middle shelf of her refrigerator held six bottles of Three Floyds Dark Lord, an impossible-to-find imperial stout that Rory managed to keep well stocked through an Indiana connection. Each twenty-two ounce bottle was positioned label out and in flawless rows—the only way Dark Lord should be shelved. She plucked one from the front, popped the cap, poured it into the tall glass, and topped it off with blackcurrant cordial. With an alcohol content of fifteen percent, the beer was stronger than most wines and

Exactly twenty-four dolls stood on the shelves. Any less left a vacancy that gnawed at Rory until the empty slot was filled. She'd tried it before—removing one doll without replacing it with another. The unfilled space created an imbalance in her mind that prevented sleep and work and rational thought. The nagging annoyance dissipated, Rory had discovered, only after she filled the vacancy with another doll to make the shelving complete. She'd come to terms with this affliction years ago, and had finally stopped battling it. It had been embedded in her since she was a young child standing in Aunt Greta's house staring at doll-lined shelves. Rory's love of restoration originated during her formative years when she spent her summers with Greta bringing broken dolls back to perfection. Now Rory's den had looked the same for more than a decade and was a replica of Aunt Greta's house from years ago, the built-ins lined with some of her most triumphant restorations. Never a vacancy present.

A thin drawer was positioned under each shelf, in which rested "before" pictures of each doll featured on the ledge above. The 8-by-10 glossy photos depicted cracked faces, missing eyes, jagged tears that spilled white stuffing, stained garments, missing limbs, and faded porcelain that had shed its glaze over years of life. The images in the drawers stood in stark contrast to the immaculate dolls standing on the shelves above, which Rory had meticulously brought back to life.

Sitting at her workbench, she turned on her gooseneck lamp and directed its beam to the ruined Kestner doll Camille Byrd's father had used to lure Rory into reconstructing his daughter's death. She took another sip of Dark Lord and began her cursory examination, photographing the damaged doll from every angle until finally laying it flat and taking a conclusive picture that would become the "before" image against which her restoration would be gauged. The beer buzz, coupled with the preoccupation of a new project— both Camille Byrd's childhood doll, and the woman herself—was enough to penetrate the deep folds of Rory's brain and distract her from the gnawing image of the files waiting for resolution in her father's law office. The distraction of a new project was just sufficient to push into the shadows of her mind the thought of her father dying alone in his home.

CHAPTER 9

Stateville Correctional Center, October 17, 2019

*H*IS KILLING SPREE DECADES AGO HAD, FOR A SHORT TIME, MADE him a celebrity. But soon after his conviction, the world moved on and had mostly forgotten about The Thief. Only in recent months had his star begun to rise again as journalists relived the summer of 1979 by recounting the women who had been informally counted as his victims. Family members were tracked down. Friends, now gray and wrinkled by age, spoke of long-forgotten kinships with those they lost. Ambitious newscasters replayed old footage in an attempt to recapture the panic of the city during that sweltering summer when The Thief ran loose through the shadowed streets of Chicago, stealing young women never to be seen again.

And now, as his celebrity began its slow ascent, he would need to rely on the one man who had helped him most over the years. He had access to the prison e-mail system, but it was a tedious process to receive and deliver messages, and prison rules placed strict word counts on his e-mails. It was faster and easier to write his letters by hand and send them through the post office, which he had done several times in the last three weeks without a response. The United States Postal Service—jail mail—had always been his swiftest form of communication. Faster even than a phone call, which required him to make a formal request, wait for approval, and then schedule a date and time to use the prison pay phone. It had always been his preference when he needed to get ahold of his attorney to simply pen a letter, stuff it in an envelope, and drop it in the mail. But after two weeks without a reply, he decided to petition for a phone call. With his final parole board hearing fast approaching, his attorney had been in constant contact with him regarding the details of his impending release. But for the last two weeks, his attorney had been silent and unreachable.

The Thief lay on his bunk now and folded his hands across his chest as he waited. There was an imbalance in the universe. He could feel it in his gut. Passing time had never been a challenge. At least, not for many years. But of late, since the parole board had stamped him *approved,* time became something more difficult to manage. His sentence was coming to an end, and he allowed himself to taste what waited on the outside. It was a dangerous practice to entertain thoughts about the freedoms that might soon come to him. It was especially dangerous to imagine the satisfaction of finding her. Still, despite the hazards, he closed his eyes as he lay on his bunk and imagined finally coming face-to-face with her. What a joyous moment it would be. The woman who had put him here would finally receive retribution.

"Forsicks," the guard said, interrupting his thoughts. "You got phone privileges today?"

He sat up quickly and stood from his bed.

"Yes, sir."

The guard turned his head and in a booming voice yelled down the length of the cell block. "One-two-two-seven-six-five-nine-four-six." His voice echoed off the walls and conjured prisoners to the front of their cells, where they stuck their arms through the bars and rested their elbows on the metal as they watched what was transpiring.

Forsicks's cell door rattled open and the guard motioned for him to take the lead as they walked down the long galley. Seeing nothing exciting, the other prisoners melted back into their cells. A door buzzed as they approached the end of the gangplank and Forsicks pushed through it. Another guard was waiting for him on the other side. He did a quick pat down, and then motioned him toward an isolated pay phone on the wall.

Forsicks went through the practiced routine of navigating the automated prison phone system that allowed outgoing collect calls, dialed the number from memory, and listened to the staticky ring through the receiver. After the eighth loop of buzzing, the call went to voice mail, where he learned that his attorney's mailbox was full.

The universe was off. Something was wrong. All of his fantasies about finding her began to fade.

CHICAGO
August 1979

*T*HE VOMITING CONTINUED FOR THE ENTIRE WEEK AFTER HER EN-counter with the stranger in the alley. Her head swam with vertigo and her stomach roiled with nausea every time Angela thought of that morning. The dirty couch had sat abandoned for the entire day. The garbage men hadn't touched it. The couch sat at an odd angle at the precipice of the open garage door, and Angela imagined they assumed it was there temporarily while the garage was being cleaned. She had watched through the slit in the curtain that covered the kitchen window as the garbage truck stopped in the alley and the guys emptied her overflowing trashcans into the back of the truck before hopping back onto the fender as the driver continued down the alley. Angela couldn't bring herself to open the kitchen door and run to the alley to ask them to haul the couch away.

It was early afternoon when Angela had heard the honking that day. Her neighbor was attempting to pull his car into the garage directly across from Angela's, but couldn't make it past the couch to cut the tight angle. As was typical in Chicago, the constant honking of one's horn was the chosen solution to nearly every problem a driver faced, from slow-moving traffic, to kids playing ball in the street, to a deserted couch in an alley. When the honking reached five nerve-racking minutes, Angela had finally gotten up the nerve to leave the house. She pulled the couch back into the garage, shut the door, and hurried back inside to bolt the door behind her. *Once. Twice. Three times, to be sure.*

She told Thomas about the day's adventure as soon as he'd gotten home. He suggested they call the police, but when they discussed it further, Angela was at a loss for exactly what she would be reporting. That a stranger, and likely a neighbor, had been kind enough to offer his assistance? That a cat had frightened her the night before and filled her with the sense that she was being watched? Angela knew how that conversation would go. She could already see the sideways glances the officers would give each other while Angela stuttered through her explanation, all the time doing her best to avoid eye contact. The nervous plucking of her eyebrows would be looked upon like a contagious disease until the officers excused themselves to speak with Thomas in private about his paranoid wife, who was clearly making more out of things than was there. The further she discussed the incident with Thomas, the more absurd it sounded to call the police.

More pressing now, a week later, was Angela's fear that she was on the verge of an obsessive-compulsive breakdown. That she even recognized its imminent approach, like thunderclouds on the horizon, could be considered progress. Years before, the affliction would descend upon her without warning to steal a week or a month as the demands of her mind sent her on meaningless tasks of redundancy. But in the new paradigm of her life, Angela not only sensed the collapse approaching, she fought like hell to prevent it. While she battled her condition, she also worked hard to hide the worst of her symptoms from Thomas. The lack of eyelashes was camouflaged by a thick application of mascara to the few follicles that remained, and a shadowing pencil bolstered her thinning eyebrows. Despite the sweltering heat, Angela had taken to wearing jeans and long shirts in lieu of shorts and tank tops in order to hide the bloody scabs that marked her shoulders and thighs from her nervous scratching.

The masking of her symptoms, however, was a venomous crutch that made things worse. The better Angela was able to conceal her habits of self-mutilation, the more dramatic her dependency on them became. She tried to stop herself with subtle tricks that had worked in the past. She kept the tips of her fingers slick with Vaseline to make more difficult the grasping of her eyebrow follicles.

And she clipped her nails down to the soft pads of her fingers to make them benign tools as she dug into her skin. She was managing thus far to keep the worst of her breakdown hidden.

The vomiting, however, was becoming a problem. Thomas noticed it the other morning. When he checked on her, Angela had told him it was the result of bad Chinese food. In reality, the nausea came every time she worked herself into a frenzy with thoughts of the stranger from the alley. Each morning after Thomas left for work, Angela spent hours pulling the curtains of the kitchen door to the side so she could stare out into the alley. A routine developed: pull curtain, check alley, secure lock, lift phone, listen for dial tone, repeat. The only thing that broke the cycle was the need to vomit. Her stomach turned whenever the image popped into her mind of the man standing in the alley and peering through the open garage door and into her kitchen, which sent her to the bathroom in violent flurries of retching.

It was during a rare moment of lucidity a week after her encounter in the alley, when Angela had discovered an expired bottle of Valium from her previous doctor. Swallowing a tablet every six hours, Angela found, took the edge off, allowed her to sleep at night, and brought her mind back from the encounter in the garage. It was a temporary fix until she could reason with herself and calm her mind. She had beaten the obsessiveness before. She could do it again.

Under the calming effects of the Valium, Angela convinced herself that it was possible, and even likely, that her encounter in the alley was nothing more than a Good Samaritan offering his help. And it was very *un*likely that the horror of the missing women could stretch this far out to the fringe of the city limits, where she lived a quiet life. She took a deep breath and tried to steady her shaking fingers as she poured her morning coffee. She stopped her gaze before she could look for the hundredth time out the back window and into the alley. Instead, she forced her thoughts to focus on the missing women and the profiles she had created. It had been days since she thought of them.

She retrieved the press clippings from the chest in her bedroom and spread them across the kitchen table. For two hours, Angela studied the missing women and the notes she had made about each of them. Perhaps it was the clean slate of her mind coming off a lost week of paranoia, or the Valium freeing her thoughts to flow in ways they hadn't in the weeks before, but as she read through the profiles, she saw something she had missed previously. Her mind ran through the catalogued information, like scrolling through microfilm at the library. Articles she had read over the past years suddenly came together in her mind and she saw a pattern that had always been there, waiting to be discovered, but to this point had gone unnoticed. Her mind raced and she jotted notes, but the bleached-out exertion from fighting her OCD for the last week had frayed her neurons and brought self-doubt. Surely, she was wrong.

Pushing her insecurities aside, Angela scribbled notes frantically as thoughts spilled from her mind, fearful that if she didn't capture them on the page they'd be lost forever. She recalled with great clarity the newspaper articles she had read years earlier and scribbled names and dates from the images that sped through her mind. When she finished, she looked at the clock. It was approaching the noon hour. She had sat down at the kitchen table three hours ago, but it felt like only minutes.

Quickly dressing in jeans and a long-sleeved shirt, Angela stuffed her notes into her purse. A wave of nausea came over her as she imagined leaving the house, but she had no choice. She had to get to the library to confirm her suspicions. She knew, too, she would have to take another precaution. She needed confirmation that her thoughts were lucid and coherent, and not the result of her paranoia. And that confirmation could come from only one person.

Angela picked up the phone and dialed her friend Catherine's number.

"Hello?"

"Catherine," Angela said in a soft voice.

"Angela?"

"Yes, it's me."

"Are you feeling better? Thomas told Bill that you've been ill since the night we had dinner together."

Perhaps, Angela considered, she hadn't been hiding her symptoms as well as she imagined.

"I'm fine, but I need to talk with you. Can we meet?"

"Sure. Is something wrong?"

"No. I just need some help. Can I stop by in a while?"

"Of course," Catherine said.

Angela hung up without saying good-bye, ran to the bathroom, and then vomited.

CHICAGO
August 1979

ANGELA MITCHELL SPENT TWO HOURS AMONG THE LIBRARY SHELVES, pulling books and skimming pages. She sat at the microfilm station and spun old rolls of newspaper articles that dated back to the summer of 1970, nearly a decade earlier. She scribbled notes until her uncanny mind saw clearly the pattern she suspected existed. She spent thirty minutes plotting her findings onto graph paper and creating a line chart that translated her findings to paper form so others might understand her discovery.

She organized her notes, returned the microfilm to the shelf, and hurried from the library. Catherine's house was just two blocks from her own, and at 3:00 P.M., Angela pushed through the wrought iron gate that led to the front stoop. Even before Angela could knock, Catherine opened the door.

"Woman, it's ninety degrees outside," Catherine said as Angela walked up the front steps. "Why are you covered in denim?"

Angela looked at her jeans and button-down shirt. She was less concerned with how her fashion choices would react to the sweltering heat as she was with hiding the scabbed-over claw marks that covered her arms and legs.

"I'm behind on laundry," she finally said.

"Come into the air conditioning." Catherine pushed open the screen door and waved Angela inside.

They sat at the kitchen table. "So what got you so sick? Stomach bug?"

"Yes," Angela said, glancing quickly into Catherine's eyes, her first bit of eye contact, then back down to the table. "But I've been over it for the last few days. You know how Thomas worries."

Thomas had pushed hard during the first year or two of marriage for Angela to mix with his friends' wives. But Angela had always felt judged by them. They whispered about her when they thought she wasn't listening, and treated her like a child when she didn't respond to their boisterous ways. Catherine Blackwell was different. Angela felt accepted when she was with Catherine, who never asked foolish questions or gave confused looks when Angela grew quiet with anxiety. Catherine had always made her feel comfortable, and stood by her whenever anyone treated Angela badly. The first time the two ventured to lunch together, a condescending waitress had scolded Angela for not speaking loudly enough.

Speak up, honey.

Her name is Angela, not Honey, Catherine had said. *And she's almost thirty years old, not twelve.*

From that moment, Catherine Blackwell was not only her protector, she was Angela Mitchell's closest friend.

"Can I get you something to drink?"

"No, no," Angela said. "Thanks, though."

"So what's so urgent?"

"I know this is going to sound crazy," Angela said, pulling a folder from her purse. It held newspaper clippings and her biographies of the missing women, in addition to the reams of paper from her latest research trip to the library. "But I've been looking into the women who have gone missing."

This caught Catherine's attention. "Looking into them how?"

"I've been collecting bits of information about them from the papers and from newscasts."

Catherine pulled one of the pages across the table. It was a *Chicago Tribune* article about Samantha Rodgers, the latest girl who had disappeared from the streets of Chicago. Catherine had watched one of the news reports about the missing girl with Angela when they all had dinner together the week before. The girl's picture was at the top of the article, a crease bent through her photo, where the clipping had been folded and stashed in Angela's binder.

"Why are you collecting all this?" Catherine asked.

Angela looked up.

"I'm obsess—" Angela caught herself. Speaking the word "obsessed" out loud would be confessing to her friend the dark affliction that had plagued her life. It was unlikely, Angela understood, that Catherine hadn't already recognized the signs of her condition, but Angela stopped herself, nonetheless.

"I can't stop thinking about them," she finally said.

"Why?"

"It's hard to explain. When my mind gets focused on something, it's hard for me to . . . let it go. So I started collecting information about the girls, and I think I've found something."

Angela spread the information across the table. She had printed articles from newspapers and microfilm at the library, as well as pages from the books she had referenced, and her own notes that filled the first third of her spiral notebook.

"Five girls have gone missing since spring. Here are the dates each disappeared." Angela pointed to a different page. "Here is a list describing each victim—age, race, ethnicity, occupation, and physical characteristics, like hair color, skin tone, eye color. You get the idea."

Angela pushed the handwritten list to Catherine.

"The police say each disappearance is random. They believe the same man has taken all of these women, but they believe there is no connection between each woman. From what I can tell, they're right about that. The women, in relation to one another, have no association. But the police say The Thief strikes unsystematically. That's not true."

Catherine looked at Angela. "How long have you been working on this?"

"All summer. Since the women started to go missing. It's all I do, really. All I've been able to think about. But in reality, I realized this morning that I've been working on it much longer than just this summer. I just wasn't aware of it until now. Until I put it together."

"What did you put together?"

Angela lifted a random sheet of paper from within the scattered Xeroxed pages. "Look at this. I categorized all the characteristics of each missing girl—age, race, occupation, physical qualities—all the things on that list you're looking at—and then I went back to look not just at missing persons cases, but also homicides in and around Chicago that involved women who match those characteristics."

Angela produced the handmade chart she had created at the library.

"Look here." She pointed at the graph paper. "On the bottom of my graph are years starting in 1960 and going all the way through to today, the summer of 1979." Angela ran her finger from left to right across the bottom of the page. "On the vertical axis is the number of homicides of women who fall into the category of these missing women. Again, age, sex, race, physical characteristics. Now look, from 1960 to 1970, the number of homicides that involved women who match these descriptions was flat."

On the graph, a horizontal line ran from 1960 to 1970 without any substantial spikes or dips.

"But in 1970," Angela said, "there was a sudden uptick in homicides involving these types of women."

On the chart, Angela's handwritten line spiked upward dramatically in 1970.

"These are *all* the homicides in Chicago?" Catherine asked.

"No. In 1970, there were more than eight hundred homicides in and around Chicago. This graph only represents homicides involving women who match the characteristics of the five women who have gone missing this summer." Angela tapped the page again, tracing her finger over her graph. "The increase in homicides begins in 1970 and continues until 1972, then tapers out but stays high relative to the entire decade of the 1960s. Then, this year, 1979, there is a sudden drop again back to levels equal to the sixties."

Catherine was nodding her head as she listened. "I see the increase and the decrease. But what does it mean?"

"Here's my theory," Angela said. "The same person who is taking women this summer has been killing these types of women since around 1970. Between 1970 and 1978, he was careless and brazen. But since the beginning of this year, he's been more diligent. Instead of the police finding a body some weeks after a girl goes missing, now the women just disappear with no bodies being discovered."

Catherine squinted her eyes as she began to see Angela's theory come together. "You're saying this person's reign of terror spans, not just to this summer, but for the entire decade."

Angela made eye contact again. Her second time. "Yes."

Catherine sat back in her chair. "This is some crazy stuff you're telling me."

"But you see how it's possible, right?" Angela asked.

"When you present it to me this way, yes. That's assuming all your facts are correct."

"They are."

"And you got all this information from the library?"

"It's all there for anyone to find. You just have to look in the right places and with the right ideas in mind. This guy, The Thief, he has a *type*. And he's been preying on a specific type of woman for ten years."

"So why has this guy suddenly become so careful this year? Why is he hiding the bodies so much better?"

"Good question," Angela said. "What happened last year? What was the big story around here?"

Catherine shook her head. "I don't know."

Angela pulled more pages from her folder and passed them to Catherine. "Out in Des Plaines?"

Catherine's eyes widened slightly when it came to her as she read the headline: KILLER CLOWN CLAIMS 33 AS MORE BODIES DISCOVERED.

"John Wayne Gacy," she said.

"Correct. The police discovered a serial killer named John Wayne Gacy, who killed more than thirty young men and buried them in the crawl space of his home."

"And what? The Thief got spooked by Gacy's arrest?"

"Correct. Police activity picked up. The public was more diligent. And if the authorities had any ability to see patterns, they would have picked up on this one." Angela tapped her homemade chart again. "So he changed from a killer to a thief. He still kills these women, I'm certain of it. He just hides their bodies better."

"Angela, sweetheart," Catherine said. "I don't really know what to say. If this is correct, even if it's only partially accurate, you need to take this to the police."

Angela looked at Catherine again. "That's why I need your help."

"Anything."

"I can't go to the police. They'll look at me . . ." Angela made brief eye contact again. "You know what they'll think."

"Bring Thomas with you."

Angela was already shaking her head. "I can't tell Thomas about this. He's already worried about how I spend my days. If he knows I've been obsessing—"

The sound of her own voice uttering *that word* again caused Angela to scratch her shoulder through the fabric of her shirt. Frustration flared when her benign fingernails, clipped to the nubs, were unable to produce the searing pain she hoped for.

"Thomas would think this is an unhealthy way for me to spend my time."

"But if it's true, Angela. If what you've discovered is true, this transcends what Thomas thinks about how you spend your time." Catherine tapped the graph. "If this is true, then telling the police could save lives."

The front door opened and Catherine's husband yelled into the house.

"Catherine, you home?"

"In here, hon."

In a panic, Angela began gathering her research and stuffing pages back into the file folder as Bill Blackwell walked into the kitchen. He wore dirty jeans and a shirt covered in bits of concrete. Angela immediately recognized the appearance, since it was how Thomas often came home after work. Catherine's husband wore a bandana, which hung loose around his neck. Angela remembered the red marks on his skin and his remarks from the other night about mosquitoes and an allergic reaction and his foreman quitting, which forced Bill to run the crews. Angela hadn't even been aware that night, preoccupied as she was with her thoughts of the missing women, that she had comprehended Bill Blackwell's words. Angela's mind worked that way, absorbing everything around her and storing it all in the deep recesses of her brain. The catalogued information randomly floated from her subconscious until she was aware of its presence. It happened to her often. Her mind would whisper to her that she was aware of something, even if she didn't quite grasp precisely what it was she understood. Then, later, the stored image or nugget of knowledge would break loose from the anchor in her mind and rise to the surface. But there was something else that caught her attention now. Angela tried not to look, tunneling her vision to the task of organizing her papers so she could leave as quickly as possible.

"Angela," Bill said. "How are you? I didn't know you guys were getting together today."

Angela smiled and offered a quick glance at Bill Blackwell. Then the other image that had caught her attention came into focus. She saw another man in the background.

"This is Leonard Williams," Bill said as the man walked into the kitchen. "He's been working up at the Kenosha shop for me. I stopped home for a quick bite to eat before heading out to a job on the west side."

When Leonard Williams appeared from the hallway and entered the kitchen, Angela immediately recognized him as the man from the alley who had tried to help with the couch. His dark eyes were less shadowed now than they had been when the morning sun had backlit his frame that day, but the dark charcoal of his orbits was unmistakable. Angela's throat closed in a momentary spasm of panic, and for an instant, she was unable to breathe, causing her eyes to widen and bulge as she stared at the stranger from the alley. The man who had pushed her into a week of hysterics that had ignited her obsessive-compulsive habits.

She finally pushed air into her lungs and returned to shuffling papers into her purse, some of which scattered to the floor. She hurriedly tried to retrieve them and stop others from falling, but succeeded only in scattering more pages from the table.

"Wow, wow, wow," Bill said. "Take it easy."

He glanced wide-eyed at Catherine before picking up a few loose papers from the kitchen floor and handing them to Angela, who took them quickly without looking at him. Angela didn't need to look into Bill Blackwell's eyes to see the disgusted look on his face. She sensed it. It was an expression that sent Angela back to her childhood. Most people had looked at her this way throughout her adolescence, and today Angela felt much of the confidence she had earned in the last few years slipping away. She muttered a nearly silent thank you while stuffing the pages into her bag.

"Let me help you," Catherine said, taking control of the situation and organizing the pages into a neat stack for Angela to place back into her purse.

"Angela stopped by for coffee," Catherine said. "Just a quick visit."

Bill looked at the dry coffeepot, empty since this morning.

"Got it," he said. "You feeling better? Thomas said you were under the weather."

Angela nodded quickly. "Yes. Thank you." She looked at Catherine. "Call me later so we can talk."

"Will do."

Angela walked past Catherine's husband and the man from the alley, hurried to the front foyer, pushed through the screen door, and raced down the steps, quickly walking along the sidewalk with her purse clutched under her arm.

Inside the house, Bill Blackwell stood next to Catherine and watched Angela rush down the block. He kept his voice quiet so Leonard Williams, whom Thomas had just hired as a foreman, wouldn't hear. He didn't want his words getting back to his partner.

"I'd never say anything to Thomas, but what the hell is wrong with her? Is she a little . . . dense? Like retarded?"

Catherine turned her head and stared into her husband's eyes. "She's anything but stupid, you idiot."

"Then why does she act like that?"

"Because she's a goddamn genius, Bill. And people treat her like a leper."

CHAPTER 10
Chicago, October 21, 2019

*R*ORY ENTERED THE SMALL LAW FIRM AND CLICKED ON THE LIGHTS. She walked past Celia's desk and into her father's office, where the stacks of files had shrunk since her initial visit. She still remembered the day Celia had dribbled tears onto her neck. A week later, the thought continued to bubble her skin with goose bumps and call for extra scrubbing each morning in the shower.

Despite her hysterics, Celia was quite efficient. She and the paralegal had notified all of the firm's current clients about the death of Frank Moore, and the need for them to find new counsel. From Celia's diligent work and research, nearly every client was either represented by a new firm or had strong leads on where to take their cases. A letter had gone out to all former clients explaining the news. In just one week, Celia's work was completed, her desk emptied, and the rest of the dissolution of Frank Moore's firm rested on Rory's shoulders.

Rory, too, had been busy. She'd placed calls to all clients whose cases were approaching trial and explained the situation—extensions were being filed until new counsel could be assigned. Nearly every case had been shuffled, and when she walked into her father's office this morning, there was only a single, lone folder waiting on his desk. It was as enigmatic as it was troubling, and so far, Rory had not been able to reassign it. Mostly because the judge she had spoken to about the case had requested a meeting before Rory did anything else, but also because the closer Rory looked into the details of the file, the more curious she became about how this case had fallen into her father's hands.

She spent an hour at her father's desk, searching the Internet for any information she could find about the client. Rory had never known of the case during her time at the firm. But given her limited role within the Moore Law Group, this was not startling news. She had never heard of most of her father's clients, but this one carried such magnitude that she was interested to know how he had kept such tight wraps on it. Her father's history with this client was extensive, and untangling the firm from the situation would not be as simple as a few phone calls looking for reassignment.

At 10:00 A.M., Rory shut down the computer, grabbed the lone file that remained on her father's desk, and locked the empty law office on the way out. She climbed into her car and drove downtown to the Daley Center. Inside, she made it through security, and, a few minutes later, rode the elevator with the security guard to the twenty-sixth floor, where the Circuit Court of Cook County was located. The guard led her down a hallway to the judge's chambers and knocked on a closed door. A moment later, the door opened and a distinguished-looking older man appeared, white hair and wire-rimmed glasses. He was dressed in a suit and tie.

"Rory Moore?" the judge asked.

"Yes, Your Honor," Rory said as the guard tipped his hat and was gone.

"Russell Boyle. Come on in."

Rory walked into the judge's chambers and took a seat in front of his desk. The judge sat in his deep-set leather throne and swiveled to face Rory.

"I've been trying to get ahold of your father for a couple of weeks. Sorry to hear about his passing. I was just made aware of the circumstances."

"Thank you."

"Thank *you* for coming down here on such short notice. I don't mean this to sound harsh, but for many reasons other than the obvious, your father's death comes at a terrible time. Frank and I were working on a delicate case, and the situation needs attention." Judge Boyle lifted a file from his desk.

"Yes, sir," Rory said. "It's the last bit of my father's business that I'm trying to take care of."

"Are you familiar with this case?"

"No, sir. I wasn't familiar with any of my father's cases."

"Weren't you a partner in the firm?"

"A partner? No, sir. My father's law firm was a one-man shop. He had no partners. Certainly not me. I did some side work for him when he needed help, but I wasn't active in the firm."

"What was your role at the firm, Ms. Moore?"

Rory tried to find the correct words to describe what, exactly, she did for her father. Her lightning-fast mind and borderline photographic memory allowed her to read briefs and comprehend the law and its loopholes better than her father had ever understood it. When Frank Moore got stuck on a case, he asked his daughter for help. Despite that she had never stepped foot in a courtroom, Rory had always been able to put together a winning strategy for just about every case for which her father had sought her counsel.

"Mostly research," Rory finally said.

"But you *are* an attorney, Ms. Moore. Is that correct?"

The technical answer was *yes,* but all she wanted to do was lie.

"I'm not practicing any longer."

"Are you licensed in Illinois?"

"Yes, sir, but only as a supplement to my employment with the Chicago Police Depart—"

Judge Boyle handed Rory a file in midsentence. "Good. Then you're more than qualified to handle this situation."

Rory took the file.

"Let me get you up to speed. Your father's client is preparing for parole, and it's a touchy situation."

Rory opened the file and began reading.

"He's due in front of the parole board one final time to review my recommendations for the conditions of his release, which is scheduled for November third. The hearing will be the day before. Your father and I were hashing out the details, and I'm afraid you're going to have to put on your lawyer shoes for the hearing. It's mostly a formality, as the board will go along with all of my recommendations, and I've already approved all of theirs. But, nonetheless, we all need to cross our *t*'s and dot our *i*'s on this one. You'll have to appear with him."

"Sir, I'm not sure that's a good idea."

"I've dragged my feet on this for as long as possible, but the parole board has made their decision and I've spoken to the governor about it. There's no way to stop this from happening, so I'm going to make sure it goes as smoothly as possible now. There was a shitload, excuse my French, of details I worked out with your father. Many terms of the release were negotiated. We had everything just about settled."

Judge Boyle pointed at the file in Rory's hands.

"Make yourself familiar with the details so we can discuss the final terms next time you and I meet."

"Your Honor, I'm working to reassign all my father's cases. I'm not taking them on myself."

"I'm afraid that's not an option in this case. Unless you think you can find someone to handle it for you by next week."

"Can I request an extension?"

"Your father has already requested several. I can't kick this down the road any longer. There's too much attention on the case. Your client has been in the news lately, and he's due in front of the board in two weeks. Before then, and when you're familiar with the case, you and I will talk about the specifics of his parole. Let's get this man's affairs in order, and get his file the hell off my docket."

"Sir, I'm not suited for a courtroom. Or parole boards. Or for lawyering, in general."

Judge Boyle was already out of his majestic leather chair and on his way to the door of his chambers.

"I suggest you find a way to remedy that situation before you come out of retirement next week."

He opened the door and stood next to it. Rory took her cue to leave, her knees buckling slightly when she stood. After she gained her bearings, Rory cleared her throat.

"What did this guy do that makes a simple parole so complicated?"

"He killed a whole slew of people back in 1979. And now a few idiots on a parole board think it's a good idea to let him out of jail."

CHICAGO
August 1979

ANGELA JOGGED THE TWO BLOCKS HOME FROM CATHERINE'S HOUSE, raced up her steps, and pushed through her front door. She rattled the frame closed and twisted the dead bolt with trembling fingers. Her breathing was labored from her frantic march home, during which she constantly looked over her shoulder to make sure no one was following her. With the door securely latched, she leaned her forehead against the frame, her breaths shallow from having come face-to-face with the stranger from the alley. She tried for the last week to stop the image of his deep-set eyes from trickling into her mind. She'd done a good job today of replacing that image of the stranger's face with those of the missing women as she worked out her theory that The Thief had been lurking for much longer than this summer. But now, since seeing the man at Catherine's and knowing Thomas and Bill had hired him, Angela's tightly tethered paranoia had broken loose.

She spent an hour checking the locks and windows, picking up the phone a hundred times in a row. She called Thomas's office, but there was no answer. Her index finger became raw from punching the numbers on the phone. She settled into a mindless loop of dialing Thomas's office number into the phone, pacing to the back door, peeling the curtains to the side, and staring out into the alley. Back and forth for hours until she finally heard the deep rumble of Thomas's Ford truck turn down the alley, and saw the garage door begin to open. The growl of her husband's truck, a noise that usually irked her the way all loud noises did, today brought comfort.

Angela's skin was burning as she waited for Thomas in the kitchen. When the door opened, Angela immediately recognized the concern on her husband's face.

"What's the matter?" he asked, rushing to her.

"I saw him again," Angela said, but Thomas was paying no attention to her words.

He grasped her wrists gently and examined her hands, lifting them to his face to get a better look. For the first time, Angela noticed her bloody fingertips. Thomas moved his hands to her upper arms, pulling her sleeves away. Angela had unknowingly removed the long-sleeved, button-down shirt she had worn to the library, which Catherine had questioned. She stood now in a white T-shirt, the sleeves of which were soaked with bloodstains from where she had dug at her shoulders and opened the scabs that were hidden there.

"What's going on?" Thomas said. "You're covered in blood, Angela."

She felt him wipe her forehead and eyebrows, where her bloody fingertips had left crimson streaks from pulling at her lashes.

"He was at Catherine's. Bill hired him."

"Slow down," Thomas said, looking into her eyes. "Slow down and breathe."

Angela swallowed hard and tried to control her frantic respiration. She was like a child who had cried ferociously and was now trying to speak. She exhaled a few times and allowed Thomas's grip on her shoulders to right her mind.

"I was at Catherine's house today."

"Okay?"

"And Bill came home."

"Okay?"

"And he was with the man from the alley. From when I tried to get rid of the couch."

"Who was it?"

"Bill said he works for you. He runs the warehouse up north."

Thomas furrowed his brow, and then cocked his head. "The Kenosha warehouse? That's Leonard."

"He was in Catherine's house. He looked right at me."

"Leonard Williams? Are you talking about Leonard?"

"Yes!" Angela screamed. "He was the man from the alley."

"Angela, it's okay."

Thomas tried to pull her into his chest, but she resisted like a child working to prevent a parent from lifting them.

"But . . . I saw him in the alley."

"Leonard lives in the area. He was probably out walking that morning. This is good news, Angela. You see? Leonard is harmless. He runs one of our warehouses. That's all."

Angela felt Thomas pull her close again, this time allowing it. She rested her head on his shoulder, her chest still heaving, but no comfort came from her husband's embrace. Worry was all she could do and all she could feel. It was all her mind would allow. It filled her chest, her head, her soul.

Thomas whispered into her ear. "I think it's time you start seeing your doctor again."

CHAPTER 11
Chicago, October 22, 2019

*I*T WAS MIDMORNING ON THE DAY AFTER HER MEETING WITH JUDGE Boyle, court was in session, and the hallways were vacant when Rory walked through the Dirksen Federal Courthouse in The Loop. Her combat boots rattled with her gait and echoed off the walls. Rory found the courtroom, pulled her gray coat tight to her neck, opened the heavy door, and slid silently into the back row. The pews were mostly empty, but for the first three, which were lined with young men and women Rory guessed were students of the distinguished Lane Phillips. Groupies, she thought, who followed the good doctor everywhere he went. Lane's court appearances brought high fervor for the young lads who hoped to see their mentor in rare form on the stand. Rory admitted that a Dr. Lane Phillips court appearance could rival any other type of entertainment.

Lane was testifying as an expert witness for the prosecution in the case of a double murder that took place the year before—a man was accused of killing his wife and mother in a fit of rage. Rory hadn't seen much of him in the last week because he had been preparing for his time on the stand.

"Dr. Phillips," the attorney asked from behind the podium. "You mentioned earlier that your specialty is in forensic psychology. Is that correct?"

"Correct," Dr. Phillips said from the witness chair.

Lane Phillips was approaching fifty, but looked like he was in his thirties, with mismanaged hair and the remnants of a once-prominent dimple on his right cheek, which flashed when he smiled. His casual attitude toward anything that came his way made him popular with the students, who looked up to him like a deity. His laissez-faire style—messy hair, black jeans, worn sport coat, and no tie—surely spoke to the young audience that filled the front pews. Whenever Lane spent the night at Rory's place, he never took more than ten minutes to shower and dress in the morning. His efficiency made Rory Moore, who was far from girlish, look like a beauty queen.

Lane's appearance stiffly contrasted with the sharp-suited attorney cross-examining him, whose hair was perfect and whose cuff links shined brightly as they peeked from under the sleeves of his tailored suit. Even before Rory took into consideration the discussion between the two men, it was obvious they were rivals.

"Is it also true, Doctor, that you serve often as an expert witness in high-profile cases?"

"The profile of a case is not a variable in my decision to serve as a witness."

"Very well," the attorney said, walking from behind the podium. "But it is true that you often testify as an expert witness in cases of homicide, is it not?"

"Yes, that's true."

"Usually, your expertise is sought to help the jury understand the mind-set of the one who stands accused of murder. Is that correct?"

"Oftentimes, yes," Dr. Phillips said. Lane sat upright with his hands folded in his lap, oozing a calm confidence against the attorney's aggression.

"In this case today, you've offered the jury quite a detailed *look,* so to say, into the mind of my client. Is that fair to say?"

"I offered my opinion on your client's mind-set when he killed his wife and mother, yes."

The attorney let out a subtle laugh. "Objection, Your Honor."

"Dr. Phillips," the judge said. "Please limit your comments to the questions being asked and offer no more conjecture on guilt or innocence."

"Excuse me, Your Honor," Dr. Phillips said, looking back to the attorney. "I offered my opinion on what someone might be thinking *if* they had shot and killed their wife and mother."

This got a subtle reaction from the students.

The attorney nodded his head and offered a small smile as he ran his tongue against the inside of his cheek.

"So, as in today's earlier testimony, and in the many other cases in which you've served as an expert into the criminal mind, one might guess that you are employed by a government agency. Say, the FBI?"

He shook his head. "No."

"No? Wouldn't a distinguished mind such as yours be put to good use in the Criminal Investigative Division or the Behavioral Science Unit within the Federal Bureau of Investigation?"

Dr. Phillips opened his palms. "Perhaps."

The attorney took a few steps forward. "You must, instead, be in private practice, then? Counseling such individuals on a regular basis. Surely, *that* is how you came to be such an expert on the criminal mind."

"No," Lane said calmly. "I'm not in private practice."

"No?" The attorney shook his head. "Then please tell us, Dr. Phillips, with all of your advanced degrees and your many publications in forensic psychology, where exactly do you work?"

"The Murder Accountability Project."

"Yes," the attorney said, gathering papers and reading from them. "The Murder Accountability Project. That's your pet project that has supposedly developed an algorithm to detect serial killers. Do I have that right?"

"Not really, no," Lane said.

"Please enlighten us, then."

"First, it's not a pet project. It's a legitimate LLC corporation that pays my employees and me a salary. And I didn't *supposedly* develop anything. I *actually* developed an algorithm that tracks similarities between homicides across the country to look for trends. These trends can then lead to patterns, which can help law enforcement solve homicides."

"And all these homicides you help to solve, how many of the accused perpetrators do you deal with personally as a psychologist?"

"My program identifies trends to help law enforcement track potential killers. Once we see a pattern, the authorities take over the case."

"So the answer to how many of these alleged murderers you end up counseling as a psychologist would be *zero*. Is that correct?"

"I'm not directly involved with any of the accused that my program has helped identify."

"So calling yourself an expert in psychology when you no longer practice the profession is a bit misleading, is it not?"

"No, sir. Misleading is dressing in a shiny suit and calling yourself an attorney, when really you're just a hack throwing insults to distract the jury."

Lane's students tried unsuccessfully to mute their laughter.

"Dr. Phillips," the judge said.

Lane nodded. "Excuse me, Your Honor."

The attorney, unfazed, went back at his papers. "You are also a professor at the University of Chicago. Is that correct?"

Lane looked back at his rival. "Yes."

"A professor of what, exactly?"

"Criminal and forensic psychology."

"I see," the attorney said again, walking back to the podium with a trying-too-hard confused look on his face and scratching his sideburn. "So you run a business that claims to identify killers, but you don't work in any capacity of psychology with those killers. And you *teach* the psychology of the criminal mind to young college students. I'm struggling to understand where your *practical* experience comes from, Dr. Phillips? I mean, you've offered so much information about my client's mind-set, and what he must have been thinking in the days leading up to the night his wife and mother were killed. Insights such as the ones you offered have to come from *practical, clinical* experience working with men and women convicted of violent crimes. But it looks to me like the prosecution has put on the stand a so-called expert witness who runs a business that sells algorithms and data to the police, and who teaches psychology to college kids. Doctor, have you heard of the axiom 'those who cannot *do*, teach'?"

"Objection!" the prosecutor said as she stood from behind the table.

"Withdrawn, Your Honor. I have no more questions for Dr. Phillips."

The DA was heading to the witness-box. "Dr. Phillips, prior to taking a university faculty position and starting the Murder Accountability Project, where were you employed?"

"At the Federal Bureau of Investigation."

"For how long?"

"Ten years."

"And what was your role within the Bureau?"

"I was hired as a forensic psychologist."

"And your job was to analyze crimes to determine the type of person who may have committed them. Is that accurate?"

"Yes, I was a profiler."

"During your tenure at the Bureau, you worked on over one hundred fifty cases. What was your clearance rate in those cases, where your expertise in profiling the perpetrator led to an arrest?"

"I had a close rate of ninety-two percent."

"The national average for clearance rate of homicides is sixty-four percent. Your success rate was thirty points higher than that. Before your tenure with the Bureau, Dr. Phillips, you wrote a thesis on the criminal mind titled *Some Choose Darkness*. That thesis is still widely heralded as a comprehensive look into the minds of killers and why they kill. Please tell us, Dr. Phillips, how you gained such insight."

"I spent two years during my PhD studies on sabbatical, during which I traveled the world interviewing convicted killers, understanding motive, mind-set, empathy, and patterns of how a human being decides to take another's life. The dissertation is a well-received and peer-reviewed document."

"In fact," the DA said, "more than ten years after your thesis was published, it is still popular in the forensic community. Am I correct?"

"That's correct."

"In fact, your thesis is used as the main training tool around which the FBI teaches new hires who join the Bureau as profilers. Is that correct?"

"Yes."

"In addition to your dissertation, you also compiled your findings on serial killers of the last one hundred years into a true-crime book. Is that correct?"

"Yes."

"As of the latest printing, how many copies of that book are in print?"

"About six million."

"No more questions, Your Honor."

CHAPTER 12
Chicago, October 22, 2019

*R*ORY ENTERED THE TAVERN ON THE AFTERNOON AFTER LANE'S courtroom appearance. She and Lane sat at the corner of the bar and ordered drinks. Rory took off her beanie hat and removed her glasses. There were few people in this world Rory Moore felt comfortable around, Lane Phillips was one of them. The bartender placed a Surly Darkness stout in front of her, and a light beer in front of Lane. Rory made an ugly face when she looked at Lane's beer.

"What?" he asked.

"Your beer is the same color as urine."

"That dark stuff hurts my stomach."

"*You* hurt my stomach," Rory said. "Why do you put yourself through that crap?"

"On the stand? Every expert witness has his credentials questioned. It's part of the gig. Gotta have thick skin to deal with it, and you have to see it for what it is. The defense is attacking me to distract the jury from the fact that his client killed his wife. If my credentials need to get shredded in order for my opinions to be heard, that's okay with me, as long as the son of a bitch is found guilty."

"I hate bullies."

"He's just doing his job."

"Lawyers are the scum of the earth," Rory said, taking a sip of stout.

"Says the lawyer next to me. And he's right, by the way. I haven't practiced psychology for years. And I haven't dealt directly with the criminally insane for more than a decade."

"That might be about to change. I need a little help."

"With the Camille Byrd reconstruction?"

Rory thought briefly of Camille Byrd, whose photo she had pinned to her corkboard days before. Her father had died of a heart attack just after she agreed to take the case, and tying up his affairs had been an all-encompassing task. A pang of heartache struck as Camille's face popped into her thoughts. Rory had all but abandoned the case, and the guilt of leaving a cold case unattended suddenly felt heavy on her shoulders. She made a mental note to put in some hours on the reconstruction, once she had this last file of her father's settled.

"No, something else," she finally said.

Rory reached into her purse and pulled out the file Judge Boyle had given her.

"I've got my father's firm pretty well settled, besides this one case."

She pushed the folder across the bar, and saw Lane's posture straighten. Paging through a criminal's file gave him a thrill. And despite any stiff-suited attorney trying to convince people otherwise, Lane Phillips was one of the best at dissecting the mind of a killer. He'd resigned from the FBI not because his profiling skills were suspect, but because he was too proficient at it. Diving into criminal minds left him shaky and tormented by what he found there. He understood their minds so well that it left a haunting impression he had difficulty shaking off. So when his true-crime book, which chronicled the minds of the most notorious serial killers of the last one hundred years, including personal interviews with many of them, sold more than two million copies during its first year in print, he quit the Bureau and started the Murder Accountability Project with Rory. The MAP was an effort to track unsolved homicides and identify patterns that might highlight similarities between crimes, often pointing to serial killings. Rory and Lane's skills complemented each other. She was able to reconstruct homicides better than anyone in the country, and Lane

Phillips was one of the world's foremost authorities on serial killings.

"Ever hear of this guy?" Rory asked as Lane paged through the file.

"Yeah. They called him The Thief. But, Christ, that was forty years ago. Your father represented this guy?"

"Apparently. I'm still sorting the details. Garrison Ford, the big criminal defense firm, originally handled the case. My father worked at Garrison Ford after leaving the public defender's office, but his tenure was short. Just a couple of years. When my father left to start his own firm, he took this case with him."

Lane turned a few pages in the file. "When was the last time your father worked at Garrison Ford?"

"Nineteen eighty-two," Rory said. "And he's had this guy as a client ever since."

"Doing what?" Lane asked.

"That's what I'm trying to figure out. After Garrison Ford mounted an unsuccessful defense at trial, my father worked on appeals and represented him at parole hearings. The guy also has a small fortune from before he was put away, and it looks like my dad oversaw the money. Set up a trust and protected it for three decades. Settled some debts, looked after some property, and paid himself out of the trust for legal services rendered."

Lane turned the page. "And visited this guy a lot. Look at all these visitor log entries."

"Yes, my father had quite a relationship with this man."

"So what's the issue? Pawn this case off like you've done with all the others."

"I can't. This guy's been granted parole. My father was working with the judge on the details when he died, and His Honor is under some pressure to get it off his docket, so he's not letting me delay it."

Lane took a sip of beer as he continued to page through the file.

Rory picked up her stout. "Tell me about this guy. I looked him up. He was convicted on a single count of Murder Two. Doesn't seem like it would be so spectacular that he made parole after forty years. But when I talked with the judge, he said the guy killed a whole bunch of people."

"Oh, boy," Lane said, looking up from the file and staring at Rory.

"What?" Rory asked.

"Something's piqued your interest about this case, hasn't it?"

"Stop it, Lane."

"I know how you operate, Rory. Something about your father's involvement in this case has planted itself in that brain of yours and now you can't let it go."

With her father gone, Lane Phillips was the only other person who fully understood Rory's obsession with things unknown. His history as a psychologist stopped Rory from pretending he was incorrect. Dr. Phillips knew the workings of the human brain well, and Rory's, in particular, better than most. This quirk in her personality was what made her such a sought-after forensic reconstructionist. Until she had all the answers about a case, she was helpless to stop her mind from working to find them. Especially if an initial glance at a case held something that made no sense, and her father's involvement with the man the papers called The Thief made no sense at all.

"Tell me about this guy," she said again.

Lane wrapped his hand around the bottom of his beer mug, spun it in place as he collected his thoughts on the long-ago case. "The prosecution pushed for Murder One, the jury came back with second-degree for the lone victim. But this guy was suspected in many other cases of missing women," Lane said. "Five or six . . . I'd have to look it up."

"Five or six homicides? Nothing in his file mentions other victims. And it would be impossible to make parole if he killed so many."

"He was *suspected* of more killings, never charged. And you won't find anything formally linking him to the other killings. Just rumor and conjecture."

"Why did they go after him for only one homicide if they thought there were more?"

Lane closed the file. "A few reasons. The city was in a panic in the late seventies. You had the Son of Sam still lingering on people's minds—he was the nut who killed a bunch of people in New York in 1976. Then, here in Chicago, we had the horror of John Wayne Gacy having killed and buried thirty-some boys in his crawl space. Then, during the summer of 1979, women started disappearing and the city bubbled with fear. The whole summer was filled with heat and anxiety. Eventually, toward the end of summer, the police found their man. But the way they discovered him was very unorthodox, and it was entirely thanks to an autistic woman who pieced it all together."

Rory leaned forward across the bar to listen more intently. She was more interested now than she had been.

"The method in which this woman gathered and delivered the evidence was very strange, and the DA knew none of the evidence would stand up in court. Most was flat-out inadmissible. Neither side wanted a trial. If the prosecution failed to convince the jury of his guilt, this guy would walk. If they succeeded, he'd be eligible for the death penalty, which was still around in 1979. So a trial was risky for both sides. In the end, the DA made the choice to go after him on the single homicide. They had shaky evidence, a lot of circumstance, and no body."

"No body?"

"No. That's why it was such a risk to go to trial, and why they went after him for only the single victim. No bodies were ever found, besides one that they could never tie to him in any meaningful way. And with no body, the jury came back with a guilty verdict for Murder Two. The conviction sent him away for sixty years, but allowed for parole after thirty. The sentence put the city's fears to rest."

"And now, after ten years of parole hearings and forty years in jail, he's about to be granted his freedom."

Lane shook his head. "I studied this case for my book, but the details never made it past the final edits. That woman who figured it all out. Goddamn, I still remember the headlines. 'Schizophrenic Woman Brings Down The Thief.'"

"Schizophrenic?"

"No one knew anything about autism back then. Plus, 'Schizophrenic' sold more papers."

85

Rory looked into the black abyss of her Surly Darkness stout, lifted the mug, and swallowed the rest of the beer. She wanted to order another. She longed for a touch of dizziness to soften her thoughts about this autistic woman she knew nothing about. She knew those curiosities were taking root in her mind and that they would be impossible to ignore. She stared up at Lane.

"What ever happened to her? The autistic woman?"

Lane tapped the file with his finger. "Her name was Angela Mitchell. He killed her before she had a chance to testify."

CHICAGO
August 1979

*T*WO DAYS AFTER HER BREAKDOWN, ANGELA WAS AT THE DOCTOR'S office, sitting on the table in a thin gown and pulling at her eyelashes.

"Relax, darling," the nurse said as she prepped the syringe. "I just need two vials. You won't feel a thing."

Angela looked the other way when the nurse pressed the needle to the inside of her elbow, but it wasn't the threat of a needle that had her on edge. Her panic attack had set Thomas's radar on high alert, and he'd forced her to see the doctor before things got out of control. Little did he know that things were far beyond that. Baring her paranoia to Thomas had set loose even more angst now that she was at the clinic. She'd been through this routine before. Most of her adolescence had been spent in doctors' offices and on psychiatrists' couches. Back when she was under the rule of her parents, doctors and shrinks were her way of life. Her parents believed that if Angela saw enough of them, and the right ones, they could psychoanalyze her back to health. When none of the therapists could do for their daughter what Angela's parents demanded, they admitted her to a juvenile psychiatric facility.

Angela was seventeen when her parents forced her into that place, and she spent seven months there until she discharged herself on her eighteenth birthday. It was only with the help of a dear friend that Angela had escaped that life. She had been on a (mostly) smooth trajectory for the last several years. Since meeting Thomas, she'd tightly managed her anxiety and had even felt like she was starting to fit into society. Her autism was something no one understood, including the many doctors who pretended otherwise, and Angela had long ago stopped trying to explain to others how her mind operated. She had learned over many years of criticism and failure that no one could fully comprehend the way her thoughts were organized. Yet, here she was again, waiting for a doctor to explain what was wrong with her.

She knew, though, that Thomas meant well. His eagerness for her to seek psychiatric help was simply his way of trying to protect her. He didn't know her full history. Angela had tried her best to keep hidden the dark days of her teenage years. And until just recently, the ruse had worked. Thomas had opened her life to new opportunities. He made her feel safe. But despite the progress, the events of the summer had made her realize how frail a hold she had on it all. The missing women who had run through the folds of her mind, and the idea that they were part of a longer string of violence, had started Angela down a road with no turnoffs. Despite Angela recognizing that her obsession with these women was unhealthy, she felt a connection to them that she couldn't ignore.

The stranger from the alley, who had reappeared in Catherine's kitchen, had set loose her anxiety in ways that transported her through the years and back to her adolescence. The obsessive-compulsive disorder she thought she had tethered and stowed in a locked-off compartment of her psyche had been reawakened to wreak havoc, like when she was younger. On top of it all, she feared that her affliction would push Thomas away. She feared now that Thomas had gotten a clear look at her paranoia; the anchor that had steadied her for the last couple of years was breaking free from its mooring to leave Angela adrift and alone. So many worries ran through her mind, she had trouble keeping track of them all.

"All done, darling," the nurse said, bringing Angela's thoughts back to the present. The nurse held two vials of deep red blood in her gloved hand.

"The doctor will be right in."

A few minutes later, the doctor entered the room and performed a cursory exam.

"Have you had panic attacks in the past?" the doctor asked while he scribbled in the chart.

"No," she said. "I mean . . . when I was younger, but they didn't call them that."

The doctor took a minute to finish writing, and then looked at Angela. "You used to take lithium as a teenager. Was it effective?"

Angela, who normally would shy away from a man staring at her, peered back with an intensity that surprised even herself. The horrors of her teenage years fueled her rage.

"No! He forced me to take it, and my parents went along with him."

"Who?"

"The psychiatrist my parents sent me to. The one who kept me locked away in the psychiatric hospital. He believed I had a behavioral disorder, and that I was a manic-depressive. They used lithium to sedate me. Besides putting me to sleep, it gave me wild hallucinations."

The doctor paused before nodding. "Yes, not everyone responds to it." He pulled a prescription pad from the breast pocket of his jacket and jotted on it. He tore the page free and handed her the slip. "This is for Valium, it will take the edge off with none of the side effects of lithium."

He jotted again onto the pad and tore a second slip free.

"And here is the name of a psychiatrist. I think you should talk with someone. I've been referring many of my female patients to him lately. The missing women from the city have gotten a lot of people spooked. Talking with someone will help. In the meantime, push fluids until the vomiting passes. The Valium should help, and, Mrs. Mitchell," the doctor said as he stood, "the police are good at what they do. They'll catch this guy. That will be the best cure for everything you've got going on."

On the way out of the clinic, Angela crumpled the paper that held the shrink's name, dropped it in the trash bin, and climbed into her car. She walked into the pharmacy ten minutes later to fill her Valium prescription.

CHAPTER 13
Chicago, October 23, 2019

*R*ORY PUT A CALL IN TO DETECTIVE DAVIDSON. HE OWED HER AFTER the setup with Camille Byrd's father; now she was calling in the favor. She needed everything he could find on the old case from 1979. Having scoured the dark corners of Cook County federal buildings in search of what Rory needed, Ron came through, delivering three boxes of information to her door earlier in the afternoon. Now the boxes were stacked next to her desk while Rory pored over the details.

She had emptied the first box and spread the contents onto her desk. The facts about the 1979 case fascinated her. More than anything, the enigmatic woman named Angela Mitchell, who had managed to identify a serial killer, drew all of Rory's attention. Rory felt a strange connection to the woman from four decades ago. Angela Mitchell had done, essentially, what Rory did now—she put names and narratives to victims in order to reconstruct crimes.

The defense team who represented The Thief, of which her father was a member, had created a biography of Angela Mitchell. It described her as a "socially awkward twenty-nine year-old woman who suffered from autism and a limited ability to understand her surroundings." An obsessive-compulsive personality disorder, the report continued, limited her abilities to handle the activities of daily living; and at the time during which she collected the "evidence" the prosecution had been allowed to present at trial, she was on heavy doses of Valium. The report went on in length about Angela's troubled adolescence, her time spent in a juvenile psychiatric hospital, and her estrangement from her parents. Taken on its surface, the account painted an unflattering image of Angela Mitchell.

The more Rory read, though, the more connected she felt to the woman from years ago. Their stories were similar in many ways. Although Rory was never estranged from her parents, quite the opposite, and she had never been forced into a psych ward, Rory's childhood had been plagued by many of the same ailments as Angela's. Instead of shipping Rory off to doctors and hospitals, her parents had sent her to Aunt Greta's house during the summers and on most weekends. Although no medication was forced on Rory, Aunt Greta offered different remedies for Rory's social anxiety. Without her great-aunt, Rory's childhood might have been written about using the identical language as Angela Mitchell's.

She pushed the thought of Angela Mitchell's supposed Valium addiction from her mind, working hard to prevent the comparison to the glass of Three Floyds Dark Lord stout that rested in front of her. It was three o'clock in the afternoon and Rory was on her second glass, her head vertiginous with the early effects of the alcohol. In a show of rebellion to her own thoughts, she lifted the glass, took a long swallow, and then spent two hours on the 1979 file, lost in the details of Angela Mitchell and what she had managed to do. Rory made it through two full boxes, but left the third untouched for now. She turned to her desktop and typed the name *Angela Mitchell* into the search engine. After scrolling through pages of links that had nothing to do with The Thief from 1979, Rory finally came across a few general articles that rehashed some details about the case. None of the online hits held revelations that were not already in the boxes next to her.

She was ready to shut down her computer when she came to a link for a Facebook page titled *Justice for Angela*. The page had twelve hundred followers and the last post had been made two years prior, a short paragraph dated August 31, 2017:

> Today marks the 38th anniversary of my dear friend
> Angela Mitchell's disappearance. So many decades later,
> and there are still no leads on the case. Few members of the
> Chicago Police Department even remember Angela, and

those that do are long retired and gave up hope long ago of discovering what really happened to her during the summer of 1979. Those of us who are part of this online community looking for answers know that no resolutions were provided during the farce of a trial that took place in 1980. With each passing year, it seems more and more likely that the only one who could shed light on the truth is sitting in jail. He, of course, refuses to utter a word about Angela.

As always, anyone with tips or information about Angela Mitchell can comment on this thread and I'll follow up with you personally. The smallest detail, even this many years later, could be helpful.

The Facebook post included a grainy image of Angela Mitchell. It was actually a photo of a photo. The person who posted it had used a cell phone to capture the old Polaroid picture, which was yellowed and faded by age, the camera's flash reflecting off the upper corner of the plastic photograph. Rory looked at Angela Mitchell. She was a petite woman, who, in the photo, stood next to a taller woman, who Rory assumed was the author of the Facebook post. In the snapshot, Angela smiled shyly at the camera, her gaze slightly down and to the left, unable, Rory understood, to stare directly into the camera's lens. Rory had the same affliction.

Lane had been correct with his assumption earlier at the bar. The seed of curiosity had been planted in Rory's mind, and stopping it from growing was as impossible as stopping the sun from rising. She was initially curious about the case because of her father's involvement. But now, since learning more about the mysterious woman at the center of it, Rory felt the familiar pull of interest she knew she couldn't ignore. It was the same feeling she encountered at the start of a reconstruction. Some part of her mind would be unable to rest until she knew everything there was to know about Angela Mitchell.

She finally looked away from the gritty Facebook image and did something she would never normally consider. She clicked the mouse over the comment section and typed quickly: My name is Rory Moore. I need some details about Angela Mitchell. Please contact me.

Rory hit the return key before she could reconsider, scrolled to the top of the Facebook page, clicked the *About* icon, and pulled up information on the person who created the page. The woman claimed to be Angela Mitchell's closest friend from the summer of 1979. Her name was Catherine Blackwell.

CHICAGO
August 1979

*T*HE VALIUM WAS HELPING. SHE HADN'T VOMITED IN THREE DAYS, AND the headaches came less often. The medication was dulling the urge to dig at her scabbed shoulders, and the drug's overall effect was blunting her paranoia and keeping Thomas's concerns at bay. Angela was taking twice the suggested dosage, though, and she worried not only about overmedicating herself, but also about what would happen when the pills ran out. Thomas had been watching her closely since the breakdown, and Angela worked hard to keep things together and convince him that since her visit with the doctor she was feeling well. That she had her short relapse under control. That the identity of the stranger from the alley, while at first disconcerting, had now led to relief. And, most important, that she didn't need to see a psychiatrist.

The acting and camouflaging of her symptoms was exhausting, and Angela wasn't sure how much longer she could keep up the ruse. But a reprieve was coming. Thomas was scheduled to inspect a work site in Indianapolis over the weekend and meet with the builder, who was planning a 150-home subdivision. Thomas and Bill were bidding on the job and he would be gone all of Saturday and most of Sunday. Talk of canceling the trip had started after Thomas came home a few days before to find Angela covered in blood and melting down in ways she had never before displayed to her husband. But desperately needing both time away from Thomas's suffocating concern, and the opportunity to explore her suspicions about Leonard Williams, Angela had used all her willpower and double the usual dosage of Valium to put up a façade of normalness and well-being. Now, Saturday morning, Angela gave one more push while she and Thomas sat at the kitchen table and drank their morning coffee.

"Just go," Angela said. "I'm feeling much better."

Thomas looked at her. "You're taking the medication, right?"

"I am. It's helping."

"I'm worried about being gone overnight. Bill should be able to handle this without me."

"I'll be fine," Angela said, trying to hide the urgency in her voice. "And we need this contract. It would make our year."

"We're doing fine," Thomas said. "It would be nice, but we don't *need* it."

"Go," she said, looking him in the eye the way she seldom did anyone else. "I'm okay."

An hour after she watched Thomas back his truck out of the garage and drive down the alley on his way to Indiana, Angela pulled away from the curb and headed for the highway. Thomas and Bill had four warehouses spread between Kenosha, Wisconsin, the north and west sides of the city, and Hammond, Indiana. Leonard Williams ran the warehouse in Kenosha, so with Thomas gone, Angela was on her way to the Wisconsin location.

Kenosha was about an hour and a half from the city, and Angela consulted her map after she turned off the highway. Eventually she turned down the long road that led to her husband's Wisconsin office and construction warehouse. A trail of dust floated behind her vehicle as she drove. Situated at the end of a long industrial park, the office was one of many single-story buildings that lined the gravel road. When Angela pulled up to the office on Saturday morning, hers was the only vehicle present. She put the car into park, but left the engine running and the air-conditioning raging as she listened to the radio. There had been a development overnight in the case of the summer's missing women and WGN offered the latest details.

"We can confirm," the reporter said through the radio, "that the body found early this morning is suspected to be that of Samantha Rodgers, who had gone missing three weeks ago and was considered to be The Thief's fifth, and most recent, victim."

Sitting in her car, Angela's mind flashed to the night she and Catherine had watched the news report in her living room about the missing woman named Samantha Rodgers. She had since created a biography on the woman and Angela knew all the details about her disappearance: the date she went missing, the last place she was seen, the last time her parents and friends had spoken with her, and the exact location where the cab had dropped her the night she disappeared—Western and Kedzie, a mere block from her apartment. Angela knew the details about Samantha Rodgers before the reporter spoke. In fact, she knew much more than the news story offered. Angela knew the girl so well that her heart ached at the idea that there was no hope she would be found alive.

"We are still waiting for the Chicago Police Department to confirm the victim's identity, but it is widely believed that the body of Samantha Rodgers has been found in a wooded area in Forest Glen, miles away from the victim's apartment in Wicker Park. We will stay on top of any new developments and interrupt regularly scheduled programming with any breaking news."

As Angela shut off the car's engine, she realized her heart was drumming. When she pulled the keys from the ignition, they jingled with the tremor in her hand. She steadied herself as she climbed from the car and looked around. She knew the warehouse would be quiet at this time on a Saturday morning, the work crews were already out to job sites.

She walked across the gravel lot. The office door was locked when she tried the handle. Before she left her house, Angela had retrieved a set of keys attached to a Chicago Bears keychain, which rested in the back of the kitchen drawer. Pulling the ring from her purse, she went one-by-one until she inserted the correct key into the door handle and twisted it open. She slipped into the office and closed the door behind her, looking back through the window and out into the parking lot. Her car sat all alone, the dust storm she had caused by driving down the industrial road had dissipated to a white cloud that hazed the area. Angela took a moment to look toward the far end of the road, which was empty and quiet. She locked the door and turned away from the window.

She went past the desk in the front office and pulled open the drawers to the file cabinets that lined the back wall. It took ten minutes of fingering through the files for Angela to find the employment records. Mitchell-Blackwell Construction had seventy-seven employees. It took only a minute to locate the file that held the name *Leonard Williams;* she pulled the file and sat on the floor to read it.

The first page held a Xeroxed photo of Leonard Williams's driver's license. A feverous chill claimed Angela's shoulders as she stared at the dark-set eyes and expressionless face of the man who had approached her weeks ago in the alley behind her home. Angela learned that he was fifty-two years old, previously employed by another construction outfit in the western suburb of Wood Dale, and had come to Mitchell-Blackwell with glowing letters of recommendation from his previous employer. He was married, with two children. As she paged through the thin file, something pulled at her mind. It was the way her brain operated. There was something she had seen, but not recognized. Some bit of relevance that had buried itself in her subconscious, but which hadn't yet floated to the surface of her awareness. Angela had always been able to sense this acute mindfulness of something critical, even if she wasn't able to immediately identify it.

She blinked away the glitch in her thoughts, ignored the soft whisper that echoed in the far-off parts of her mind, and continued to flip through the file—1099 forms, employment contracts, workmen's compensation paperwork, and union credentials—until it finally dawned on her. Until the whisper turned into a scream. She turned back to the opening page of the file and looked at Leonard Williams's driver's license again. Her vision narrowed to focus on his address. He lived in Forest Glen, the same neighborhood where Samantha Rodgers's body had just been discovered.

CHICAGO
August 1979

ANGELA JOTTED LEONARD WILLIAMS'S ADDRESS ONTO A PIECE OF scratch paper, replaced the file, and closed the cabinet. She walked around the secretary's desk and to the side door that led to the warehouse, pushed it open and entered the cavernous space. The rafter ceilings were three stories high and light penetrated the grimy windows in a cloudy gray film that left Angela squinting in the murkiness. She found the light switch and clicked the warehouse to life with fluorescent bulbs that blinked and warmed.

Giant trucks occupied the space, and pallets of dry concrete lined the walls, packaged in green bags and stacked high. Other equipment she didn't recognize or understand hung from the walls and stood in tall piles in the middle of the warehouse. Angela walked around the equipment. This was the place Leonard Williams operated and supervised.

In the back she came to a filmy window that looked out onto the parking lot. She saw her car isolated in the gravel lot, and again looked to the end of the long road that led from the main thoroughfare to the warehouse. It was desolate, and the emptiness of the place suddenly brought Angela aching lungs and shallow breaths. She felt the twinge of an impending attack, and fought against the pull of her mind to go to that dark place and entertain disturbing thoughts of Leonard Williams from the morning in the alley, his shadow climbing over her legs as he came closer to her, his black eyes, and his body silhouetted by the steep angle of the sun. But she felt something else, too—something that made it easier than normal to get past the roadblocks in her mind. The same stutter in her thoughts from a few moments earlier—while she looked through Leonard Williams's file, and unknowingly saw his address—was happening again now as she stared out the window. Something screamed for her attention.

She was in the corner of the warehouse, with the back wall immediately to her left and the sidewall with the grimy window in front of her. Something was off. As Angela looked again out at the parking lot, she remembered the image from when she had climbed from her car. She had parked at the edge of the warehouse, yet her car was many feet to the left of the window she was staring through. Angela looked at the back wall and realized the warehouse did not end where she stood, but continued beyond this point.

Moving away from the window, she walked along the back wall. It was covered in wooden shelving that rose up a full story. Heavy equipment and pallets of material filled the shelves. A forklift was parked nearby to claim the items from the higher shelves. As Angela walked along the back wall, she noticed a break in the shelving, in front of which sat a pallet of concrete. Behind the pallet a tarp hung like a curtain and partially covered a door. An eerie feeling came over her as she looked back through the warehouse toward the office. The rafters creaked with the wind. The roll of her stomach returned. She had swallowed two Valium on the way over, and resisted the urge to fish another from the bottle. She turned back to the partially hidden door, squeezed her small frame past the stacked bags of concrete, and tried the handle. Locked. She opened her purse and pulled out the keys attached to the Chicago Bears ring. She stuck one after the other into the doorknob until, on her fifth try, the lock twisted open.

Angela pushed the door, allowing it to swing on the hinges and glide into the darkened room until it struck the wall after a full 180-degree turn. She reached her arm in and felt for a light switch. The overhead lights brought the space to life, and she slowly walked into the large storage area. Rows of shelving lined the walls. Another wall was lined with barrel-sized oilcans. The floor was caked with mud, unlike the dusty concrete slab of the warehouse.

On the floor next to the large oilcans was a dirty tarp, a shovel, rope, and a stack of cinder blocks. She lifted the top from one of the cans and peered inside. It was dark and empty. As Angela slowly turned in the storage room, her skin was itchy and flushed. She took deep breaths to settle her stomach, but still bile rose in her throat. In the darkened corner, she saw a strange contraption hanging from the tall ceiling. She walked closer to get a better look. Bolted to the ceiling was an M-shaped wooden beam. Five pulleys were fastened at each point of the M, through which thick rope was strung. The rope hung down from each end of the beam like the loose limbs of a willow tree. Six feet separated the two ends of the rope. Angela walked even closer. Attached to each end of the rope was a strap of red nylon tied in a noose. It reminded her of some contraption from medieval times.

Angela held the nylon noose in her hand, pinching the soft, red material between her thumb and forefinger, when she heard a thud outside. She released the noose, ran to the door of the storage room, and peeked out into the warehouse. It was still dingy and gray, and the large overhead doors were closed. She heard the pounding once again. Squeezing between the shelving and pallet of concrete that hid the storage room door, Angela ran back to the window and looked out at the parking lot. One of the concrete trucks had returned and was dumping waste into a reservoir across the parking lot. The truck was backed up against a retaining wall, with its tank at a ninety-degree angle as workers barked orders to the driver.

Angela ran the length of the warehouse and into the office. She locked the door on the way out and hurried to her car as the workers continued their dumping fifty yards away. She steadied herself by leaning on the hood and breathing in the humid summer air. When the nausea passed, Angela climbed into the driver's seat and reached for her purse. She pulled out her bottle of Valium, swallowed another pill, and tore out of the parking lot, accelerating down the industrial road and kicking up a cloud of dust in the process. The M-shaped contraption and dual nooses burned in her vision like the afterimage of a flashbulb, just like the reporter's image from the night she watched the news report about Samantha Rodgers. And then something else . . . another whisper, far in the recesses of her mind, just a slight murmur, asking to be heard. She knew she should stop and listen to it, attempt to decipher what it was trying to tell her, but she was hardly aware of it as she sped along the gravel road, fighting to breathe and control her shaking hands, let alone able to comprehend its muddled message.

CHAPTER 14
Chicago, October 24, 2019

*R*ORY HAD NEVER APPRECIATED POSTCOITAL AFFECTION AND, IN FACT, needed her space after intimacy. Having slept together for ten years, Lane no longer questioned Rory's stealthy escape from the bedroom after sex. During the early phase of their relationship, she used to wait until Lane was asleep before attempting her get-away, but now it was just expected. She was slow and quiet as she slipped from beneath the covers, pulling a tank top over her head and tiptoeing downstairs.

In the kitchen, she opened the refrigerator, spilling soft light across the floor as she grabbed a Dark Lord. In her office, Rory sat at her desk and opened the file that waited there. With the rest of the house dark, her workspace was lit only by the soft auburn glow of the desk lamp. She took a sip of stout and began reading.

The Thief had hired the law firm of Garrison Ford immediately after his arrest. The 1979 retainer had been $25,000, which was paid with a cashier's check. The total fee for representation, which included the failed defense and the contentious trial, was close to $120,000—also paid via cashier's check in four lumps between the summer of 1979 and the winter of 1981. All of this information was contained in the third and final box Ron Davidson had delivered, along with the file from her father's office and the information Judge Boyle had provided.

Rory took a sip of beer and turned the page. The best she could piece together, her father had become involved with The

Thief during the appeals process, after the sixty-year sentence had been handed down. Garrison Ford continued to bill for services into 1982, when her father left the firm to start his own practice. Cross-referencing documents she unearthed from her father's file cabinets at his law office, Rory found a transition of invoicing that started in the later half of 1982. The first check was written to the Moore Law Group on October 5, 1982, to finance the second round of appeals.

Rory found that all reimbursements—old Xerox copies of hand-written checks—were full lump-sum payments. Over another beer, she learned that in addition to being a cold-blooded killer, her father's client was also a millionaire. At the time of his arrest, he had a net worth of $1.2 million. The man's financials were intimately detailed in his file because, in addition to handling appeals and representation at parole hearings, the man had also hired her father to look after his fortune during his incarceration, a task that included resolving debts, bringing his estate into order, and liqui-dating assets. Dipping into the dark side of criminal defense, Rory saw how her father had structured this man's fortune in an oasis of LLC corporations and trusts to hide assets and protect against the threat of civil lawsuits. Sheltered as it was, had the families of his other alleged victims gone after him, a large portion of his money would be off-limits.

But no civil suits were ever filed. Without bodies, Rory knew, a civil suit would be deemed frivolous. The remains of only one woman were found during the summer of 1979. Her name was Samantha Rodgers, and although there had been an attempt, Rory read, to tie The Thief to this woman, the attorneys at Garrison Ford had managed to convince the judge that any evidence linking their client to Samantha Rodgers was purely circumstantial. The judge agreed and the prosecution dropped their pursuit, instead focusing on Angela Mitchell.

Her father's client's money stayed protected, and, all told, when the killer settled into his cell in the early 1980s, he did so with more than $900,000 resting in a bank account. Through the 1980s, Rory's father had drawn from those funds to pay his legal fees dur-ing the lengthy appeals process, which dragged on for a decade.

In addition to checks rendered for legal services, Rory also came across additional payments categorized as "retainer fees." Over the course of the 1980s, the Moore Law Group had been paid more than $200,000. It was a steep sum to simply file appeals. The roots of her curiosity stretched deeper into her mind as she recognized that her father's connection to this man went beyond the typical attorney-client relationship.

What were you doing for this guy, Dad?

Rory read the details of the appeals her father had crafted, which highlighted the prosecution's weaknesses. They included, conveniently, that the district attorney could produce no physical evidence against his client, including the body of his alleged victim. Adding to the absence of Angela Mitchell's remains, Rory's father had argued that the woman was mentally retarded, as was stated in the 1979 brief. The term "cognitively challenged" was still decades away, and labeling her as "autistic" was less dramatic, too medical, and didn't fit the narrative. A mentally retarded schizophrenic was much more powerful. But no matter which adjectives had been used to describe Angela Mitchell, none were quite right. As Rory learned more about what the woman had done, and the lives she had surely saved, nowhere in the documents was Angela Mitchell described as "hero."

According to the statement by the prosecutor, Angela had spent the last days of her life compiling evidence that pointed a strong finger at the 1979 killer. She was killed during the process.

CHICAGO
August 1979

*I*T WAS SUNDAY MORNING, LESS THAN TWENTY-FOUR HOURS SINCE her bizarre discovery in the warehouse, and Angela had not slept a minute. She was up all night updating the biographies of the missing women, and adding everything to her notes that she had found in the last three days about Leonard Williams. After leaving the warehouse yesterday, she had spent hours at the library, spinning microfilm and researching hanging and strangulation deaths associated with women in and around Chicago. Below the graph diagram Angela had put together depicting the trend of killings over the last decade, she now added relevant information from her library research. She was trying to make sense of the contraption she had found in the hidden storage room, and believed she was onto something. Of the women on her graph who fit the description, who fell into the profile, and who had been killed in and around Chicago, most had been strangled. On the last page of her file, Angela had drawn the odd, M-shaped wooden beam with the dual hanging nooses.

Ever since rushing from the warehouse to pore through microfilm at the library, the entire time she was creating her documents and graphs and working out her theory about Leonard Williams, all through the night and up until this morning when she arrived at Catherine's house, that soft whisper in her mind nagged and annoyed. Angela never stopped her work to listen, and feared the voice that was calling her was a side effect of the Valium, which she was swallowing at an alarming rate. Or it was the logical and reasonable part of her mind working to be heard, trying to tell her that she was overmedicating herself and that her ideas about the missing women were ridiculous.

She sat at Catherine's kitchen table now, pushed the whisper of that voice away, and showed her work to her friend. Catherine sat patiently and listened to Angela tell the story of her trip to the warehouse, her discovery that Leonard Williams lived so close to where Samantha Rodgers's body had been found, that of the women who had been killed and who matched the description of the missing women from this summer—all had been strangled. And finally she showed Catherine the bizarre image she had drawn of the dual noose contraption.

Catherine took a sip of coffee when Angela finally looked at her. "You know I always support you," Catherine said. "But . . ."

"But what?" Angela asked.

"I think everything that's going on this summer has set you off."

"What do you mean?"

"I think you're very nervous about what's going on. So am I. But I think you feel like it's your responsibility to figure this out, and, Angela, some of what you're showing me is . . ."

"Is what?"

"It's hard to digest. All the research you've done on the missing women, and how they might be connected to a decadelong string of murder."

"I think they are."

"But now you're telling me you think you know who did this, and that it's a man who works for Bill and Thomas."

Angela looked away from Catherine and back to her notes, her cheeks suddenly red and searing. She gathered the papers and stuffed them into the file folder. Her research and her theories, all contained in the file folder, sat on the kitchen table like some foreign and unwanted artifact found in the wild. Neither knew quite what to do with it or how to handle it—if it were worth anything at all, or just a useless bit of something unearthed and dragged inside.

"I think Leonard Williams scared you in the alley," Catherine finally said, placing her hand on Angela's. "And I think that's made you look at him in a way that most wouldn't see him. From what I know, he's a family man. He's got a wife and kids, Angela. He's not some deranged serial killer. I don't think you've done anything foolish, let me be clear. But reasonably looking at all of this, I don't know that I totally agree with everything you're suggesting. Angela, I'm not sure . . . I'm not sure I totally believe all of this."

Angela swallowed hard at the rejection. Her surroundings faded as memories of her childhood flooded her mind. Her teachers' disparaging comments anytime Angela made a remark in school, her parents' constant refusal to listen to Angela's reasoning on any subject, her psychiatrist's outright dismissal of her pleas for help when the lithium drew wild hallucinations in her vision. All the images from her childhood carried her away, and only when she heard talking did she come back to the present. When she did, she found Bill Blackwell standing next to Catherine.

There was a far-off echo. Angela tried to hear it, but it was hollow and muted. She saw Bill's lips moving and realized the man was speaking to her. She blinked her eyes.

"The second time in a week that I come home to a surprise," she heard Bill say. "Is Thomas back from Indiana yet?"

Angela focused her eyes on the bandana around Catherine's husband's neck. She realized the soft echoing voice she had heard a moment before was not that of Bill Blackwell, but instead the whispered voice she had been hearing since her visit to the Kenosha warehouse. It was finally loud enough to decipher. It was screaming, in fact, as she stared at the man in front of her. Angela's mind flashed to the night they all ate dinner in her home. She remembered Bill's red neck, explained then as an allergic reaction to insect repellent and the remnants of mosquito bites. She remembered his bandana from the last time she sat in this kitchen with Catherine. And now today, she looked at his bandana-covered neck to see deep red marks on his skin. Marks that could come from a noose.

Angela stood quickly. The kitchen chair toppled backward and ricocheted off the kitchen floor. She backed away and, without saying a word, turned and hurried out the front door. Her thick file folder remained on the table.

CHAPTER 15
Chicago, October 25, 2019

*R*ORY MADE IT THROUGH THE SCREENING PROCESS AGAIN AND ENtered the judge's chambers after the security guard had escorted her through the hallways. Now she sat, just like she had at their original meeting, in front of the desk while the judge took to his throne behind it, the high-back leather chair rising well above his head as he sat.

"Lots to cover," Judge Boyle said. "Have you made yourself familiar with your client?"

"Your client." The sound of it bothered Rory in many ways. She didn't have "clients." Her life revolved around "cases." Her life revolved around helping *victims,* not the men accused of killing them. An acidic burn rose up her esophagus and settled in the back of her throat. But Rory swallowed it down. Her interest in Angela Mitchell was stronger than her GERD, and her father's mysterious role in The Thief's life had won a spot in her psyche. She knew she couldn't dump this case until she learned what, exactly, her father had been doing with this man for all these years.

"Yes, sir," Rory finally said.

"Excellent. Your father and I had worked out many of the stipulations relating to this man's release. Here are a few of them."

Judge Boyle handed a single piece of paper across his desk. On it was a long list of bullet points. He read from his own copy.

"There was a request to forgo a halfway house as a living requirement. Considering your client's notoriety, his age, and his financial means, I've agreed to this request. He is required to stay in Illinois for twenty-four months, however. Your client owns a home in the state, out near Starved Rock State Park. It's about an hour outside of the city. Frank had requested that your client be allowed to keep this as his residence, and I've agreed. However, there is a list of stipulations that will need to be met. You and the social worker, as well as your client's assigned parole officer, will need to visit the property ahead of time and make certain it meets the requirements."

"What requirements, sir?"

Judge Boyle pushed another sheet of paper across his desk.

"It needs to have a landline for phone, as your client will be required to check in daily with his parole officer for the first three months. Internet access is not mandatory, but suggested. The property needs to have a USPS mailing address. POB addresses are not allowed. Photos of the home will also need to be taken and placed in the formal file. Your trip to the home should be scheduled this week. You'll coordinate it with Naomi Brown, the social worker?"

The judge posed the statement as a question, but Rory understood his tone to be less of a request than an order. She nodded.

"There is a substantial sum of money that your client will have access to upon his release. Your father had financial power of attorney for the last four decades. Now that Frank is gone, the money will be handled exclusively by your client. That's over eight hundred thousand dollars, counselor. He's never been in this new world of digital banking. He'll need some help getting settled. So, of course, release the funds to him, but I'll expect you to be his steward. For the first eighteen months after his release, you'll be required to provide me with financial updates to prove that he will not squander his fortune or become"—the judge paused—"a victim . . . of financial predators looking to take advantage of him. The State of Illinois has spent enough money on this man. I'd like to make sure we spend no more after he is released."

Rory made notes.

"Finally," the judge said, "he is sixty-eight years old. He obviously has the means not to work, and his notoriety prevents him from meaningful employment. It's best for now that your client disappear for a while. Maybe forever. The property near Starved Rock has been held in a trust, so his name is not attached to it. He will be difficult to track down after release. Of course, everyone in authority who needs to find him will have easy access. But the trolls will be looking for him, and it's up to you to help him stay anonymous. Your father had done a lot of work, to this end."

The judge closed the file and stood, as if he had even more pressing issues to attend to. "Is there anything else?"

"Yes," Rory said. She swallowed down the acid again. "I'll have to see him before the formal parole hearing to go over a few other things. To my knowledge, he doesn't even know his attorney has died."

The circumstance of seeing a stranger in the close quarters of a visitation room, of having to look him in the eye and explain that she was his new attorney, was something Rory would have normally run from. Typically, she'd have done anything to avoid such a thing, arms up and slithering from its hold like a child escaping her mother's grip. But Rory was after something. She didn't give a shit about the man they called The Thief. She wanted to know what her father was doing for him, because she knew damn well it wasn't simply tending to his legal needs.

"That can be arranged," Judge Boyle said. "I'll put in the request so that it's expedited."

CHICAGO
August 1979

ANGELA'S BIRTHDAY FELL ON TUESDAY, TWO DAYS AFTER CATHERINE had rejected her, the way everyone from Angela's adolescence had done. Two days after she saw Bill Blackwell's neck, and the ugly red gouges he hid with a bandana. Two days since Angela had put all the haunting pieces to this summer together. Two full days, and she had done nothing. It had been two days of very little sleep, her mind allowing only thoughts about the missing women, and questioning her belief that Bill Blackwell was part of it all. That the peculiar practice of dual hanging was the method he had used to kill the women. Two days of questioning her theory that the disappearances were part of a much broader string of homicides, which dated back an entire decade. Two days of panic and doubt. And if Angela doubted herself, she couldn't blame Catherine for rebuking her.

"Is the wine okay?" Thomas asked, bringing Angela back from her thoughts.

Knowing she didn't like crowds, Thomas made early dinner reservations. Now, on her birthday, they sat at a candlelit table, sipping red wine, while the restaurant was only sparsely occupied. Angela did her best with the acidic cabernet that was upsetting her frail stomach.

She smiled. "It's good."

She had been close to confessing everything to Thomas when he arrived home on Sunday night. But instead, she kept things bottled up, allowing her mind to run wild. She had, Angela knew, lost all control of her thoughts. Not even the Valium was able to corral her psyche. The lack of sleep had her ragged and on edge.

She wrestled with her uneasy stomach through dinner, and then declined dessert.

"You don't want dessert on your birthday?" Thomas asked.

"I'm not in the mood for sweets. But you go ahead."

"No, we'll skip it tonight. I have something for you," Thomas said, producing a small wrapped present from the breast pocket of his jacket.

Everything that had transpired since that day in the garage when Angela had attempted to move the old couch out to the alley for trash pickup—her encounter with Leonard Williams, her overwhelming bout of obsessive compulsion that had stolen an entire week, the forming of her theory about the missing women dating back for a decade, the report of Samantha Rodgers's body being found, and, most recently, her bizarre discovery in the warehouse, her research about the disturbing practice of dual asphyxiation and thoughts of Bill Blackwell being involved in all of it—had caused Angela to forget about the necklace she found in the old picnic basket.

The events of the past week had nearly caused her to forget her birthday altogether. Now, as she sat with the gift in front of her, she was grateful for having forgotten about the necklace. Had it been present in her mind, she wouldn't have been able to play off being surprised.

"Can I open it?" she asked.

"Of course," Thomas said.

Angela pulled the wrapped box in front of her. She carefully tore away the paper and opened the top of the small box. She squinted her eyes at the diamond earrings that rested on the felt interior, with no attempt to hide her confusion.

"You don't like them?" Thomas asked.

She looked up at her husband, who was staring with a confused look on his face that matched Angela's.

"No, no," she quickly said. "I love them. I just . . ." She shook her head. "They're beautiful."

"We can exchange them if they're not what you like. You pointed them out a few months ago when we were shopping. I thought they'd make the perfect surprise."

Angela nodded. "They do. They're perfect."

As she slipped the diamonds through the piercings in her earlobes, her mind could think of nothing but the necklace she had found hidden at the bottom of the picnic basket in her garage.

Angela lay in bed pretending to enjoy her husband's attention. Although their sex life had never been passionate, she and Thomas shared chemistry in the bedroom and their lovemaking had always been enjoyable. But tonight, her mind was elsewhere. When he rolled off her, she lay with her head on his shoulder until she was certain he was sleeping. Then, to the sounds of his rhythmic breathing, Angela slipped out of bed. She pulled on her robe and sunk her feet into stockings. It was just past eleven, a time of night she would never typically consider venturing outside. The thought of making the journey to the garage in the dead of night had her fingertips tingling and the scabs on her shoulders begging to be ruptured. But another urge overshadowed her fear and trumped even the strongest pull from the self-destructive parts of her mind— curiosity.

She knew sleep would never come, even with the liberal use of Valium, until she understood the mystery of the necklace. Angela avoided the light switches until she made it to the kitchen, where she turned on the dim light over the stove. She felt the flush in her cheeks and the familiar queasiness in her stomach as she looked through the kitchen window to the garage. Her pounding pulse and the audible rush of blood through the vessels of her head were her body's way of begging Angela to wait until morning, but she could not.

Unlatching the back door, she stepped out into the night. The sweltering summer heat relinquished none of its power even this late, and Angela felt the humid air dampen her face. The neighborhood was quiet. She kept the patio light extinguished and carried a small flashlight with her. An impending panic attack made her breathing shallow. She hurried to the utility door at the back of the garage and ducked inside, bringing the interior to life with her flashlight.

The dirty couch was still against the wall. She turned her attention to the cluttered shelves and found the picnic basket. Pulling it from its spot, she opened the top and shined her light inside. The thin necklace box remained just where she had left it. Angela reached into the basket and pulled it out. Opening the box, she found the necklace as it reflected the flashlight's brightness.

In the darkened garage, she reached up to pinch the dangling earrings that hung from her lobes. She swallowed a sudden bolus of saliva that had formed in the back of her throat as she contemplated what it could mean. Thomas had been working late this summer, at least two or three nights a week. She remembered a string of phone calls last month when no one spoke after Angela had answered. A few times the caller had hung up just after Angela had uttered the word "hello." She knew he'd hired a new secretary that summer. Now, as Angela stood in the darkened garage, she fought against the screams of her mind that told her Thomas was having an affair. The nausea returned and her stomach rolled. She retched once, then quickly dropped the necklace back into the basket and replaced it on the shelf. She raced through the utility door and vomited onto a small patch of grass in the backyard.

Breathing heavily, she gulped the sticky summer air until a second wave of nausea passed. Then she hustled back into the house. She closed and locked the kitchen door just as the lights flashed on. When Angela turned around, Thomas stood in the kitchen, wearing only his boxer shorts.

"What's going on?" he asked.

Angela patted her nightgown, a nervous reaction to hide her confusion. It did just the opposite. "I thought I heard the trashcans rattling again. The top had fallen off," she said, immediately judging her lie to be somewhere between awful and completely unbelievable.

"Why didn't you wake me?" he asked.

"I just . . . didn't want the neighbors to hear it. Mr. Peterson has been edgy since I blocked the driveway with the couch."

Thomas walked to the back door and pulled the curtains to the side.

"The utility door to the garage is open," he said, looking at her.

"Is it? I hadn't noticed." Angela felt her stomach roiling again.

Thomas unlocked the kitchen door and walked out to the garage. The sticky night air drifted into the house as Angela watched him enter the garage and turn on the lights. He disappeared out of sight for a full minute, during which the knot in her stomach tightened and pulled her to the washroom. She vomited again before steadying herself against the wall and resting her forehead on the back of her hand. She heard the floorboards squeak and, through watery eyes, saw Thomas standing in the bathroom doorway.

"Are you all right?" he asked.

"Not feeling well again."

"This is why you should have woken me," he said, taking her under the arm and leading her back upstairs. She allowed him to guide her into bed.

"I saw that you vomited outside," he said as he pulled the covers over her. "I'm calling the doctor in the morning. I know you've been resisting, Angela. But it's time to see the psychiatrist. Someone has to help you through this, and I don't know what else to do for you."

Angela had nearly run through her Valium. She'd need more, so she didn't protest. As Thomas climbed into bed next to her, Angela closed her eyes, but never slept.

CHAPTER 16
Chicago, October 25, 2019

*T*HE FRACTURE HAD COME TOGETHER NICELY, BUT IT HAD TAKEN A larger amount of epoxy than she preferred using. The additional adhesive was needed to ensure the eye socket of Camille Byrd's childhood doll remained intact. Rory was unable to get herself into the correct mind-set to reconstruct the woman's murder, so she concentrated on Camille Byrd's doll instead. Once Rory immersed herself in the restoration, she found the doll's eye was the most challenging to repair. She had rebuilt the eye socket with a papier-mâché-and-plaster combination, a technique Sabine Esche had written about. Now that the epoxy and plaster had set, and the eye was seated in the orbit, Rory was pleased with the result. When the doll was laid down, there was just a slight delay in the closure of the eyelid, which only the most astute observer would notice.

She sanded the adhesive so that the seam of the original fracture was smooth. When Rory closed her eyes and ran her fingers over the doll's cheek, the fracture was undetectable. The *feel* of the doll's face had been perfectly restored. The *appearance* of Camille Byrd's childhood doll, however, still left much to be desired. The additional epoxy and heavy polishing had left a badly discolored patch that ran, like a stream on a map, from the hairline down to the edge of the jaw. The curved ribbon of tarnished porcelain looked like a poorly healed scar. Rory knew the skills she had utilized to repair the fracture and reconstruct the eye socket were unmatched. She also knew where her weakness lay, and that was in bringing porcelain back to its original state. For this task, she would go to a master. To the one person who was better than she was.

It was approaching midnight when Rory walked into the nursing home. She had gained permission from the staff, and had been granted the access code to the front entrance, to visit so late at night. The nurses knew Greta rarely slept at night, and that Rory's best chance for a coherent conversation usually came after midnight. Her last two visits with Aunt Greta had been failures. Since the passing of her father, Rory had trouble connecting with her great-aunt. With no children of her own, Aunt Greta's family consisted of her nephew—Frank Moore—and his daughter. Rory's father had been more like a grandson to Greta, and Rory like a great-grandchild. Over the course of her life, Rory had learned many things from Greta, including her love for restoring china dolls. It had once been their most cherished activity, restoring old dolls that had lined the walls of Greta's house. Their mutual love of antique-doll restoration was the foundation of their relationship, and was how the two had become so close through Rory's childhood. Now, since dementia had stolen Greta's mind, the old dolls Rory brought to her bedside provided a different conduit to the past. They provided access to a part of Greta's history that was filled with joy, rather than the agonizing moments of Greta's life that the dementia usually dredged up.

Tonight's visit also carried selfish undertones. Since she had requested a meeting with The Thief, a tremor had taken hold of Rory's hands, the way they used to tremble as a child. Anxiety had plagued her since a young age, and the only way Rory managed her childhood was through the calming nature of Aunt Greta and the dolls they restored together. Rory's parents had known the effect Greta had on their child, and had shuttled Rory away when signs of her disorder became apparent. After a long weekend, or sometimes an extended stay that lasted a week or more, Rory would return to her parents' house restored and renewed, much like the dolls she and Greta worked on. Tonight Rory needed the same healing powers Greta had delivered to her when she was a lost child.

Rory carried Camille Byrd's Kestner doll into the darkened room. Aunt Greta sat upright in bed with her eyes open, staring at nothing. Rory visited during the night not only because it was the most likely time to catch Greta in a coherent state, but also because Rory knew that sleep rarely came to her great-aunt during the small hours of night. The thought of Aunt Greta lying awake, staring into space, was never a comforting one. The woman had given Rory so much in life that Rory refused to allow her to spend the last stretch of her life alone.

"Hey, old lady," Rory said when she approached the bedside.

Greta's eyes flicked to the side, catching a glimpse of Rory for just an instant.

"I tried to save you. There was too much blood."

"I know," Rory said. "You did the best you could. And you helped many, many patients during your career."

"There's too much blood. We have to go to the hospital."

"Aunt Greta, everything is okay now. Everyone is safe."

"We have to go. I need help. There's too much blood."

Rory paused a moment as she stared at her. Finally she took her hand and squeezed gently. "You promised you'd help me with a restoration. Do you remember?"

Rory placed the box containing the Kestner doll on the bed. She immediately saw her aunt's demeanor change. Greta looked down at the doll, whose damaged face was visible through the window in the lid.

"I had to use a lot of epoxy to fix the fracture, which required a great deal of sanding to smooth. I have it repaired perfectly, but need some help getting the porcelain back to its original color."

Greta sat more upright in bed as Rory opened the box, removed the doll, and placed it on her aunt's lap. Rory found the controls and lifted the back of the bed upward so that Greta was fully erect.

"I brought your pastels," Rory said, removing from her backpack a large assortment of fingernail polish–sized glass bottles filled with different colors. She wheeled the bedside table over and set the paints on the surface.

"I need better light," Greta said. Her voice was scratchy and hoarse, different now than the high-pitched ramblings when she was trapped in the throes of dementia.

Rory pulled over the lamp, clicked on the overhead lights, and watched her go to work. She was immediately transported to her childhood, to Greta's home, to the room lined with dolls, and the workstation where she and Greta had spent hours and hours.

"Hey," Rory said while Greta painted a foundation coating over the repaired fracture. She kept her eyes on the Kestner doll as she spoke. "I've got to do something that's got me . . . scared."

Rory never used the words "nervous" or "anxious." To do so would be to admit too much. Greta kept working, not even a glance in Rory's direction. She was lost in the restoration.

"I've got to meet with someone Dad used to work with. A client."

Rory waited a moment for any indication that Greta had heard her.

"He's a bad man. An evil man, from what I know. But I have no choice but to meet with him."

Greta finally stopped stroking her brush over the doll's face to look at Rory. "You always have a choice."

Rory paused a moment. "I guess that's true."

Greta went back to the doll, all her concentration channeled on coloring the repaired fracture streaming down from the eye socket.

Of course, Greta's words were accurate. Rory could have simply told the judge that she would not take the case. Was she legally obligated to do so? It was a gray area. Being a partner in her father's law firm put Rory next in line to take his cases, but had she simply refused to do so, there was little Judge Boyle could have done. The truth was that Rory had already made the choice. She was meeting with this man for a reason. She had chosen to visit him face-to-face because there was something her father had been hiding. Rory wanted to know what it was, and the only person who could tell her was the man sitting in jail, waiting on his parole.

Greta spoke again as she attended to the doll, her brushstrokes even and purposeful as the fissure began to disappear. "Nothing can scare you unless you allow it to scare you."

Rory smiled and sat back in her chair. She loved the rare moments when she was able to connect with Greta, whose mind lately had seemingly been ravaged and stolen.

Two hours later, the first coat was finished and drying. To a casual observer, Camille Byrd's doll looked perfect. But Rory knew it would take two more coats of paint and polish before it was truly flawless. For this, she was grateful. It meant she would soon have an opportunity to reconnect with her great-aunt again.

CHICAGO
August 1979

*T*HE DAY AFTER HER BIRTHDAY WAS SPENT UNDER THOMAS'S WATCHFUL eye. Angela did her best to keep things together as she acclimated herself to the idea of seeing a psychiatrist. There was no way to avoid it, and she knew Thomas would press the issue. Wild bouts of memories came back to her as she remembered her teen years spent under the authoritarian rule of her doctor, in whom her parents had placed their trust that he would control her wild outbursts, her self-inflicted wounds, and morph their introverted child into a "normal" outgoing teenager.

Angela had swallowed the last of her Valium after her venture to the garage the night before, and when the sun brightened the frames of the bedroom windows this morning, she was eager for the world to pull her from another night of torment. Alone in bed now, once the nine o'clock hour came, she heard Thomas making phone calls. One of his calls was to Dr. Solomon, Angela knew, asking for a referral to a shrink. Angela had never mentioned to Thomas that Dr. Solomon's original recommendation had found its way into the trash, or that the doctor's last few phone calls had gone unreturned.

Angela finally climbed from bed as Thomas continued to talk on the phone, his deep voice rumbling from the kitchen. She showered and dressed. When she walked downstairs, Thomas was drinking coffee at the kitchen table and analyzing a spreadsheet for work.

"I made coffee," he said. "Are you feeling better?"

"A little, yes," Angela lied as she poured a cup and sat across from him.

"I called the doctor," Thomas said. "He's out of the office until tomorrow. I left a message. I think I should go with you when you see the psychiatrist."

Angela didn't protest, just nodded.

"And I've got a problem with the job in Indiana. They need me to come down and have a look. At this time of morning, I'll miss rush hour, will get down there by early afternoon. Then I'll get back by tonight. Shouldn't be later than eight."

Angela felt for the first time that she might have overdone it with the Valium. A wave of indifference had come over her since she swallowed the last of the pills after her trip to the garage the previous night. The necklace hidden in the picnic basket, and thoughts of Thomas's infidelity, ricocheted through her mind. She thought of his late nights at the office, and his spree of out-of-town jobs that had him frequently spending nights away from home. Add that to Catherine's dismissal of her findings, and Angela felt alone and isolated with no one to turn to. That wasn't true, she reminded herself. Through the fog of hazy thoughts, she knew she'd always have one person in her life she could trust. And the offer to help Angela *at any time, for any reason,* had been unconditional. Angela had never thought she would need that help. Not since she had been saved, when she was eighteen, had she needed help. Since then, she had been on her own, free from the confines of her parents and the shrinks and the psychiatric facility where they held her prisoner. But this morning, for the first time in years, Angela needed help. After all these years, she wondered if the offer still stood.

"Will you be okay by yourself?" Thomas asked. "I can call Catherine to see if she could stay with you today."

"No," Angela said.

Her mind wandered back to her childhood when her parents watched her like hawks, always fearing the worst if they left Angela alone. And Catherine was no longer someone she could confide in.

"I'll be fine."

Thomas nodded, taking a long look at his wife. "The girl at Dr. Solomon's office said he sometimes returns calls from home, so if the phone rings, make sure to answer it. She said he's been trying to reach you, that he's called a couple of times."

Angela stared at her coffee. She felt the walls of her world constricting on her. She had erased Dr. Solomon's messages from the answering machine with the illogical thinking that if she erased the messages she'd never have to talk with him. With the nonsensical reasoning that deleting Dr. Solomon's voice and his request for a return call would prevent her from having to return to the world of psychiatrists. Finally Angela looked up at her husband and shrugged. "He hasn't called, that I know of. But I'll make sure to answer if the phone rings."

Thirty minutes later, she watched as Thomas backed out of the garage and into the alley. He pulled slowly away, headed back to Indiana for the day. The rumble of the truck's engine was barely out of earshot by the time Angela was on the move. She had been unable to follow the news for the past couple of days, knowing that Thomas would not like the idea of stirring her paranoia with news articles about the girl whose body had been found the week before.

Now, with Thomas gone, Angela felt a sudden urge for the latest details of the case. She longed for anything to take her mind off the idea that Thomas could be having an affair. She hadn't seen or heard any updates about Samantha Rodgers since she had listened to the radio report the morning at the warehouse. She turned on the television, but with Thomas's late start this morning, all she found was the start of daytime television. The morning newscasts had ended more than an hour ago. She clicked on the radio next and tuned to 780AM for the latest news. Ten minutes of stock market talk and commercials passed before she decided to look for the newspaper.

The front stoop was empty and the driveway bare when she looked for the *Tribune*. She figured Thomas had already fetched it, and she checked the bathroom, a disgusting habit she'd never been able to break him of. When she was unable to locate the paper in the house, she decided to check the trash. She walked to the alley and lifted the lid to the trashcan. Inside, on top of black plastic Glad bags, rested an unread *Tribune* still wrapped in the plastic bag in which it was delivered. Angela rescued it from the trash and hurried inside.

The *Tribune* was filled with stories of The Thief and details about the only victim whose body had been found. Angela pulled at her eyelashes as she carefully read the articles, one at a time, and then delicately clipped them from the paper with a scissors to add to her growing file. She turned the page and started a new article that covered Samantha Rodgers and the shallow grave where her body was found. Angela's skin tingled as she read the story:

> *The body of Samantha Rodgers was discovered in a wooded area of Forest Glen, less than a mile from the main road. Deep bruising found on her neck, discovered during autopsy, suggests that she was strangled. The Chicago Police are asking for any information about the victim from the night she disappeared, and are leaning hard on Samantha Rodgers's parents' suggestion that on the night she went missing, Samantha was wearing a peridot-and-diamond necklace she had received for her graduation the month before. The police are approaching all city and suburban pawn shops to see if a necklace matching the parents' description will be found, hoping for the first lead in the summer's missing persons cases.*
>
> *The necklace in question carries an engraving of the victim's initials and birth date on the back: SR 7-29-57.*
>
> *Any information can be reported to the phone number below.*

Angela looked up from the paper. Her world narrowed in a migrainous aura of tunnel vision that captured only the utility door to the garage as she gazed through the kitchen window. She was on her feet in a flash, following the periscope of vision and heading out the back door.

CHAPTER 17
Chicago, October 26, 2019

*R*ORY WAS IN FULL BATTLE GEAR—GLASSES, BEANIE HAT, GRAY jacket, and lace-up combat boots. Her face burned crimson as she sat in her car in the parking lot. She took deep breaths as she thought of sitting across from her father's oldest client, a cold and calculating killer, pretending to hammer out the details of his release. An odd guilt came over her when she considered the notion that her dead father had some nefarious business relationship with this killer from 1979.

"Nothing can scare you unless you allow it to scare you." She took a few more calming breaths, and allowed the attack to escape her lungs with each exhale. When her hands were steady, and her lungs freely expanding and contracting without the hiccup rhythm of panic, Rory opened the car door, stood from the passenger seat, and sucked in the cool fall morning. She stood in front of Stateville Correctional Center in Crest Hill, Illinois. It was where The Thief had been housed for the past forty years.

She had her identification prepared, the paperwork filled out ahead of time, and a copy of Judge Boyle's orders to permit the impromptu visit. Still, processing moved slowly. She was finally called to the window to fill out additional visitation forms. A woman slid the partition window to the side and looked up from her computer.

"Name, please?"

"Rory Moore."

"Relationship to the inmate?"

"Attorney."

The woman typed on her computer for a moment.

"Name of the inmate?"

Rory looked at the file in her hands, read the name from the bottom flap.

"Thomas Mitchell."

CHICAGO
August 1979

*T*HE UTILITY DOOR TO THE BACK OF THE GARAGE WAS WIDE OPEN AS Angela pulled the picnic basket off the shelf. The wicker top rolled a few feet away when she dropped it, spinning on its edge like a coin as it twirled several times before coming to a rest. Angela had the necklace in her hand, dropping the case that held it to the ground, and was closely examining it. The green peridot and surrounding diamonds were dull this morning in the poorly lit garage, different from the morning when she had first discovered it. Back then, she had sat with the bright morning sun bringing the gemstone to life. So much was different now than had been that morning, like the light of her life had been drained from her, just like from the gemstones.

The tremor returned to her hands as she slowly turned the necklace over and strained her eyes to look for an engraving. She held the necklace up to the light that spilled through the window until she could clearly see the engraving on the back: *SR 7-29-57*.

Angela Mitchell's world ended that day in her garage. Some indecipherable correlation formed in her mind between the morning she had attempted to move the couch to the trash and today. Her life had been on a downward trajectory since then, and this morning, it had finally crashed in a fiery explosion.

She slowly looked back to the shelves in front of her and, without consciously knowing what she was doing, rummaged through other containers. She went through one box after the other until she came to a plastic carton that held Christmas decorations. She slid it from overhead, placed it on the garage floor, and lifted the lid. Inside were strings of Christmas lights tightly wound, sitting on top of an object that she could not immediately identify. Pulling the strings of lights from the box, Angela found a purse underneath. It was nothing she had ever owned. With a feeling of foreboding in the pit of her stomach and with trembling fingers, she unzipped the purse. Makeup and lipstick greeted her. A crumpled pack of Pall Malls and a lighter. A small wallet. She pulled the wallet from the purse as the cigarettes tumbled to the floor. She dropped the purse and turned the wallet over in her hands. She was light-headed. Her peripheral vision was blotched with dancing stars. She thumbed the driver's license out of the wallet and saw a picture of a blond-haired woman. Angela recognized her immediately as Clarissa Manning, the first victim who had gone missing in May. Angela had created an extensive biography on her, like she had on all the others.

Angela had no way of fully understanding the horrors she had stumbled onto in the storage room at the Kenosha warehouse, but early waves of comprehension began rolling onto the shores of her mind as she thought of the dual nooses and again about the news reports detailing the bruising on Samantha Rodgers's neck. She couldn't bring her mind to understand what might have transpired there.

As it all came to her, and while she stood with Clarissa Manning's ID card in one hand, Samantha Rodgers's necklace in the other, a rattling noise screamed for her attention. Angela's vision was still tunneled as she stared at the relics that belonged to the missing women. She finally had the answer to why she had been on edge all summer. She finally knew the reason why the long-dead obsessions and compulsions from her past had risen from the graves where she had buried them. As much as she tried to convince herself, it had nothing to do with the stranger from the alley, or with Bill Blackwell. Her sense of fear had been so acute this summer because she had been so close to the man responsible for taking the women.

The clattering noise continued until it finally pulled Angela back to the present. She stared wide-eyed at the back wall of the garage until her mind eventually processed the noise she was hearing. It was the rattle of the garage door opener overhead engaging the chains, the squeak of the springs as they twisted the door upward, and the rumble of Thomas's Ford truck approaching up the alley.

He was supposed to be in Indiana. He was supposed to be surveying a future job site. Angela looked down at her feet, the rushing of blood loud in her ears. There, on the garage floor, was the open plastic container, the lid slid to the side. Three strings of Christmas lights were haphazardly stacked next to it, and Clarissa Manning's purse, which had landed upside down, spewed its contents of makeup, lipstick, cigarette lighter, and loose change. The picnic basket and its cover, which had spun to a stop several feet away, lay there, too.

The rumble of Thomas's truck grew louder as the garage door continued to rise.

CHAPTER 18
Chicago, October 26, 2019

*R*ORY SAT IN THE BOOTH ACROSS FROM THOMAS MITCHELL. SHE knew from her father's file that he was sixty-eight years old, but the man across from her looked younger. Deep crevices ran from his nostrils, around his lips, and died somewhere near his chin. But otherwise, his face was chiseled and young-looking. If Rory didn't know better, she'd guess he was in his early fifties.

His expression was stoic when she sat in front of him, his hand-cuffed wrists resting on the table, his fingers folded as if in prayer, and an aura of patience emanating from him. He lifted the phone and placed it to his ear. Rory did the same.

"Mr. Mitchell, my name is Rory Moore."

"They said my attorney was here to see me."

"I'm sorry to inform you that Frank Moore passed away last month. I'm his daughter."

Rory noticed something in the man's eyes, whether it was emotion or simply contemplation was difficult to determine.

"Will this delay my release?"

"No. I've taken over the case and am handling the details."

"Are you a lawyer?"

Rory hesitated, just like when Judge Boyle asked her the same question.

"Yes," she finally said. "I worked occasionally with my father, and I've met with the judge who is overseeing your parole."

Thomas Mitchell said nothing, so Rory went on.

"The judge and my father were negotiating the terms of your parole. I'm familiar with the details."

Rory opened the file in front of her.

"You have some assets." She pulled a page from the stack. "Just over eight hundred thousand dollars remain in your account. If you're smart with your money, it should last for the rest of your life."

He nodded.

"My father had financial power of attorney. Those rights have transferred to me, and the judge has asked that I help you get established financially after your release. The world of banking has changed since you were a free man. The judge has asked that I help you with your finances for the first year and a half after your release."

"What about my living arrangements? I don't want to live in a halfway house," he said. "Frank was working on that for me."

"The judge has granted your request to live in the home located near Starved Rock. I see that you inherited the cabin from an uncle in 1994. My father placed it in a trust for you and it's been under management ever since as a rental property. The judge has ordered me, along with your social worker, Naomi Brown, and parole officer, Ezra Parker, to inspect the residence before your release."

"Fine," The Thief said. "Please make sure the heat is on."

Rory paused at his subtle attempt at humor.

"Have you been to this cabin before?"

"When I was a kid. I was surprised my uncle willed it to me. But I'm happy to have it, and Frank has kept it anonymous."

Rory had paged briefly through her father's work related to the inherited property. It made sense now that he had placed it in a trust to keep the owner nameless.

"There is a long list of requirements you'll be expected to follow during your first twelve months of release." Rory pulled another page from the folder. "You'll need to meet and speak regularly to your parole officer. You'll also be assigned a social worker, who will make sure you are getting settled. There is a list of doctors here that you will be required to see. An internist who will run regular drug testing, and a psychologist you will be required to meet with every other week. All of this is set up to help reintegrate you into society."

"There's not going to be any *reintegration*. I'll have folks trying to hunt me down. And if any of them find out where I'm living, it'll be the end of me. Frank anticipated this and took measures to assure my privacy. And for the same reason, I doubt it would be helpful to make me find work. No organization will want me, and I'll run into the same problem of people finding me. I have plenty of money to live a quiet life, which is what I intend to do."

"The judge has waived the work requirement based on your age, notoriety, and your financial means. Paperwork that covers all of these stipulations will be delivered to you for your signature. Once the papers are signed, the parole will move forward. Your release is scheduled for November third. Questions?"

"Yeah. What happened to Frank?"

Rory observed the man through the glass. The way he said her father's name felt personal.

"He had a heart attack."

"Damn shame."

Rory squinted her eyes behind her thick glasses. "You and my father seem to have had a close relationship."

"We did. He was my attorney, and other than the people on the inside, he was the only one I was regularly in contact with."

Rory wanted to ask what her father had done for Thomas Mitchell for forty years. It was more than appeal and parole hearings. She wanted to ask why this man had paid her father nearly $200,000 in retainer fees.

As if The Thief had read her mind, he said, "Listen, I'm sorry to hear about Frank. He was the closest thing I had to a friend. But I've got to concentrate on getting out of here, and keeping myself anonymous after I do. Can you help with this?"

His friend. Rory's phone vibrated in her back pocket. Then again, and again. Three notifications in a row. She offered Thomas Mitchell a forced smile, retrieved her phone from her pocket, and looked at the screen: **Rory. Very interested in talking with you about Angela Mitchell. I'm in Chicago and would love to meet, Catherine Blackwell.**

132

Rory had nearly forgotten about the message she left in the comments of Catherine Blackwell's Facebook page. She looked back to Thomas Mitchell. There was a woman still looking for justice forty years after this man had killed his wife. Rory's fingers itched with the urge to type a message back to Catherine Blackwell.

"Your parole is still scheduled for next week," Rory said, looking up from her phone. "Nothing's changed."

Thomas Mitchell nodded his head, hung up the phone, and pressed the call button underneath it. A moment later, a guard appeared and ushered him away.

CHICAGO
August 1979

*T*HOMAS PULLED HIS TRUCK INTO THE ALLEY AND PRESSED THE automatic garage door opener. As he approached the back of his home, he saw the top of the trashcan strewn into the middle of the alley. He stepped on the brake and shifted the Ford into park, then climbed out and retrieved the top. When he placed the lid back into place, he noticed that the newspaper he had deposited in the trash earlier in the day was gone. He rested a rock on top of the can and looked across the small backyard to the kitchen window, where he'd left Angela less than an hour ago. His senses were on fire since the night of her birthday when he'd found her in the garage. After twenty minutes on the Kennedy Expressway this morning, he felt something was wrong. He decided his trip to Indiana could wait. Things might be falling apart at home, and he had to deal with it.

Climbing back into his truck, he pulled into the garage and immediately noticed the boxes and cartons on the shelf were out of place. He knew this part of the garage well. It's where he hid his treasures. Now, as he stared at the shelving, he knew he'd made a mistake by leaving things unattended. Since she'd been through the boxes, who knew what she might have found?

He killed the truck's engine, climbed from the cab, and closed the truck's door. Thomas stood in front of the shelf and took inventory. He could tell that she had moved things around, but was unsure what, exactly, she had gotten into. As he started toward the utility door that led to the backyard, he noticed quarters, dimes, and pennies scattered across the floor. Turning back to the shelf, he reached for the clear plastic box that held three strings of Christmas lights and one of the girls' purses. He had placed it there immediately afterward, but hadn't disposed of it yet. It was difficult to get rid of their things. He liked to savor them for a time, until The Rush was gone. He should have kept the items at the warehouse, but there was a perverse pleasure in keeping their personal items so close to his home.

Pulling the box from the shelf, he opened the lid and found the three strings of lights wound in tight circles resting on top of the purse, just as he had left them. He leaned his waist against the box and pinned it to the shelf so his hands were free, then moved the lights and picked up the purse. Unzipping it, he poked around at the contents. Cigarettes and a lighter. Random makeup. He fingered the wallet and then lifted it out. It was a thin item, with a zipper that led to a small compartment for loose change, and slots for charge cards. Thomas looked down at the floor and the strewn quarters and dimes.

He turned the skinny wallet over and noticed an empty slot on the front where a driver's license would be slid for easy access. He thumbed through the pockets inside, and continued to poke around the purse but was unable to find the girl's ID card. He leaned his body slightly to his right, keeping the box pinned to the shelf, and peered through the curtains of the utility door to survey the back of his home. He could see into the empty kitchen.

His forehead wrinkled as he considered the possibility of his wife having discovered his secret. The implications would be disastrous. He dropped the purse back into the box, not bothering to rezip it. He dropped the wallet haphazardly on top of it, and then tossed the lights in. Sliding the box back onto the shelf, he next reached for the picnic basket and threw the lid to the ground. He ripped the tablecloth out of the basket and found it empty.

Dropping the basket onto the ground, Thomas exited the utility door of the garage, walked across the backyard, and turned the knob on the kitchen door. It opened.

"Angela," he yelled as he walked inside.

No answer.

"Angela?"

He heard a metallic thud in the basement and headed for the stairs. He took them quickly. When he reached the landing at the bottom, he saw a light in the laundry room. The dryer was running, and the lid to the washing machine was open as water filled the bin and Angela tossed clothes in.

He startled her when he approached and she let out a piercing shriek. Her body shook and she crumpled to the floor of the laundry room.

"Sorry," Thomas said. "You didn't answer when I called."

Angela looked up, running a hand through her hair.

"The washer and dryer were running. I didn't hear you."

"Sorry to startle you," he said, reaching down and helping her to her feet. He looked around the room, assessing the situation. "The back door was unlocked. I thought we talked about keeping the doors secured."

"Oh," Angela said. "I must have forgotten to lock it."

"Did you go out?"

"Yes. This morning. I took a bag of garbage out."

Thomas remembered the trashcan, the missing newspaper, and the top that had rolled into the middle of the alley.

"What are you doing home?" Angela asked.

The washing machine made a thundering sound and started gyrating as the barrel engaged and splashed water around. Angela noticed and closed the lid to muffle the sound. The dryer hummed and gave off heat.

"I decided to go tomorrow," Thomas said.

Angela nodded. He sensed her anxiety, a different kind than normal.

"Come upstairs," Angela said, picking up the empty laundry basket. "I'll make you some lunch."

Thomas watched her hurry across the basement and up the stairs. Alone in the laundry room, he looked around again. He sensed in his gut that something was wrong. He lifted the lid to the washing machine and saw the drum filled with water and the agitator twisting the submerged clothing back and forth into a frothy foam. He stood for another minute and listened to the sounds around him.

Finally his gaze came to rest on the dryer. He listened to it hum, and then identified what was wrong. It wasn't a noise that had piqued his suspicion, it was the absence of one. The dryer hummed quietly, but he heard nothing tumbling inside. No clanking of buttons and buckles on the metal interior. No thudding of wet clothes falling from top to bottom as the drum spun.

He reached down and opened the dryer door. Dry, hot air mushroomed out of the machine. When it passed, he looked into the dryer. It was empty.

CHICAGO
August 1979

IT WAS THURSDAY MORNING, THE DAY AFTER THOMAS HAD ARRIVED home unexpectedly and surprised her in the garage. Twenty-two hours since she saw Clarissa Manning's face staring back at her from the driver's license she had found hidden in the shelves of her garage. Less than one full day since she had identified the mysterious necklace she had found weeks ago as belonging to Samantha Rodgers. Were there other pieces of jewelry there, too, belonging to the other women whose biographies she had compiled? Angela had spent most of Wednesday night pretending to sleep while her mind imagined the women's possessions hiding on the garage shelves.

Like a slowly building pressure cooker, her paranoia grew each hour. She was convinced that Thomas knew about her discoveries. She had put the containers back on the garage shelf so haphazardly that he had to suspect she had been snooping through them. Thomas had canceled his trip to Indiana for today, and hadn't gone to work. His concern about Angela seeing the doctor had been replaced now by a different preoccupation—the garage. She watched him all morning through the kitchen window, pulling at her lashes and pinching her eyebrows. Thomas would appear every so often in the frame of the utility door when he walked from the back of the garage out to his truck in the alley, arms filled with boxes and cartons.

She ran through the moment when the garage door had started

opening the morning before. Somehow managing to get things back on the shelf, Angela had rushed into the kitchen and thought briefly of locking herself in the bathroom, to claim illness. Surely, she had been sick enough over the past couple of weeks for it to be a believable ruse. But she chose the basement and the laundry room instead. With the washer and dryer running she could pretend not to hear him come home, and then could feign being startled when he finally found her. It had provided her with an extra few minutes to hide Clarissa Manning's driver's license, which she had slipped down the front of her pants. Samantha Rodgers's necklace had gone into the washing machine, along with the clothes that had been on the floor. Her skin had bubbled with itch and burn when she left Thomas alone in the laundry room. He had stayed there for a minute or two after Angela retreated upstairs, and she had worried that he would reach into the foaming water and somehow retrieve the necklace.

Now, as she sat in the kitchen on Thursday morning, her mind frantically scrolled through her options. She needed to find a way out of the house and away from her husband. She contemplated her options as she sat in the kitchen and watched Thomas empty the garage. She stopped herself from her initial instinct to run—to run through the front door and never stop. But where would she go? To Catherine's? Certainly not. To the police? Possibly, she thought. But then she imagined the disparaging look in their eyes when Angela revealed her fantastic story. They would likely pack her into a squad car and drive her home and back to Thomas.

The phone rang. As Thomas loaded his truck with boxes, Angela pulled her gaze from the activities taking place outside. She walked over to the phone and lifted the receiver.

"Hello?"

"Mrs. Mitchell, this is Dr. Solomon. I've been trying to reach you."

She paused for a moment, upset with herself for having answered the phone.

"Mrs. Mitchell, are you there?"

"Yes," Angela said in a soft voice. "I'm sorry I haven't been able to call back."

"Mrs. Mitchell, I need you to stop taking the Valium I prescribed."

The bottle was empty. It wouldn't be a problem.

"Mrs. Mitchell?"

"I'm here."

"Stop taking the Valium and come back in to the office."

Dr. Solomon continued to talk, his voice static-filled and echoing as he explained to Angela the findings from his exam. Angela let the receiver fall to her shoulder as she released her grip on it. It bounced off her chest and hung from the wall mount, twirling in a circle. She thought she heard Dr. Solomon's voice again, asking if she was still there. Angela sunk to the floor, her back pressed against the wall. If the bottle of Valium was not empty, she'd have swallowed the rest of it.

CHICAGO
August 1979

SHE LAY AWAKE THURSDAY NIGHT, THE NEWLY EMPTIED GARAGE RUN-ning through her mind. All that was left were the only things that mattered—Samantha Rodgers's necklace and Clarissa Manning's driver's license—both of which Angela had hidden. Thomas had barely spoken to her since he found her in the laundry room, so she had no idea if he knew she'd found the relics.

In addition to the image of the now-barren garage shelves constantly blinking in her mind, Dr. Solomon's voice played over and over in her ears, like a record stuck and repeating. She hadn't slept the previous few nights and finally, with the bed empty next to her while Thomas continued his purging downstairs, fatigue overcame her and she drifted into a fitful trance.

Her sleep-deprived mind took her back to the hidden storage room in the Kenosha warehouse. She walked through the dingy, unlit space, the gray light of early morning barely brightening the windows high in the rafters. When she headed to the back of the warehouse, she twisted the handle on the storage room door and it creaked open. When the groaning door hinges quieted, Angela heard something else. It was a soft moaning. She stepped into the dark storage room and found Clarissa Manning hanging from one of the twin nooses. *Help me,* the missing girl said. She was holding a bundle of something in her arms. Angela walked closer to see what it was. As her eyesight adjusted to the darkened space, she saw an infant child wrapped in the green tarp that had been hanging in front of the door. As she reached for the bundle, the baby began to shriek.

Angela bolted upright in bed. She gasped for breath as if finally surfacing from minutes beneath water. Clarissa Manning's moans and soft pleas for help from her nightmare were replaced now by the growl of Thomas's truck. She threw the covers to the side and raced to the window. She saw Thomas pull his truck down the alley, the bed filled with boxes and cartons from the garage and the basement.

Angela quickly dressed. She knew she had only a small window of time. When she raced down the stairs, she saw that Thomas had been through every corner of the house. Angela had forgotten her file folder at Catherine's on Sunday morning, when she raced out of the house after Bill had come home. Now she was happy to have left the research file behind. If she had kept it hidden in the bedroom trunk, where she had always placed it when she was not working on it, Thomas would surely have discovered it. Angela badly wanted to bring that file with her, but knew there was no way to retrieve it. She had no time.

Clarissa Manning's driver's license had not been moved since she stuffed it down the front of her pants. She retrieved it now, and ran down the basement steps. When she reached the landing, she saw that Thomas had been through every inch of the space. Drawers were opened and the contents spewed haphazardly to the sides and onto the ground. Shelves were emptied, and Angela could hardly remember what had once filled them. An eerie chill came over her body as she imagined all the evidence she might have been living with for the past two years. She wondered how many more items had been stashed here, and whether she could have done anything to thwart Thomas's reign of terror, which she was sure had been going on for a decade. On the now-empty shelves may have been everything she needed to prove her theory. Still, though, she believed she had enough.

She ran to the washing machine and lifted the lid. The clothes she had put there the previous morning were flat and damp, the spin cycle having stuck them to the walls of the drum. She ripped one item after the other free until she heard a clanking within the machine. Angela reached in and found Samantha Rodgers's necklace. A slight bit of peace found her gut, now that she knew Thomas hadn't discovered it.

Back upstairs, she spent thirty desperate minutes jotting notes about her discoveries over the last week. Angela had passed the dark hours of night listening to Thomas rustle through the house, moving from the basement to the backyard and out to his truck as he emptied the house of evidence. She had listened, and prayed. Drifted between panic and fitful sleep, where she had dreamt of Clarissa Manning hanging from a noose. She fought against her urge to run and scream and cry. She had held her breath, and formulated a plan.

CHAPTER 19
Chicago, October 27, 2019

 M EETING WITH NEW PEOPLE RANKED RIGHT UP THERE WITH ROOT canals. Rory did better when the stranger was otherworldly, a victim who needed Rory to reconstruct their death and discover what had happened to them. She had a harder time with the living. They interacted and questioned and judged. But the meeting with Catherine Blackwell presented an opportunity Rory would find nowhere else. The lure to talk with someone who had known Angela Mitchell was all consuming. Rory had an unexplainable urge to know everything about her.

It was noon when Rory walked up the steps of the bungalow house and rang the bell. Although she had never created a mental image of Catherine Blackwell, other than the grainy Facebook image, Rory was surprised to see a white-haired lady when the door opened. Rory guessed she was seventy, perhaps older. The math made sense if she was a friend to Angela Mitchell in 1979.

"Rory?" Catherine asked.

"Yes, Ms. Blackwell?"

"Call me Catherine. Come in."

Rory walked inside and followed the woman into the kitchen.

"Can I take your coat?"

Rory unconsciously had her fist tight on the top button, which was latched and secured at the base of her throat.

"No, thank you."

Rory managed to remove her beanie hat, but that was as far as she would go.

"Can I get you a coffee?"

"I'm okay."

Catherine poured herself a cup and they both sat at the kitchen table. Stacked on the table were several binders of information.

"I was very excited to receive your message," Catherine said. "I haven't had much traffic on my Facebook page lately."

"I was glad to find you," Rory said, pushing her glasses up her nose.

"I've become a bit of a sleuth in my old age," Catherine said. "And I'm proud to be a friend to the digital age rather than a stranger, as many people my age are. After I saw your comment on my Facebook page, I did some snooping. You have quite a reputation in the world of forensic investigation."

Rory nodded, averted her eyes, and reached again for the collar of her coat, making sure the top button was still secured. It made her feel safe and protected, anonymous somehow, even though she was anything but.

"Yes. I work for the Chicago Police Department as a special counsel, of sorts."

"And with the Murder Accountability Project," Catherine said with a smile. "Is that why you contacted me? Are the Chicago Police looking into Angela again?"

Rory paused. *Looking into her?*

"No, I'm afraid not. My curiosity about Angela Mitchell is mine alone." Rory shifted in her chair, leaned a little closer. "How did you know Angela? If you don't mind me asking."

Catherine smiled, setting her gaze on the steaming coffee. "We were dear friends. I mean, it was so long ago." She looked up. "Maybe I embellish our friendship when I think of it now. Perhaps I make more of it than it really was. But Angela meant a lot to me. She was a special woman, indeed."

"Special in what way?" Rory asked, although she believed she knew the answer.

"Angela was a beloved friend, but also a terribly troubled woman. She had a lot of . . . issues. Maybe that's why she and I were so close. She didn't have much of a support system. She was estranged from her parents, from what little she told me about them, and she had no other family to lean on. Angela was what we would now label autistic, but back then she was just horribly misunderstood by most. She was also an obsessive-compulsive. She suffered from debilitating bouts of paranoia. But despite it all, somehow she and I settled into a perfectly normal friendship that I cherished. During the summer of 1979, before she disappeared, she was going through another spate of her illness and I'm afraid . . ."

Rory waited a moment. "Afraid what?"

"I'm afraid I treated her no better than any of the people she tried to avoid."

"What happened?"

Catherine took a sip of coffee to steel herself. "I'm sure you are aware of the missing women from 1979."

Rory nodded. From what Lane had told her, she knew a brief amount about the women who went missing. None had been linked to Thomas Mitchell, despite wide speculation that he was responsible for their deaths.

"Angela had become consumed with the missing women that summer. She came up with a theory of who took them, and how he had killed them. But they were wild ideas, perhaps considered by some to be a conspiracy theory, of a decadelong string of missing women who had all succumbed to the same man. She had researched it all. She had reams of material and graphs and a detailed model of how it had all transpired. Similar women killed in similar ways, all in a tight location in and around the city."

Rory's breath caught in her throat. She thought about her work at the Murder Accountability Project, her and Lane's efforts to find similarities between homicides that might point to trends and serial killings. She thought of the cases that had been solved because of their algorithm. Angela Mitchell had been doing something similar before computers were widely used, before algorithms could be produced, before the Internet existed and put information at one's fingertips. The roots of Rory's curiosity about Angela Mitchell grew deeper, stretching into the folds of her mind.

"Here," Catherine said. "Take a look at her research."

Catherine pushed a three-ring binder across the table.

"This is everything Angela compiled that summer on the missing women, and all her theories on what happened to them."

Rory slowly pulled the binder in front of her and opened the cover. It was strange to see such a large volume of work with so much of it handwritten. There were many pages that looked to have been copied from books, the shadows of the old Xerox machine present on each page. But most of it was written by hand in neat print. Rory remembered the piggish writing from the detective's notes on the Camille Byrd case. Angela Mitchell's penmanship was immaculate.

Rory turned page after page that described the women who had disappeared in 1979, full biographies that must have taken hours to compile. She read each name, the details of their lives and disappearances sketched in her memory the way everything she looked at was imaged and categorized. Only the body of one woman featured in the biographies was ever found. Her name was Samantha Rodgers, and Angela had gone to long lengths to describe the woman.

Rory turned a page and came to a detailed drawing.

"What's this?"

Catherine leaned over the table to get a better look.

"Oh," she said. "That was one of Angela's final theories. She told me she found that contraption at Thomas's warehouse, hidden in a back room. Angela believed it was how he killed the women, hanging them in some fashion. I'm afraid that was all too much for me."

Rory analyzed the bizarre drawing that depicted two nooses juxtaposed to one another, the rope between them winding through a triple pulley system that took on the shape of an M and looked barbaric.

"And I'm sad to admit," Catherine continued, "that when Angela showed me all of this just before she disappeared, I turned my back on her. I told Angela her theories were over the top. That she couldn't possibly be right. I told her that the summer and the missing women had gotten the best of her, and that she was on the wrong track. I tried to convince her that she was in no danger. But then . . ." Catherine looked away from Rory, down into her coffee again. Her voice was lower when she finally spoke. "Then she was gone."

Rory didn't recognize what was happening at first, and then she noticed that Catherine Blackwell had begun to cry. Rory stirred with anxiety. She was incapable of comforting strangers.

"There, there," Rory heard herself say, wondering where the words came from or what on earth they meant. Rory cleared her throat and continued on. "Why do you have all of Angela's notes?"

"Just before she went missing, she left them at my house— whether she did it accidentally or on purpose, I've never known for sure."

"Why didn't you give them to the police?"

"Because the police were never going to charge Thomas with anything but Angela's murder. That was clear from the start."

"But this drawing." Rory pointed to the binder. "Didn't the police find this device at Thomas's warehouse?"

"His warehouse burned to the ground. He made sure there was nothing to find."

Rory took one last look at Angela Mitchell's notes before she closed the binder. "I'm curious about the Facebook page. You call it *Justice for Angela* and ask for anyone with information to come forward. What exactly are you looking for all these years later?"

Catherine collected herself and looked up at Rory. "Answers," she said, wiping her eyes with a tissue. "I've been looking for answers for decades. The Facebook page is just a more public way for me to do it."

"But that's what I'm having trouble understanding. What *kind* of answers? There was a trial, and a conviction."

Catherine smiled. It was more a disappointed look than it was a kind gesture. "That trial provided no closure. It provided the City of Chicago and all its frightened residents with peace of mind. But it answered no questions about Angela Mitchell. It's been forty years, and I still want to know what happened to her."

Rory stared at Catherine Blackwell, narrowed her eyes, and cocked her head just a bit. "Her husband killed her."

"Oh," Catherine said, shaking her head. "I'm afraid that's just not true. See, there's something you need to know about Angela."

Rory waited. "What's that?"

"She was fiercely intelligent. Much too smart for Thomas to have killed her. Angela disappeared on her own accord. I turned my back on her just before she left, and I've never forgiven myself for it. I hope someday to tell her how sorry I am for how I treated her."

Rory leaned closer, resting her elbows on the kitchen table. "You think Angela is still alive?"

Catherine nodded. "I know she is. And I pray you'll help me find her."

CHICAGO
August 1979

*I*T WAS APPROACHING MIDNIGHT WHEN THOMAS MITCHELL PULLED INTO the parking lot of his Kenosha warehouse. The long industrial road that led to his secluded lot had always made for perfect cover. During the day, he could see a car approaching as soon as it turned down the smoky road and threw dust into the air. At night, headlights announced another's presence as clearly as a lighthouse spotlight. And if someone attempted a stealth approach, the gravel road would betray the vehicle with loud crunches well ahead of their arrival.

Until recently, though, he had never been concerned with such things. He had covered his tracks well, and had a nice distance between the locations of the bodies and his warehouse. But he'd made a grave error by underestimating his wife. Mostly, he overlooked her aptitude for suspicion. Now he needed to take precautions while he considered the best way to deal with her. It was a risk to leave her alone in the house, but he had no choice but to visit the warehouse. The unknown, of course, was how much Angela had found, and what, exactly, she knew. The safest assumption was that she knew everything, even though this was impossible.

He thought briefly of the previous night when he emptied the house. He considered taking her here to the warehouse to end things properly, but several obstacles stood in the way of that decision. The greatest of which would be that he'd have to report his wife missing. She would be added to the list of victims claimed by the man the police called The Thief, and the pressure on him would be uncomfortable. Part of him was enthralled with pretending to be stricken by the horror gripping the city this summer. But the logistics of that move were complicated, and Thomas had decided, instead, to take a different route. He had hauled everything he collected from the garage shelves and the basement crawl space—a decade of memorabilia, much of which he didn't remember—into his warehouse and to the storage room in the back.

He had precautions set in place in case things started falling apart, or if he ever made a mistake. He never thought the threat would come from inside his own home, and the dilemma had put him in a crunch. His wife was typically a very predictable person. He never had trouble manipulating her emotions, or controlling her movements. He was sure with time he could learn everything she had discovered, and mold it in a way that would convince her that she had made a great mistake. But to do that required time, and he wasn't sure how much of that he had.

When the bed of his truck was empty, he crawled under each of his cement trucks and punctured the gas tanks. The smell of fuel was pungent when he locked the doors ten minutes later. As he drove down the dusty road and out of the complex, he saw in the rearview mirror the subtle glow of flames starting to rise from the warehouse.

CHICAGO
August 1979

*T*HE PACKAGE WAS DROPPED SATURDAY MORNING, ALONG WITH A large stack of mail, on the reception desk at the front of the police station. It sat unattended for two hours before the clerk got around to sorting the pile. The package—an oversized, thick-padded manila envelope—was finally placed in the detectives' bin, where it sat for another hour. Just after lunch, one of the detectives picked up the envelope and inspected it. There was a name and a return address in the upper left corner.

Belching from fast food and soda, he brought it to his desk, sat down, and tore open the package. Peering inside first, he eventually dumped the contents onto his desk. Across the desktop blotter spilled a photo ID, a necklace of diamonds and green gemstone, newspaper clippings, and a handwritten letter. The detective slowly inspected the necklace, then stopped when he saw the name on the driver's license. When he finally got around to reading the newspaper article and letter, he quickly picked up his desk phone and dialed. It was Saturday afternoon and the staff was thin.

"Hey, boss," the detective said. "Sorry to bother you on a weekend, but I got something you need to see."

Two hours later, calls had been made, facts had been checked, and at three o'clock on Saturday afternoon, the detectives dropped everything back into the envelope, slipped their arms into suit coats, and headed out of the precinct offices.

CHICAGO
August 1979

*T*WO DAYS AFTER THE WAREHOUSE BURNED TO THE GROUND, THOMAS Mitchell was gravely concerned. He was inundated with police reports, insurance claims, employees and clients inquiring about being paid, and outstanding jobs waiting for completion. He had anticipated all of it, and knew there was no other way. But the planned commotion was not what had him out of sorts. He'd come home in the early hours of morning after torching his warehouse with the stale smell of whiskey on his breath from his stop at the bar, and had passed out on the couch.

When he woke late Saturday morning, he had a long list of errands to run. He first noticed the unmarked squad car parked across the street that afternoon. When he made a run to the insurance adjustor's office, he saw the same car in his rearview mirror. He had other places to go, but didn't dare drag the tail anywhere that was unsafe. When he pulled back into his garage hours later, he walked to the front room and peeled the curtains to the side to see the car back in its spot, parked across the street.

By evening, he started making calls because it was what a concerned husband was supposed to do. He called Catherine Blackwell, and even resorted to calling Angela's parents. No one had heard from her, which he knew would be the response. But what he wanted was a record of his concern so that if anyone looked, they'd see his desperate attempts to find his wife.

It was nine o'clock at night when he had exhausted his options, and considered that the next logical step would be to call the police. He swallowed hard at the thought. He had taken care of the warehouse; the garage and basement were empty. Despite his precautions, he had a strong sense that things were falling apart, and that he might have to put his final safety effort into place: run.

He had money stashed for that exact reason, but before he had a chance to seriously consider this last option, there was a knock on the front door. He looked around his empty house, then slowly walked to the foyer and opened the door. Two men in suits stood on his porch. The humid summer night layered their foreheads with perspiration.

"Thomas Mitchell?"

"Yes?"

The man pulled a badge from his waist and held it in front of Thomas's face.

"Chicago Police. We'd like to speak with your wife."

A grave look came over Thomas's face, and he tried hard to morph his distress of self-preservation into something that might be mistaken for spousal concern. He cleared his throat.

"I'm afraid I haven't heard from her all day."

CHAPTER 20
Chicago, October 27, 2019

*T*HEY WERE STILL SEATED AT CATHERINE BLACKWELL'S KITCHEN TABLE. Catherine had poured herself another coffee. Rory had declined again.

"You see, outside of a standard Google search," Catherine said, "I'm afraid I don't make a very good detective. It's been forty years and I know as much about what happened to Angela now as I did back then. The Facebook page was my effort to include others in my search for Angela, which was why I was so excited to hear from you."

"I'm not sure I'd be able to help you," Rory said.

It was a ridiculous statement and Rory knew it as soon as the words floated from her lips. Rory Moore was the perfect person to help Catherine find answers. She reconstructed deaths for a living. She pieced together bits of evidence that had been overlooked by everyone else. She pored through information and found answers where everyone else saw only questions. If Angela Mitchell were alive, Rory was better equipped to find her than anyone else.

"Then why did you contact me?" Catherine asked.

Rory adjusted her glasses. "I heard about the case," she lied. "It's been in the news lately, with Thomas Mitchell's upcoming parole. I was curious. That's all. I'm sorry to have raised your hopes, but I'm not the one to help you, and . . ."

Rory stopped herself, then spoke again.

"Catherine, I don't mean to be dismissive. But have you considered that perhaps the reason you've found no answers for forty years is because there are no answers to find? Have you considered that Thomas Mitchell actually *did* kill Angela, as he was charged?"

"Many times, dear. Many, many times over the years. But there's been one thing that's always convinced me otherwise. One thing that's made me sure she's still alive."

"What's that?"

"A couple of years after Angela went missing, a man came poking around. He contacted me to ask questions about Angela. Seemed to know a lot about me and my relationship with Angela."

"After the trial? This man came around after the conviction?"

"Yes," Catherine said. From the stack of binders, she pulled a leather-bound folder in front of her and turned the pages. "I recorded everything back then. Oh, where is it?" She turned a few more pages. "Yes. Here it is. On November 23, 1981, I was visited by someone who claimed to be looking into the death of Angela Mitchell."

Rory paused, working it out in her head.

"If this man came after the trial was over, what was he looking for?"

"He never came right out and said it, but I knew what was happening. He believed Angela was alive, and he was looking for her."

A flutter went through Rory's chest. "What did you tell him?"

"Nothing. I refused to speak with him. I knew what was going on, and I wasn't going to help in any way."

Rory squinted her eyes. "What was going on?"

"Thomas was looking for Angela. If he could find her, his sentence would be overturned and he'd be a free man, despite the many other women he killed. The women Angela had discovered. The women she became obsessed with. Thomas hired this man to find Angela, I'm sure of it. And ever since that moment, I've known she was alive. She's been hiding for forty years."

Rory became dizzy. A spinning light-headedness meant to fog her mind, a defense mechanism, perhaps. But her thoughts were clear and she knew the answer to her question before she formed it.

"What was his name?" she asked quickly.

"Who?"

"The man. The man who came asking questions. Do you know his name?"

"Yes, I recorded everything," Catherine said, looking at the page in front of her. She ran her finger down the print, stopping near the bottom and pausing a moment before looking back at Rory.

"His name was Frank Moore."

PART II

THE RECONSTRUCTION

CHICAGO
November 1981

*F*RANK MOORE WAS TWO YEARS REMOVED FROM HIS STINT AT THE PUB-
lic defender's office in Cook County when he signed on at Garrison
Ford. The public defender's gig was a rite of passage for most criminal defense attorneys, a way to rapidly acquire a large number of
cases, learn the law, get in front of judges, and endure the spoils of
wild courtroom failures. It was a part of every great defender's
coming of age, a painful post–law school education necessary to
forge a successful career defending criminals. Frank's record over
the first two years of his career had been good enough to land him
a job at Garrison Ford, one of Chicago's largest and most accomplished criminal defense firms. He joined in the summer of 1979
with grand visions, monumental goals, and a true passion for protecting the rights of those who sought his help. Had someone told
Frank Moore back then that he'd spend most of his career running
a one-man shop, far from the spotlight of Garrison Ford's high-
profile cases, he'd have never believed them. He was young and
hungry and filled with fire. Nothing was going to get in his way.
That is, until he was assigned to the case that would change his life
forever.

The summer of '79 had been plagued by the disappearances of
six women, and the city was on edge. When the police found their
man, Frank's phone rang. His boss, a partner in the firm, needed
his help on a sensitive case. A man named Thomas Mitchell, who
had notoriously been dubbed The Thief, had hired Garrison Ford

to defend him against the charge of killing his wife. For a high-profile firm, it didn't get much better. Frank Moore, young and bright and ambitious, would do the scut work of research and briefs. He jumped at the opportunity.

Over the following two years, between the summer of 1979 and the fall of 1981, the case took nasty and insurmountable turns. In the end, Garrison Ford had presented a failed defense of Thomas Mitchell, and The Thief was sentenced to sixty years for the murder of his wife. After the trial, Frank Moore became lead counsel on Thomas Mitchell's appeals. It was during the appeals process, when Frank met often with his client to discuss strategy, he first started to believe Thomas Mitchell's wife might be alive.

"I've filed the notice of appeal," Frank said. "Next I'll finish my brief and submit it in the next week or ten days."

"And the brief goes after her?" Thomas Mitchell asked.

They were seated in a private interview room at Stateville Correctional Center, which was reserved for privileged attorney-client meetings. Frank was on one side of the table, and his client—handcuffed and orange jumpsuited—on the other. Frank knew it was possible that someone from the prison was listening to their conversation, but not likely. And he didn't really care.

"It goes after how the defense obtained the alleged evidence against you. It goes after the judge's decision to allow that evidence to be presented in court."

"Good. Go after the judge and go after the evidence, but go after her, too. She was having a nervous breakdown when she did this to me. She was swallowing Valium at three times the rate it had been prescribed. Plus, mentally, she was not all there."

"We have a lot of ammunition, Thomas. My first brief will be based mostly on the legality of the evidence presented against you, the complete circumstantiality of it all, and the argument that none of it should have been allowed in court. If our initial appeal is denied, and there is a very good chance it will be, then our next appeal will include details about your wife's mental state when she disappeared. Remember, the appeals process allows us to continue to the federal level through the writ of habeas corpus, if needed. And there's a lot of work to be done on the state level before we even consider that route. Hopefully, someone in their right mind within the appeals court makes the sound and just decision about this. So I'll make a strong opening argument in this initial appeal to the state. But we'll save details about your wife for later, if we need them, including the fact that you were convicted of second-degree murder without the prosecution producing a body."

"They can't produce a body, because there *is* no body. Where are you on that? Any progress?"

Frank gathered some papers and placed them into his bag. Pulled out a different stack and looked at it. "Her parents were a dead end. They hadn't seen her for many years before she disappeared. Only a few times since she turned eighteen, they told me."

"Could you read them?" Thomas asked. "You didn't get a sense that they were lying to you?"

"They weren't lying."

"She had to have help. A woman like Angela, she doesn't just go off on her own. She'd be too scared. Sometimes she couldn't bring herself to leave the house. Now I'm supposed to believe she up and vanished all on her own. No, someone helped her. Someone is *still* helping her. Her parents are the most likely ones. Did you tell them you were looking for her?"

"Thomas"—Frank put his elbows on the table and leaned closer to his client—"They were very upset. They believe, like the rest of the country, that Angela is dead. I didn't tell them who I was or that I thought their daughter was still alive. I made up a story about the possibility of a civil suit."

"Maybe you should have told them what you're really after."

"That's not the right approach. They believe their daughter is dead, I'm not going to fill them with false hope that she's alive."

"It's *not* false. She's alive."

Frank nodded his head. "But I'm not the one to tell them that. I'll conduct my search for her the way I think is best."

"Did you talk with Catherine?"

"Catherine Blackwell, your business partner's wife. Yes. I visited her a couple of weeks ago. She's still very distraught at the mention of you or Angela. We didn't have a fruitful conversation."

"Do you believe me?"

Frank stared at his client—convicted of killing his wife, accused of killing many more—and paused too long before he answered. "I'm looking for her, aren't I? If I didn't believe you, do you think I'd be spending all my time on this? And by the way, I've got to start billing for my time."

"I've got money."

"It's going to be expensive."

"I'll pay you whatever it costs to find her. But I want you to do this quietly. Don't involve your firm. I'll pay you separately."

"I haven't even told my wife what I'm doing. Do you think I'm about to tell the partners at Garrison Ford? On the record, you and I are working on your appeals. Off the record, you're retaining my services independently to look into a personal matter, settle your debts, handle your finances, negotiate your way out of the business you still technically co-own, deal with your property, et cetera. I'll write up the paperwork."

"What's next?" The Thief asked.

"I'll file the notice of appeal this week."

"No. What next with your search for her?"

"Oh," Frank said, collecting his papers to leave. "The psychiatric facility where she spent her teen years."

CHAPTER 21
Chicago, October 28, 2019

*L*ANE PHILLIPS STOKED THE DYING EMBERS AND BROUGHT THE OR-
ange glowing logs back to life. He stacked two more splinters of
wood on top, watched the flames grow, and sat on the couch, where
his laptop was open. Rory was next to him, her own computer on
her lap as she typed away. Fall had come quickly, descending on
them from the heavens as cold Canadian air swept across the
Midwest to send temperatures into the forties. It felt too soon to
turn on the heat, so they opted for their first fire of the season.

"So your father was forever tied to this man, and now you
are, too?"

"Not forever," Rory said. "But for at least eighteen months. I'll
represent him at the final hearing, review all the stipulations one
more time, and hand him off to his parole officer. The judge ordered me to look after his finances with monthly reports for a year
and a half, since he's got a solid nest egg stashed away, and my father was listed as the financial power of attorney. So I'll make sure
he doesn't go broke. Then he's on his own."

"And why the order to go out to Starved Rock?"

"The judge waived the requirement to live in a halfway house
due to his notoriety. He inherited a cabin near Starved Rock in the
nineties from an uncle. My father put it in a trust and handed it off
to a management company. The property has been a vacation
rental for all these years. He's going to live there, so the judge ordered me to tag along with the social worker and the parole officer

to have a look at the place ahead of the release. Make sure it meets all the requirements."

"I'm going with you," Lane said.

Rory hadn't told Lane about her meeting with Catherine Blackwell. She allowed him to believe her nervousness had started with her visit to Stateville Correctional Center. It was a logical conclusion, as compared to the real source of Rory's distress—that her father had been trying to find Angela Mitchell before he died. And more troubling than the discovery itself was what it was doing to Rory. That walled-off place in her mind had been disturbed, the once-calm waters clouded now with muck and filth. The only way to restore clarity was to figure out what her father had found. The only way to tame those waters back to peace, and to quiet that place in her mind, was to look for Angela herself. To ignore this urge was to stoke the flames of a sickness she had managed to control for many years. She knew the best way to extinguish the impulse was to nurture it, like Aunt Greta had taught her as a child when Rory defused her fanatical impulses by mastering the detailed craft of restoring china dolls. The burning question now, though, was if Rory would be reconstructing the woman's death, or following the footsteps of a woman who was still very much alive.

"Fine," Rory said. "Come with me." She looked up from her laptop and offered a rare glimpse of emotion. "Thanks. I didn't want to go alone."

A pang of guilt prickled her neck for keeping her secret from Lane. The man had done nothing more than love her—and all of her flaws—for the better part of a decade. Didn't he deserve to hear this part of her life? Perhaps so, but she couldn't bring herself to tell him. Rory pointed to Lane's computer, then looked back to her own.

"Let's go, we're way behind. What have you got?"

Lane continued to stare for a moment, as if he sensed something more she wasn't saying. Rory felt his stare, but kept her attention on the laptop.

"Okay," Lane said, giving in and looking at his own computer monitor. He scrolled through the pages. "I've been watching an area outside of Detroit, southeast portion of the city and into the adjoining counties. It's been coming up on the algorithm. Several hits in just the last four months. There have been twelve homicides in the last two years where the victims have been homeless women or prostitutes, all African-American. Little or no family support, a few who were only identified at the morgue through fingerprinting and matching to the Michigan fingerprint identification program of convicted criminals. Basically, no one knew they had been killed. No family, no friends."

Rory was typing on her computer. "Easy targets with little risk."

"Correct," Lane said.

"How did the algorithm pick them up?"

"Manner of death."

Each week, Lane and Rory ran through trends picked up by the algorithm Lane had created. It took into account several different factors about crimes reported from across the country, looking for trends and similarities. Doing so allowed them to recognize commonalities between homicides in a particular geographic region. When enough markers and tags showed up in the same location, Lane and Rory were alerted. Then they jumped in and started digging. To date, the Murder Accountability Project had identified twelve serial killers—defined as a single person having committed at least three homicides—across America in which arrests were made. Many more hot spots were trending, where local police were following up on leads. Tonight's meeting was a weekly occurrence where Rory and Lane pointed out marks that were trending on the software. Sometimes it was a cluster of homicides in a tightly focused location, or a group of homicides carried out with the same suspected weapon, or on the same type of victim. It might be how a body was disposed of. It could be the occupation of the victim. The algorithm tracked over five thousand indicators looking for similarities.

When they could make a strong enough case, Rory and Lane took their findings to the authorities in that area. With Lane's reputation as a forensic psychologist and criminal profiler for the FBI's Behavioral Science Unit, and Rory's credentials as a recon-

167

structionist who pieced together the very findings the algorithm looked for, they made the perfect team. Police departments listened to their conclusions, and many had started using Lane's software to track homicides on their own.

"All of them were killed by some sort of blunt-force trauma—blows to the side of the head—and then the bodies were disposed of in Dumpsters."

They were in the process of logging the names of the twelve Detroit victims, and cataloguing their findings, when the doorbell rang. Rory looked at her watch. It was almost ten o'clock. She walked to the front door and peered through the peephole. Ron Davidson stood on her porch.

"Shit," she said before pulling the door open. "Hey, Ron."

"Gray," he said in a measured tone. "You're not returning my calls again."

Rory exhaled loudly. "Sorry. I've been busy with this . . . thing. For my dad."

"I've heard all about it since you asked me for those old records." He leaned closer to the screen door. "Christ, Gray. Your dad repped this guy?"

Rory nodded. "Looks like it, yeah."

"Did the boxes from 1979 have what you needed?"

"Yes. Or . . . I'm not sure. I haven't been through them all yet." Her hand habitually moved to her face to adjust her glasses, but she realized she wasn't wearing them. She never did when she was alone with Lane. "Thanks for coming through on those."

"No problem. I owed you for taking Camille Byrd's case."

The two stood without speaking for a moment, Detective Davidson on the front porch and Rory inside behind the screen door.

"Can I come in?" Ron asked.

"Yeah, sorry. Of course," Rory said, opening the door.

She led her boss into the living room, where Lane was still tapping away on his computer across from the roaring fire.

"Lane," Rory said. "Ron's here, we've got to talk."

Lane looked up. "Ron, how are you?"

"Doing good, Doc."

The two shook hands.

"Sorry to interrupt," Ron said. "I'll just be a minute."

"No worries," Lane said.

"In here," Rory said, walking Detective Davidson past the darkened den, where all her dolls stood on the shadowed shelves, and into her office. In addition to the three boxes from 1979 that rested by her desk, the contents of which were spread across the surface, Camille Byrd's photograph also hung from the corkboard with the few scant notes Rory had made nearly two weeks ago about the autopsy findings.

"Walter Byrd contacted me," Ron said. "He says he hasn't heard from you. He said he called a few times, but never got a call back. Sounds familiar."

"I don't have anything to tell him yet."

"Then tell him *that*, Rory. But tell him *something*."

"I feel like crap, Ron. I agreed to take the reconstruction, then my father died, and I've been tied up in dissolving his law firm and . . . everything else I ran into. I haven't put many hours on the case."

"I'm sorry for the timing, Rory. I know you've got a lot on your plate."

Rory looked over at her desk and saw the remnants of her research from the 1979 case strewn across the surface. She remembered sitting at the desk a few nights before, stumbling across her father's notes and wondering what he had been doing for Thomas Mitchell throughout all the years he represented the man. Now she knew.

"I'll get back to Camille Byrd. I promise."

"Have you looked into it at all?"

"Just a glance," Rory said, remembering the night she'd paged through the medical examiner's report, the image of Camille's bruised and damaged throat sparking in her mind. Rory glanced over at the picture of Camille Byrd on the corkboard. She felt the spidery tentacles of guilt crawl up her back. She had dreamt of Camille Byrd two nights earlier, coming across her body as it lay in Grant Park. Rory had tried to apologize for ignoring the case, but the girl was dead and cold in her dream when Rory shook her. As she stared now at the photo and into the dead girl's eyes, Rory felt the urge to hide behind her thick-rimmed glasses, turn up the collar of her coat, and look away.

"I'll put some hours on it."

"When?"

"Soon, I promise."

Her phone rang from her back pocket. Rory held up a finger.

"Sorry." She retrieved her phone and checked the number. Although not in her list of contacts, Rory immediately recognized the number. It had been burned into her memory the way everything else was, but this particular phone number held a greater significance than simply her remarkable memory. The last time she received a call from this extension, she had learned that her father was dead. Was it irony, Rory wondered, that she had also been with Ron Davidson when she had accepted the last call?

"Celia," Rory said to her father's administrative assistant. "Is something wrong?"

"Oh, hello," Celia said, caught off guard. "No, nothing's wrong. Well, I'm not sure. I have to see you. I have something of your father's that I'm not sure what to do with. Can we meet this week?"

Rory spun through her schedule. She had to make the trip out to Thomas Mitchell's cabin, meet with Judge Boyle and the parole board for the final hearing, finish the legal paperwork to get her newest and only client out of jail—which was scheduled to happen in one week, get his finances in order, and now dedicate some time to Camille Byrd's reconstruction. All of this while putting off the burning desire to start her own search for Angela Mitchell and figure out what had happened to her.

"I'm swamped at the moment, Celia," Rory said, knowing that her father's law firm was all but shut down and wrapped up besides the Thomas Mitchell affair. "Can we put it off for a couple of weeks?"

There was a pause before the soft voice answered: "I really need to see you, Rory."

She thought she heard quiet weeping. Rory remembered Celia's tears dripping onto her neck when the woman had embraced her at her father's law office.

"Yes," Rory said. "Then we'll meet this week. I'll call you tomorrow to find the best time."

She heard more sniffling and ended the call without waiting for confirmation. She placed the phone in her back pocket and looked at her boss.

"Give me another week, Ron. In the meantime, I'll call Mr. Byrd and give him an update."

The detective nodded. "Okay. But I need something soon, Rory. Something new. Anything."

"I'll have something to you by next week," she said.

CHICAGO
November 1981

FRANK MOORE HAD TRACKED HER GENEALOGY, THE BEST HE COULD figure. If Angela Mitchell were alive, she would likely rely on friends or family. This was his hope, anyway. Because the other possibility—that she had disappeared on her own—presented an insurmountable obstacle he'd never be able to scale. How would he find her if she had simply vanished? What if she had left the state to hide in a corner of the country where no one would look? Based on what Frank knew about the woman, this was a very conceivable possibility.

Angela Mitchell had been a loner her whole life, moving from her parents' custody as a child, to an extended stint at a juvenile psychiatric hospital in downstate Illinois that lasted until she was released at age eighteen. From there, Frank's research got murky. Her parents had been out of the picture since she became a legal adult, and Frank's trip down to St. Louis to visit them had been fruitless. Angela Mitchell's parents hadn't seen or heard from her in years prior to her disappearance. They hadn't even known she married. The next time she showed up on Frank's sketchy timeline was when she met Thomas Mitchell in Chicago, had a short courtship, and then married. She had no close friends besides a woman named Catherine Blackwell, who was the wife of Thomas's former business partner. Frank's journey to the Blackwell residence had been unsuccessful, a little strange, and ultimately a waste of time and energy.

Through archival information he found at the library and some names given to him by Angela's parents, Frank had made a list of distant relatives to call on. These were cousins, and siblings of her parents, and cousins of her parents, and other further removed folks that had at one time or another been part of Angela's life before she met Thomas Mitchell.

For the past three months, Frank had been looking for any hint that his client's wife was still alive, as Thomas Mitchell swore she was. A twenty-eight-year-old associate, Frank was anxious to prove himself at Garrison Ford. He filled his days by slogging through research and briefs, and occasionally making an appearance in court to assist the partner to whom he was assigned. He spent his nights hunting down a woman who was likely dead and buried. Newly married, with a nurse for a wife who worked the afternoon shift at the hospital, he had the time to look. He was happy being paid to chase a ghost. But God almighty, he could only imagine what would happen if he actually found her. His client would be free, the conviction overturned, and Frank's stock at Garrison Ford would rise quickly. Perhaps he'd make partner before forty.

The latest lead was written on a scrap of paper—a name and address—and stuck with Scotch Tape to his dashboard. The rural road, an hour and a half west of the city, was empty. Frank couldn't imagine there ever being much traffic this far out in the sticks, and he drove freely as the sun set in front of him. Cornfields stretched out on either side of the road, as far as he could see. The once-tall stalks were now cropped down to nothing. Large bales of hay, spun in tight spirals, studded the field in random patterns.

He came to a T in the road, checked his map, and turned left. After another three miles, he eventually saw the top of the two-story building rising above the otherwise-flat terrain. The campus sprawled out over many acres. In the middle of nowhere, the white structure looked like a prison. Frank was sure it felt that way to many of its patients. He turned into the parking lot and pulled past the sign indicating that he had arrived at BAYER GROUP JUVENILE PSYCHIATRIC FACILITY. He found a spot and parked. Inside, he signed in.

"Which resident are you visiting?" the receptionist asked.

"No resident," Frank said, standing in his wrinkled suit after making the long drive from the Garrison Ford offices. "I'm here to see Dr. Jefferson."

"Do you have an appointment?"

"Yes. I called earlier in the week."

"Let me find him," the receptionist said.

Frank paced the waiting room for five minutes until the door opened.

"Mr. Moore?"

Frank turned around to see a thin man with tiny glasses and a long white coat.

"Dale Jefferson, we spoke on the phone."

"Yes," Frank said, walking over and shaking hands. "Thanks for taking a meeting."

"Sorry it's not under better circumstances," Dr. Jefferson said. "Come back to my office."

Frank followed the doctor into the psychiatric facility, through a long white corridor, and into his office. The space was decorated like a living room—a couch, coffee table, and two end chairs. A wall of built-in shelving held volumes of textbooks. Dr. Jefferson sat in one of the chairs and motioned for Frank to take a spot on the couch. A file was resting on the coffee table and Dr. Jefferson picked it up as he sat.

"It's a terrible shame about Angela. I was unaware of the situation at first because the news media never used her maiden name. And, sadly, Thomas Mitchell has gotten more attention than any of his victims. Society is more interested in The Thief than the lives he stole."

Frank was not here to debate the psychology of society, and wasn't about to mention that his client was convicted of killing only one woman, not a slew of women. In fact, Frank hadn't mentioned his association with Thomas Mitchell to anyone he had encountered during his months-long search for Angela. The court of public opinion had pinned all the missing women from the summer of 1979 on Thomas Mitchell, and Frank knew he needed to hide his motives for why he was asking about a woman who had supposedly been killed more than two years ago.

"Yes," Frank finally said. "It's a shame."

"You said Angela's family is looking into a civil lawsuit?"

"Yes," Frank said, crossing his legs. A poker player might see this as a nervous reaction to hide his lie. "I'm looking into matters myself to see if a civil suit is possible, given the circumstances."

"You'll excuse me," Dr. Jefferson said. "The man must be very troubled, but if they're not going to put him to death for what he did, then I say lock him up for life and drain him of all his resources."

"Well," Frank said, clearing his throat, "I'm going to see what I can do."

"Do you represent Angela's parents?"

Frank paused briefly. "Yes."

"From what I remember, they didn't have a wonderful relationship with Angela. Always terrible to see fractured relations between parents and child. And now, never to be repaired."

"Yes. It's a shame," Frank said again.

"Do you have children, Mr. Moore?"

"I'm just married. Maybe in a year or two my wife and I will try."

Dr. Jefferson held up the file. "What can I help you with?"

"Civil suits can be nasty, so I want to find out as much about Angela as possible. I know she spent time here during her teen years, and I'm wondering if I could ask a few questions."

"Of course."

Frank removed a piece of paper from his breast pocket. "Angela came here in 1967 when she was seventeen years old."

"That's correct."

"How long was Angela here?"

"Seven months. She left on her eighteenth birthday. I'm afraid we didn't help Angela as much as we, or her parents, had hoped."

"So, once she became an adult, she left on her own?"

"Yes. Bayer Group is a juvenile facility. We only treat youths who are younger than eighteen and under a parent's or guardian's supervision. Once they become legal adults, they stay only if they choose to do so. Angela did not."

"And what was Angela admitted for?"

Dr. Jefferson read from the file.

"'Oppositional defiant disorder, social anxiety, and obsessive-compulsive disorder.' She was also autistic, which complicated her treatment."

"So, when Angela turned eighteen and you could no longer legally keep her here, her parents picked her up? Do you know what happened to Angela after her time here?"

"It wasn't her parents," Dr. Jefferson said. "Like I mentioned, that relationship was fractured. During Angela's time here, I felt like we were making such poor progress that I suggested to her parents that perhaps Angela should be discharged and return when she had an attitude that might be more receptive to accepting help. Her parents were against discharging her. I'm afraid at that point they had reached the end of their patience with her."

Frank sat forward on the couch. "So what? They dumped her here?"

Dr. Jefferson shrugged. "I wouldn't put it that way. They wanted to get Angela help, and they felt unable to help her on their own."

"So she turns eighteen. You can't keep her here. Where did she go? Back with her parents?"

Dr. Jefferson shook his head. "No. Angela was released of her own accord. She was legal at that point."

"Yes, but she was just eighteen, with no job, no money, and, I presume, no transportation. Where did she go? She just walked out into the cornfields?"

"One of our counselors tried following up for a few weeks, but never heard back from her. The last address we had for her was in Peoria, Illinois."

"What was in Peoria?"

"The best I remember, a friend of Angela's lived there. The friend signed in the day Angela was discharged. Helped her pack her things. According to our records, Angela left with her."

"Do you have a name for this woman?" Frank asked quickly, then paused to control his excitement. This was the first real lead he'd come across while searching for anyone who might be connected to Angela Mitchell during her adult years. "If she's a relative, we may be able to add her name to the civil suit."

176

"Of course," Dr. Jefferson said, paging through the file until he removed a single slip of paper and pushed it in front of Frank. "Last name was Schreiber. She was one of our on-call nurses. Not sure this is the correct address anymore. That was a number of years ago."

CHAPTER 22
Chicago, October 29, 2019

*T*HEY DROVE TOGETHER AND FOLLOWED THE CAR IN FRONT OF THEM, which held the social worker and the parole officer. Thomas Mitchell had inherited the cabin in 1994 when his uncle died. Rory had tracked the property the best she could from her father's paperwork. The uncle had died of pancreatic cancer and had willed the cabin to his nephew. Rory's father had placed the cabin into a trust. A rental company had taken good care of the place, and according to the financial documents she found in the file, the property had provided a nice source of income over the years. It was a two-bedroom A-frame just outside of Starved Rock State Park, about an hour from the city.

Located so close to the park and the Illinois River, the cabin had been easy to rent over the years. The rental income had been self-sustaining and allowed the management company to stay current with upkeep. Rory's father had dismissed the management company the previous year, and had carefully documented his monthly trips to keep the cabin updated, surely anticipating his client's arrival.

When they reached the outskirts of Starved Rock, the social worker slowed in front of her. Rory assumed she was consulting her GPS. The lead car took off again, and Rory followed it through winding roads on the north side of the park. They traveled across bridges, where short waterfalls fell over bluffs and where evergreen pines rose up into the clear October sky. Had she not been on a journey to see the future home of a suspected serial killer, the setting would be majestic.

After fifteen minutes of slow going, stopping at each intersection before deciding which direction to turn, Rory and Lane arrived at the entrance to a long dirt driveway canopied tightly by foliage that had started to morph to fall colors. A mailbox stood isolated, just to the side of the drive, and Rory figured she could check off at least one of the judge's requests. If anyone wanted to send The Thief a letter, he'd receive it via the United States Postal Service.

She turned onto the driveway and followed the social worker along the uneven path for a hundred yards. The cocooned driveway eventually opened to a clearing in which stood a cedar-sided A-frame cabin. The piece of land was impressive. Rory's mind imagined an aerial view of the property, which was cut into a densely forested area. The clearing where the cabin stood was five acres of grass and gravel and clay that butted up against the thick forest around it. The end of the driveway led in a circle around the cabin. As Rory drove the loop around, she spotted the river through the trees off to her right. A path was cut in the forest, and a set of stairs led down to a dock that ran out into the water.

"Well," Lane said from the passenger seat, staring out his window, "you can't argue that this is anything but the perfect place for a suspected serial killer to hide for the rest of his life."

Rory shook her head. "And I was thinking how beautiful this place had been for the families that rented it all these years."

"No you weren't. You wouldn't reconstruct deaths for a living if you were really thinking that."

Rory pulled around the cabin and parked. She grabbed her thick-rimmed glasses from the dashboard, put them on her face, and pulled her beanie hat down her forehead. "Yeah, you're right," she said, opening the car door. "This place is creepy as hell. Be right back."

Rory climbed from the car and met Naomi Brown, the social worker, at the front of the cabin, inspecting the residence as she did. Rory had the key, which she had found in her father's office.

"Have you been to your client's home before?" Naomi asked.

"He's not my client, exactly," Rory said, shaking her head and adjusting her glasses. "No, I haven't seen the place."

The social worker looked at Rory for a moment. It was the confused look Rory often received and always hated.

Rory twirled her finger in the air and pointed at the cabin. "Let's get this out of the way."

"There is a list of requirements," Naomi said. "Including a functioning landline, a current U.S. Postal Service address, and other items. It's mostly a formality, but since the judge is agreeing to this unique living arrangement, we need to check all the boxes."

"Then let's check them," Rory said as she climbed the steps to the front porch. The wooden boards creaked under her weight. She inserted the key in the door and pushed it open. Ezra Parker, the parole officer, snapped photos of the outside before entering. Inside, they found a well-kept home furnished the way any rental property might be, with a couch and chairs positioned around a stone fireplace in the front room. A kitchen was off to the left, and another room for dining. A screened-in porch on the back of the home offered a view of the sprawling acres that led to the forest, through which the river was visible and reflecting the October sky. Stairs led upstairs to two bedrooms.

The group took thirty minutes to inspect the place. Naomi Brown checked all the boxes to show that the home met the judge's requirements. Ezra Parker snapped all the required photos.

"Until your client acquires an automobile," Naomi said, "there is a convenience store half a mile down the road."

Rory nodded. She had a sudden desire to leave the place, realizing that her authority over Thomas Mitchell's finances would likely require her to help him with purchases, such as a car. As they headed to the front door, they noticed the red footprints they had all tracked in from outside. Rory looked down at her combat boots, noticing for the first time that they were covered in a crimson dust.

"Sorry about that," Naomi said. "We should have removed our shoes."

"What the hell is it?" Rory asked, lifting her foot to examine the bottom of her boot.

"Red clay," Ezra said. "It's common around Starved Rock. The soil is saturated with it. It gets everywhere. Your car will be a mess, too."

Rory looked at the bloodred footprints.

"Time to go," she said. "I'll call someone to clean the cabin before his release."

CHICAGO
November 1981

*T*HREE DAYS OF PHONE CALLS HAD GONE UNANSWERED BEFORE FRANK decided to make the drive out to Peoria and have a look himself. Angela Mitchell had been discharged from Bayer Group Juvenile Psychiatric Facility in 1968, thirteen years ago, and it was very possible that whoever had once lived at the address Dr. Jefferson provided no longer did so today. But since it was his first legitimate discovery he'd come across while looking for any trace of Angela Mitchell in her adult life, prior to marrying Thomas Mitchell, it was worth the drive.

He made the trip on Saturday morning when traffic out of the city was light and the drive time was just over two hours. He drove past acres of harvested cornfields—not very different from his drive out to Bayer Group the other day. Tractors sat parked in the middle of the fields, and silos rose up occasionally on the otherwise-flat horizon. When he turned onto a long stretch of two-lane road, address numbers were stenciled on roadside mailboxes situated next to long, stretching driveways that led to isolated homes nestled on large plots of land, each property far from its neighbors. He found the address that was listed in Angela Mitchell's file.

The driveway was winding as he turned onto it. Dogs appeared from behind the house as he pulled his car to the end of the drive, barking and following the car as he came to a stop. Frank slowly opened the door. Two German shepherds greeted him and barked for his attention, both jostling to position their heads under his hand. He obliged by petting them while he stared at the farm-house.

The front door opened and a woman walked onto the porch. She stared down at him. Frank held up his hand in an amicable wave and walked toward her. The dogs barked and followed, jumping and leaning into his legs.

"They won't hurt ya," the woman said from the porch. "Leave the man alone! Go on, get in the backyard!"

The dogs barked and abandoned their playful assault and disappeared behind the house. Frank walked to the foot of the porch stairs.

"Ms. Schreiber? Do I have the name right?"

As Frank approached, he got a better look at the woman, who he guessed was in her late fifties or early sixties.

"Yeah, that's me. What can I help ya with?" she asked. "You selling encyclopedias or vacuum cleaners or some such?"

"No," Frank said with a laugh. "My name is Frank Moore, I'm an attorney. I'm here to ask a few questions about Angela Mitchell. Or Angela Barron, to use her maiden name. I believe you knew her?"

Frank saw the woman's face go slack. Her jaw loosened and her mouth opened. Her eyes widened as if Frank had pulled a gun from his waistband and pointed it at her. She took a step backward, her free hand reaching for the door handle.

Frank lifted his hands. "I'm just here to talk."

"I got nothing to say. Now get off my property or I'll call the police."

"I'm not here to cause any trouble, ma'am. I'm looking into a civil lawsuit that might help Angela's family."

"I want you to leave my property." Her eyes were wide and feral. "Right now!"

The woman's demands turned the scene quickly into something Frank had not anticipated.

"Okay," Frank said, reaching into his pocket and pulling out his business card. "If you decide you want to talk about Angela, give me a call. My number is on this card."

"Tubs! Harold!"

At the sound of their names, the dogs barreled from behind the house. This time, their demeanor was aggressive. Their playful yelps had morphed to growls. Frank dropped his business card as he backpedaled. The dogs nipped at his ankles as he hurried to his car, and then they bared their teeth with vicious snaps, once he had locked himself inside. His forehead was slick with perspiration as he started the engine and glanced back to the front porch. The woman was gone, but Frank saw the curtains in the front window bend slightly.

The white speck of his business card caught his eye. It was lying on the ground where he had dropped it. He pulled a U-turn and headed up the long drive and away from the barking dogs. He knew he had discovered something, but Frank Moore had no idea what it was.

CHAPTER 23
Chicago, October 29, 2019

*T*HE CHINA DOLL RESTED ON THE PASSENGER SEAT AS RORY DROVE south out of the city. She took the Kennedy Expressway until it turned into I-94, then followed I-80 east for a short spurt to exit at Calumet Avenue. She pulled into the town of Munster, Indiana, fifty minutes after she left her house in Chicago. Three Floyds Brewery was long closed when she turned into the parking lot. The last time she'd been to the brewery was in May for Dark Lord Day, a ticketed twelve-hour event where stout lovers got the only chance of the year to buy their favorite beer. Rory attended because it was one of the rare public events she enjoyed, because beer flowed liberally, and Lane had expressed interest. She didn't go for the reason everyone else did—to stock up on Dark Lord, although she did that, too. For most regular folks, when their Dark Lord supply was gone, they had to wait until the next year to find more. Rory, thankfully, was not a member of the regular folk.

She grabbed the doll from the passenger seat and stepped out of the car. Her breath was visible in the chilled night air. She pulled her beanie hat low on her head, adjusted her glasses, and started toward the building. The parking lot was lit by a single yellow halogen bulb at the top of the tall post in the middle of the parking area. As she walked along the blacktop, the golden glow of the halogen mixed with her still-red footprints to create an orange trail away from her car. Rory noticed the strange footprints and stomped her combat boots to rid them of the last of the red clay that remained from Starved Rock earlier in the day. The memory of the bloodred prints she had tracked through the cabin gave her a shiver. Hence, the trip to Munster to settle her nerves. Her fridge at home was empty.

She walked to the side of the brewery and knocked on a gray metal door. It opened almost immediately.

"Rory the Doll Lady," a large man said. His thick beard dribbled down to his chest and was striped with gray. He wore a *3 Floyds Brewing Co.* ball cap. "You almost made it six months."

Rory had left Dark Lord Day in May with what most would consider a year's worth of stout. But she had been on hiatus for most of that time, and her alcohol consumption always increased when she was on a break. And the most recent developments in her life had caused her to prematurely run through the rest.

"Kip," Rory said. "Always nice to see you." She held up the doll. "Simon and Halbig. It's German, rare, and in pristine condition."

The large man took the doll and inspected it like he knew what he was looking at. He stroked his long beard.

"Can I find this at Walmart?"

"Not a chance."

"Taylor's been begging for one. She heard about the doll I gave Becky over the holidays."

Rory knew Kip had handfuls of grandchildren. Always looking to one-up his rival grandparents at birthdays and Christmas time, restored china dolls had been his go-to gift for the past two or three years. They were rare and expensive and could not be one-upped by his competition. Rory wasn't sure what she'd do when Kip had charmed all his granddaughters with her rare dolls. She'd have to ration her Dark Lord like everyone else. Until then, she bartered.

"Retail?" Kip asked.

Rory shrugged. "Probably four hundred."

"And what are you asking?"

"Two cases."

"Straight up?" Kip asked.

"I'm feeling generous."

Kip stroked his beard once more while he looked at the Simon & Halbig doll. "You got papers on it?"

"Come on," Rory said, reaching into the pocket of her gray coat and producing the original papers describing the doll. She'd picked it up the previous year at auction for next to nothing. It had been in terrible condition with multiple fractures running through the porcelain and clumps of missing hair. Rory had expertly managed the fractures, erasing them to near invisibility. She relied on Aunt Greta to come up with a solution for the bald patches on the skull, which, of course, the old lady did. When Rory handed the doll over tonight, it looked brand-new. Had she returned to the same auction hall where she found it, unloading it would bring a payday far north of $400.

Kip nodded as he took the papers. "Be right out."

A few minutes later, they walked across the parking lot. Kip pushed a dolly with two cases of stout stacked on it. He loaded them into Rory's car and closed the trunk. Rory climbed behind the wheel and started the engine. She rolled down the window when Kip knocked.

"You walk through a pumpkin patch on your way here?" Kip asked, looking at the orange, lunarlike footprints around the car.

"Not a pumpkin patch," Rory said, pushing her glasses up her nose. "But a real frickin' mess, that's for sure." She attempted a smile. "It's why I'm here at midnight, let's just leave it at that."

"Yeah. When I got your call, I figured you were in bad need of a fix."

"It's beer, Kip. Not heroin."

"A fix is a fix."

Kip reached into his coat pocket and pulled out a bottle of Dark Lord, frosted from having come straight out of the cooler. He produced a Swiss Army knife from his other pocket. The Dark Lord emblem was inscribed across the front of it. Peeling it open, the double-side blade shined on one side with the sharpness of a scalpel. The other side sported a bottle opener. Kip popped the cap and handed it to Rory through the window.

"Watch yourself on I-80. Goddamn state troopers got eagle eyes."

Rory smiled and took the ice-cold bottle. "Thanks, Kip. I'll see you in May."

"Here," he said, handing her the Swiss Army knife as well. "I know that doll's worth more than a couple cases of beer."

Rory nodded her thanks, then pulled out of the brewery's parking lot and onto Indiana Parkway. A few minutes later, she was on the highway with her cruise control set at one mile per hour slower than the posted speed limit. She sipped her Dark Lord and enjoyed the ride back to the city.

Rory found herself parked in front of her father's house. It was close to one in the morning. She was becoming unhealthily fixated on the woman from 1979. Angela Mitchell had somehow reached back across the years to grab hold of some part of Rory's consciousness. Like a tuning fork that has been tapped, the vibration from the mystery surrounding the woman was at once barely audible but yet impossible to ignore.

At first, she failed to understand why Angela Mitchell had such a hold on her. Or, at least, Rory wouldn't admit it. To do so required self-reflection, and the acknowledgment of her own flaws and idiosyncrasies. Baring her soul had always been difficult, even if she were doing so only to herself. The connection had started when Rory learned that Angela was autistic. The link had strengthened when Rory read the descriptions that painted Angela as an introverted woman on the outskirts of society, someone who never truly fit in and who had few, if any, close relationships in her life. A woman who had been too scared to go to the authorities even when she suspected her husband was a killer. Since she had learned that Catherine Blackwell believed Angela Mitchell could still be alive, Rory's mind was in overdrive. That her father had once searched for her, and perhaps had spent much of his life looking, had produced an unhealthy obsession with Angela Mitchell. From the low vibration in her mind, a single question formed: What did her father find? It was too much for Rory to neatly pack away, compartmentalize, and forget about. Rory knew she would use all her skills and talent to reconstruct Angela's whereabouts.

She climbed from her car and strapped her backpack over her shoulder. Opening the trunk, she grabbed a second Dark Lord from one of the cases and then used her key to enter her childhood home. A wave of emotions suddenly washed over her. Rory couldn't remember the last time she cried. In fact, she was unsure if she had ever experienced the emotion during her adult life. She didn't think so, and wasn't about to start now just from walking across the threshold to her childhood. Her father was gone. He had carried with him a great secret. It was enough for her to be curious. Crying would produce nothing useful.

She closed the door behind her, walked into her father's office, and sat behind his desk. She used Kip's Swiss Army knife to pop the top on her stout, and looked around the darkened room. Rory's greatest gift was her ability to piece together cold cases, to pore over the facts and discover things other investigators missed until a picture of the crime—and sometimes the perpetrator—became clear in her mind. Her understanding of a killer's thinking and motive came from examining the carnage he left behind. The frustration with attempting to reconstruct anything about Angela Mitchell lay in the fact that there had been nothing left behind. Thomas Mitchell left no carnage, and this made Rory wonder about the man's guilt. Was it possible, she asked herself, that he had spent forty years in jail for a crime he didn't commit? The more puzzling dilemma was whether he had spent decades in jail for a crime that had never happened.

She clicked on the desk lamp in her father's office and pulled Lane Phillips's thesis from her backpack. He had written it for his dissertation more than a decade ago. It was a dark and ominous look into the minds of convicted killers. A tour de force that came from Lane's two-year crusade, during which he personally interviewed more than one hundred convicted serial killers around the world. The thesis still echoed in the hallways of the FBI, even though Lane had long ago moved on from his time as a profiler there. It was also Rory's go-to reference material when she needed to remind herself how to think like a killer, a useful technique when trying to piece together a crime. Rory took a sip of Dark Lord and turned to the cover page: *Some Choose Darkness* By Lane Phillips.

She'd read the thesis many times, and was always drawn to the same section. She turned to it now. The heading always put a flutter in her chest: "Why Killers Kill."

She read Lane's discernments on what made a person choose to end another's life: the rationalizing that occurred, the blocking of emotion, the pouring of societal norms and moral obligations into a black hole of the mind. This concept got back to the core of his thesis: At some point in every killer's existence, a choice is made. Some choose darkness, others are chosen by it.

Rory finished her beer while she sat in her dead father's darkened office. She looked around her childhood home, the quiet of the empty rooms allowing her mind to form the questions that gnawed at her. She thought about Angela Mitchell. She wondered if the mysterious woman had chosen darkness all those years ago, or if darkness had chosen her.

CHICAGO
November 1981

*F*RANK MOORE CONTINUED TO KEEP HIS HUNT FOR THE GHOST OF Angela Mitchell to himself, sharing none of his investigation with his bosses at Garrison Ford. And he hadn't yet mentioned anything to his wife. He had been named lead counsel for Thomas Mitchell's appeals, a task he was handling with efficiency and skill. Frank had kept private the fact that the man had hired him to look for his dead wife. He had received the request with confusion and suspicion, but since his bizarre encounter at the farmhouse in Peoria, and perhaps for the first time, Frank considered that Angela Mitchell might actually be alive.

He sat at his desk at Garrison Ford, the phone to his ear. Next to him was the thick folder of research. It held all the information he had collected thus far on Angela Mitchell, her troubled adolescence, her stint at Bayer Group Juvenile Psychiatric Facility when she was seventeen years old, and Frank's conversation with Dr. Jefferson. The file ended with the address of the farmhouse in Peoria and the name of the woman who had driven Angela from Bayer Group the day she discharged herself on her eighteenth birthday—Margaret Schreiber.

He spent a week researching the woman. His phone calls to the county and the literature he had managed to obtain from public records told him that she had owned the home for eleven years. She held a mortgage and was current on her taxes. She was a certified nurse-midwife at the local hospital in Peoria. Over the past few days, Frank had pulled permits from public county records and nursing licenses from the Illinois Department of Professional Regulation. He made phony phone calls to inquire about the hospital's services, and had pieced together an impressive biography of Margaret Schreiber.

"She left Bayer Group on her eighteenth birthday," Frank said into the phone. "I found the woman who picked her up."

"It wasn't her parents?" Thomas Mitchell asked in a static-filled voice from prison.

"No. She signed herself out, but a woman named Margaret Schreiber helped her. It's my only lead so far. The only non-family member whom I can link to her before she met you. I'm running with it for now."

"Have you talked with her?"

"Briefly," Frank said.

"Did you ask about Angela?"

"I mentioned her."

"And? You think she knows something?"

Frank remembered Margaret Schreiber as she backpedaled through the front door of her farmhouse. He remembered the fear in her eyes. He remembered the curtains as they shifted slightly when the woman peeked through the window as he drove away. She was hiding something, and Frank had a good idea what it was.

"I'm not sure," he finally said. "But when I know more, I'll be in touch."

Frank hung up the phone and logged the fifteen-minute call to the Thomas Mitchell file and tacked it onto the appeals billing. His secretary walked into his office.

"I'm heading to lunch," she said. "Here are your messages from the morning." She held yellow slips of paper in her hand. "Your wife called. She's going to work early and won't see you tonight. Howard Garrison stopped by, wants you to come see him. And a strange message from someone who wouldn't give her name. She said, hold on . . . it was a bit strange."

Frank felt a numbness run through him as the secretary shuffled the paper slips.

"Here it is. She said . . ." Frank's secretary looked up from the message to stare at him with raised eyebrows. "'Sorry about the dogs'? And she'd like to talk with you as soon as possible." The secretary handed him the message. "You know what that's all about?"

"Long story," Frank said, standing quickly and hurrying around his desk. "I'll call my wife later. Tell Mr. Garrison I got hung up with something. I'll see him tomorrow."

"She wouldn't leave a phone number," the secretary said as Frank hurried out of the office.

"That's okay. I don't need one."

He jogged out of his office, chasing the ghost of a woman who disappeared two years ago.

CHAPTER 24
Chicago, October 30, 2019

AFTER RORY'S MOTHER, MARLA, DIED SIX YEARS EARLIER, HER FATHER had threatened to downsize to a condo, but could never bring himself to do it. Instead, he kept the three-bedroom house, where Rory was raised, and lived in the too-large space in order to keep the memory of his wife alive. It dawned on Rory the night before that with her father gone, she'd have to empty the place like she had done the law office, box everything up, and stick a FOR SALE sign in the front lawn. After too many Dark Lords, she had lain on the sofa with a strong beer buzz. She contemplated the sad and unenviable task of clearing out her childhood home of all its memories to allow a different family to start the process of painting a new story over the ones that were here now. She had contemplated it all while using the alcohol to numb her senses. Eventually she dozed off and was gone to the world.

Rory woke now in her father's office. Sunlight skewed through the window and across her face, causing her to shield her eyes as she woke. A dull headache greeted her as she sat up on the couch and rubbed her temples. Her father had died in this room. It was where Celia had found him, and Rory felt some cathartic sense of peace for having stayed here through the night. Maybe she offered her father's spirit a night of company. Maybe she was still drunk on Dark Lord.

The empty bottles of stout sat on her father's desk, and the computer exposed the last of her voyeuristic attempt to discover what her father had learned about Angela Mitchell before his death. If he had found anything at all, he didn't put it onto his computer. She cleared the bottles from the desk, sat again in the chair where her father had died, and used her phone to find the websites of three moving companies, the numbers of which she jotted on a sticky note. There were a number of storage facilities in the area, and she picked a few at random. She spent thirty minutes making calls and arranging times. When she was finished, she shut down the computer and looked around the room. Her father's office appeared different in the morning light than it had in the dark hours of the previous night. She noticed the cabinet door at the bottom of the desk was opened a crack, and saw the knob to a safe peeking from the crevice between the edge of the door and the frame of the desk. Rory pulled the door open.

The safe was built into the desk, and she immediately spun the dial, trying common combinations of numbers. They all failed. She spun through her birth date, then her mother's and father's. When she finally tried her parents' wedding anniversary, the door swung open. Crouching down below the desk, Rory peered into the vault of the small safe. A thick folder sat on the shelf. She retrieved it and placed it on the desk. She opened the cover and found Thomas Mitchell's parole letters dating back two decades, all marked *Denied*. Her father's appeal letters were attached to each denial. When Rory made it to the bottom of the stack, she found a letter from the parole board that suggested great progress by Frank Moore's client, and a changing in the board members' thinking. Two more letters praised the evolution and rehabilitation of Thomas Mitchell, and then, at the bottom of the stack, the parole letter marked *Approved*.

Rory paged back through the stack, glancing at the dates on top of each letter, her mind registering and cataloguing each month, day, and year. Her father had been part of all of the hearings and appeals dating back to the 1980s. She stacked the appeal letters and parole board correspondence to the side. The next stack of papers was handwritten letters from Thomas Mitchell. The penmanship was perfect block, all-caps letters that looked as though they were traced from the print of an old-fashioned typewriter. Rory recalled the detectives' chicken scratch from the many reports she had read throughout her career. Thomas Mitchell's writing was in stark contrast, evidence of a man with nothing but time in front of him. There was no urgency to his work. There was no reason to rush. His writing was deliberate, each letter a perfect match to the one preceding it. As Rory skimmed the page, she noticed the repetitive way the man composed his *A*'s. He used no crosshatch, and the letter looked simply like an inverted *V.* The character jumped from the page in every word where it was present:

I, THOMAS MITCHELL, ELECT MY ATTORNEY, FRANK MOORE, TO BE PRESENT AND TO SPEAK ON MY BEHALF ON THE MATTER OF MY LATEST PAROLE HEARING.

The unique symbol gave Rory a nauseous feeling, as if the missing crosshatch represented a sinister deletion of something more significant in the man's soul. She pushed the letters to the side and pulled the last pile of papers in front of her. The stack was a rubber-banded collection on top of which was her father's writing: *Angela Mitchell.*

Rory's breath caught in her throat. Chronicled in the pages was what appeared to be her father's research into the life of Angela Mitchell, her family, friends, and acquaintances. A long list of names, with check marks and notes next to each one. She recognized Catherine Blackwell's name. She moved her finger down the page, reading each name.

"Your friend said I might find you here."

The voice startled her, and the breath Rory held in her throat came out with a yelp. She looked up to see Celia standing in the doorway.

Rory put her hand over her chest. "Christ, Celia. You scared the hell out of me."

"Sorry. I knocked, no one answered. But I saw your car outside."

Rory stacked the papers together. "What are you doing here, Celia?"

"You never called me back. I went to your house this morning. Your friend said to look for you here."

Rory vaguely remembered a drunken call to Lane the night before while she snooped through her father's computer.

"Sorry," Rory said. "I've just had so much going on."

Rory recognized something in Celia's expression.

"Is something the matter?"

"I'm afraid your father has left me with a burden I can't handle," Celia said, holding a small object in her hand. "He gave me this a long time ago. Told me to keep it to myself."

Rory squinted her eyes; her contact lenses were dry from having slept in them and she couldn't make out the object in Celia's hand.

"What is it?"

"It's the key to his safe-deposit box."

CHICAGO
November 1981

FRANK STOPPED HIS CAR AT THE EDGE OF THE LONG DRIVEWAY. THE farmhouse stood in the distance. It was late afternoon and the shadows of maple trees stretched across the property. He turned the wheel and advanced up the extended drive. The dogs appeared from behind the house to chase his car, hopping at the excitement of a visitor. Frank worried that they would sense his fear from the last time he was here, when he had barely made it to the safety of his car as they tried to rip him to shreds.

He wasn't about to open the door, but he shut off the engine and waited while the dogs barked and announced his presence. After a minute, the woman appeared on the front porch and shouted at the dogs, and they promptly ran to the back of the house. Frank stood slowly from his car.

"C'mon inside," the woman said.

Frank walked up the steps and onto the creaky front porch. The woman opened the screen door and Frank followed her inside. They entered the sitting room off the foyer. A large bay window looked out over the fields behind the property. The woman appeared older, now that Frank had a good look at her, perhaps a bit haggard, as if life had treated her badly. She ran a hand through her coarse gray hair as she sat on the sofa.

Frank was prepared for small talk, but didn't need to be. He had his story prepared, but wouldn't use it.

"Why are you asking about Angela?"

The directness of the question caught Frank by surprise, and he felt the sudden need to tell the truth. For months, he'd lied about what he was doing. For months, he'd been deceptive as he tried to find any useful thread that might lead to the whereabouts of a woman he was rapidly believing might be alive. But for some unexplained reason, the woman in front of him now seemed as though she'd be impervious to his stories. "I've been hired to see if Angela is . . ."

Frank struggled with his words for a moment.

"Is what?"

"Is still alive."

The woman shook her head. "She warned me that he'd come looking for her."

A tremble went through him. A buzzing deep in his soul. "Who warned you?"

The woman looked at him. A dead stare that was unrelenting.

"Angela."

Frank felt as though he were falling. The air drained from his lungs, and when he spoke again, his voice was soft and weak.

"She warned you that *who* would come looking for her?"

The woman's voice was equally frail when she answered.

"Thomas. She said he'd never stop looking for her."

CHAPTER 25
Chicago, October 30, 2019

"W HERE DID YOU FIND IT?" RORY ASKED, LOOKING AT THE key in Celia's hand.

Rory had been through every square inch of her father's law office. It was empty.

"I loved your father," Celia said in a voice congested from crying. "We loved each other, Rory. We didn't tell you, because Frank thought you'd be upset that we were together."

Rory sat up in the chair, reached to adjust her glasses before realizing they were on the coffee table next to the couch, where she had slept. Her beanie hat was there, too. As she stood from her father's chair, she did so barefoot, her combat boots in a heap next to the table. All Rory's protective gear was gone as she listened to Celia confess to a relationship with her father.

"It was a year or so after your mother passed. Frank worried that you'd think we were together before that. But we never were, Rory. I would never do that. Your father was so sad after Marla passed. My own husband had died years before, and we just found each other and fell in love."

"Okay," Rory said, holding up her hands. "I don't really want to know any more, Celia. Not right now."

Her head ached from too much Dark Lord, but through the pounding, Rory pieced things together. The relationship explained Celia's wild emotions at the funeral, and her near-debilitating, tear-dripping embrace when Rory met her to start the process of dissolving the law office. A profound sadness came over her as Rory considered the last few years of her father's life. He had gone through a deep and agonizing depression after Rory's mother had passed. And during the last year, Rory had sensed that her father had been overly stressed. Perhaps it was because he had found happiness with another woman, but couldn't share his newfound joy with his daughter. Rory had always been his to protect, and her father had gone to great lengths throughout his life to make sure Rory was never hurt by anything he did. Now Rory had discovered a part of his life she wished she could have enjoyed with him. The crying she worked so hard to prevent last night nearly came to her now before she managed to stop her eyes from welling with tears.

"I'm sorry to tell you this way, Rory. I've struggled with it ever since Frank died. I even thought about never telling you. And perhaps that would have been the easiest solution, except for this."

Celia walked over and pushed the key across the desk. "Your father had a safe-deposit box. He told me that if anything ever happened to him, I was supposed to take what was in the box and keep it to myself."

Rory composed herself, picked up the key. "What's in it?"

"I have no idea. I think money, but I don't feel right keeping it. Frank promised that he'd always take care of me . . . you know, financially. But if he left money behind, it belongs to you."

Rory picked up the key and ran her fingers over the grooves on the blade. An eerie feeling ran up her sternum and through her neck to cause her ears to ring. The hair follicles on her head tingled. She looked at the stack of papers she had just discovered in her father's safe and knew it was not money he wanted Celia to hide.

Rory parked her car in the bank's parking lot just before nine o'clock. Celia sat next to her in the passenger seat. The Dark Lord headache still gripped her temples and her mouth was cotton dry. She was adorned in her protective armor—hat, glasses, gray jacket, and Madden Girl Eloisee combat boots.

On the ride over from her father's house, Celia explained that a year after they started dating, Frank had asked her to sign papers that put her on the safe-deposit box as a registered holder. Celia had never asked about the contents of the box; she only knew that it had caused Frank much distress when he asked Celia to watch over them. As they waited in the car, Rory took a quick sideways glance through the edge of her glasses and noticed Celia staring at her. The woman was anxious to talk about her relationship with Rory's father. Rory was anxious for a Diet Coke and some privacy. Mercifully, a bank employee unlocked the front doors just as the car's digital clock blinked to 9:00 A.M.

Rory pointed through the windshield. "Bank's open."

They each climbed from the car and made it across the lot. Inside, they rode the elevator to the bottom floor and approached the reception desk. A woman smiled at them. Rory allowed Celia to take the lead.

"We need access to Box 411."

"Are you both registered holders?" the woman asked.

"No," Celia said. "Just me."

"Only registered holders are allowed into the vault, but you're welcome to wait in the reception area just outside."

"That's perfect," Rory said. "Thank you."

Celia handed over her ID and signed a card. The bank employee made a copy, checked Celia's signature to the one on file, and retrieved the master key from a locked cabinet on the back wall. The woman disappeared briefly as she walked around the corner, then opened the door to where Celia and Rory waited.

"Right this way," the woman said.

They walked to the other side of the floor where thick metal bars separated the reception area from the vault of safe-deposit boxes. The gate had been opened earlier in the morning, as had the vault door beyond. The woman pointed to a waiting area with tall, round tables. Rory walked over and watched Celia walk with the woman past the gates and into the vault. A few minutes later, Celia reappeared with a thin metal box in her hands.

The woman smiled. "Let me know when you're finished."

Celia placed the box onto the surface of the tall table. "I'll leave you alone," she said to Rory.

Rory nodded, kept her gaze on the box. When she was alone in the room, she lifted the lid and stared at the contents. There were just a few pages inside. She lifted the first packet, which was her father's last will and testament. She turned the pages slowly, found nothing out of sorts, and placed it to the side. When she examined the next document in the box, the room began spinning. Slowly at first, but faster with each passing moment. She placed her hands on the table to steady herself as she lifted the page and read it.

The room rotated with such ferocity that Rory reached for her temple as she studied the page, knocking her glasses to the floor. She took the last article from the bottom of the box, another single document, stumbled backward until she collided with the wall. Her beanie hat fell from her sweaty scalp and she sunk to the floor as she read.

CHICAGO
November 1981

"A NGELA WARNED YOU THAT HER HUSBAND WOULD COME LOOK-ing for her?" Frank asked.

The woman stayed silent.

"Angela is alive?"

Margaret looked away from him, out the window and to the vast expanse of land behind the house. "How did you find me?"

Frank accepted the dodge without pushback. He knew he was on the cusp of a monumental discovery. "You were listed on the Bayer Group's log as the one who picked Angela up on her eighteenth birthday when she left the psychiatric hospital."

"Damn it," she said. "We thought long and hard about any trail that might lead to me. Anything that might link us to one another. We thought we were safe."

She pulled her gaze from the window. "So now I know *how* you found me. But I need to know *why* you're looking. Did he send you?"

Frank swallowed hard. A sinister sense of dread hung in the room, and his connection to Thomas Mitchell never felt so wrong.

"There are some people who . . . believe Angela is still alive. That she disappeared to get away from her husband. The police were convinced he killed her, and the district attorney mounted a good-enough case to convict him. But I'm wondering if they were all wrong."

"Did he send you?" she asked again.

He felt a seismic shift in what he was trying to accomplish. His journey had been set to help his client, but now he felt as though he were putting lives at risk. Frank nodded.

"Yes," he finally said. "Thomas Mitchell hired me to find his wife."

The woman's eyes widened with fear. "You mustn't ever tell him what you've discovered. Do you understand? He must never find me."

"Were they wrong?" Frank asked. "Were the police and the prosecution wrong? Did Thomas Mitchell kill his wife?"

"No," Margaret said. "But he killed so many other women."

"Where is Angela?"

"He killed all those women, just like she said. And she told me he would come looking for her. She told me he'd hire people to find her. It took two years, but Angela was correct."

Frank kept to himself that he had already discussed this lead with his client, something he now regretted. Some part of him felt that doing so was a grave mistake.

"Tell me what happened," he said. "I can help you. If you need help, I promise I'll find a way."

From another room, far off in the farmhouse, there was a squeal. Frank looked out into the hallway when he heard it. It came again and again. Louder and louder. Crying.

"Come with me," the woman said.

She stood from the couch, walked into the foyer, and started up the stairs. Frank noticed the perspiration beading down from his temples. He followed the woman to the base of the stairs. An odd premonition came over him that if he continued up the staircase, his life would never be the same. But the lure of Angela Mitchell, the ghost he had been chasing, was too great to prevent his steps. He heard the floorboards creak under his feet as he followed the woman up the stairs. With each stride, the cries grew louder. More than cries now, they were shrieks.

At the top of the landing, the gray-haired woman turned and entered a room. Frank paused when he reached the last step, then looked down the long staircase he had just ascended. The wooden railing and the rungs within it blurred in his vision. The foyer below, and the front door, and the dying afternoon sunlight pouring through the window, all swirled together in a distorted image. He still had time. The opportunity was still in front of him. He could race down the stairs and to his car. He could drive away from this farmhouse and never come back. He could tell his client it was a dead end. He could lie.

In the end, though, he didn't run. Instead, he turned and walked to the open doorway through which the woman had disappeared. A baby carriage stood in the corner. The small child standing in the crib, red-faced and angry, was the source of the crying. The screams were so visceral now that Frank had the urge to cover his ears, but curiosity pulled him into the room. When he walked through the threshold, the cries subsided as the gray-haired woman lifted the baby into her arms.

As Frank entered the room, a strange sensation came over him. It felt as though a thousand sets of eyes were watching him. Then he realized why. Three of the four walls in the nursery contained built-in shelves. Each shelf was lined with antique china dolls in perfect rows, three on each shelf. They looked immaculate as they glowed under the lighting with their unblinking eyes focused on him.

"He mustn't ever find her," the woman said.

PART III

THE FARMHOUSE

CHICAGO
May 1982

FRANK MOORE TURNED HIS CAR ONTO THE COUNTY ROAD AND ACCEL-erated down the long stretch of two-lane highway flanked by freshly planted cornfields. His wife sat next to him in the passenger seat. The sun was behind them this Saturday morning and cast a slanted shadow of their car onto the road in front of them. It had rained for most of the month of April, but so far May was doing a splendid job of ushering spring along, bringing sunshine and flowers. For Frank and Marla Moore, the season brought hope as well.

"How did you find this family?" Marla asked.

"It's a long story," Frank said. "But I've been searching since we heard the wait list was so long. I received a phone call last week."

"You met them without me?"

"Just to make sure it was legitimate. You've been through so much already with . . ." Frank's voice trailed off. He wanted to avoid talking about the miscarriages. They always sent Marla into bouts of depression, and today was meant to be a joyous day, even if it was filled with deceit.

"I've heard stories of people being scammed for money when they don't go through a formal agency," Frank said. "I wanted to make sure this was on the up-and-up before I got you excited."

"Is it?"

Frank paused. "Yeah, it's legit."

"You're sure about this?" she asked.

Frank looked at his wife. "I'm sure."

Frank saw Marla smile for the first time in months. An hour later, they pulled to the edge of the farmhouse. A waist-high, white painted wooden fence surrounded the property and went on for acres.

"Are you ready?" he asked.

"Is this real?"

Frank nodded his head slowly. "It is."

He turned into the driveway and coasted along the gravel until he stopped the car in the same spot he always did. Six months had passed since the first time he came to this house. He'd lost count of the number of visits he'd made since he first stumbled onto his discovery. He wished he had more time to figure it all out, but no matter how long he waited, the blueprint to their plan would never be perfect. It would be dangerous. It might even be disastrous. But perfect? Not a chance in hell.

He'd never kept a secret from Marla in the short few years that they had been married, and he'd gone into his relationship with the idea of never keeping anything from her. But life sometimes delivers unforeseen opportunities. Unexpected callings that make certain transgressions palatable in the grand scheme of it all, when life asks of you more than you ever thought you could give.

The dogs knew him now. They were playful and relaxed as they hopped next to him as he walked to the porch with his wife's hand in his own.

The door opened and the woman smiled.

"Marla?"

Frank's wife swallowed hard and nodded. "Margaret?"

"Oh, dear, no. No one but my grandmother ever called me Margaret. Please call me Greta." She pushed the screen door open. "Come on in. I can't wait for you to meet her."

CHAPTER 26
Chicago, October 30, 2019

*R*ORY CARRIED THE KESTNER DOLL INTO THE NURSING HOME. SHE found Greta sitting in her chair. It was the first time in weeks, since before her father had died, Rory had seen her out of bed. A strange feeling washed over her when she stared at her aunt. A lifetime of memories flashed in her mind—images of long weekends spent at the farmhouse, passing the days restoring the china dolls with Greta. The satisfaction Rory felt when Greta allowed her to place a finished doll on the shelf in the room upstairs was like nothing else she had ever experienced. An obsessive-compulsive disorder, diagnosed when Rory was six years old, had threatened her childhood. But somehow, in the room upstairs at Aunt Greta's farmhouse, Rory was able to tend to the needs of her mind.

Working on the dolls purged all the tenuous demands of her brain. Rory's habits, and the mandate for perfection, not only went by without judgment or worry when she worked with her aunt, but the time Rory spent in that room upstairs *demanded* all the redundant and meticulous acts that were an unwanted nuisance during the rest of her life. As soon as Rory discovered this outlet, the rest of her days were untouched by the requests of her mind. In adulthood, Rory began her own collection and applied to it the craft Greta had taught her. When Greta's health began to fail, she made it clear that the upstairs room in the farmhouse belonged to Rory, and that she alone was in charge of watching over the collection. Those dolls now lined the shelves in Rory's den.

But her childhood felt different now. Nothing seemed the same since Rory had opened that safe-deposit box to find a birth certificate listing Greta as her birth mother, and documents showing Frank and Marla Moore as her adoptive parents. Rory understood so little and wanted so many answers.

"Hey, old lady," Rory said.

Greta glanced at Rory before looking back at the muted television.

"I tried to save you. There was too much blood."

Rory took a deep breath, angry with herself for the sudden frustration she felt toward Greta. A moment of pause reminded Rory that Greta could no more control the random thoughts that popped into her mind and were spewed from her mouth than Rory could control a sneeze.

"He's coming. You told me. But there's too much blood."

"Okay," Rory said. "It's okay.

"He'll come for you. But we have to stop the bleeding."

Rory closed her eyes briefly. She hadn't asked anything of Greta for many years. In fact, their roles had been reversed over the course of their lives. Greta, once the caretaker who settled Rory's anxiety, was now the patient, and it was Rory who calmed her great-aunt during bouts of unrest such as this. The fact that Rory wanted answers tonight that only Greta could provide was not an excuse to abandon her when she was in distress. Rory took a cleansing breath and walked to the side of the chair. She knew the best remedy for Greta's turmoil. It was the same one that had saved Rory as a child.

"We've got to finish this Kestner," Rory said. "The owner is getting impatient. You promised me one more coat would do it."

Greta blinked at the sight of the doll, as if the Kestner pulled her across the years, away from the tortured memories of the past and back to the present. She gestured for the doll. Rory kept her eyes on the woman she had known as her great-aunt for her entire life. Up until her dead father's lover had given her a key to a safe-deposit box that told her otherwise. She eventually took Camille Byrd's Kestner doll out of the box and laid it carefully on Greta's lap. From the

212

closet, Rory wheeled the art kit she had brought a few nights before, set the pastel paints on the rolling table, and pulled it over to Greta's side.

"In sunlight," Rory said, pointing to the doll's left cheek, "the hues match perfectly. But incandescent brings out the flaws, and fluorescent bleaches it out."

"One more coat," Greta said. "And I'll polish the undamaged side to bring it all together."

Rory sat on the edge of the bed and watched her work. The sight of Greta restoring a doll transported Rory back to the farmhouse, to the long summer days and quiet nights. She spent every summer of her childhood at Greta's place. During the school year, if a bout of obsession took hold of her, Rory's parents would pull her from school early on Friday for a long weekend at the farmhouse. There was no better remedy for her OCD and anxiety than a visit to the country and the restorations that waited there. Now, as Rory sat staring at Greta, the relaxed feelings she usually experienced while restoring a doll were replaced instead with thousands of questions.

"Are you working?" Greta asked, pulling Rory back from her thoughts.

"Yes," she said.

"Tell me."

Rory paused. She hadn't had a meaningful conversation with Greta in weeks. Tonight, though, presented a rare window of lucidity, where her aunt was interactive and coherent.

"That Kestner. It belongs to a dead girl."

The brush in Greta's hand stopped. She looked at Rory.

"She was killed last year. Her father asked me to look into it."

"What happened to her?"

Rory blinked several times, aware again of how badly she had neglected the case. A small part of her was concerned that Ron Davidson would be disappointed in her. A bigger part worried about Walter Byrd, who had put his faith in Rory to find justice for his daughter. But mostly, Rory's heart ached for Camille Byrd, whose spirit waited for Rory to come for it, find it, and help it to a place of proper rest. Take it from its frozen grave in Grant Park and lay it carefully where it belonged so the girl could find peace.

Rory remembered another dream she'd had about the dead girl. Of walking through Grant Park and trying unsuccessfully to wake her as Rory shook Camille's cold shoulder as she lay lifeless on the grassy knoll. Rory refocused her eyes, returning from the wandering abyss of her thoughts. Greta was staring at her.

"I don't know yet."

Greta stared at her for a minute, then went back to work. An hour later, Greta finished polishing and coloring the cheek and forehead. She dusted the face one last time until the Kestner doll, once damaged and in disrepair, looked flawless.

"Greta," Rory said. "It's absolutely perfect." She remembered the deep fissure that had run through the left eye socket when she first examined the doll at the library. When Rory laid the doll horizontally, the left eye closed in perfect unison with the right. The cheeks matched one another, and the fracture that had started at the hairline and run down to the chin was gone.

"As close as we'll get. The girl's father will be happy with what you've done."

"What *you've* done as well."

Greta looked back to the doll. Rory watched her, concerned that she had suddenly fallen into a lost moment and that her mind would be gone for the rest of the visit. The abrupt changes in demeanor happened so often now that Rory was no longer shocked by them—Greta, present and alert one moment, gone the next.

But instead of staring off into a void of dementia, Greta spoke as she examined the doll.

"It reminds me of when you were young," Greta said.

Rory nodded. "Me too."

Greta smiled. "Sometimes those summers seem like yesterday."

"Greta," Rory said, standing from the edge of the bed and moving closer. "Why did my parents bring me to your place so often? Why did I spend every summer of my childhood at the farmhouse?"

A long stretch of silence followed before Greta pulled her gaze from the Kestner doll and looked at Rory. "You were a nervous child, but found peace at my house."

Rory couldn't argue this fact. All the anxiety that surrounded her days, the angst that rose like early-morning fog off a lake, faded away when she was at Greta's farmhouse. But Rory now understood there was another reason for her time there.

"Was the time I spent with you an *arrangement*, Greta? Something you worked out with Frank and Marla?"

Greta blinked, but didn't answer. She brought her gaze back to the doll in her lap.

"I found the papers, Greta. Dad had a safe-deposit box where he kept them. My birth certificate. The adoption papers."

Rory stared at Aunt Greta for a full minute without talking, allowing the confession of her discovery to settle between them. She wanted to press for answers. Wanted to hear the truth from the only person left living who could provide it. But Rory saw Greta's eyes retreating to that faraway place, perhaps intentionally. More likely, though, just the result of the small stretch of coherence having spent its worth before the dementia pulled Greta's mind back to oblivion.

As she watched Greta, Rory sensed a longing from the woman she had known her whole life. A woman who had saved Rory's childhood from what might have been years of torment and ridicule. A woman she had always thought of as her great-aunt, but whose identity now had been jumbled in Rory's perception, like a fully set dining table once perfect and ordered being tipped on its side. The pieces suddenly too muddled to sort. Rory saw it in her eyes, a sense of sorrow that the restoration of the Kestner doll was over. It had been a channel to the past. To the summers and weekends when a young girl developed a lifelong friendship and unbreakable bond with a middle-aged woman she knew as her aunt.

"I wish I could have saved you as easily as Rory and I save the dolls," Greta said, her eyes now vacant and set on the television.

"I *am* Rory." She crouched next to the chair. "Greta? Can you hear me?"

"Yes, we'll hide you. He'll come, like you said. I tried to save you, but there was too much blood."

Rory closed her eyes briefly. Greta was gone. The visit was over. She stood up, lifted the doll from Greta's lap, and carefully laid it in the box.

CHICAGO
May 1982

*F*RANK AND MARLA SAT NEXT TO EACH OTHER ON THE COUCH. THE VIS-itations had taken place every weekend for the past month, with Frank and Marla making the trips out to Peoria each Saturday and Sunday to spend the days at Greta Schreiber's farmhouse, getting to know the child. The girl was asleep now. Marla had just finished reading *Goodnight Moon* while the child lay in her arms. It was a rit-ual she was starting to love, Frank could see. Marla hadn't wanted to put the child down, and only released her when Greta suggested they talk about the future.

Frank knew the first part of his plan was working. His wife was becoming emotionally attached to the little girl. It was a critical part of his strategy. The bedrock, in fact, that needed to be laid in order for it all to work. Now, as the child slept, Frank was about to present the proposal to his wife. The specifics of which, Frank was sure, would sound simultaneously too good to be true and too out-rageous to be possible.

"For this to work," Frank said to Greta, "Marla needs to know everything. If we're going to pull this off, there can be no secrets. We'll help in any way possible, you have my word. I know much of the story, but not all of it. I want my wife to know everything. Please start from the beginning so we're all on the same page."

Greta nodded. Her hair seemed to have whitened a shade since Frank first stepped foot on the farmhouse property the previous fall. Clearly, the stress she was carrying on her shoulders was crush-ing her.

"I'm a nurse," Greta said. She was speaking to Marla, as Frank had previously heard this portion of the story. "I work for the hospital here in town as a midwife. I make house calls to assist patients who have chosen to undergo a more natural childbirth in the home. I also counsel young women at Bayer Group."

Frank turned to Marla. "Bayer Group Juvenile Psychiatric Facility."

Frank watched Marla nod, as if any of this made sense to her. He knew her mind was fixated on the child and the possibility that she would be theirs.

"I work with the girls at Bayer Group who were pregnant, or who had once been pregnant. I counsel them on what to expect. I've been doing it for many years, and it was during my time at Bayer Group that I met Angela. She was seventeen then."

Marla looked away from the bassinet. "Who?"

"Angela Mitchell," Frank said.

Marla looked at her husband. Her eyes were squinted and her forehead wrinkled. "The girl who was killed a few years ago? The girl from the summer of 1979?"

Frank nodded. "Yes."

Marla cocked her head. "Your firm represents Thomas Mitchell," Marla said. "You're working on his appeals."

"Yes," Frank said, taking Marla's hand. "I told you we needed to understand the full story before we move forward. That's why we're here."

Frank took a second to stare at his wife, making sure she was on board for what was about to transpire. Finally she nodded. They both looked at Greta.

"Angela was at Bayer Group for several months when she was seventeen years old. This was in 1967." Greta shook her head. "Hard to believe that was fifteen years ago. Whenever I went to Bayer Group to counsel my patients, I noticed this introverted girl off in the corner by herself. One day, I approached her, not as a nurse or as a counselor, just out of concern. I was hoping to make this young woman feel not so alone."

"Hi," Greta said as she sat across from the quiet girl she always saw sitting alone.

The girl didn't look at her, or acknowledge her presence in any way.

"I'm Greta. I'm a nurse here."

This caused the girl to glance quickly in her direction and then back to her lap.

"I'm not taking the medication," the girl said. "I don't care who you are or how nice you pretend to be."

"Oh, I'm not a psychiatric nurse. I work with some of the girls here, talking with them about the future."

Greta leaned a little closer.

"Are they giving you medication you don't want?"

"Yes," the girl said.

Greta looked around the rec room. The television was playing and a couple of girls were on the couch in front of it. No one else was in the room.

"What are they giving you? Maybe I could talk with someone?"

The girl looked at her. Greta saw fear in her eyes, and a glimmer of hope, too, at the idea that Greta may be able to help.

"Lithium. All it does is make me sleep and cause wild dreams. Sometimes the dreams even come while I'm awake."

"That's called hallucinating, and it's a common side effect of lithium." Greta scooted her chair closer. "Have you told your doctor about it?"

"Yes, but he doesn't care. They just want me to sleep and stay sedated."

"When you say 'they,' who are you talking about?"

"My parents and the doctors." The girl looked at Greta. "Will you help me? No one in here will help me."

Greta reached down and took the girl's hand. Greta felt her recoil, but after a moment, the girl squeezed back.

"What's your name, dear?"

"Angela."

"I'm going to help you, Angela. I'll find a way to help you."

CHAPTER 27
Chicago, November 1, 2019

*R*ORY SAT IN HER OFFICE WITH CAMILLE BYRD'S PHOTO LOOKING down on her from the corkboard. On the desk in front of her were the documents she had recovered from her father's safe-deposit box. She stared at the adoption papers until her vision blurred. Her mind was beginning to strain in the unhealthy way Rory always worked to avoid. The redundant considerations that prevented clear thinking had started to descend on her, and like a cornered animal, she fought back at them. She knew the consequences of succumbing to them. She pushed the torment aside and swiped the adoption papers to the floor. Then she went back to the pages she had found in her father's desk safe and rifled through the parole board's letters. She read through years of appeals made by her father when he was a young attorney with Garrison Ford, arguments that poked holes in the prosecution's case that her father argued was built solely on circumstantial evidence. She read her father's scathing description of Angela Mitchell as an overmedicated autistic woman who struggled socially and who did not have a firm grasp on reality. Rory tried to convince herself that the pages in front of her were merely her father's attempt to fulfill the oath he took to protect all those who sought his help. But something about the research told a different story.

It was subtle, what was coming to the surface of her attention. Elusive enough that Rory was sure no one else would see it. There was a change in tone. Rory picked up on it as she read through her father's appeal letters. The tenor of the arguments changed throughout the years, even if the content and facts within the letters remained the same. Perhaps, Rory thought, after years of failure, her father had lost a bit of passion trying to defend Thomas Mitchell. Perhaps, after two decades of redundancy, he had given up hope that any appeal would make a difference. But Rory couldn't stop herself from thinking that maybe something else was happening. That perhaps her father's letters held a different motive. That maybe her father never wanted Thomas Mitchell out of jail.

She poured another Dark Lord and continued to read.

CHICAGO
May 1982

*T*HE CHILD REMAINED SLEEPING AS GRETA CONTINUED HER STORY about Angela Mitchell and how the two had come to know each other. Frank and Marla Moore listened from the couch as Greta poured coffee.

"I slipped Angela my phone number that day we first met in the corner of the rec room at Bayer Group. She was alone in the world with no one, not even her parents, to turn to. I had to help her. I spoke with both her doctor and the director of Bayer Group. My boss at the hospital back then was close with the medical director over there, and with some pushing, I was able to get Angela's parents more involved and have the lithium stopped. It took a few weeks, and during the whole process, I met regularly with Angela. Not in any formal manner, just as . . . I guess you'd call us friends."

Greta sat on the couch and sipped her coffee. She looked at Frank. "And that's how you found me. Because of my friendship with Angela. When she turned eighteen, Bayer Group could no longer keep her unless she chose to stay. She did not. She called me to pick her up. I pressed her to contact her parents, but that relationship was too fractured to repair. So I obliged. She signed herself out of Bayer Group, but my name was on the log that day as the one who picked her up. The best I can tell, it was our only mistake. I brought Angela here to the farmhouse. She stayed for a year, working and saving money until she had enough to move on. When she was nineteen, she left for the city. That was 1968. She found a job and was managing on her own. She called every so often. Even called to tell me she had met a man," Greta said. "Unfortunately, that man was Thomas Mitchell."

She took another sip of coffee.

Marla and Frank were sitting on the edge of the couch. Marla was listening intently, and Frank sensed that she was working to make the final connection.

"So you and Angela stayed in touch?" Frank asked to move the conversation along.

"Not really," Greta said. "For a while we did. For a few years, she'd call every once in a while to tell me how she was doing. She told me her parents had moved to St. Louis, that she had found a job, that she had her own apartment. I was very encouraging, and I always invited her out to the farmhouse if she wanted a visit. But then she met Thomas, and after that she stopped calling. Years went by and I didn't hear a thing from her."

Greta paused again to sip her coffee. She replaced the cup on the saucer and looked back at Frank and Marla.

"Then, in the summer of 1979, I saw the news reports."

"That Angela had disappeared?" Marla asked.

"Yes. My heart broke when I saw her face on the television. And when the news came out that her husband was the man responsible for all those missing women from that summer, I felt that I had failed Angela. I had worked so hard to help her when I first found her sitting at the table all alone at Bayer Group. We had become close during the year she spent here. But then, I just let her leave. I let her walk off into the world. When I heard what happened to her, I was stricken with guilt that I hadn't done more to guide her life. For those two days my heart ached in a way I'd never experienced."

"For what two days?" Marla asked.

Greta looked at Frank. He nodded. Frank Moore needed his wife to hear it all.

*　*　*

223

Greta Schreiber sat at the workbench in the room upstairs. The wall shelves were decorated with porcelain china dolls arranged in perfect rows. She had started a new project two days before, just after news spread about the most recent events in Chicago. Angela, the girl she had befriended at Bayer Group years earlier, and who had spent an entire year at the farmhouse when she was eighteen years old, had gone missing and was suspected to be the latest victim of the man authorities called The Thief. The startling revelation that this man was Angela's husband had sent Greta pacing the kitchen for the better part of the night. But now, the damaged doll in front of her was providing the distraction she needed. The hairline fracture, which ran across the crown of the skull, down over the ear, and to the base of the jaw, required just enough attention that for as long as she worked on it, she didn't think of the young girl she once knew.

A noise pulled her concentration away from the restoration. She heard an automobile's wheels crunching over the gravel of the long driveway that led from the main road to the farmhouse. Greta stood from the workbench and walked over to the window, peeling the curtains to the side. She saw a silver sedan pulling slowly down the drive, a gray cloud of dust floating behind it. Tubs and Harold barked and jumped alongside the approaching vehicle.

She stayed at the window while she watched the car approach, and only when it stopped with no sign of the driver leaving the vehicle did Greta turn from the window and head down the stairs. A moment later, she opened the front door and walked onto the porch. The car was parked at the front of her lot, the driver sitting behind the wheel. The windshield reflected the blue sky and maple trees to prevent a clear look at the person behind the wheel. Greta waited until finally the driver's-side door opened. A thin woman climbed from the car, a hooded sweatshirt drooping from her frail frame. She lifted both hands to her head and pulled the hood down.

"Sweet Jesus," Greta said, bounding from the porch and down the steps. When she reached the woman, she hugged her tightly.

The woman whispered into Greta's ear.

"I need your help."

Greta backed away, taking Angela's face in her hands. She had the appearance of an alopecia patient. Her eyebrows were missing, and the lashes on her lids were present only in random clusters. Scratch marks climbed her *neck and stretched beyond the collar of her sweatshirt. Greta remembered a similar appearance from when she had first met Angela at Bayer Group, but today's version was severely pronounced.*

"We need to call the police. People think you're dead."

"No. We can't call the police. We can't call anyone. He can never find us. Promise me, Greta. Promise you'll never let him find us."

CHAPTER 28
Chicago, November 1, 2019

*R*ORY PUSHED THE APPEALS LETTERS TO THE SIDE AND PULLED IN front of her the stack with Angela Mitchell's name scrawled across the top. The pages chronicled her father's search for the woman after she disappeared in 1979. Rory had been reading these pages the morning Celia found her in her father's office. She had been scanning the names of the people her father contacted during his search when Celia showed up with the safe-deposit box's key.

Rory forced the rest of it from her mind—the idea that her father was subtly trying to keep Thomas Mitchell in jail—and concentrated only on that which was in front of her. There was something ominous about seeing proof that her father had been searching for Angela Mitchell. Catherine Blackwell's notes left little doubt that it was true, but some part of Rory refused to believe it. Now, as she sat staring at her late father's notes that recorded his search for Angela, she could no longer deny it. The woman was out there somewhere.

Rory read about her father's trip to St. Louis to talk with Angela's parents. She read about his visit to Catherine Blackwell's house on the north side of Chicago. She read about his trip to a psychiatric hospital where Angela had been treated when she was a teenager. Rory pored through her father's investigation into the whereabouts of Angela Mitchell with a rabid thirst for details, turning the pages with fervor and frenzy until she came to the name of a nurse—the nurse who had driven Angela Mitchell away from the hospital on her eighteenth birthday. Rory's vision funneled until a strange kaleidoscope of images danced in front of her when she saw the woman's name: *Margaret Schreiber.*

She had trouble breathing, her lungs heavy with panic and confusion, unable to expand or contract. Her father had been searching for Angela Mitchell, retracing her life and following her past to a juvenile psychiatric hospital—where she had been befriended by the woman Rory had believed her whole life to be her great-aunt, but whose identity had been blurred by the adoption papers and birth certificates. None of it registered in Rory's mind. Her confusion could be chalked up to denial, but she knew it was more than that. She had been trained to see things others did not. To root through details of cases and reconstruct a picture of events that was invisible to others. But discovering a connection between Greta and Angela sent her mind spiraling. A deep ache started below her sternum and rose like bubbling lava from the crater of a long-dormant volcano. Rory couldn't remember the last panic attack she'd had. It would have been as a child. It would have been before she found the healing outlet in the upstairs room of Greta's farmhouse.

She swallowed the rest of her Dark Lord, hoping the fluid would physically wash away the rising fear, and that the alcohol would dull her senses. She ran to the refrigerator and popped the top on another beer, stood in the darkened kitchen and raised the bottle to her mouth. In a few swallows it was half gone. Dizzy, she stumbled to her den and clicked on the lights. She stared at the china dolls that lined the shelves. The room was a replica of the farmhouse and she hoped the sight of the restored dolls would dampen the panic that coursed through her body.

Rory needed to occupy her mind with something other than thoughts of Greta and her parents and how they might be linked to Angela Mitchell. Having just completed the restoration of Camille Byrd's doll, she had no current projects to work on. She opened the chest that sat in the corner and pulled out a doll she had purchased at auction. It was tattered and ruined and would take a great deal of skill and concentration to restore. Rory sat at her workbench and tried to analyze the damage, but her mind would not take the bait. The usual lure of the doll's needs was trumped tonight by the discovery that Greta had known Angela. Her go-to method of skirting a panic attack was failing.

She left the den, grabbed another Dark Lord, and ran out to her car. She pulled from the curb with her headlights bringing to life the dark and empty Chicago streets. She drove without thinking. She knew the address from the file. It was on the north side. She took side streets and tried to control her speed. She was in no condition to be behind the wheel, both from too many Dark Lords and because she was not in her right mind. Twenty minutes later, she pulled past the bungalow where Angela Mitchell had lived in 1979. The houses were close together, and the entire block was silent and dark, with only front-porch lights shining in the darkness.

Rory stared at the front of the house for a few minutes, sensing the strong connection she had felt since first learning about Angela Mitchell. A relationship had formed, like with the subjects of the crimes she reconstructed, between her and Angela. Rory felt an obligation to find the woman. To let her know that there was someone who understood her struggles and her pain.

Pulling past the house, she turned the corner and crept into the alley behind the home. A chain-link fence protected the small back-yard of Angela Mitchell's previous residence. A detached garage opened into the alley. Rory stood from her car and walked in front of it. She stared at the back of the home. She wondered what had transpired here all those years ago, and how it was connected to all the people in her life.

The car's headlights cast her shadow along the pavement of the alley, her legs forming an inverted V. As Rory stared at her shadow, she sensed something inside her, something tugging for her attention. She could not place the feeling or determine why the sight of her shadow gave her such a chill until she realized that the headlights threw a silhouette on the ground in the exact same way Thomas Mitchell designed his *A*'s in his perfect block penmanship with no crosshatch—Λ. Then it occurred to her. As she stood in the dark alley and stared at her shadow, she realized that she had not only come to Angela's home, but to Thomas Mitchell's as well. The revelation hollowed her chest and gave resurgence to her hyper-ventilating lungs. But it was impossible for Rory to understand the real reason for her clairvoyance. She was standing in the exact same spot where Angela Mitchell stood forty years earlier, just as determined to uncover what had happened to the women who went missing that summer as Rory was today.

The back-porch light came on and caught her attention. Then the kitchen window flashed with light from inside. The rear door opened.

"Can I help you with something?" a man yelled from the door frame. "Or maybe I should call the cops and see if they can help? Or maybe I'll come out there and utilize my Second Amendment rights for someone trespassing on my property."

Jolted by the sudden confrontation, Rory turned and hurried back into her car. Her shadow darting and then disappearing.

"Get the hell out of here!" she heard the man yell as she climbed behind the wheel. She pulled out of the alley, sideswiping a trash-can in the process.

CHICAGO
May 1982

FRANK AND MARLA REMAINED ON THE COUCH AS GRETA TOLD HER story. Marla leaned forward when she asked her next question.

"Angela Mitchell was never killed by her husband?"

"No," Greta said. "But he would have killed her if she hadn't left."

Marla took a quick glance at her husband, then back to Greta. "What happened to her?"

Greta hesitated.

"Where is she, Greta? And what does it have to do with our adoption?"

Greta shook her head, looked over at Frank as well.

Frank nodded. "We need to know everything, Greta. I made a promise to help you, but we both have to hear the whole story."

Greta took another sip of coffee and then gently replaced the cup on the saucer. "After Angela told me, I knew there was no turning back."

Two days after Angela appeared in her driveway, Greta drove to the reservoir that sat a mile from the farmhouse. Angela followed in her own car. They waited until dusk, until the summer sky was brushed lavender and the clouds caught the remnants of the setting sun on their underbellies and blushed a cherry red. It was just dark enough to provide cover, but light enough to guide their actions. Greta parked a hundred yards from the reservoir, and then climbed into the passenger seat of Angela's car for the last leg of the journey. Angela pulled her car over the long grass and to the edge of the drop-off that led to the water. They both got out.

Greta looked around to make sure they were alone; then she reached through the driver's-side window to make sure the car was in neutral. They positioned themselves behind the rear bumper, dug their heels into the ground, and pushed. When the front wheels crested the bank, gravity took over. Greta and Angela watched as the car careened into the reservoir and disappeared beneath the water. They waited for ten minutes as the water bubbled while the car released trapped air from below. When it became too dark to see the disturbance on the surface, they walked to Greta's car.

On the way back to the farmhouse, Greta looked over at Angela.

"How far along are you?"

"I'm not sure."

"Have you been vomiting?"

"Yes," Angela said, "for a couple of weeks. I thought it was nerves until the doctor called."

"Okay," Greta said. "Probably a month or two. That means you're due in the spring. We'll have no problem delivering in my house. I've done it dozens of times. Our issue will be keeping you and the baby hidden. We'll have to file the proper documentation. And even if we skip that process, eventually there will be school registration and life in general. I can keep you hidden. For a while, anyway. Everyone thinks you're dead. But after you deliver, we'll have to figure out a long-term plan. Hiding a child is nearly impossible."

"He can never know he has a child, Greta. Promise me you'll find a way."

Greta nodded her head slowly. She had no idea how she could agree to something so impossible, but still she said, "I promise."

CHAPTER 29
Chicago, November 1, 2019

*R*ORY PULLED HER CAR TO THE FRONT OF HER HOUSE, THE passenger-side wheel hopping the curb as she did so. She stumbled up the stairs, keyed the front door, and headed up to her bedroom. She hadn't experienced such a powerful attack since childhood, and she understood the devastating effects they could have if she failed to stifle it. She fell into bed. Rising above the white noise in her mind—above the revelation that her parents had hidden her adoption, beyond the notion that Aunt Greta was not the person she had always believed her to be, and louder than the incessant whispers that she was due in front of Judge Boyle and the parole board with Thomas Mitchell tomorrow—were the unrelenting calls from Angela Mitchell.

Atop the panic was the lure of a mysterious woman who was somehow linked to all the people Rory had loved in her life. It was a pull Rory could not ignore. It reminded her of her childhood, when a similar sensation had taken hold of her. She folded the pillow over her head and pressed it to her ears to quiet the whispers that came from within.

Rory worked to control her breathing. She closed her eyes and cleared her thoughts. There was a process—a way to manage the attacks. She tried to remember the tricks. The breathing exercises that always brought her to a proverbial fork in the road. In one direction was a restless night during which her mind would not cease, with wild and relentless thoughts keeping her awake. In the other direction was the calming lure of sleep and the charm of shutting down her brain, allowing dreams to run effortlessly through the folds of her mind.

She worked for thirty minutes on her breathing, pushing all other thoughts from her mind other than an image of her lungs expanding and contracting. Finally she skirted onto this other road, the peaceful road, and soon her breathing was deep and rhythmic.

Rory woke in the bedroom of the old farmhouse.

It happened every so often. A few times every summer. Aunt Greta would put her to bed, tuck her in, and shut off the lights.

"Remember," Aunt Greta would say, standing in the doorway. "Nothing can scare you unless you allow it to scare you."

Greta would close the bedroom door and Rory would fall peacefully to sleep, the way she always did during her stays at the farmhouse, where the angst and worry had never been able to find her. Rory would typically sleep straight through until morning. But tonight was one of the times she woke in the small hours of night, her body filled with energy that put a buzz in her chest and in her head and in her fingers and toes. She literally vibrated with vigor, overcome with an awesome desire to explore. The sensation had her tossing and turning in bed. The first few times she had encountered this phenomenon Rory fought against it. She kicked the covers and reset the pillows until sunlight filled the window frame the next morning, spilling around the blinds to finally push away the urge to wander into the night and discover the source of her unrest.

Rory was careful never to mention this feeling of angst to anyone. Her parents sent her to Aunt Greta's farmhouse to escape the anxiety she felt during the rest of her life—to dispel it, really—and if they knew about these rare bouts of midnight disquiet, they might decide that Rory's visits to Aunt Greta's were no longer serving their purpose. She loved her long weekends and summers in this peaceful place, so Rory kept the odd nights of sleeplessness a secret. That, and because describing the middle-of-the-night sensation as anxiety wasn't quite right. Rory felt no worry when these spells of wakefulness came to her at the farmhouse, only the temptation of the unknown and the call for her to climb from bed and explore its meaning.

She was ten years old the night she decided to give in to the lure. When Rory woke, fully alert and without a trace of grogginess, the bedside clock told her it was 2:04 A.M. Her chest vibrated with the familiar curiosity she had come to know after many summers at her aunt's farmhouse. Throwing the covers aside, she climbed from bed, pulled by an invisible need. She opened her bedroom door and endured the whine of the hinges. She crept silently past Aunt Greta's bedroom, beyond the second doorway that led to the workshop, where the restored dolls stood in perfect rows on the shelves, and down the stairs. She opened the back door and slipped out into the night. The stars shimmered down on her from the heavens, obscured occasionally by thin sheets of shadowed clouds traced silver by the moon. Far off in the distance, a lightning storm ignited the horizon with off-and-on flickers of brightness, delivering a low rumble of thunder minutes later.

Standing on the back porch, Rory gave in to the pull in her chest. Her feet followed like a magnet drawn to a giant slab of faraway metal. She walked without effort through the field behind the house, found the low, two-rung wooden fence at the edge of the property, and followed it, her hand gliding over its smooth surface as she walked. Near the back of the property, where the fence cornered and turned at a ninety-degree angle, Rory found what was summoning her. On the ground, she saw the flowers she had watched Aunt Greta collect earlier in the day.

Every morning, Rory observed Greta gather flowers from the garden. It was Rory's job to bundle them with twist ties. Rory always asked Greta about the flowers, and she had asked that day as well. She questioned what Greta did with them each day, and where they ended up. Rory's inquisitions were met with vague answers. Tonight, however, she found them. The roses had been placed on the ground in a gentle heap, isolated and alone in the back corner of the property.

Another lightning strike appeared far off on the horizon, adding just enough light to the gray glow of the moon to bring to life the cherry petals. Rory crouched down and removed a rose from the bunch, lifted it to her nose, and inhaled the sweetness. The buzzing in her chest dissipated, and a soothing calm came over her. The feeling of tranquility had always drawn her back to her great-aunt's farmhouse. Tonight, under the tarnished glow of the moon, she harnessed that serenity in a single rose placed to her nose.

When another lightning strike brightened the area, Rory bent down and gently replaced the rose on the pile, then turned and ran back through the gray night until she reached the house. She climbed into bed. Sleep came instantly. Throughout the rest of her childhood, and for all the remaining summers that Rory stayed at Greta's farmhouse, the mysterious middle-of-the-night insomnia never again found her.

CHICAGO
May 1982

"I'M GOING TO QUIT MY JOB," FRANK SAID. "I NEED TO LEAVE Garrison Ford."

"To get away from him?" Marla asked. Her eyes were red-rimmed from crying.

"No. To take him with me. I need to keep Thomas Mitchell as close as possible if this is going to work. I need to be the only one he hires to look for Angela. The only one he trusts."

"He'll never stop looking," Greta said. "Angela was adamant about that. If it's not Frank, then it will be someone else."

"I need to control the information he receives," Frank continued. "He needs to believe I'm making progress. I'll find something to feed him for a while, but ultimately my search will come up empty. I'll make him believe me. What's important is for him to think I'm looking for her. As long as he believes this, he won't look himself. He won't employ anyone else. The man trusts me, and I plan to build and keep that trust."

"For how long?"

"For her entire life," Frank said.

Marla looked off. Her eyes wandered to the stairs, and Frank knew she was thinking of the child sleeping in her crib.

"What will we do for money, Frank? How will we support ourselves?"

"I'll hang my own shingle. I've got enough experience to go off on my own. And he's willing to pay me for my services."

"Thomas Mitchell?"

"Yes. He needs an attorney to file his appeals and handle his finances. And he'll pay me on the side to continue my search. He'll be my first client."

"Frank," Marla said. "It's just . . . not what I imagined."

"Please," Greta said, looking at Marla. "I need your help. *We* need your help. You're the perfect couple to love this child. Imagine what sort of life she might have if the truth is ever discovered. Imagine if the public discovers that Thomas has a child from the wife he was imprisoned for killing. And how could she ever live a normal life, knowing her father killed a string of women?"

Marla began crying again. All three of them had been pulled into an impossible situation. All three thought of the child sleeping peacefully in her crib. An innocent child who deserved none of what waited for her. Marla slowly shifted her gaze to Greta.

"Where is she? Where's Angela?"

Greta let out a long breath, and then it was she who began to cry. "I tried to save her. There was too much blood."

Something was wrong. The bleeding was intense and constant as Greta examined Angela's pelvis. Preeclampsia had forced bed rest for the past few weeks, and spotting had gotten Greta concerned. But Angela had insisted Greta treat her without involving a physician. It was too risky, she had argued. And Greta couldn't disagree that with Angela's face on the news during Thomas's trial, she would be immediately recognized. So Greta had treated the blood pressure issues, forced bed rest, and monitored her like a hawk. But Angela had woken tonight, her water having broken. She was hemorrhaging badly. Now she was in the throes of delivery.

"Push, Angela. Push."

"I can't," Angela said.

She was covered in sweat as she lay on the bed. A surgical gown hung in front of her to block the view of her lower half. Greta's head was only intermittently visible as she worked to deliver the baby.

"I know it hurts, but you have to push, Angela!"

"No. I can't. I just can't."

"Okay," Greta said, shaking her head. "We're going to the hospital, sweetheart. Something is wrong. You're bleeding too much."

"No! We can't go to the hospital. He'll be set free. And he'll know about the baby. Please!"

Greta looked back down. The hemorrhaging had intensified. She swallowed down the fear that rose in her throat, then nodded her head. She worried about the baby, but more so about Angela. Her home, despite the equipment she had gathered over the past few months, was simply not equipped to handle such complications. Greta was not equipped, either.

"Then I need you to push. Do you hear me?"

Angela did. She pushed and pushed.

PART IV

THE CHOICE

CHAPTER 30
Chicago, November 2, 2019

*T*HE COURTROOM HEARING WAS A FORMALITY, COMPLETELY UNNECESsary, and the last place Rory wanted to be this morning. Still reeling from her panic attack, mildly hungover, and with her mind squarely preoccupied with the enigmatic dream she'd had the night before, she was desperate to get to the nursing home and ask Greta about her connection to Angela Mitchell. But Frank Moore had agreed to this hearing months ago as a way to provide a final voice to the board members, who were allowing this man to walk free two decades before his sentence was complete. Present with Rory in the courtroom were the six members of the parole board, a designated representative from the district attorney's office, who looked like he was straight out of law school, and a court clerk, as well as Naomi Brown and Ezra Parker, the social worker and parole officer who had accompanied Rory to the Starved Rock cabin. They all wore some form of appropriate attire for a courtroom, except Rory.

She looked more like the parolee than his attorney, dressed as she was in gray jeans and a dark T-shirt. She couldn't get away with wearing her beanie hat in court, so she allowed her wavy brunette hair to fall to either side of her face like barely parted window curtains. She made sure her glasses were in place, and when she walked into the courtroom, her combat boots rattled and drew everyone's attention. She had warned Judge Boyle that she was not meant for a courtroom. The stares would normally have sent her into a state of panic, but she spent most of her angst during the height of her attack the previous night when she drunkenly drove to Angela Mitchell's old house. It had once been Thomas Mitchell's house as well, she thought just as the side door of the courtroom opened and two bailiffs appeared. They led Thomas Mitchell into court and sat him next to Rory. Judge Boyle materialized through a different door and took his spot on the bench.

"Good morning," the judge said, his voice echoing through the nearly empty courtroom. "This will be a brief hearing."

The judge kept his gaze on the papers in front of him and never looked up to see those present in his courtroom. He appeared to be as excited about this morning's proceedings as Rory.

"Ms. Moore, I've brought the board up on the latest circumstances of the passing of Mr. Mitchell's previous attorney, and that as his new representative you've agreed to all the previous stipulations."

They covered again the living arrangements, regular check-ins with the parole officer, restriction on drugs and alcohol, drug testing, and on and on.

"Yes, sir. Yes, ma'am," Thomas said whenever a member of the board addressed him.

The formalities took fifteen minutes. Once everyone was satisfied, the judge shuffled some papers.

"Mr. Mitchell, your release tomorrow will be tricky," Judge Boyle said. "There is intense media attention surrounding the exact details, and Ms. Moore and I have discussed the importance of you staying anonymous. The press release lists a ten A.M. release. I'd like to keep that as the formal time listed, but release you instead at four-thirty A.M. It will still be dark. The warden has agreed to this, and to an east-side exit. I think this will be the best way to keep things discreet and allow you to get to your residence without notice."

Unstated, but agreed upon long ago, was that his attorney would be the one driving him from jail. He had no one else in his life. And now, Thomas Mitchell no longer had Frank Moore.

Judge Boyle looked at Rory. "Transportation has been arranged?"

Rory nodded.

"Mr. Mitchell. You've been an exemplary inmate. The state hereby agrees to your release at four-thirty tomorrow morning, November third. I hope you make much of your life from this point forward. Good luck to you."

"Thank you, Your Honor," Thomas said.

The judge banged his gavel and was up and gone, his robe drifting like a cape in the wind.

Thomas looked at the board members, bowed his head. "Thank you."

He was gracious and kind. A perfect gentleman. Rehabilitated and ready to integrate back into society.

CHAPTER 31
Chicago, November 3, 2019

WITH LANE NEXT TO HER IN BED, RORY WATCHED THE BEDSIDE clock tick, tick, tick, minute after minute, until it reached three o'clock. She hadn't slept, hadn't even closed her eyes. She had considered a middle-of-the-night visit to see Aunt Greta. Greta would typically have been the perfect person to calm Rory's nerves about sitting alone in her car with Thomas Mitchell, but Rory knew that the next time she saw Greta, she needed to take advantage of whatever small window of opportunity presented itself to ask about Angela. She would need to be clear and concise, and to do this, Rory needed to gather her wits. During the dark hours of night, as Lane slept next to her, she decided to tackle the obstacle of delivering Thomas Mitchell to the Starved Rock cabin before seeing Greta. At 3:15 A.M., she pushed the covers to the side and climbed from bed.

The warm flow of water crashed over her head. She spent more time in the shower than usual before she finally shut off the spigot and readied herself for what was coming. Twenty minutes later, she was dressed in her usual battle gear. She laced up her combat boots and was about to head out the front door and into the darkness when she saw Lane dressed and waiting in the darned front room. He sat with crossed legs and his arm draped over the back of the couch, staring into the black fireplace.

"What are you doing?"

Lane turned at the sound of her voice.

"Not a chance I'm letting you go by yourself."

"Lane—" Rory started to say, but he was already up and out the door. A few seconds later, she heard her car door slam.

"Thank God," she whispered to herself.

At four-fifteen, they pulled to the east gate at Stateville Correctional Center in Crest Hill, Illinois, and waited. The headlights illuminated the chain-link fencing. At precisely 4:30 A.M., the side door opened and spilled yellow light into the predawn darkness. Figures appeared, silhouetted by the brightness inside the building that cast their shadows in front of them like long, slender ghosts. The scene brought Rory briefly back to the other night, when she stood in the alley behind Angela's previous home—Thomas Mitchell's home—and stepped in front of her car's headlight to cause her shadow to creep out in front of her.

The chain-link fencing parted as the figures approached, and when the group reached the edge of the enclosure, only one of them continued on. Rory's sternum ached as Thomas Mitchell walked through the darkness, opened the door, and climbed into the backseat.

The ride to Starved Rock took just over an hour. There was no conversation in the dark car, only the hum of highway as they sped along I-80 guided by the brightness of the headlamps. She took the appropriate exit and navigated the side streets with the aid of Lane's GPS, eventually slowing when she approached the nearly hidden driveway that led to the secluded cabin.

"Wow," Thomas said from the backseat. He was staring through the side window. The first glimmers of dawn were on the horizon, ushering away the dark night and replacing it with a soft blue. "It's been a long time."

Rory didn't know if he was talking about the cabin or the sunrise. She didn't ask, just turned onto the drive. The car rocked as she steered along the canopied drive, finally emerging into the clearing where the A-frame cabin sat in the teal glow of morning. She put the car into park when she reached the end of the driveway, turned and draped her right arm across the front seats so that her hand was touching Lane's shoulder.

She handed a key over the seat.

"I only found one key in my father's office."

Thomas took it and climbed from the rear of the vehicle. He carried with him a zipped plastic bag the guards had provided. It represented everything he owned in the world. Rory stood from the driver's seat, popped the trunk, and removed a small backpack. They both approached the front porch.

"There's no food," Rory said.

Her father would have probably stocked the fridge. Rory never considered it.

"But there's a convenience store about half a mile down the main road."

Thomas nodded. "I remember."

She handed him an envelope of money she had withdrawn from his account using the password set up by her father.

"Here's some cash to get you started. There's also an ATM card in there with access to one of your accounts. Pass code is on a sticky note. Are you familiar with ATMs?"

He nodded. "We had a card system inside. I'll figure it out."

"ATM machine is at the convenience store. Food and clothes will be your first necessities." She handed him the backpack. "I put this together for you. It'll do until we can get you a vehicle. But you'll need a driver's license first. We'll have to work on all that. You think you can survive on a week's worth of clothing and the convenience store for a few days while I work out the details?"

"I'll manage. Thank you."

He keyed the front door and stepped inside. After a quick look around, he was back in the doorway. "Thanks for the lift."

"Answer the phone if it rings. Your parole officer will be calling today to give you instructions. His name is Ezra Parker. You're required to check in with him every day."

"Will do."

"Here's his card. Keep it by the phone."

He took the card from her hand.

"Got it."

Rory nodded. "We'll talk soon."

It was getting brighter as she walked back to the car, the sun's yellow glimmer through the trees made Rory feel as if she had emerged from a dangerous journey.

At just after 8:00 A.M., Rory and Lane pulled to the curb outside her house. Her nerves were frayed, she was sleep deprived, and the adrenaline rush was on a steep decline. She was exhausted when she walked across the front lawn and up the steps to her porch. Lane put his arm around her. With her father gone and Greta too elderly to embrace her, there was only one person left in her life whose touch she enjoyed. She put her head on his shoulder and they climbed the stairs to her front stoop.

"I'll make coffee?" Rory asked.

"You don't drink coffee."

"I'll open a couple Diet Cokes."

"No," Lane said. "I've got a class this morning. I'm already late. You should get some sleep. You were up all night."

"I have to see Aunt Greta."

"Now?"

"Something's come up. I have to talk with her."

"Get some sleep. I have a faculty dinner tonight. I'm giving the keynote address. But I'll try to skip out afterward and come see you."

She let him kiss her.

"Okay?" Lane asked.

Rory nodded. Her eyes were droopy with fatigue. "Okay."

She turned and entered the house. After the door was closed, Lane looked down at the porch, which was covered in ruddy dust. He noticed the trail of bloodred footprints from Rory's boots. They led from the street, across the front lawn, and up to the patio.

CHAPTER 32
Starved Rock, Illinois, November 3, 2019

*T*HOMAS MITCHELL CLOSED THE DOOR TO THE CABIN AND WATCHED through the window as Frank Moore's daughter drove the circular path around the cottage and disappeared into the forested drive from which they had come. Once she was gone, he looked around his new home, checking each room. He walked back out onto the front porch and into the dawning morning. It was the first time in forty years that he witnessed a sunrise. He sucked in the scent of the pine trees, his brain tricking him at first into believing he smelled the usual antiseptic bleach that had greeted him for the last many decades. But no, he tasted only the fresh scents of morning, of freedom, of opportunity.

So much had transpired at this place. He had history here, at his uncle's cabin tucked away in the woods. And there was more to come. The final chapter of his life was about to be written here. He planned to find her. To bring her here, the way he should have done years before.

He took just a moment to enjoy the rising sun before he went back into the cabin and sat on the couch. Across the coffee table, he spread the contents of the plastic bag the guard had given him when he stood at the precipice of the open gate at Stateville Correctional Center. The trinkets and possessions he had accumulated during his life in prison had been left in his jail cell. He knew the guards had pocketed the knickknacks to sell to rabid fans. The Thief still had a following. But all that mattered to him were his papers. The tedious and meticulous notes he had taken over the years. They were a verbatim list of everything he had ever spoken about to Frank Moore. Every lead the attorney had ever brought him during the search for his wife. Every person Frank had contacted. Years of plotting had boiled the list down to an essential few. Thomas knew where to start. He planned to waste no time. Forty years of waiting were about to end.

Hours later, the sun was high above and his white skin burned under the unfamiliar rays. His shirt was soaked through with perspiration as he stepped onto the shovel for the thousandth time. The mound of dirt had grown thigh-high and it took a good stride down to reach the bottom of the hole. He spent another hour widening it, and another squaring off the corners. It had been so long since he'd dug a grave that he nearly forgot the thrill it brought. It meant The Rush was coming.

The anticipation surged through him. He swiped his forearm across his face to clear the sweat; then he speared the shovel into the earth again. And again. And again.

CHAPTER 33
Chicago, November 3, 2019

A BUZZING WOKE RORY FROM A DREAMLESS SLEEP. THE BEDROOM WINdows displayed a fading chestnut sky as night fell. The combination of her first panic attack in nearly three decades, more than twenty-four hours without sleep, and the tormented task of driving Thomas Mitchell from jail had resulted in total exhaustion. She was disorientated when she woke. The buzzing came again. She searched for the source until she heard it once more and finally recognized that her phone was vibrating. She grabbed it from her bedside table, expecting to see Lane's number. Instead, though, it was someone else. The series of numbers immediately registered. Dragging the slider to the right, she placed the phone to her ear.

"Mr. Byrd?"

"Yes, hi. Rory?"

Rory waited, still groggy and suddenly aware that she sounded so.

"Sorry. Did I wake you?"

"No," she said. There was a long pause as Rory stood from bed and walked to the window. It was past 5:00 P.M. and the sun had set. She realized that she'd slept the entire day.

"Hello?"

"Yes," Rory said. "I'm here."

"I was calling to get an update about the case. To see if you've made any progress."

Rory blinked the sleep from her eyes. "I'm afraid not. I mean, I haven't gotten to it yet. But I promise I will. In the meantime, I've finished Camille's doll. I just need to make some last alterations. I'll call you next week and we'll arrange to meet."

There was another pause. "That would be fine."

Rory ended the call. She checked her text messages, but found none. She tried Lane, but got no answer. His class had ended hours ago. He was probably on his way to dinner. He wouldn't be back for another few hours. She climbed back into bed to wait for him. She needed to close her eyes for just a moment. When she did, it took only seconds for sleep to take her again.

CHAPTER 34
Chicago, November 3, 2019

*C*ATHERINE BLACKWELL FINISHED THE TEN O'CLOCK NEWS AND SHUT off the television. The lead story had been the release of Thomas Mitchell, aka The Thief, from Stateville Correctional Center earlier in the day. With no footage of the release, reporters speculated that he had been discharged early in the morning under cover of darkness. That, or there had been a delay. Authorities and prison spokespeople offered no updates, and likely would not until the following morning. Still, reporters stood vigil outside the correction center, hoping to break the news if The Thief ended up walking from behind the prison walls into the hot lights of their cameras.

What a shame, Catherine thought. *What a terrible shame.*

She walked into the kitchen, removed a glass container of milk from the refrigerator, and poured it into the bowl on the ground. The sound of the cap suctioning off the jar brought her cat roaming from under the bed in the other room to lap at the cool milk. Catherine went to the sink and placed the empty bottle into the garbage bag, tied it tightly, and carried it to the back door. The cat was immediately on her heels.

"You want to explore, don't you?" Catherine said. "Come on."

She opened the back door and the cat ran out into the night. Catherine walked to the alley behind her house and lifted the top to the large plastic garbage can to drop the bag inside. The cat was at her side again.

"Not feeling adventurous tonight? Go find a mouse."

But the cat was unusually needy this evening, not wanting to leave Catherine's side. Catherine sensed something ominous as she stood in the alley. The cat hissed into the night.

"What's wrong? What do you see out there?"

The cat hissed once more before darting from Catherine's side, swallowed quickly by the black night. As Catherine squinted into the darkness, feet shuffled behind her. She turned quickly, startled. Their eyes met and she let out a short scream, which was quickly stifled by his hand.

CHAPTER 35
Chicago, November 3, 2019

GRETA SCHREIBER LAY IN BED, EYES CLOSED AND IN A WILD STATE OF dementia. Her mind flashed with images from the past. Quick bursts of colorful mirages from a previous life.

"Where is she?" a voice came from the darkness.

"I tried to save you," Greta said. "There was too much blood."

The farmhouse flickered in her mind. The makeshift delivery room. Angela lying on the bed. The blood. The doubt. The terror.

A grave worry filled Greta's chest, now like it had that day.

"Where is she?" the voice asked again.

"We have to go to the hospital," Greta said. "Something's wrong. There's too much blood."

"I'll ask one more time," the voice said from the darkness. "You picked her up from the psychiatric hospital. I know she came to you for help. Where is she now?"

Greta opened her eyes. The farmhouse disappeared, replaced by a hospital room, a blue glowing television, and a looming figure standing over her bed. The figure leaned closer so that his face was inches from hers.

"Where. Is. She."

Greta blinked. Her mind cleared. She knew the face in front of her. She'd seen him on the news all those years ago. He was older now than when she had watched updates of his conviction on television while Angela sat next to her. Older than the photos that had appeared in the papers. But she was sure it was him. It was not a surprise that he was here, nor was this day unexpected. Frank had worried about it for years and had voiced his concern to Greta many times.

"Last time," the man said. "Where is—"

"Nowhere." Greta's voice was gravelly and inaudible.

The man leaned closer so that his ear was close to her lips. The blue glow of the television disappeared from Greta's vision when the man bent over her.

"Again," he said.

"Nowhere you'll ever find her. Nowhere you'll ever go."

The blue light came back as the man stood up. Then it quickly disappeared again. Greta felt the pillow press against her face. She kept her arms at her sides and never tried to resist. Her mind drifted off.

I tried to save you. There was too much blood.

CHAPTER 36
Chicago, November 4, 2019

*I*T HAD BEEN MORE THAN FORTY-EIGHT HOURS SINCE HER PANIC ATTACK and Rory was starting to feel her body balance itself. The sleep had helped, and now she was ready to face the source of her angst. Greta was linked to Angela Mitchell, and Rory had finally made it to the nursing home to ask her about it. Camille Byrd's Kestner doll lay in its box on the passenger seat. It would be good ammunition for when Rory asked Greta the tough questions she had planned. Rory would not let her off the hook today. Today she needed answers. She needed to understand the mysterious veil that had fallen over her life, a web that connected everyone she loved to a woman who supposedly died forty years ago.

As she pulled into the lot, Rory saw red flashing lights from an ambulance and fire truck that were parked in the turnabout in front of the building. Greta had been a resident here long enough that red lights and sirens were routine for Rory. Throughout nearly every resident's tenure, they suffered some sort of medical crisis that required a trip to the hospital. Emergency vehicles parked out front were a daily ritual.

Rory walked in front of the fire truck, whose engine was roaring. In the lobby, she scribbled her name into the visitor log and paused as she went through the process of printing Greta's name and room number, and then signing her own along the narrow line. Rory had gone through the routine so many times over the years that the practice had attached itself to the image of her aging great-aunt sitting in her room and staring at the blue light of the television. But something caught her attention as she stared at the visitor log today. A vague, subconscious intuition made her hesitate as she penned her name. Before she had a chance to decipher the premonition, Greta's nurse appeared in the corner of Rory's eye. She was walking in a hurried fashion, an urgency to her pace. Rory looked up from the sign-in sheet, dropped the pen to the floor. Things slowed. The rushing nurse took on an underwater motion, her hair flowing behind her in slow motion.

Rory felt the woman take her hand, her eyes dripping with sympathy.

"I'm afraid your aunt has passed, Rory."

Rory blinked as the world caught up and began again in real time. The noises of the lobby came back to her. The people moved around her with normal gaits and at a normal speed. The framed picture on the lobby wall blinked red with the flashing lights outside.

"She was perfectly happy when she went to sleep last night," the nurse said. "We found her this morning. She passed overnight. Peacefully and with no distress."

Rory stood still and offered no reply, the Kestner doll secured under her arm.

"Would you like to see her?"

Rory nodded. She would.

CHAPTER 37
Chicago, November 4, 2019

*R*ORY LAY IN BED, SHE COULDN'T SHAKE THE IMAGE OF THE ZIPPER pulling the gap in the body bag together, Aunt Greta's face disappearing. With it, a part of Rory vanished, too. She had fought against it when Celia called a month ago to tell Rory that her father was dead. And she battled to prevent it when she walked into her childhood home and was assaulted by memories of a life gone by. She tried to resist again tonight, but had no chance of stopping the tears this time. She cried like she never remembered doing as a child, and had certainly never done as an adult.

It wasn't that Rory Moore didn't feel the emotions of pain or sadness, she did. But those things affected *her* differently than they affected *most*. Those sensations altered her mood and changed her thinking. They pulled her back from interactions and made her want to hide from the world. They made her want to be alone. Rarely, however, did pain cause the socially accepted form of bereavement—hysterical crying. Tonight was one of those rare occasions. Rory lay on her side, head sunk in the pillow, and wept.

So many things were gone. Greta had been Rory's last living relative. Besides Lane Phillips, Rory loved no one else in this world. But the anguish she felt now carried another significance. In addition to the end of her lineage, gone, too, was Rory's chance for answers about the adoption papers. About Frank and Marla Moore. About her summers at the farmhouse. About her true relationship to Greta. And about Greta's link to Angela Mitchell. Ever since

Rory started reconstructing her death, the mysterious woman seemed to be tied to everything in Rory's life. It was a connection that felt otherworldly, stronger than the usual relationship Rory developed with the victims of the crimes she reconstructed. And so it was that on the night Greta died, she could think of nothing but Angela Mitchell.

Regret was her companion as Rory closed her eyes, seasoning the tears that ran down her cheeks to soak the pillow. Soon sleep was pulling her. She surrendered easily to it, because within the slumber was something else: the familiar lure she had known as a child, the temptation that had drawn her from bed and ushered her to the prairie behind the farmhouse, where she once found peace. Tonight, though, as her eyes fluttered under her lids, she recognized that it was someone different that pulled her mind. Still, it was irresistible.

It was dark and quiet when Rory walked into Grant Park. The Chicago skyline shined in the distance, intermittent windows lit yellow in the skyscrapers that were set against a black sky. Rory squinted against the darkness. She walked past Buckingham Fountain and to the cobblestone path flanked by birch trees until she came to the clearing where Camille Byrd's body had been found nearly two years prior. The girl was there now, sitting alone in the grassy knoll. The halogen bulb of a lamppost highlighted her body. A brick wall in the background caught her shadow. She looked tranquil with her legs crossed in a yoga pose, a blanket cloaked over her shoulders. The girl lifted a hand when Rory appeared, a gentle wave that filled Rory's heart simultaneously with peace and sorrow.

Camille held something in her lap, and as Rory walked onto the grass and approached the girl, she got a better look at what it was. The Kestner doll was splayed over the girl's crossed legs. Camille ran her hand over the doll's knotted hair. Rory squinted in the darkness and saw the jagged fracture down the left side of the doll's face, the eye socket split open like a chestnut.

"I'm sorry I've neglected your case," Rory said. "I'm sorry I've ignored you."

The girl smiled. It was a radiant smile that put a serene mood over the area where someone had dumped her body. There was no anger or disappointment in her eyes.

"You haven't ignored me," Camille said. "You've thought of me more than anyone else."

"I promise to get to your case. I promise to find the person who did this to you."

"I know you'll come back to me."

Rory took a step closer. The Kestner looked as ruined as the day Walter Byrd had given it to her.

"You become close with the people whose deaths you reconstruct. You always have. It's the way you figure things out that no one else can. And you'll solve your own riddle as well. All the answers are in front of you. All the things that are troubling you. All the things that make no sense . . ." Camille ran her hand over the doll's face. "The truth is easy to miss, even when it's right in front of us."

Camille shifted the doll in her arms, stared into its eyes.

"You and Greta did such a great job on her."

At the mention of her name, Rory's mind ignited with images of Greta as she babbled with dementia each time Rory walked into her room, confused and overwhelmed by Rory's presence.

"I tried to save you. There was too much blood."

Rory remembered the fear in Greta's eyes each time she visited. The distress that lasted a few desperate seconds until Greta snapped back from the tortured memories of her past.

"I wish I could have saved you as easily as Rory and I save the dolls."

The world began to spin as Rory remembered the mysterious pull that had taken hold of her as a ten-year-old girl, the one that ushered her to the prairie behind the farmhouse. Everything blurred around her as she thought of the roses heaped in a pile on the ground, of their sweet scent that filled her body when she placed them to her nose, of the peace that came to her.

As quickly as the spinning started, the world stopped. Rory found herself alone. Camille Byrd was gone. In her place on the grassy knoll was a bundle of roses and the Kestner doll, restored to perfection.

Greta's voice echoed in her ears:

"I tried to save you. There was too much blood."

"There's too much blood. We have to go to the hospital."

"He's coming. You told me. He'll come for you."

Then Camille Byrd's voice:

"The truth is easy to miss, even when it's right in front of us."

As Rory stood in the grassy knoll of Grant Park, it all made sense. The connection she felt to Angela Mitchell and all the similarities that linked them, her father's appeal letters that screamed to Rory an ulterior motive about never wanting Thomas Mitchell out of jail, Greta's connection to Angela, her career as a midwife, the adoption to Frank and Marla Moore, her father's stress during the final year of his life as he could no longer stop Thomas Mitchell's release from jail.

And something else that tugged at her. It was so close to surfacing, but the harder she reached into the far recesses of her mind to retrieve it, the more she stirred in bed. Rory moaned now as she tried to pull herself from sleep. As Rory tried to run, she heard Camille Byrd's voice. When she turned, the girl was back on the grass, standing with the blanket cloaked over her shoulders. The yellow halogen painted Camille's shadow on the wall behind her, and the image triggered Rory's mind. She understood what had been bothering her, and she knew it was Camille who had helped her epiphany.

"Thank you for restoring my doll. It means everything to my father."

When Rory looked, the Kestner was flawless as it rested in Camille's arms. The girl waved again and then Rory ran and ran.

CHAPTER 38
Chicago, November 5, 2019

S HE WOKE WITH A JOLT, KICKING HERSELF AWAKE. THE SHEETS WERE tangled around her legs and it took her a moment to free them. Covered in sweat, she felt her heart thundering as she remembered her dream. When she replayed the image of Camille Byrd's shadow cast on the brick wall, Rory jumped from bed. She stepped into a pair of jeans, pulled on a T-shirt, and sunk her feet into her combat boots. She draped her beanie hat over her head as she crashed through the front door and climbed into her car.

At just past midnight, there was no traffic and she reached the nursing home in fifteen minutes. She sped into the turnabout, where the ambulance and fire truck had been parked the day before, left her car running and the driver's-side door open as she ran into the building.

Rory had made many midnight trips to the nursing home over the years, and knew the place would be asleep. There was a young man tending the front desk when Rory rattled into the lobby in her combat boots.

"Hi," the man whispered in a voice meant to display the serenity of the place at such an hour. "Are you here to see a resident?"

"I need to see the visitor log from yesterday."

"Do you need to sign in?"

"No, I just need to look through the log from yesterday."

"Are you looking for a specific resident?"

Rory took a breath. She could play this one of two ways. Force the issue by threatening to have Ron Davidson of the CPD down here in a matter of minutes to find the log for her—or play the sympathy card. She chose the latter.

"My aunt passed yesterday. Her dear friend came to see her just before she died, and I've forgotten her name. I'm sure she signed in, and I was hoping to recognize her name."

"Oh." The young man was immediately defenseless. "Of course."

He opened a drawer behind the desk and pulled out a thick three-ring binder. He placed it on the counter, spun it so that it was upright for Rory, and opened the cover. Bound neatly into the rings were the year of visitor log sign-in sheets. Yesterday's was on top. Rory placed her finger on the first line of the page and quickly skimmed down the names until she saw it.

Her fierce mind flashed with images of Thomas Mitchell's penmanship from reading the letters he had written to her father. The Thief's writing had been meticulous, all caps, and in perfect rows despite the lineless paper on which it was printed. Rory remembered the unique way in which he wrote his *A*'s as inverted *V*'s.

The character had jumped from the page in every word where it was present. The unusual symbol filled her vision now as she remembered the font. The nursing home began to spin, just like in her dream. She remembered Camille Byrd's image from her dream, when the girl stood and the halogen light painted her shadow on the brick wall. It reminded Rory of the night she stood in the alley behind Angela Mitchell's house, her legs forming the same inverted V. Rory remembered, too, the eerie sensation that had come over her that night. She had felt it again yesterday when she signed the visitor log—a premonition she had been unable to place. It had screamed for her attention just before the nurse appeared out of the corner of her eye, hurrying toward her to break the news about Greta. Now, measured and with a gentle push from Camille Byrd, Rory was able to comprehend it. Thomas Mitchell's penmanship was present on the page in front of her. The same inverted *V*'s.

The person who had come to see the resident in room 121 had written Greta's name in perfect block, all-caps letters: *MARGARET SCHREIBER.*

CHAPTER 39
Starved Rock, Illinois, November 5, 2019

*I*T WAS APPROACHING 2:00 A.M. WHEN RORY TOOK THE HIGHWAY EXIT. I-80 had been empty, but for the rare set of isolated headlights, and now she found herself truly alone as she took the sleepy country roads that led toward Starved Rock State Park and the cabin that waited in the woods. She'd driven the route twice before, and this third outing came from memory. She didn't hesitate at the forks, didn't contemplate the T's. She knew the way. The route had burned itself into her memory the way everything else did. The same way all the details of her life were stored and categorized.

Rory wasn't always aware of the things her mind noticed or picked up on, and could not readily comprehend the enormous volume of material her memory logged. But since her dream, since finding Camille Byrd's spirit nestled in the grassy knoll in Grant Park, all the cryptic elements of her childhood and the farmhouse—of Aunt Greta and her parents, of her visits to the nursing home and the dolls she restored, of Greta's seemingly random mutterings, of the mysterious pull that had once drawn her to the back property of the farmhouse as a young child, of the instant attraction she felt toward Angela Mitchell, and of the nearly identical symptoms they shared of social anxiety and obsessive compulsion—all came to her with vivid clarity. She knew what it all meant. She had finally grasped that elusive element of her existence that had been out of reach for so long, and it had taken nothing more than a push from the spirit of a dead girl who waited for her help.

"The truth is easy to miss, even when it's right in front of us."

Rory's epiphany had brought her to this place tonight. She was at the precipice of darkness, and her soul felt tainted by it. She was unsure if it was possible to correct this mutation at the core of her existence, but anger drove her to try. She made the final turn of her journey. Her headlamps were the only source of light in the otherwise-black night. Until she turned them off. Then only the moon was present, and it offered little guidance. She pulled her car to the side of the road, crunched over the gravel, and turned off the engine. Two hundred yards ahead was the canopied driveway that led to Thomas Mitchell's cabin.

She picked up her phone for the hundredth time, stared at the lit display. She'd had Lane's number plugged in and ready to connect multiple times throughout the drive to Starved Rock, but had stopped herself from calling. The same for Ron Davidson's number, which she had also pulled up during the hour drive. To call either of the men in her life would have prevented her from doing what she was about to do. Rory decided that only one man would be part of her life tonight—the one who had played a silent and unknown role in her existence. The man who had, perhaps, formed her character. The one who had taken from her more than she could reclaim tonight.

As she climbed from her car and eased the door closed, she wondered if extinguishing the source of a fire could stifle the flames that blazed in adjacent structures? The silence of the night overwhelmed her ability to answer her own question as she headed toward the canopied drive. Halfway between her parked car and the cabin's driveway, Rory found a path that led into the forest. She clicked to life the flashlight on her cell phone and followed the trail. Two hundred yards later, she heard the gentle gurgling of water and knew the river was up ahead. When she came to the clearing, the river bled to either side and reflected the moon off its surface like a mystical snake slithering through the night. She followed the riverbank for another two hundred yards until she found the dock she had seen during her first visit to the cabin with the parole officer, Ezra Parker, and the social worker, Naomi Brown. There was a long stretch of neglected stairs that led from the water's edge up the steep embankment. She took them cautiously, one at a time, as her sternum began to throb and her head became flush with blood.

At the top of the stairs, she saw the cabin sitting in the middle of five acres. The square clearing was surrounded by forest. As she slowly set off for the structure, the moon cast a faint shadow next to her. It was her only companion.

CHAPTER 40
Starved Rock, Illinois, November 5, 2019

SHE APPROACHED FROM THE REAR. THE WINDOWS OF THE CABIN WERE dark, the sort of darkness that made Rory think she was looking into a black hole. Rory slowly navigated her way from the edge of the forest and across the long stretch of grass behind the cabin. She crept without the aid of her flashlight. The grass beneath her boots felt level and her steps were unchallenged. But as she came to within fifty yards of the cabin, she took a step but found no earth beneath her. She stumbled forward, falling a full three feet until her feet finally hit the ground. By then, it was too late to right herself. She crashed face-first onto the ground, the damp odor of soil heavy in her nostrils.

She lay still for a moment, attempting to gain her bearings. She felt for her phone, which was thrown from her hand on impact. When she found it, she turned on the flashlight. As she looked around, it was clear that she was in a freshly dug hole. Above her, a mound of dirt sat in the dark. Climbing to her knees, Rory slowly stood from the pit, the top of which was up to her waist. Her breathing was labored when she looked back to the cabin. It remained dark and quiet.

She climbed from the hole, shut off her cell phone, and started off again toward the cabin. When she came to the gravel drive that encircled the cottage, she remembered bending her car around its curves two mornings before. She followed it again now to the front of the cabin and reached into the pocket of her coat to feel for the only weapon she thought to bring—the Swiss Army knife Kip had given her.

She peeled open the blade as she crossed the gravel, her combat boots crunching over the rocks and the red clay that covered the ground. Her first stride onto the stairs caused the porch to creak under her weight. In the dead of night, it may have been a cannon shot. After a moment of pause, Rory continued to the next step, and then the next, until she was standing at the front door of the cabin. To pause now would be to lose her nerve. She grasped the handle and twisted. The door opened without protest, the hinges squeaking softly as the handle floated from her grip. She waited thirty seconds, felt a tremor rattling her fingers. Darkness welcomed her as she stepped inside.

Her mind pulled up the blueprint of the floor plan from her only other time in the cabin, back when she came here with the social worker and parole officer. Despite the darkness, she knew there were three rooms on the first floor—front room, kitchen, and a porch at the back of the house. The stairs to the left of the front door led to two bedrooms and a hall bath. He would be upstairs. He would be sleeping. Just like Greta had likely been when he entered her room.

She started up the stairs, the blade vibrating in her grip.

The bedrooms were empty. The beds were bare, absent of sheets or blankets. Rory descended the stairs, clicked on her phone's flashlight, and splayed it across the front room. On the coffee table were papers scattered in a cluttered mess. She lifted one of the pages and saw his meticulous block penmanship chronicling his years-long search for his wife. An eerie stimulus simmered just below her sternum. Unable to help herself, Rory sat on the couch, placed the Swiss Army knife on the table, and flipped through the pages. It would have been easy for her to become lost in the words, to surrender to the call to reconstruct his path over the years and see how far his research had taken him. And she might have succumbed to this temptation had she not come across the handwritten map.

Written in his distinct block lettering, the inverted *V*'s jumped out at her everywhere they appeared. She tried to understand what

268

she was reading. It looked to be a plat of survey for the cabin and the land on which it sat. Architectural renderings of the property and its boundaries. On the formal diagram, rectangular boxes had been drawn by hand. They were organized in a grid formation and covered the open area behind the cabin. In each of the boxes, a name was written. Rory immediately recognized the names as the women who had gone missing in 1979. She dropped the survey to the ground when she realized she was holding a map of a makeshift graveyard, and that she had likely just pulled herself from a freshly dug grave.

CHAPTER 41
Starved Rock, Illinois, November 5, 2019

S HE STOOD IN THE FRONT ROOM OF THE CABIN, THE PLAT OF SURVEY and the graveyard map at her feet, and her body temperature quickly on the rise. She felt the perspiration on the back of her neck, and recognized her inability to inhale. A similar episode had gripped her a few nights before when she struggled to piece together her discoveries about Greta and Angela. And now, here again, she felt the impending doom of a panic attack.

Rory ripped the beanie hat off her head and fumbled with the buttons of her jacket. As her pulse raced at an unhealthy clip, she felt cool air on her throat when she unclasped the top of her coat. It provided a moment of clarity and an overwhelming urge to get out of the cabin. Her lungs ached badly enough that she finally sucked for air. With her cell phone flashlight still shining, Rory grabbed the Swiss Army knife from the table, hurried across the front room and through the kitchen. She pushed open the door that led to the porch with a plan to cut across the back of the property, find the stairs to the river, and race to her car. But when she stepped onto the porch, all thoughts of leaving this place evaporated. A woman sat slumped in a chair, a nylon noose around her neck and her hands bound behind her back. The subtle tremor that had vibrated Rory's fingers now rippled through her entire body as she walked closer and realized she was looking at Catherine Blackwell.

The noose around her neck was attached to a rope that snaked upward to a large wooden contraption bolted to the porch ceiling. Rory ran her cell phone light over it. The rope slithered around three pulleys—up, down, up, down—before the other end fell to the floor a few feet away from Catherine. The apparatus took on the shape of an M and Rory instantly remembered it from Angela's drawings. She had discovered a similar tool in her husband's warehouse.

Rory pulled the beam of her light down from the ceiling and hurried to Catherine's side.

"Catherine, can you hear me?"

As soon as she spoke the words, Rory knew they were worthless. The woman's eyes stayed closed, her body was cold. Rory swiped the face of her phone. It took three attempts, her shaking fingers unable to activate the slider. When she finally had the phone open, she hesitated for an instant, contemplating whether to call Ron Davidson or dial 911. During her indecision, she saw the light out in the distance. Through the screen of the porch, out across the back of the property, she spotted a wobbling light. The long beam of the flashlight cut through the darkness and bounced in a rhythmic cadence as the person who carried it made his way toward the cabin.

Remembering her initial view of the cabin from when she had crested the stairs from the riverbank a few minutes earlier, Rory realized the glow of her phone would stand out in the darkness. She quickly doused the light by covering her phone with her hand and pressing it to her chest. Still crouching next to Catherine's body, she turned her flashlight off and dropped the phone in her pocket. Then she turned and ran back through the door and into the kitchen.

As she quietly closed the door to the porch, she saw the bouncing flashlight approaching. The distance had been cut in half, he was perhaps thirty seconds from reaching the cabin. In the darkness, Rory fumbled around the kitchen for somewhere to hide. She realized that she had stopped breathing again and was momentarily distressed at the idea of having to remember to inhale. On the wall adjacent to the porch, she felt the handle of the pantry door.

She opened it and slipped inside just as she heard the outside door to the porch squeak open.

"Have you got one more round in you? I'm sure you do."

Rory trembled in the pantry as she heard Thomas Mitchell's voice.

CHAPTER 42
Starved Rock, Illinois, November 5, 2019

*R*ORY WORKED TO CONTROL HER BREATHING AS SHE STOOD IN THE pantry, the door of which she had pulled to her nose like the lid of a casket. Mold and dust filled her nostrils, and tears blurred her vision. A sliver of visibility was available between the door and the frame. Her sternum ached and her ears thundered with the rush of circulation as she watched Thomas Mitchell prepare a meal in the kitchen. He stood just five or six feet from her as he mixed food in a metal bowl and then ate while he stood, clinically separated from the enjoyment of taste, interested only in the need for sustenance.

He had turned on the lights when he entered the cabin, giving Rory a clear view of the kitchen and porch. As she moved her gaze around, she noticed the red footprints she had tracked across the floor. She looked to the area immediately in front of the pantry and saw the hurried scuff marks she created when she had slid into her hiding spot. Her panic rose, and she concentrated on reviving her lungs and leveling off her breathing. It sounded to her as if she took each breath through a bullhorn, and that any second, Thomas would walk to the pantry, open the door, and discover his prize. She was prepared to scratch and claw, to gouge and punch. She wouldn't hesitate to bite any piece of anatomy that came close to her if she had to. The only thing she wouldn't do was die at this man's hand. Too many other women had. It was why Rory was staring at him now when she could have been racing down the canopied drive and out to her car. It had taken her this long to realize it.

As usual, her conscious mind took a moment to catch up to the small triggers of her subconscious. But she knew now why she hadn't run out the front door when she had the chance. Or why she had turned her phone off rather than dial 911. The same way Camille Byrd's spirit had spoken to her a few hours before, there were others who needed Rory's help. Others who waited for peace and closure. They were buried behind this cabin, where they had lain in turmoil for forty years. Rory could no more turn her back to those women now than she could to Camille Byrd. Rory didn't need Lane or Ron or anyone else to help the women who waited for her. The women needed Rory, and Rory needed to answer their calls for help.

Just as these thoughts materialized in her mind, Thomas placed the metal bowl from which he had been eating onto the kitchen counter and walked toward her. Rory retreated an inch or two, as far as she could in the cramped space, receding farther into the darkness of the pantry. Her lungs became so difficult to fill she was certain her efforts had betrayed her hiding spot. She closed her eyes, waiting for the sliver of light that crept into the pantry to explode as Thomas opened the door. The brightness would be her prompt to attack. To fight like hell. For herself. For Catherine. For the lost souls behind the cabin. Her muscles tensed as she readied to pounce. But instead, music drowned out her heaving breaths.

Her eyes blinked open and she set her gaze back to the crevice between the door and the frame. She scanned the kitchen, but he was gone. She heard Mozart's Requiem fill the cabin, soft at first and then louder. And louder. And louder. Finally he appeared. He walked past the pantry and out to the porch.

CHAPTER 43
Starved Rock, Illinois, November 5, 2019

*T*HE MUSIC WAS DEAFENING IN THE CABIN, BUT HERE ON THE PORCH, it was just right. He hoped it was loud enough to stir her, to bring her back. He longed for the lyrical chorus of Mozart's Requiem to wake her and tell her what was to come. She had barely survived the last round, and he wasn't sure she was still alive. He refused to check now. He didn't want to know if she was gone. He'd missed The Rush more than he imagined, and longed for it once more.

His two leads had run sour. One was too old to offer much, even if he believed she knew the truth. He hadn't the time to elicit it from her. He thought he'd have more luck with the one in front of him, but she proved to be just as useless to his search for Angela. And when he didn't know where to go next, he succumbed to his long-subdued urging for The Rush. Now, as the ode to lost souls spilled from the cabin and filled his ears, Thomas stepped up onto the stool six feet from Catherine Blackwell. He slipped the nylon noose around his neck, instantaneously feeling the surge of endorphins fill his body. Tightening the strap, he slowly eased himself off the stool and watched as she levitated from the chair. It was a glorious sight. Coupled with both the charm of the music and The Rush that surged through his body, Thomas Mitchell slipped off to euphoria.

He closed his eyes for a moment. Despite being out of practice, he reminded himself of the dangers of overindulgence. The Rush was a cryptic practice. It provided the closest thing this world offered to bliss, dangled it on a stick in front of him and begged him to come for it. But Thomas knew The Grim Reaper held that stick, and to abuse The Rush or take too much of it would spell the end. Perhaps that was the lure. Ecstasy and mortality divided by such a fine line.

He was there now, euphoric as his body shook with The Rush. He slivered his eyes open to take in the sight of the woman floating in front of him. He witnessed her magically hanging in the air. It was magnificent and perfect. Until it wasn't. Until a flash of something appeared in his peripheral vision. It startled him. He opened his eyes fully, grasping for the noose around his neck and searching with his foot for the stool.

CHAPTER 44
Starved Rock, Illinois, November 5, 2019

*R*ORY WATCHED FROM THE PANTRY AS THOMAS PULLED A STOOL TO the center of the porch. He fidgeted with the noose overhead. Finally he mounted the stool, hooked the nylon around his neck, and slowly lowered himself off the stool while Catherine simultaneously rose into the air across from him, like a magician levitating his subject. The sight stole what little breath Rory had left.

Through the crack in the pantry door, Rory witnessed the strange scene play out before her. She had reconstructed cases that dealt with the despicable practice of autoerotic asphyxiation, and had read articles about the perverted individuals who reached sexual gratification from its practice. But the scene unfolding in front of her was something entirely different. It was not sexual in nature, but perverted in another, more disturbing way. The high Thomas Mitchell was reaching came not from any perverse use of sex, but rather from the pleasure of watching another die.

Rory saw Catherine's legs dangle limply as she rose, the weight of Thomas's body on the other side of the pulley system dragging her upward. Rory remembered the dual pulley system Angela had drawn in her notes chronicling what she had discovered in Thomas's warehouse. He had re-created that system here in his cabin, and across from him now was his wife's only friend. Someone who he surely believed had helped Angela disappear forty years earlier. How terribly wrong he had it, Rory thought.

As he lowered himself in a slow, guided movement, he kept one foot on the stool as a fail-safe, placing his weight back onto its surface when the tension became too great and he neared unconsciousness. When he put his weight back on the stool, he rose higher and allowed Catherine to sink back to the ground. Rory watched the eerie seesawing while the classical music blared through the cabin.

When she saw Thomas take his weight off the stool again and sink downward, coming to a rest twelve inches from the cabin floor, with the noose tight around his neck and his face boiling to a deep crimson, Rory felt the pull in her chest. It was as powerful as when she was a child at Greta's farmhouse. She quickly pushed open the pantry door, the sounds of her movements camouflaged by Mozart. She reached into the pocket of her coat and retrieved the Dark Lord Swiss Army knife. Unfolding the device, the blade caught the light from the porch. Her movements as she charged through the porch door startled Thomas, who worked frantically to gain leverage on the stool under him. His bloodred face took on another shade, deeper now. Purple.

He worked to gain footing on the stool, his legs flailing until his right foot touched the top surface. If given another few seconds, he would have had the stool underneath him and the pressure relieved from his neck. Rory made sure to take those seconds from him. She walked slowly over to him, their eyes meeting—hers calm and calculating, his bulging and panicked. For once Rory had no inclination to avoid eye contact. She thought of Aunt Greta alone in her room the night Thomas had found her. She thought of the women buried beneath the ground behind the cabin. She thought of Catherine. She thought of Angela.

Rory folded the Swiss Army knife closed. She wouldn't need it after all. Just as Thomas placed his foot on the stool, Rory kicked it out from under him. His body dropped down a few inches, recoiling with the jolt. She watched as he reached for his neck, trying unsuccessfully to pry his fingers between the noose and his skin. As he thrashed about, Rory took a good, long moment to stare at him before whispering in his ear. His bulging eyes appeared to widen; then she turned to tend to Catherine.

She couldn't leave her strung up like cattle. It took a few minutes before Rory had her body lying peacefully on the ground of the porch. Then, with Thomas still meekly thrashing, she walked into the kitchen and lifted the phone from the cradle. The card had been stuck into the crevice between the phone jack and the wall. Rory dialed the number, waited for a voice to answer, and then laid the phone on the kitchen table.

When Rory finally walked from the cabin, she left the front door open. She could still faintly hear Mozart's Requiem when she reached her car.

CHAPTER 45
Chicago, November 5, 2019

*I*T WAS SIX IN THE MORNING WHEN RORY PULLED TO THE CURB OUTSIDE her house. She hurried barefoot up the steps and fumbled with the lock. Inside, she went straight to the front room, gathered newspapers from the bin next to the hearth, and placed them under the logs in the fireplace. She lit a match and touched the flame to the paper, then carefully kindled the fire until it was blazing. More logs went on top, stacked in a precise teepee to allow maximum heat.

Then she undressed and threw her clothes into the fire. First her jeans and T-shirt; next her coat and beanie hat. She waited a moment for the flames to take the fabric. The fire grew strong as it absorbed the clothing. When they were gone, floating up the chimney in small remnants of ash, Rory grabbed her Madden Girl Eloisee combat boots. They were covered in the red clay from her trek through the forest and to the Starved Rock cabin. She placed them in the fire.

Standing in her underwear, she watched the boots begin to melt before she walked upstairs and climbed into bed.

Lane Phillips keyed the front door and walked into Rory's house. It was just before noon and she hadn't answered her phone. He'd called several times. He noticed the glowing logs of a dying fire in the front room.

"Rory?" he called.

No answer.

He checked the study. Empty. The den next. Also empty—besides the dolls that lined the shelves. He walked upstairs and found her asleep. Rory Moore would never be considered a morning person, but sleeping until noon was not common, either. Lane walked over to the bed to check on her. The covers rose and fell with her rhythmic breathing, and Lane couldn't remember the last time he'd seen Rory sleep so soundly.

He noticed the corner of papers poking from under the blanket. He pulled the comforter to the side to find a tattered copy of his thesis. The corners were turned up from frequent readings, the pages crumpled. Lane flipped through the document and saw Rory's notes in the margin of many pages. Toward the end, he found a dog-eared page in the section analyzing why killers kill, and the psychological mechanisms that bring an individual to the precipice of deciding to take another's life. In the middle of the page, a passage was highlighted. He read the yellow glowing sentence: *Some choose darkness, others are chosen by it.*

The page was damp, with circular stains, as if someone had dribbled water onto the paper. *Water,* Lane thought, *or tears?* The doorbell rang and Lane looked up from his thesis. Rory didn't stir. The bell rang again. He placed the document on the nightstand and headed down the stairs. He opened the front door to find Ron Davidson standing on the front porch.

CHAPTER 46
Chicago, November 5, 2019

"*R*ORY?"

Her eyelids fluttered. She heard her name again.

"Rory."

When she opened her eyes, she saw Lane standing over the bed. He touched her cheek.

"Hey, you feeling okay?"

"Yeah," Rory said, sitting up. "I'm fine."

Her mind ignited with quick snippets of her time at the Starved Rock cabin. Of Catherine Blackwell hovering off the ground. Of Thomas Mitchell in his bizarre state of ecstasy. Of her hiding spot in the pantry and the thin slice of light between the door and the frame. Of the classical music. It still rang in her ears.

"What time is it?"

"Noon," Lane said. "Did you hear me about Ron?"

"No, what about him?"

"He's here, downstairs. Said he needs to talk with you. Something urgent."

Rory blinked a few times. She saw her copy of Lane's thesis resting on the nightstand. She had been reading it earlier, before sleep took her to a deep, dreamless rest.

Rory ran a hand through her hair as she nodded. "Tell him I need a minute."

* * *

The three of them sat in the front room fifteen minutes later.

"I got a call early this morning from the LaSalle County Sheriff's Office," Ron said. He was sitting on the couch across from the fireplace, Rory and Lane on adjacent chairs next to him. The fireplace was to Rory's left, Lane's right, and directly in front of the head of Chicago Homicide. If Rory could have chosen, she'd have ushered Ron into the kitchen for this meeting. Instead, when she finally walked down the stairs, he and Lane were sitting in the front room.

"LaSalle County?" Rory asked.

"Starved Rock," Ron said. "We're still piecing together the details, but it looks like Thomas Mitchell killed himself."

Rory kept her face stoic. It was how she would typically react to this news, and she wanted to look typical today.

"How?" she asked.

"Looks like he hanged himself. But details are still coming in. I only talked for a few minutes with the detective in charge. There was another body at the cabin, a woman. It sounded like he tortured her in some way. The county guys are still putting the scene together."

"How'd they find him?"

"He called his parole officer early this morning, about three o'clock. Left the phone on the table while he hanged himself. Least that's what they think. The forensics crew is still putting the scene together. Because he was your client, I thought I'd stop by to let you know. I'm getting ready to head out there now."

Rory nodded. "Thanks." She looked at Lane, then back to the detective. "Sorry I seem off, I'm trying to process everything."

Mostly, Rory was worried that she'd left her fingerprints on the phone or somewhere else in the cabin. Or that she hadn't managed to sweep away the red imprints of her combat boots on the way out.

"Well, there's more to process," Ron said.

"Yeah? What else could there be?"

"The state guys found a plat of survey at the cabin that looks like a map of the burial grounds for several women who went missing in 1979. All the women who were suspected to have been abducted by Thomas Mitchell."

"Sweet Jesus," Lane said.

"Sounds like he abducted them from Chicago, killed them, and then buried them behind his uncle's cabin. When the uncle died, he willed the place to his nephew. Son of a bitch probably knew what Thomas was doing all along."

Rory shook her head. "I don't know what to say."

"My guys will be part of the investigation, since the victims were from Chicago. Cook County Sheriff's Office as well."

"Makes sense," Rory said.

"Say, Gray, when were you last out at Starved Rock?"

Rory looked at Ron. "Uh, you know, the other morning. When Lane and I dropped him off."

"Doc?" Ron asked. "That the last time you were there?"

"Yeah," Lane said. "Why? What's up?"

"Just crossing my *t*'s. The LaSalle County guys are bound to ask. Just giving you two a heads-up. Since you were at the cabin, they'll probably ask to talk with you."

"Sure," Lane said.

Rory nodded. "Of course."

A glowing log popped in the fireplace—a loud crack that caught everyone's attention. Rory looked for the first time at the spot where she had burned her clothing a few hours earlier. A muscle in her neck twitched when she saw the remnants of one of her combat boots sitting on top of the ashes. It was the front half—toe and sole, about four inches of leather and rubber that the fire had failed to swallow. The boot stuck out from a glowing log as obvious as dead fish floating in an aquarium. It was covered in the red dust from the clay terrain of the Starved Rock cabin. She looked at the area in front of the hearth and noticed a faint patch of bloodred dust from where she had placed her boots while she waited for her clothes to burn.

In the split second after the log crackled, and during the time it took Rory to recognize her errors, she saw Lane stand from his chair and grab the poker.

"Whatever you need from us," Lane said, standing in front of the fireplace and blocking Ron's view of the logs. "We'll do whatever helps your guys."

He threw a few slivers of wood on top of the glowing logs, causing a stream of embers to puff from the orange glow. The logs caught immediately and rejuvenated the flames. Rory had a clear view into the fireplace, and watched as Lane put the tip of the poker to the remnant of her cherry-red boot and pushed it into the flames. It caught and melted away to nothing.

Lane threw another log on the fire and hung the poker with the other fireplace tools. Rory watched as Lane slid the throw rug, which lay on the hardwood in front of the hearth, to his left until it covered the smear of crimson.

"Needless to say," Ron continued, "we've got a goddamn mess on our hands. The media are going to have a field day with this. Being that he was your client, the state guys are going to want to talk with you, too, Rory. I'm heading there now, if you want to tag along."

Rory suddenly wanted Ron Davidson out of her house. And the last place on earth she wanted to go was back to that cabin.

"Yeah," she said, nodding her head. "Probably be a good idea."

Lane had sat back down in the chair across from her. He, too, was nodding. They made eye contact, staring at each other with volumes of wordless conversation happening between them.

"Probably a good idea," Lane repeated.

"Give me a minute?" Rory asked.

"Of course," Ron said. He stood from the couch. "I'll call and let my guys know we're on the way."

Ron walked to the front door, his phone already to his ear. Rory continued to look at Lane after Ron was gone. She wanted to talk with him, to tell him everything.

"You better get dressed," Lane said.

Ten minutes later, Rory found Ron on the front porch. He held up a finger as he finished his call. When he slipped his phone into his breast pocket a minute later, he did so with a quizzical look.

"You ready?" he asked.

"Yeah," Rory said, adjusting her glasses. "What's the matter?"

Ron looked down at her feet. "I've never seen you without your boots on."

Rory pulled her beanie cap down on her head. She'd found a

spare in her closet. She had a replacement for her coat, too, which was now buttoned up to her neck. But she had owned only one pair of boots. Ten years old, perfectly formed to her feet, and now melted to a pile of ash.

"Well," she said. "It's a mess out there. I don't want to ruin them."

She walked past her boss and climbed into the front seat of his unmarked cruiser.

CHAPTER 47
Peoria, Illinois, December 5, 2019

*T*WO ITEMS RESTED ON THE PASSENGER SEAT WAITING FOR DELIVERY. Rory pulled to a stop in the parking lot of the Harold Washington Library Center. She picked up one of the items—Camille Byrd's Kestner doll—and carried it into the lobby. She spotted Walter Byrd standing in nearly the exact spot where she had met him weeks before. When she approached, his stare was set firmly on the box in her hands. Rory adjusted her glasses.

"Sorry it took me so long to get this back to you."

"Is it finished?" Mr. Byrd asked.

Rory pointed to the doors of the library. "I'll show you how it turned out. I think you're going to be pleased with it."

They walked into the library and found an empty table in the back corner. Rory placed the box on the surface and opened the top. She carefully removed Camille's doll and handed it to him. Walter Byrd took the doll in his hands, swallowed hard, and ran his hand over the surface of its face. Rory saw the man's eyes glaze over with tears. He looked up at her.

"Thank you," he said. "It's truly remarkable."

Rory averted her eyes and nodded. "I wanted to let you know," she said, "that Camille's case is all I will be working on now. I've got one more thing to take care of, and then all my attention will be on your daughter."

Mr. Byrd looked up from the doll. "Thank you," he said again.

Rory wanted to tell the man that his daughter had helped her in ways that were unimaginable. They were unexplainable as well, and no one would understand how the soul of a dead girl who waited for Rory's help had pushed her to the precipice of her epiphany. So, instead, she said, "I feel a connection to Camille, and a need to help her. I promise I will."

She turned and walked out of the library, leaving Camille Byrd's father holding the now-flawless restoration of his child's doll. Outside, she headed to her car to deliver the second item that waited on her front seat.

She drove the long, straight country road as the barren cornfields blurred past in her peripheral vision. It was late afternoon and the sun was approaching the horizon, sitting out in front of her on the flat landscape. The sky was cloudless, melting from cotton blue to a deep shade of salmon as the day fell away.

The body of every woman who went missing in 1979 had been located behind the cabin in Starved Rock. The identities had been made via dental records, and the victims' families had finally found closure. Sadly, many of the women's family members had passed before the discovery. Most of the parents had died without knowing for certain the fate of their daughters. But their siblings were living and many were present at the press conference when Detective Davidson explained the discovery to the world. The news media covered the story at a frantic pace. Thomas Mitchell, the events of the summer of 1979, and the tragic discovery at the cabin in Starved Rock forty years later would forever be folklore for true-crime junkies. It was sure to be revisited at some point when a filmmaker decided to create a documentary about the case. When that happened, Rory wanted no one knocking on her door and asking questions. She wanted only to be a small footnote in the Thomas Mitchell saga, the attorney who briefly represented him during his parole. She didn't even want that mentioned, but she knew there was no way around it. What she desperately sought was to hide the truth. The truth about Angela Mitchell, her escape to Greta's farmhouse, and the child she bore before she died. A child whose blood ran thick with Thomas Mitchell's DNA.

For Christ's sake, Rory thought, *what a field day the nuts on the Internet would have with all that.*

It was no wonder the people who loved her most took such extraordinary measures to bury the secrets of the past. Rory planned to do all she could to keep them underground. She knew it would take effort. People would continue to dig. There was a buzzing conversation, mostly relegated to chat rooms and Reddit threads, about one victim whose body had not been found buried at Thomas Mitchell's cabin. That of his wife, Angela—the woman who had started her own investigation in 1979 and had become the nucleus of The Thief's downfall.

One phase of the public's conversation fed into the deep sympathy that since Angela's remains had not been unearthed, and now that Thomas Mitchell was gone, the whereabouts of her body would forever stay a mystery. The other dialogue was conspiratorial, with theorists suggesting that there was a simple explanation for why her body was not found at the Starved Rock cabin: Angela Mitchell was still alive. Conspiracy theories always trumped sympathy, and over the past month this discourse became louder and louder until it dominated the conversation. True-crime buffs jumped on the bandwagon to claim that Angela Mitchell was out there somewhere. They promised to keep searching for her.

As Rory drove the lonely country road, though, she knew the truth. She finally understood it all. Not only had she reconstructed Angela's death, but she had pieced together her own childhood. The missing fragments came together in a way that both shocked and settled Rory's soul. It was a reconstruction that had taken a lifetime to assemble. Careful deliberation and months of searching told her she was the only one left who knew the truth, and she had no intention of sharing her knowledge with the world.

She had briefly considered confiding in Ron Davidson, telling him everything. She should have, probably. But the repercussions were too unpredictable. If she confessed to Ron, she feared smart people would start asking questions, and if put onto a scent, investigators would start sniffing. If one of them began to dig the way Rory had dug, she worried they'd find the same lineage she unearthed. It was a secret Rory planned to carry to her grave.

The only people who knew the truth were gone, and she was satisfied that wherever they were now, somewhere off in the by-and-by, they were watching her as she made this final journey. They were proud of her. A deep sense of peace came to her as she drove. It was a reconciliation never before experienced that allowed her to feel free and alive, liberated somehow. She had made her choice, and she was comfortable with it.

The long road came to a T, where Rory turned left. A moment later, the farmhouse appeared before her. She hadn't been here in some time. Aunt Greta had moved to the nursing home several years before, and until today, Rory never had reason to return. As soon as she saw the old farmhouse, though, with its blue painted cedar and wraparound porch, she realized how much she missed it. Her memories transported her to the summers she spent there as a child.

With her mind flooded by flashbacks, Rory turned up the gravel driveway. She parked at the front, where the gravel ended and the never-ending expanse of grass began. A moment passed as she waited for anyone to appear from inside. She wasn't sure how she would proceed if the new owners were home. But what she needed to do could not wait. The pull in her chest was too strong to ignore. After a few minutes, the farmhouse stayed still and quiet in the fading light of dusk, silhouetted by the lavender horizon. Rory looked at herself in the rearview mirror. Even during the long ride out to the country, she kept her thick plastic glasses on her face, and the beanie cap slung low on her forehead. She reached up and pulled them off. Today, of all times, she couldn't hide. Didn't want to hide. Didn't need to.

She dropped her hat and glasses on the passenger seat, and picked up the other item that had made the trip with her. She opened the door and climbed out into the evening. She walked to the side of the farmhouse and into the backyard. The rear porch was to her left, and she remembered in vivid detail the night when she was ten years old, when the buzzing in her chest had pulled her out of bed and into this field during the middle of the night. She remembered the smoky glow of the moon and the far-off thunderstorm that ignited the horizon with intermittent pulses of lightning. Tonight the fading sun burned lilac on the horizon, the sky above a dark cobalt.

Rory found the low, two-tiered stable fence that ran the length of the property. She followed it again now, the same way she had the night the amazing calm had come over her. Nearly thirty years later and Rory finally understood the meaning of that night. The lure in her chest, the magnetism that had pulled her, and the sense of peace that had washed over her when she had lifted that rose and had inhaled the sweetness of its scent.

Rory followed the fence to the back edge of the property, where it turned at a ninety-degree angle and ran off to her left. Once she arrived at the corner of the prairie, Rory looked down at the ground. The only other time in her life when she stood in this spot, she had found the flowers she always watched Aunt Greta pick from the garden. The ones she helped bundle.

The conspiracy theorists could have their chat rooms and threads. They could keep their wild and uneducated ideas about Angela Mitchell and where she was today. None would ever know the truth. None would ever find her. Angela hadn't wanted to be found forty years ago, and she didn't want to be found today. Rory lifted the item she had carried with her from the car—a bouquet of roses tied in a tight bundle. She placed them to her nose, closed her eyes, and took in their sweet scent. Then she crouched down and laid them on the ground.

ACKNOWLEDGMENTS

A big thank you to the following people:

The entire clan at Kensington Publishing, who continue to support my novels in ways that stun me. Especially John Scognamiglio, who has fought for me more times than he lets me know.

Marlene Stringer, agent and friend, who is always two steps ahead of me.

Amy Donlea, who is the glue that holds our family together. Without you my life would be in so many scattered pieces that not even Rory Moore could put it back together.

Abby and Nolan, for being my biggest supporters, for constantly asking to read my books (you're still not old enough), and for all the wild ideas for future novels. Keep 'em coming!

Mary Murphy, for trying so hard to have coherent conversations with me about completely incoherent ideas for a manuscript that was only half written when I started bothering you for help.

Chris Murphy, for suggestions on the final draft, and for setting me straight on Dark Lord stout. We should probably share one soon.

Rich Hills, for the idea. Although I'm sure I distorted and perverted your original suggestion.

Mike Chmelar and Jill Barnum for sharing your lawyering knowledge in order to help me spring a serial killer from jail.

Thomas Hargrove, founder and chairman of the real Murder Accountability Project, for taking my calls and explaining what you do.

And to all the readers who keep buying my books. I'm forever grateful.

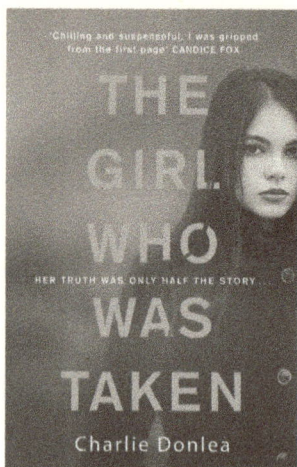

THE GIRL WHO WAS TAKEN

Charlie Donlea

Her truth is only half the story . . .

Megan McDonald is a high school senior when she disappears from the small town of Emerson Bay. Miraculously, after two weeks held captive, she escapes from a bunker hidden deep in the woods.

Now, one year on, Megan is a national celebrity thanks to her bestselling book, *Missing*. It's an inspiring story – except for one inconvenient detail.

There was a second girl who was taken. Her classmate Nicole Cutty.

Livia Cutty is a forensic pathologist. Every time a Jane Doe arrives at the morgue she wonders if it's her missing sister. However, it's the body of a young man, an apparent suicide, that finally offers the first clue to Nicole's fate. So Livia reaches out to Megan for help.

But Megan knows more than she's revealed. Flashes of memory are coming together – and they are pointing to something darker and more monstrous than anything her chilling memoir describes.

'Chilling and suspenseful. I was gripped from the first page'
Candice Fox, bestselling author of *Crimson Lake*

AVAILABLE NOW

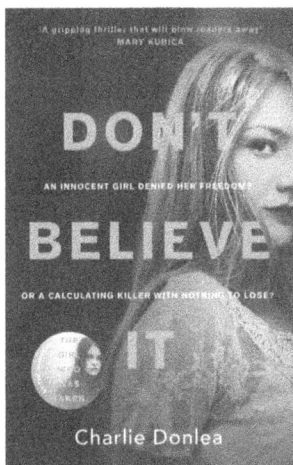

DON'T BELIEVE IT

Charlie Donlea

An innocent girl denied her freedom? Or a calculating killer with nothing to lose?

The Girl of Sugar Beach is about to become the most watched documentary in television history. The ten-part true-crime serial centers on the burning question: did Grace Sebold really murder her boyfriend, or is she the victim of a shocking miscarriage of justice?

For Grace has spent the last ten years in prison, and now she's reaching out to filmmaker Sidney Ryan in a final, desperate attempt to prove her innocence.

As the first episodes go to air, exposing startling new evidence and additional suspects, the series quickly becomes a ratings smash – and Sidney a celebrity in her own right.

Yet by delving deeper into Grace's past, Sidney is uncovering layer after layer of deception. And as she edges closer to the real heart of the story, she must decide if finding the truth is worth risking her newfound fame, her career . . . even her life.

'A perfectly executed and entirely satisfying read, *Don't Believe It* is a gripping thriller that will blow readers away, from the first page right up to the very last words. Charlie Donlea's best book yet!'
Mary Kubica, author of *Pretty Baby* and *The Good Girl*

AVAILABLE NOW

Dawn G

Grave

Intent

Copyright material © All rights reserved

Chapter 1.

Thunder clouds hung in the sky as sweat dripped down Dawn's back. Her tank top clung to her, limp and soggy.

She slid the long length of rough-sawn weatherboard down the saw bench, retrieved the pencil from behind her ear, adjusted the lamp light and ran the measuring tape along the surface of the board. Scratching a mark, she slipped the pencil back and let the tape retract with a thud.

Pulling her earmuffs on, she fired up the saw and smiled as the blade slid through the aged timber, sending sawdust flying to the back of the blade. The scent of dried hardwood tickled her nose.

A month ago, she'd have done anything not to return to her family home. It held dark memories she'd rather forget. But as she glanced at the old rusty bike hanging from the ceiling joists, and recalled learning to ride, she thought of her father in a new light.

Sighing, she removed her ear protection, lifted the board and turned – halting as the end of the timber nearly knocked a tall figure from his feet.

He dodged aside, then studied her makeshift workshop, hidden beneath the old Queenslander. Nodding, he turned to her looking mildly impressed.

'You've been busy.'

Dawn focussed on the broad chest, twinkling blue eyes and top-shelf suit in front of her, then mirrored his expression.

'Detective Ryan. You snuck up on me. You're lucky I didn't knock you on your arse.'

He crossed his arms and watched her from a safer distance, leaning against the slatted wall inside the entrance.

'I tried to get your attention, but you were making a lot of noise.'

Dawn carried the board past him, out into the humid air beyond. The threat of tropical rain loomed overhead.

'The place needed sprucing up. I'm on long service leave but I don't have much cash and my sister definitely hasn't got any to spare. *And*, I'm not afraid of a little hard work.'

'I could lend you a few dollars, if it helps.'

Dawn could see Detective Ryan's offer was legitimate. What she wasn't sure of was why he had cash to burn.

When they met last month, she'd been wrapped up in finding her sister, but in hindsight, she knew his accommodation overlooking the Endeavour River inlet and the Ralph Lauren suit he now wore, were way above his Queensland Police Service pay grade.

Dawn carried the board toward the front of the house and angled it against an A-framed ladder.

'I'm doing okay, thanks. Kind of enjoying the challenge.'

The detective followed.

'A far cry from catching bad guys.'

'That's for sure.'

She felt his eyes on her back as she climbed the staircase. Dragging the board over the ladder, she placed it against the wall and clamped it into a jig to hold it in place. Reaching for the nail gun, she fired a shot to keep it in place.

The echo resonated through the rustling gums and mango trees, heavy with ripening fruit.

'Stairs look a bit more solid since I was last here,' Ryan spoke between nail gun shots.

Dawn crossed to the ladder, climbed to the top and lifted the board in place. Lining up the next shot, she glanced his way.

'Yep. I've had over a month to get some jobs done. Tourist season is over. Sergeant Martin hasn't needed any consulting services. Not that I expected he would. It's not exactly a done thing.'

'He might now.'

Dawn fired the nail, then turned to see a sparkle in the detective's eyes. She thought he was there for a social visit. But why would he be? Ryan was a Queensland detective based in Cairns and although they spent a lot of time together when he was last in town, most of it was because her sister Lisa was missing.

'What have you got?'

Dawn stepped down from the ladder, dragging the compressor air hose back into her workshop. A loud crack sounded as she disconnected the nail gun and placed it in a moulded plastic box.

Ryan followed her once more.

'A body.'

Dawn stowed the case under the workbench and considered under what circumstances she'd be asked to consult on a suspicious death in Queensland.

'You know when I offered to consult for the local police, I didn't really expect anyone to take me up on it. I'm officially employed with South Australian Police, and out of my jurisdiction. Sure, I could do with the extra money to fix this old girl up, but...'

She waved her hand at the worn siding and skewed windows. 'I'm just another detective, so unless this is linked with South Australia, SAPOL won't want me on this. Or is this a joint operation?'

Dawn got away with insisting on consulting on the previous case because her sister was missing, and Detective Ryan showed her some professional courtesy—after it became clear she wasn't leaving it alone.

But consulting between state police agencies only happened if a case crossed state borders.

'No. Not at this stage, but I've requested your help on the case, and Sergeant Martin has agreed.'

Ryan crossed his arms, back hard against the slatted wall as he waited for a reaction.

She folded the ladder and carried it inside—secretly glad he didn't offer to help her. As she glanced at the understorey, memories flooded her mind. Not all of them were happy, but she was working through them.

Taking on a case could take her time away from her sister and the niece she never knew existed. Dawn was enjoying being in Abby's life. Did she want to be working on a case right now?

Of course she did. Being back with her sister was fun. Repairing her family home after years of neglect was fulfilling, but her work…

Dawn ushered him outside, dragged the slatted doors closed and slid the bolt across.

'Details.'

Ryan failed to hide his grin.

'Female. Forensic techs are on scene, but preliminary exam says under twenty-five.'

Dawn ascended the stairs two at a time. Ryan right behind her.

'Cause of death?'

'Hard to tell. Remains have been mauled by a croc.'

Dawn halted as her feet hit the wide, wrap-around veranda and turned to Ryan.

'Croc? You don't think the croc killed her then?'

'Body floated to the surface out at Keatings Lagoon Conservation Park. Crocs are usually pretty efficient at stowing their kills under heavy logs until they decompose. Could be a tourist. Maybe a backpacker who went for a swim and got taken, but …'

'You're not buying it.'

The screen door groaned as Dawn opened it and strode down the worn, flaking timber floor. Another project on her *to-do* list.

Ryan followed her inside.

'There's a reason the warning signs have the word "*Achtung*" on them. Germans have been known to ignore the No Swimming signs from time to time, but the Wetlands are conservation and very obviously croc-infested. They'd have to be a bloody moron.'

It wasn't exactly an answer, but Ryan was right. A local conservation area made out of low-lying marshland would hardly look like an inviting place for a quick dip.

'Who found the body?' Dawn asked as she turned the kitchen sink tap on, pumped soap onto her hands and scrubbed the dirt and sawdust away.

Ryan tossed her a handtowel.

'Someone else who thought you should be in on the case.'

'Michael?'

'Yep. Ranger Michael is on the case.'

Ryan's tone made Dawn roll her eyes. During the investigation into her sister's disappearance, he never stopped having a dig at the Indigenous ranger's Dudley-Do-Right attitude. It turned out, it wasn't an act. Michael *was* a nice guy, with a good heart.

Dawn opened her bedroom door. Ryan stepped up to follow her. Turning, she placed a hand on his broad chest.

He grinned.

'I just need to get changed.'

'And.'

'And you can wait out here.'

Dawn shoved him back into the hallway and slammed the door. There was an obvious attraction between them, and Dawn wasn't against a quick fling, but there were other reasons to keep detective Ryan out of her room.

She drew a slow breath and let it out as she scanned the pinboard behind the door. Her brother's photo was faded and tattered at the edges. There weren't many to choose from unless you counted the crime scene photos from the day he died.

She knew she couldn't face those day after day.

Staring back at her, were three young, cheeky smiles. Lisa, Fraser and her, huddled in front of the Christmas tree back when life was simple. Back before her mother disappeared. Back before Fraser died of supposed suicide. Back when Dawn held no tortured memories.

The rest of the board was covered in reports, suspect photos and large question marks.

She tapped his face in the photo, then suppressed rising emotions.

'Sorry Fraser. I'll get back to you. I promise. But I need to help Detective Ryan find out who this woman is, so we can notify her family, and maybe catch her killer.'

Chapter 2

The stifling humidity did nothing to deter the flies and mosquitoes. Dawn swatted a bug as she accepted the can of bug repellent Detective Ryan offered. Spraying her exposed arms, her hair, even the tight-fitting areas of her clothing, left a choking scent hanging in the air.

'That stuff stinks.' Dawn waved the scent away as she handed the spray back. 'You should really use something less toxic you know.'

'How about you bring your own next time?' he huffed, before tossing the can onto the back seat of his Ford Mustang. The vehicle didn't surprise her. Ryan's persona oozed muscle car, but this one was police issue.

'How'd you score this?'

She waved at the unmarked police vehicle, aware the grill lit up with blue and red lights at the touch of a button.

'I know a few people,' he grinned. 'Ford and Holden production is due to end soon. The government has finally decided they can't keep bailing out the car companies, so New South Wales and Queensland police are trialling new high-speed highway patrol models.'

'And you scored yourself a demo?'

Ryan led the way along the boardwalk.

'Yep.'

Dawn followed, warily studying her surroundings. White and purple water lilies floated in the large pond, providing ideal cover for lurking crocs. Trees bordered the water's edge and grew down into the waterline, shading the lagoon and leeching tannin into the water. The still, mirror-like surface reflected the looming thunder clouds above.

'You know I lived in Cooktown for seventeen years and never came out here.'

Ryan swatted a mozzie hard on his arm. 'Really! I can't understand why not.'

Dawn chuckled as she ducked under an overhanging branch.

'I'm guessing it's beautiful out here in winter.'

A bug crawled around her neck, seemingly impervious to the bug spray. As she chased it down the front of her tank top, she realised it was probably always insect infested out here.

Ryan raised an eyebrow as her hand plunged down her cleavage. She scowled, retrieved the beetle and presented it on her palm as if in defence of her actions.

He chuckled, then accepted a pair of gloves from Constable Reynolds, whose brown eyes twinkled with mirth as she handed Dawn a pair of gloves.

'Good to see you out here Reynolds.'

When Dawn first met the young constable, she was relegated to desk duty by the station's Senior Constable.

'I've got you to thank for that Detective.'

'Call me Dawn.'

'Never gonna happen on duty Detective.'

The woman smiled. Her eyes softer than the first time Dawn met her. The young constable waved her on.

Ryan snapped on a glove as he led her to the scene.

'We've run all the missing persons cases.'

'Anything pop?' Dawn asked.

'We have a recent one that might fit.'

They trudged down a narrow, lightly used trail making conversation difficult. Ryan vaulted over a log, then held out his hand to help her. She ignored him, stepped over and nodded for him to lead on. He grinned, then turned his back to her.

She followed, the bush growing denser and forcing them closer to the water's edge. Dawn's heartrate rose a notch as she tried not to think about the tall grass full of snakes or the dark, deep water where crocodiles stalked, hidden between the lilies, ready to lunge out of nowhere and drag their next victim into the renowned Death Roll.

Ryan's voice dragged her back to reality as they entered a wide clearing bustling with activity.

'A young woman went missing while walking her dog on Newell Beach, north of Port Douglas last Thursday. Aged twenty-four.'

'Age fits.' A muffled voice spoke from behind a surgical mask. 'We'll know more once the coroner approves an autopsy. Keep back behind the tape Ryan.'

The man waved—his eyes still focussed on the clump of flesh in front of him. This wasn't Dawn's first body. And definitely not her first floater, but the gnawed flesh, exposed bone and white, pasty appearance wasn't easy to look at.

Ryan pointed to the man hovering over the body.

'Detective Grave, meet Doctor Greg Mayfield, one of our on-call pathologists.

Cheerful hazel eyes peered over the mask as the doctor waved his gloved hand.

'I'd shake your hand…'

'All good.' Dawn flashed a grin. 'Do you have any idea of cause of death, Doctor?'

'Call me Greg. And no. I don't guess on scene. We don't even have all the body parts yet. I reckon the croc had a nibble before she floated. But…'

A voice interrupted.

'This isn't the primary crime scene, so this could be Jane Nichols.'

A stocky woman wearing overalls and shoe protectors, approached carrying her camera around her neck. Her dark brown, almost black eyes fixed on Dawn through goggles, her hand outstretched.

'Hi, I'm Tammy Gleeson.'

Dawn reached to shake, but the woman snatched the hand back, waggling her gloved finger in Dawn's face.

'Can't cross-contaminate the scene.'

Dawn scolded herself for being duped, but a glint in Tammy's eyes said she was only testing the new face and having a dig.

Dawn nodded, an unsaid *'challenge accepted'*.

'Tammy is our lead Forensic Investigator,' Ryan explained. 'Good at her job, but a major pain in the arse.'

'Pleased to meet you.' Dawn's tone said she could tell.

The woman glanced at Ryan with a raised eyebrow, then returned her gaze to Dawn.

'And you are?'

Dawn opened her mouth, but Ryan spoke for her.

'Consulting Detective Dawn Grave.'

The woman rolled her eyes, then gave Ryan a knowing look.

'Grave has extensive local knowledge.'

Ryan sounded defensive. Tammy wasn't buying it. Dawn still didn't understand why she was there but was glad to be out of the house and in the field.

Tammy waved like she was ignoring Ryan's comment.

'Whatever. Do you want to know what I've found?'

Ryan grinned. Tammy continued with a lofty tone.

'I've found nothing to indicate this is our primary crime scene.'

With a nod, she indicated the narrow dirt track they entered through and the low native grass and heavily treed waterline.

'There's no blood anywhere. No crushed foliage to indicate a struggle. No seminal fluids or discarded condoms. Not even a piece of rubbish or torn clothing here.'

Dawn thought about Michael.

'Maybe this is where the ranger pulled the body out of the water?'

'It's possible. You'll have to read his statement I guess,' Tammy shrugged.

Ryan pointed to the end of the boardwalk across the other side of the clearing.

'What about in the gazebo over there?'

A structure like a hut hung out over the water.

Dawn turned and began walking toward it.

'Ryan's right. That would be the perfect place to toss the body over.'

'I've brushed it. There are a thousand sets of prints. Everyone must come here and hang on to the railing. There's no blood. Just a load of graffiti. But you're probably right about it being our dump site.'

Dawn turned back to see Tammy holding a bag containing yellow fibres. Ryan scrutinised it. Dawn watched his face crease as his eyes studied the bag, then glanced back toward the shore to see the body being placed onto a heavy-duty plastic bag.

Tammy slipped the evidence bag into her jacket pocket.

'Looks like she went in over the railing. Caught a bit of fabric from her clothing on the way.' She turned and strode away. Her voice echoing across the lake as she spoke without turning. 'I'll let you know if I find anything else useful.'

The woman's hand gave a quick, royal wave over her head. Dawn grinned at the brush off.

'It could be an accident,' she offered as Ryan drew alongside.

'Not if it's Jane Nichols' body.'

'Maybe she ran away and hooked up with someone up this way and things went bad.'

Dawn knew she was playing devil's advocate, but a good investigation needed to take all possible scenarios into account.

'And leave her dog tied up to a park bench?'

'Maybe not.'

Dawn slipped shoe covers on and held a mask to her face as she strode down the boardwalk to the hut. Turning, she caught Ryan's eye.

'Is this dump site significant then? Or just a quiet place to get rid of evidence? Why bring the victim here? Especially if it *is* Jane Nichols.'

'With so many fingerprints and DNA samples, we won't be able to isolate our killer. So does it really matter?'

'It does if this place means something to a killer.'

Chapter 3

Dawn glanced out from the gazebo over the water as clouds continued to build overhead. Her mind was tossing over why anyone would dump a body out here, if their victim was killed near Port Douglas, nearly three hours away.

The last case they worked on together was personal for her. Thankfully, her sister was safe, but two young women were dead, and the murderer wasn't exactly a serial killer, but he certainly liked using the same dump site.

Ryan voiced what she was thinking.

'You're thinking like Archer Point?'

Dawn nodded and tried not to think about how her mother's body remained out there all alone. Knowing her mum was murdered, and catching her killer, gave Dawn some closure. But her mother's unrecovered body was a lingering reminder of all the unresolved issues in her past.

'I'm not saying there are more murders. I bloody hope there aren't, but why here?'

'Convenient.'

'You said she disappeared from Newell Beach. So why here? And no scuffle. I think she might have come out here willingly.'

Dawn turned slowly, taking in the marshy billabong edges, the boarded walkway leading to the gazebo, the thin, winding trail they took to get there.

Ryan watched her, a grin splitting his lips.

'This is why I wanted you on the case.'

'I thought you just loved my magnetic personality.'

Dawn chuckled. Ryan didn't.

'You think outside the box.'

Ryan's expression was serious.

Dawn let her thoughts manifest a moment.

'He couldn't have carried her this far, even if he were a big guy.'

'I know a few who could.'

Ryan was right. And Tammy Gleeson said there was no sign of a struggle, but her instincts were telling her this wasn't a random location. If Jane Nichols disappeared from Newell Beach, there was no reason to bring her here unless this location meant something to the killer or the victim.

'I could be wrong.' Her tone said she didn't think so. 'Maybe there was more than one person. That could explain the lack of physical evidence on the dump site, but if two people carried her along this narrow track, there'd be signs.' Dawn scanned the deep, dark water as she peered over the railing. 'Was there anything at Newell Beach to indicate she died there?'

Ryan chewed his lip.

'Not that we found.'

'Then it makes sense she died here.'

'But the techs, and the pathologist...'

'Detectives!' a voice called out. Dawn and Ryan turned to see Doctor Mayfield waving them back toward the body.

Ryan was first back to the scene.

'I think you should see this.' The pathologist glanced up. 'This is off the record, but it might help with your investigation.'

He pried open the eyelid with an instrument Dawn didn't recognise.

'Eyes take longer than most parts of the body to deteriorate. A post-mortem will give us more corroborating evidence, but I think your victim died of asphyxiation.'

'Strangled?' Ryan asked, then glanced at Dawn.

'Not necessarily. I'll check the hyoid bone and the tissue for bruising which might confirm strangulation, but for now, I can confirm her eyes show signs of petechial haemorrhaging.'

'She died here Ryan. I'm sure of it.'

'Then we need to confirm ID as soon as possible Greg,' Ryan said.

'DNA tests are taking weeks right now because the lab has a backlog.'

'They always have a backlog,' Ryan huffed.

'Can't argue with that.' The doctor began packing up his equipment.

'Greg, if this is Jane Nichols' body, it's high-profile mate. I think we can get it moved up the line.'

The pathologist zipped the bag and nodded to Constable Reynolds and two forensic techs in overalls before turning back to Ryan.

'I know it's all over the papers. Isn't that just media trying to get the word out?'

The body was lifted and carried to a waiting stretcher. Dawn stifled a shiver as her mind filled with memories of visiting the morgue to ID what could have been her sister's body.

Ryan sighed.

'Don't you read the paper?' Ryan didn't wait for an answer. 'Jane Nichols is Minister Tenneson's stepdaughter and if this is her, we're going to have one very annoyed politician publicly pressing us to find a killer.'

Greg whistled. Tammy turned with a frown, camera hovering mid-air.

'Keep that thought to yourself until we have a positive ID then, because if you get Tyson Tenneson involved and it's not his stepdaughter, then you are going to wish you never caught this case.'

For the first time since Dawn met Tammy, she seemed seriously concerned. It wasn't a flippant remark.

Ryan shoved his hands in his pockets. 'I'm not afraid of Tenneson.'

He might not be afraid, but Dawn couldn't help but wonder if there was history between him and Tenneson.

'Did you know his stepdaughter?' Dawn asked the question before she could stop herself.

Ryan slipped her a side-eye and ignored the comment.

'Just keep digging Gleeson. If our victim died somewhere here, there must be more evidence.'

Ryan turned and strode away. Dawn watched Tammy Gleeson huff, spin and carry on combing the scene. The pathologist rose with a groan, pulled his mask down and grinned over a thick, black moustache, curled at the tips like a cartoon villain.

Dawn glanced at Ryan stomping through the undergrowth and turned to the doctor.

'Does he have history with the Nichols family?'

'I don't know, but I do know he's got history with Tenneson.'

'Care to elaborate?' Dawn whispered. The pathologist opened his mouth.

'Are you coming Grave?' Ryan's voice said it wasn't a question.

Greg shrugged, then winked. 'See you around Detective.'

She suppressed a grin. He was an attractive guy, making him the ideal uncomplicated one-night-stand she preferred. The thought was appealing. But as she watched Ryan's retreating back, she thought about the past month since they worked together, and suddenly realised she'd missed working with him.

'You never know Greg.'

She turned and quickened her step to catch Ryan.

Chapter 4

Dawn clipped on her seatbelt. 'What's with you and Tenneson?'

She waited as Ryan started the car, revved the motor and ignored her as he slipped the vehicle into reverse. The V6 motor growled, matching Ryan's scowl.

He broke his sulky silence as the car lunged forward, kicking up gravel in its wake.

'If it's Jane, we should be able to get dental records and confirm from there.'

His tone was personal, not like a cop using a victim's first name in passing. She tried to refocus him on staying professional.

'Jane?'

'Until we know, we need to treat this *victim* as a new case. We'll check CCTV footage in the area. Check for any reports of missing persons from the local accommodation places.'

Ryan scanned his watch.

'Maybe an early lunch at the Top Pub? We can ask your friends if they know of anyone missing?'

Ryan steered the car from the carpark onto the main road. Dawn wondered if it was the right time to quiz him over his relationship with their possible victim. She decided to leave it until they got a positive ID.

'Do you want me to call Sergeant Martin and ask for Constable Jamison and the Senior to canvas the local backpackers and Air BnBs?'

'I think it's a waste of time, but we need to cover all bases. Give them a call.'

'You think it's Jane Nichols? Was there anything on the victim you recognised?'

Ryan's penetrating gaze swung her way for a second, then fixed back on the road without a word.

'What? You used her first name. You know her stepdad?'

Ryan's thumbs tapped the steering wheel as his chest rose and his jaw clenched.

'I didn't sleep with the woman if that's where you're going.'

'If you don't share shit, how am I supposed to not go there?' Dawn huffed. A sly grin crossed Ryan's lips.

'A bit jealous?'

'Stuff off. I'm doing the job you asked me to do.'

Dawn crossed her arms over her chest and tried not to pout.

Ryan's knuckles relaxed on the wheel as he finally sat back into the seat.

'I've met Jane Nichols a number of times. She worked in Tenneson's office from time to time, but she was a bit of a new age thinker, and they went their separate ways a while ago.'

'So she didn't get along with her stepdad?'

'No one gets along with her stepdad.'

'You mean you don't.'

Dawn dialled the station as Ryan easily found an angle park outside the pub and pulled in. The street was quiet, the town emptying as travellers headed south to escape the heavy humidity and rain of the brewing Far North Queensland wet season.

Finding a missing tourist would be easier with the town population shrinking by the day.

'No comment.'

'Very diplomatic of you.'

He ignored the jibe, opened his door and stepped out of the car as the call connected. Dawn recognised the voice.

'Jamison. It's Detective Dawn Grave. Apparently, I'm working this wetlands case with Ryan and we need a search for any missing persons in the area matching our victim. Reynolds has the details.

'Hello to you too Detective.'

'Sorry Jamison. You're right. How are you going?'

Dawn noticed Ryan leaning impatiently against the bonnet as she made idle conversation with the local constable. She didn't know him well, but when she worked with him on her sister's case, he seemed polite and maybe a little sensitive.

'I'll chase it up, but nothing's come in recently.'

'Thanks Jamison. Can you canvas all the backpackers and accommodation in the area? We'll be down the station after lunch.'

'Will do. See you then.'

Dawn hung up and glanced over to see Ryan push away from the car.

'You coming?'

Dawn stepped out, slammed the door and strode off toward the pub. Ryan was being deliberately evasive and he'd pulled her into this case for a reason. Was it because of his connection with Jane Nichols and Tenneson? Was he expecting to have issues?

'Ben.'

Dawn waved as she entered the pub through the beer garden. Humid air hung in the still, outdoor dining space, making Dawn a little homesick for her apartment in Adelaide. She was beginning to miss the warm spring days and cool nights.

'Dawn.' The publican grinned, then waved a tattooed arm as he spotted Ryan sulking behind her. 'Detective. Nice to see you again.'

'Good to see you too.'

Ryan reached for a menu and browsed, obviously leaving Dawn to ask the questions.

'Busy still?'

She started with the usual pleasantries.

'Nah. It's been a wet year already and doesn't look like letting up anytime soon. Tourists are bugging out earlier than usual. The Cape is pretty hard going now, and the fishing isn't so crash hot in the pouring rain. Plus, the crocs are getting active. Some poor bugger was snatched from the Annan River last week.'

'I've been busy on the house. Haven't paid much attention to the news. Did they find him?'

'Yep. In three different crocs.'

Dawn scrunched her nose, deciding to stick with the weather. It was a safer subject, especially after traipsing through the bush near crocodile infested waters.

'It is warming up and getting wet, that's for sure.'

Dawn lifted her shirt away from her body, aware sweat was pooling under her bra band.

'What can I get you?'

'Actually, before we order, just wondering… have you had any tourists, or backpackers disappear unexpectedly?'

Ben glanced from her to Ryan and smiled.

'Thought you might have been here for a social visit Detective.'

Ryan kept his eyes on the menu.

'Afraid not.'

Dawn cleared her throat.

'Detective Ryan has caught a case and he's asked me to give him a hand. Anyone missing Ben?'

The publican nodded knowingly at her obvious shift in conversation.

'Not that I know of. Like I said. It's been pretty quiet since last month's early storm. The threat of a cyclone usually clears the place quickly enough. The Return Servicemen's Club is *still* waiting for a new roof. Getting tradies up this way is like pulling teeth.'

'Tell me about it.'

'Yeah, how's the reno going?'

'Slowly Ben. Very slowly.'

Dawn scanned the menu.

'What can I get you Grave?' Ryan pulled out his credit card. 'I'll expense this one on the Queensland Police Service.'

'Chicken salad and a cappuccino thanks.'

'What, no wine?'

'I'm on duty.'

'No. *I'm* on duty. You're consulting.'

Ryan placed the menu on the long bar as Ben wiped a wet spot on the glossy timber.

'Just coffee thanks,' Dawn insisted.

'You heard the lady. I'll have cola, and a fisherman's basket thanks mate.'

Dawn waited for Ryan to pay, then turned and crossed the dining area to a tall wooden table, with a rugged live edge and high-gloss finish. Her phone buzzed in her pocket as she slid onto a worn vinyl-topped stool.

Retrieving the phone, she recognised the station number and answered out of habit.

'Detective Grave.'

'Dawn. Glad to have you onboard for this one.'

'Honestly didn't expect an invite Ross, but it's appreciated. What you got?'

'Nothing matching our victim. I've got Jamison and Reynolds canvassing hostels and accommodation spots for missing girls and the Senior is chasing down CCTV footage around town. There are no cameras out at Keatings Lagoon, so no luck there.'

'Thanks Ross.'

'See you a bit later.'

'Will do.'

Dawn hung up.

'Sergeant Martin has the constables out canvassing, but there are no open missing persons cases matching our victim in this region. With not a lot of people in town, we are probably going to find ourselves pursuing the Nichols' case for now.'

'We'll wait and see if Jamison or Reynolds come up with something, but I figured it would be our next step.'

Ryan reached for a coaster and tapped it on its edge against the timber top. Dawn let the silence linger a moment before asking.

'So are you going to tell me about your history with Tenneson?'

'Sounds like you'll meet him soon enough.'

Ryan flipped his coaster over as Ben arrived with their drinks. Dawn studied his face—his eyes avoiding hers. Whatever the history was between Ryan and Tenneson, it was personal, and the tension in Dawn's stomach told her it was going to cause nothing but trouble.

Chapter 5

A tingle ran down Dawn's spine as she approached the front door of the local police station. A mix of memories flooded her mind—some good—like working to find Lisa and solving two murder cases with Ryan and the team last month.

But most were painful, vivid and nauseating memories of answering endless questions after finding her brother's body in the change rooms at the town swimming pool. Then there were the tense days of arguing with the then Constable Martin over Fraser's apparent suicide.

She got nowhere at the time. But now the case was being reviewed by the coroner. Even if they reopened the case, there were no leads. To keep her mind occupied, Dawn threw herself into fixing up the family Queenslander homestead and helping her sister raise her daughter. A little girl, born of a serial paedophile who was now behind bars.

Putting Abby's father away stilled some of Dawn's demons but it didn't stop her stomach from knotting as she stepped into the foyer of the station.

'Detectives.' Constable Reynolds' smile reached her brown eyes.

Ryan returned the grin and put on his charm.

'Looking good Reynolds. Like your hair that way.'

Reynolds smoothed her ponytail reflexively. Dawn agreed, the look was more relaxed, more confident than the severely tightened bun she wore when Dawn arrived in town.

'Sergeant in?' Dawn asked, her hand hovered on the door to the back offices.

'He is.'

Reynolds pressed a button and the door buzzed. Dawn held it open as Ryan passed through. Then glanced back to Reynolds.

'Did you get anywhere with missing persons?'

'Nothing. I'll let the boss brief you though. Wouldn't want to overstep my bounds.'

Dawn kept the door ajar with her butt.

'Senior Constable Constable still giving you crap?'

Ryan snorted at the Senior's last name. It was a standing joke—one Dawn never missed an opportunity to exploit.

Reynolds grinned.

'He's warming to me.'

'Good for you. I'm pretty certain he won't be so pleasant when he sees me though.'

Reynolds sniggered as Dawn let the door shut.

'What is it with you two anyway?' Ryan asked as they strode down the wide hallway, past the rear door to the Sergeant's office, an interview room on each side, and turned right.

'I honestly have no idea. He's been an arse since we first met.'

Dawn glanced into the empty staff room as they passed, then turned right again into a wide-open office area.

A bank of desks lined each side. A central walkway led to two offices with wide walls of glass. Sergeant Martin glanced up from his desk beyond the glass to the right. Holding a phone to his ear, he waved them forward, then hung up. Stepping around his desk, he met them outside his office door.

'Got a board up.' He smiled with enthusiasm as he pointed to a whiteboard mounted on a stand with wheels. 'Not much info yet though. Still waiting on a preliminary exam by the pathologist, but just got off the phone with Greg. He managed to put a rush on a dental match.'

'Jane Nichols?' Ryan asked, his tone flat.

Dawn studied his tense expression, trying to read him, but failed.

The sergeant strolled to the whiteboard, lifted a marker from the rail and scribbled a name next to the photo of the remains.

'It certainly is.'

Dawn glanced at the photo of the bloated body in situ but didn't let her gaze linger. Instead, she focussed on the investigation.

'She disappeared a week ago.' Dawn sat on the corner of the closest desk. 'Do they have any idea how long her body has been in the water?'

Martin slipped a photo from a folder in his hand and Blu-tacked it to the centre of the board next to the crime scene photo of the body.

'Nothing confirmed yet.'

Dawn studied the board, noting the soft smile and intelligent eyes of their victim. She was blonde, petite, and pretty. Turning, she met Ryan's eyes.

'We need to get back to the original scene. Were you on the case?'

Ryan's chest rose with a deep breath.

'No. I usually catch the regional cases.'

'You said that last time. What's with that?'

Dawn waited.

Ryan shrugged, then puffed out a breath.

'Look. Full disclosure here.'

Dawn hovered, expecting to finally find out what history Ryan and Tenneson shared.

'I don't think I'm going to be welcome on this case by the Nichols family.'

'Tough titties.'

Sergeant Martin scribbled a line across the top of the whiteboard and added a single line with the date *October 9th* and the words *disappeared from Newell Beach*. He then added another cross line on the end of the timeline with today's date, *October 16th*.

'The body was found here. So I'll be calling the shots. I want you and Grave on this one.'

Dawn frowned.

'I'm only a consultant Ross.'

'About that.'

The sergeant rummaged in his pocket as a smile slowly crept across his face.

'Had a word with a friend of mine in Brisbane. He pulled your file and confirmed you did basic training in Brisbane.

The sergeant produced a leather wallet. 'We both agreed. You are too good of a resource not to utilise while you're here. Technically, you would usually need to resign to get a reciprocating role here, but we pulled a few strings.'

He flipped the wallet open in front of Dawn to reveal a Queensland Police Detective badge.

'You're official now.'

'What the…'

'It's strictly for assignments we allocate, and they all need to be cleared with your Chief in Adelaide for now. You can formally request a transfer if and when you are ready.'

'Don't I get a choice in this?'

Dawn's tone was half-hearted.

Ryan grinned as he accepted the badge from Sergeant Martin and shoved it into her hand.

'No way. You need to be on this case. No one is going to mess with you Grave. You're too smart.'

A look passed between them, but Dawn shook it off.

27

'This doesn't get you out of telling me why Tenneson and you don't get along,' she whispered.

'I'm sure you'll find out soon enough. We'll need to pay him a visit now we have a confirmed ID.'

'It's three hours away and I'm supposed to pick Abby up from school,' Dawn glanced at her watch, 'in twenty minutes.'

'We'll grab Abby, catch up with your sister, then head out first thing tomorrow morning. Alright with you?'

Ryan glanced back at the Sergeant as though the decision was made. Dawn gaped.

'What's she doing here?'

The gruff voice was unmistakeable. Dawn didn't need to turn around to know the Senior Constable wasn't any more welcoming than he'd been the first time they met. For some reason, unknown to all, he took an immediate dislike to Dawn.

She now knew he was the uncle of the young woman her brother was accused of killing. But his attitude didn't change, even after they confirmed Fraser didn't kill his niece. He didn't kill himself either and the suicide note claiming he murdered the schoolgirl, his girlfriend at the time, was written under duress.

'She's your boss. That's what,' Ryan gloated. Dawn cringed but couldn't resist pulling out her new badge.

'What the hell.'

'Let it go Rick. I cut you a bit of slack last month, with everything that was going on. But mate, Dawn is a Detective Sergeant with SAPOL and officially on loan to us now. I'm sure I can count on you to be professional.'

Jamison entered the main office before the Senior could agree. Or disagree. Something in his eyes told her the latter was more likely.

'Detective. Good to see you.'

The tall, gangly constable wore a wide grin as he reached out for Dawn's hand.

'Nice to be working with you again Constable. Did your canvassing bring us any eyewitnesses who saw anything helpful out at Keatings Lagoon recently?'

'Nah. Sorry.'

'Senior. Anything on CCTV?'

Dawn chose to take the lead and give the Senior something to focus on other than his hostility toward her.

His nostrils flared, but he appeared to shake off whatever was annoying him and composed himself.

'There's no CCTV out at the lagoon, and local coverage is basically confined to public places like the wharf area, botanical gardens and public toilets. Until we have time of death, there isn't much point trawling through all that footage.'

Dawn wanted to argue, but the Senior Constable was right. Keatings Lagoon was on the main road out of town. Even if someone was picked up on camera footage leaving town, without a murder window, they would be searching blind.

'Thanks Senior.'

Dawn turned to the sergeant.

'Sergeant, we'll make a few calls and organise interviews with the family and friends for tomorrow. I'll keep you in the loop.'

Dawn didn't wait for permission to leave. As she passed the Senior, she couldn't miss his stiff body and huff as he crossed his arms over his chest.

The last thing she heard as they rounded the corner toward the exit was the Sergeant giving out orders to get a call for witnesses into the local paper and posters printed for the supermarkets, clubs and restaurants around town – asking if anyone had seen Jane Nichols between Wednesday October 7th and Friday October 16th.

Chapter 6

Dawn negotiated the concrete pathway, dodging children as they scrambled around her. The high-pitched voices, giggles, laughter, chatter and squeals made her smile. It was a far cry from the screams of frightened children the month before.

She wondered if any of the children tormented during the siege were hanging on to unresolved issues. There was no doubt a few would be. The ordeal certainly left a mark on her. She'd come so close to losing her sister and niece.

'Auntie Dawn!'

Blonde ringlets bounced as Abby sprinted toward her.

'Hey Bub. How was your day?'

Dawn dropped to her haunches and accepted the firm embrace from her vibrant little niece.

'We played touch football and I beat Liam, but that's not really surprising because Liam is pretty shy when it comes to that rough stuff and then we did art and some spelling and we cooked damper with Michael.'

Dawn totally ignored the fact that touch football shouldn't be rough and settled on wondering how the ranger went from finding a body this morning, to doing cooking with a class of first graders?

'Michael was at school today?'

'For afternoon tea. It was sooo.. good. Hot, sticky and buttery.'

Abby rubbed her tummy with her free hand.

'Sounds like a wonderful day.'

Dawn guided Abby across the soggy lawn toward Ryan's car parked furthest from the classrooms. School pickup was bedlam most days. Today even more so. As she reached for the door handle, Abby squealed.

'Ooh. Did you get a new car? I weally liked the pretty painted van you had, but this is super.'

'The van was a hire Abby. I returned it, but no, this isn't my car.'

Dawn couldn't say she missed the ostentatiously painted camper, but she knew she needed to get her own vehicle. Something else to get on with soon.

Opening the passenger side door, she flipped the seat over so Abby could jump in the rear of the coupe.

'Detective Ryan!' Abby ignored the backseat and launched herself over the folded front seat into Ryan's lap. Her arms wrapped around his neck as she planted a kiss on his 3 o'clock shadow.

'Hello Abby.'

Did Ryan just blush?

She hid a smile.

The little girl wriggled out his lap and into the back seat.

'Are you here to take Auntie Dawn on a date?'

'Detective Ryan is on a case Abby and I'm helping him out.'

Dawn pulled the seatbelt out and strapped Abby in.

'Aren't I supposed to have a booster?' she asked with pouted lips and a stern frown.

'You're right. I'll make sure we bring it next time.'

'But Auntie Dawn. We could get in trouble.'

The little girl crossed her arms over her chest and scrutinised Dawn.

Dawn tongued her cheek and considered reminding her niece that she *was* the police, then thought better of it. Abby was right. She wasn't above the law.

'You're so clever. Yes, we could get in trouble, but it's a fine for a first offence and I'll pay it and next time, I will absolutely remember to bring your booster seat. Detective Ryan will drive very carefully too, won't you?'

Dawn glanced his way, he nodded solemnly, then turned quickly so Abby didn't see him crack a smile.

'I've been very busy all morning and I know it isn't an excuse to break the law. Laws are there for a reason.'

The little girl assessed Dawn like a high court judge, then nodded, wiped the frown from her face and continued like nothing ever happened.

'Are you staying with us Detective Ryan? I'm sure we have space in Auntie Dawn's room. You can't use the spare room because Auntie Dawn is renovating it and it's full of boxes and old stuff that's been there *forever!*'

Dawn flipped the seat over and slid in, pulling the door to and trying desperately to ignore the expression on Ryan's face.

He finally put her out of her misery.

'I've booked an apartment Abby but thank you for the offer. Maybe next time.'

He wiggled his eyebrows at Dawn, who rolled her eyes. Ryan chuckled under his breath as he backed the vehicle out of the parking spot and revved the motor to pull away.

The throaty sound of the engine made Dawn's stomach tingle. She was always a sucker for a sports car and assured herself the butterflies in her stomach had nothing to do with Ryan's mirth-filled, sparkling blue eyes.

'You'll be coming to dinner though.' Abby's tone said it wasn't a question.

'If your mum doesn't mind.'

'Oh mummy won't mind. She loves cooking for friends and the more the merrier she always says.'

Dawn let Abby's chattering wash over her on the drive home. The little girl's sweet innocent enthusiasm hammered at the barriers and sent the ghosts of Dawn's past scurrying away.

As the car bounced over the rutted driveway and the old homestead came into view, Dawn realised something else.

Renovating the old Queenslander was cathartic and painting and moving walls and fixing broken cladding was like mending the shattered pieces of her past. Each board she nailed to the side symbolised putting her life back together in a new, fresh way.

With the Sergeant presenting her with Queensland Police credentials, she was being provided with a chance to start over in her hometown.

But was this what she wanted?

Chapter 7

In the twenty years of living away from Cooktown, Dawn cooked less than fifty times. Her first job after leaving town was working a night club on the Gold Coast, serving behind the bar and drinking nearly as much as her patrons.

When she became a cop, the long hours, late nights and rocky relationships meant a steady diet of takeaway, snacks or microwave meals.

Her sister on the other hand, was a fine cook, great mum, true homemaker. When Dawn decided to take long service leave and reconnect with her sister and get to know her niece, she was unsure what she could bring to the tight little family.

But it didn't take long for her to realise that as a working mum, Lisa was busy juggling a hectic schedule. Although Dawn was working on the renovation during the day, she made time to pick Abby up from school and do meal prep ready for Lisa to cook when she got home.

The arrangement was going perfectly, giving Lisa more time to work in her holistic clinic, and less time in the kitchen afterward.

Now, as Dawn sat at the kitchen table – the aroma of a glass of red, and the scent of frying onions and garlic gave her a sense of contentment she never expected to experience again.

Dawn sipped her red wine, savouring it and promising herself that one was all she was going to have. She watched Michael setting the table with plates and cutlery and couldn't help but be happy for her sister.

Michael's dark brown eyes caught her studying him.

'Been a busy day for you.'

Dawn smiled. 'And for you I hear. Damper at the school?'

Michael nodded. 'Fun bunch of kids. It's always great to get the chance to share a bit of bush tucker and tell Dreamtime stories to the kids.'

Dawn watched the bright smile light up his face and longed for a simple life. But then work jumped into her head and she realised how much she'd missed the thrill of the chase this past month.

Who was she kidding? She loved being a detective. Thinking of work made her recall Michael was a potential witness.

'I read your statement Michael. You don't normally work out at Keatings Lagoon.'

He added a pepper grinder to the table.

'Nah. I was filling in for someone.'

'So the Indigenous rangers contract Keatings Lagoon for the National Parks as well as Archer Point?'

Michael nodded. 'Anywhere that's considered on Country, or of cultural significance comes under our scope.'

Dawn learnt a lot about the subject when Michael found Lisa's car abandoned out at Archer Point and got entwined in the case to find her sister and solve two murders. Since then, he'd been a semi-permanent fixture in the Grave household.

Lisa leant over his shoulder, kissed his cheek and snatched a plate out of his hand.

'Dishing up now Michael. Any chance you can go find the detective and little miss for me?'

'I'll do it.'

Dawn put her glass down and rounded the worn wooden table occupying the centre of the traditional kitchen. It was almost as wide as the house, opening on to the rear veranda through an old, ornately carved screen door.

Reconfiguring the floor plan to open the kitchen up to the living room was part of Dawn's future plans, but Lisa wasn't too keen on the idea.

While the entire house held dark memories for her, Lisa was much younger and for her little sister, it was a place of refuge. It held memories of their mother cooking over the very same stove occupying the back wall now.

It was a battle she might very well lose since it was Lisa who'd lived here all these years, not her.

The screen door creaked, and moisture hung heavy in the air as she stepped out onto the long, wide veranda. The sound of cicadas grew deafening, and twilight closed in, bringing the biting insects with it. Dawn expected the detective to be hightailing it back inside, but she stopped to watch the gruff alpha male sitting with the blonde angelic child on his lap.

The scene looked wrong but felt right. Abby's smile was wide, her cheeks flushed, her chatter rhythmic as she interrupted Ryan's deliberately incorrect reading of a book Dawn forgot existed.

'No. That's not right Detective. He says, "*I do not like them anywhere.*" Not "*I'd like them here and there*", see.' She pointed to the page.

'Really. You should read it to me then?'

Abby pouted. 'But I can't read properly.'

'Then you'll have to listen to it my way.'

Dawn grinned at the expression on her niece's face. If looks could kill she'd have another murder to solve.

'Stop messing about you two. Dinner is ready,'

Dawn called from the doorway. Abby catapulted from Ryan's lap. The detective rose, his eyes on Dawn as Abby flew past her and disappeared inside. Ryan collected his beer from the raw edged coffee table with milky white lacquer. Another thing in need of repair.

'You are such a stirrer you know.'

The detective drew up alongside.

'No fun in reading the classics verbatim. They get boring otherwise.'

'That's a matter of opinion.'

Ryan opened the screen door, his face close to hers. His breath ruffled her fringe.

'Everything needs a shake up from time to time.'

Dawn frowned as she concluded he wasn't talking about Dr Seuss.

As they stepped inside, Lisa pointed to a seat, 'Ryan.' She stopped speaking, her blue eyes suddenly thoughtful.

'Actually.' She wiped her hands on her floral apron, flicked her dark blonde ponytail over one shoulder and studied Ryan thoughtfully.

'I can't keep calling you Ryan. Abby is forever going to call you Detective Ryan anyway, but I think I'll use your first name, if that's alright with you. Clint, isn't it?'

Clint nodded. 'It is.' His smile softening his features even more than reading with Abby.

'Okay. Clint. Take a seat here.' Lisa pulled out a mismatched colonial chair with flaking white paint. 'Do you need a top up?'

Lisa fussed. Dawn watched.

It was obvious Lisa missed having her family around. Dawn suppressed a twinge of guilt. She didn't even know Abby was born until Lisa went missing. There were a few signs. A phone call when she was on assignment on Kangaroo Island in South Australia. A sound that could have been a baby, but at the time, she never bothered to chase it up.

It was another indicator of how wrapped up in her own world of pain she was back then.

Dawn lowered into a worn vinyl chair next to Ryan, or Clint, as her sister now insisted he should be called in her house. Dawn wasn't sure she was going to be able to get used to that.

Abby squealed with delight as Michael lifted her into a seat and shuffled it up to the table. Lisa used a clean cloth to wipe the edges of each plate like a chef, then handed them to Michael to distribute around the table.

Saliva filled Dawn's mouth as her memory recalled her mother making this very same dish—with meat though. Lisa was nearly one hundred percent vegetarian.

'I like 'pasghetti better mummy, but this is good for guests. More posh,' Abby approved as a plate of vegetarian lasagne was placed in front of her.

Michael began cutting it into manageable pieces. Dawn couldn't help but smile. The ranger was a sweet man and so focussed on family and community.

Lisa left the dishes, grabbed her plate and sat next to Michael, who poured her a wine with a grin. Lifting it to her lips, she turned to Dawn.

'You getting anywhere on this new case? Michael told me about it.'

Dawn cut a piece of lasagne and postponed shovelling it into her mouth to answer her sister.

'We have a positive ID, but it's not been released yet. We need to speak to the family tomorrow.' Dawn glanced at Abby, knowing the little girl never missed anything going on around her.

Michael lifted a forkful of food which hovered a moment.

'It's not dinner table stuff, but I heard she's related to political royalty.'

Ryan sipped his beer and swallowed hard.

'The Minister for Aboriginal and Torres Strait Islander Partnerships, Arts and Communities Affairs to be exact.' His tone said he didn't believe there was anything Royal about the man.

Michael grinned over his mouthful, then reloaded his fork before swallowing.

'Met the bloke once. Had dibs on himself if you ask me.'

'I'd have to agree with that.'

Ryan shoved a forkful of dripping cheese into his mouth. Dawn was sure he did it to prevent him from saying anything more about Tenneson. She wondered again about their history.

'When did you meet a politician Hun?'

Lisa sipped her wine, eyes fixed on her new man.

'He was up here, getting media brownie points before the last election. Opened a few of our mob's projects.'

'Like?'

Ryan held his next mouthful aloft, eyes fixed on the ranger.

'The painted memorial along the river describing Indigenous persecution and community reconciliation.'

Ryan relaxed.

Michael lifted his beer and tipped the neck toward Ryan. 'And the Keatings Lagoon Boardwalk of course.' His face split with a grin.

Dawn rolled her eyes.

'You could have led with that,' Michael chuckled as Ryan's nostrils flared.

'Looks like tomorrow's interview could prove very interesting after all.'

Chapter 8

Dawn gazed out over the ocean as Ryan's Mustang hugged each bend at breakneck speed. Beaches of pale grey sand, polished rocks and blue water whizzed by to be replaced by tiny seaside towns surrounded by lush tropical greenery.

The car slowed as a coach load of tourists came into view.

Dawn flipped through her notebook. 'We should visit Mrs Nichols first. The uniforms haven't informed her yet.'

She reached toward the car navigation system to add the address from her notes.

'I know where Mrs Nichols lives.'

Ryan kept his eyes on the road as he snuck onto the other side, trying to find a gap to overtake the coach.

'Just stay behind him. This road is too windy for overtaking a bus. And how do you know where Mrs Nichols lives? You weren't on the original abduction case. You said so yourself.'

Ryan steered the car out again. A horn blasted. Dawn's head narrowly missed the side window as Ryan jerked the car back into his lane.

'What's the bloody hurry? We aren't exactly on the clock you know.'

'Technically you are. Consultant and all that.'

'You know what I mean.'

Stay on the Captain Cook Highway for thirty-six kilometres.

The GPS chimed in. Dawn pressed the mute button.

'She might get upset if you silence her you know.'

Dawn gaped at Ryan's comment.

'GPS doesn't have feelings. You're deflecting.'

She resisted the temptation to shake her finger at him. 'Are you going to tell me how you know Tenneson and why you weren't on the case to begin with?'

'The two aren't connected. I wasn't on the case because I get rural and regional cases. I told you that already.'

Ryan wasn't exactly pouting, but his expression was close.

'And why do you get all the rural and regional cases?'

'It's a long story. My history with Tenneson on the other hand is pretty short.'

'And.'

Dawn tried not to sound too curious. Something about Ryan's body language and his knowledge of Mrs Nichols' address told her the woman might be right in the middle of the rift.

'Let's just say I've visited Lorraine Nichols' place on a number of occasions, and it wasn't work related.'

Ryan glanced her way. His eyes asking a question or was he gauging her reaction.

'You're a grown man Ryan. Who you sleep with is your business, but a married woman?'

'Who said she was married at the time?'

'So why is Tenneson pissy with you if she wasn't his lady at the time?'

'The man has an ego the size of Everest.'

'Sounds like someone else I know,' Dawn mumbled, but not quietly enough.

'Don't take my word for it Grave. You'll find out soon enough.'

Dawn bit her lip and returned her gaze to the ocean as Ryan floored the accelerator. The beautiful palms and rocky beach disappeared behind a bright red bus. Dawn blinked. A horn screamed, the bus disappeared, and her view returned.

Shaking her head, she remained quiet the rest of the drive south into Palm Cove.

Twenty-five minutes later, Ryan turned left at an enormous roundabout and drove down a tree lined street. Turning right, then left, his Mustang's throaty exhaust vibrated between the palms and tropical plantings either side of the narrow road.

Reaching the end, he turned right onto the esplanade at Palm Cove. People wandered down the street between shops and cafés, unaware of the news Dawn was about to deliver to a mother.

Dawn knew nothing about being a mum, but watching Lisa with Abby and seeing her niece held hostage last month gave her an idea of what losing a child might be like.

They drove slowly down the main esplanade, past the shops and high-end hotels until high-rise gave way to three storey homes with glass balustrading, dark moody colours, skillion roofs and walls of timber slats.

'This is it.'

Ryan parked in a *No Parking Emergency Services* slot. Dawn didn't protest. Despite the early wet season, Palm Cove was teeming with tourists taking advantage of the off-season tariffs, to stay in the hub of the rich and famous.

'Tell me how on earth you travelled in the same circles as this woman?'

Dawn gaped at the architecturally designed home as she unclipped her seatbelt. Ryan stepped out without answering.

'My bet is Tenneson will be here with her.'

'Well I know if my husband was a politician and my daughter was missing, I'd expect him to be here.'

Ryan strode toward the tall, solid sandstone wall, featuring a timber electric gate on one side and a wide security door on the other. The entrance was framed by a timber arbour and flanked by two enormous, lush green Heliconia plants with bright red flowers.

'Brace yourself,' Ryan warned.

Dawn followed, with more questions ready to fly from her lips but talking to his back wasn't an option.

Ryan pointed to the stainless-steel intercom to the right of the door.

'You should buzz them. If he hears my voice, you'll need a court order to get in.'

'What the hell did you do to annoy him so much?'

Dawn pressed the *call* button.

'What can I say? Must be my magnetic personality.'

He wasn't grinning.

'Hello. Nichols' residence.'

Dawn wondered over the woman's use of her previous married name but said nothing.

'Mrs Nichols. This is detective Grave with Cairns Major Crimes. We made an appointment to call in.'

'Yes. Of course.' The woman's tone was measured. Maybe she knew what they were there for.

The gate buzzed.

'Just push to open Detective. I'll meet you at the front door.'

Dawn did as she was instructed. The gate swung open weightlessly to reveal a hand laid stone path bordered by low tropical vegetation. Red and green flowers on spikes scattered between thick, lush dark green foliage released a scent of mulch, mixed with jasmine. Dawn's nose twitched.

Glancing at Ryan, she noted the tension in his shoulders and back.

The roof-height wooden door opened. A slim woman greeted them. Her auburn hair was cut stylishly short. The kind of hairstyle requiring fortnightly maintenance to look so good. Her grey eyes studied Dawn's a moment, then shifted to Ryan.

She gasped but recovered quickly.

'Clint. I had no idea you were looking for Jane.'

Silence hung a moment. Dawn thought she was going to have to speak for Ryan, but he found his tongue.

'I wasn't. But I am now Lorraine. Can we come in?'

'Of course. Sorry.'

She stepped back, her cheeks blushing, then waved them inside. Closing the door, she pointed left of the open foyer and rising staircase to a living room where a plush sofa and two occasional chairs were lost amongst expansive high-gloss marble floors.

The area was surrounded on two sides by a raised walkway, lined with planters and rimmed with closed doors.

'Please. You said on the phone you had news.' She led the way to the sofa, then turned to face them with tired eyes. 'Have you found Jane?'

A short man with titanium grey hair and arms the size of Dawn's thighs, cleared his throat from beyond a door above the living room. Dawn watched as he snibbed the lock and closed the door before descending the three tiled steps to the living room.

'Oh, I'm sorry Detective Grave, this is my husband, Tyson Tenneson.'

The man stared past her, glaring at Ryan, who sneered right back.

'What the hell is he doing here?'

Tenneson's crisp white shirt stretched over his ample chest. Dawn stepped between the two men.

'Mr Tenneson. We have news about Jane. Maybe we should take a seat.'

The man's steely gaze finally fell on her. She pointed to the sofa.

'I won't ask again.' His lip twisted.

Dawn resisted the urge to cross her arms over her chest.

'Then maybe you can find out about your stepdaughter from her mother because I'm not here to answer any questions that don't specifically pertain to Jane's disappearance.'

Ryan was right. The guy was a complete arse.

Mrs Nichols slipped her hair behind her ear with a shaking hand.

'Tyson please. This isn't the time.'

Did she know what was coming? Dawn wondered.

'Maybe you could fetch Mrs Nichols a cup of tea or coffee Mr Tenneson?'

Dawn tried to convey the severity of her news with her eyes, but Tenneson wasn't having any of it.

'Come this way. Whatever you've got to say to Lorraine, you can say in front of me too.'

The man turned. Lorraine's pleading eyes beckoned Dawn and Ryan to follow.

No one spoke. Dawn sat on the edge of a mocha-coloured chair facing the sofa. Ryan hovered. Tenneson patted the spot alongside him. Lorraine Nichols perched delicately with hands gripped tightly in her lap.

Ryan nodded for Dawn to lead.

'Mrs Nichols. I'm sorry to inform you. Jane's body has been recovered.'

The woman bit her cheek as her eyes glistened with tears. Tenneson reached for her hand. She pulled it away, then made eye-contact with him. Dawn watched the exchange with interest as Mrs Nichols seemed to read something in the man's eyes.

Tenneson tried again. This time, Mrs Nichols allowed the comforting grasp. A tingle ran down Dawn's spine.

'I'm so very sorry for your loss Mrs Nichols.' She gave the woman a moment to ask any questions. When she didn't, Dawn continued, trying to work out why the usual questions like, *was it an accident* or *where did you find her*, weren't uttered.

'Mrs Nichols, I wish I didn't have to tell you this, but the circumstances of Jane's death are suspicious.'

'Of course they are bloody suspicious. She wouldn't have wandered away from our beach house and left her dog tied to a friggin' bench now would she?'

'Mr Tenneson, I understand your frustration.'

'You have no…bloody… idea.'

Ryan scoffed.

'Detective Grave has a damn good idea, Tyson. Once again, you're the one with no idea what you're on about.'

Tyson vaulted from the sofa. Dawn intercepted him with her hand flat in front of the man's chest, then turned to glare at her partner. She knew he was protecting her. But this was work and she wasn't some damsel in need of rescuing.

'Gentlemen, and I use the term *very* loosely.' She glared at Ryan who shrugged like none of it was his fault. 'I have no idea why the animosity, but this isn't the time or the place for a pissing contest.'

Silence hung as Dawn wondered if the bulls in the room might charge. Both huffed. Tenneson flopped down in the seat next to Mrs Nichols whose face was now sheet white. Shock was setting in.

Crouching before the woman, she tried to make eye-contact.

'I know this is a terrible time, but we need to go over a few things.'

Lorraine's eyes studied her hands as they wrung in her lap.

'When can I see her?' Her words were barely a whisper.

Dawn wanted to hug her or grasp her trembling hands or do absolutely anything to help, but her answer was by the book.

'Once the forensic pathologist is finished and the coroner has given us a preliminary report, I'm sure we can organise for you to see Jane, but Mrs Nichols, I'm not sure that's wise.'

Tenneson's eyes questioned her. Mrs Nichols began to sob.

Dawn rose.

'Look. I'm going to make a cup of tea. Mr Tenneson,' she scanned the layout trying to find the kitchen, 'can you give me a hand?

The politician looked ready to argue as his eyes fell on Ryan with suspicion, but Dawn's expression told him it wasn't up for debate. Lorraine needed a minute to calm down so Dawn would be able to interview her before she left.

'I'll keep an eye on her,' Ryan offered and for the first time, Tenneson didn't seem willing, or able, to put up a fight.

Chapter 9

Dawn followed Tyson Tenneson up the stairs in the foyer to an open-plan living area on the second level. A wall of ceiling high windows overlooked the serene waters of Palm Cove. The central kitchen island featured a sink and a row of bar stools, overlooking a crystal blue lap pool running the width of the block.

Dawn found the kettle on the back counter and flicked the switch. A low hum told her it was on and going.

Tenneson opened an overhead cupboard and fumbled for cups.

'I'll get it. I know how she likes it.'

'Mr Tenneson, I've been told Jane was working in your office until recently.'

'That's correct.'

His eyes didn't leave the tea bags as he dropped them into each cup.

'Can you tell me what her role was?'

'Jane helped with marketing. She studied communications at university but lost interest. She was good at it though.'

'Do you know why she left?'

'No.'

The kettle popped. Tenneson hurried to pour the water, jiggling a tea bag to keep his hands and eyes busy.

'Surely she told you?'

He shrugged.

'Did she go on to other work?'

Tenneson stirred the tea, removed the tea bag and crossed the kitchen to the fridge for milk.

'What's this got to do with her disappearance and death?'

'Maybe nothing, but I've read the report on her disappearance Mr Tenneson. I'm yet to follow up with the detectives on the case, but I understand her Labrador was tied up to a park bench at the beach.'

Tenneson picked up two cups of tea and held them as he turned to face Dawn.

'So?'

'So, the dog didn't bite the person who tied it up. Do you believe Jane would have tied her dog up and abandoned it?'

'What are you saying?'

'The dog may have known the person who abducted her, which means I need to know about all the relationships in your stepdaughter's life. So once again, did she go on to work elsewhere after she left your office?'

'No. She went all hippy and wanted to run health retreats and yoga camps. If it wasn't for her mother, she'd have gotten a real job like normal people. But Lorraine spoils, spoilt her.' Tenneson passed the cups to Dawn with a sigh. 'She told her she could stay at our house on Newell Beach and run hippy, yoga, detox weekends and such.'

'And did she do that?'

'I don't know. There certainly wasn't any money being paid back to Lorraine, so if she did, she didn't make a damn dollar out of it.'

Dawn nodded to the remaining fine porcelain cups steaming on the counter.

'Let's get Mrs Nichols her tea and see if she's feeling up to answering some questions.'

Tenneson collected the cups and led the way toward the stairs.

'Actually, I have one more question Mr Tenneson.'

The man turned—frustration evident in his eyes.

'Where were you the day Jane disappeared?'

His stare turned into a glare, before his gaze dropped to the two purple and red cups in his hands. Finally, he looked Dawn in the eye.

'You can't seriously think I'm a suspect?'

Dawn smiled. She knew it was forced and she could see Tenneson knew it too.

'We must eliminate everyone as a suspect in a suspicious death Mr Tenneson. Where were you?'

Dawn knew there was no need to remind the man of the date. When loved ones went missing, everyone remembered the details. She could still remember the day her mother disappeared as if it were yesterday.

'I was with my PA in the morning. I attended a speaking engagement over lunch which ran on, as they do, and I was back here around 4 p.m.'

'And you remained home the rest of the night?'

'We both did. Yes.'

'Thank you. Let's see how your wife is doing.'

Dawn nodded toward the stairs. Tenneson studied her a moment, drew a slow breath, then started down.

They returned to find Ryan sitting on the coffee table in front of Lorraine Nichols, his hands on her shoulders. Dawn cleared her throat. Ryan didn't move.

He obviously saw nothing wrong with an investigating detective sitting close to a possible suspect, but she wasn't about to make a fuss.

'Mrs Nichols. Let's grab a tea, take a few minutes and then I'm afraid I'll need to ask you a few questions.'

Dawn held a cup of tea out for Ryan, while Mr Tenneson sat alongside his wife and passed her a cup.

Ryan took the tea in both hands, shuffled back, but didn't leave the coffee table. Dawn sat on the chair adjacent to Mrs Nichols.

'I know this isn't easy. Believe me. I've been where you are right now.' She didn't explain further. There was no need. Mrs Nichols' eyes told her she believed her.

'We need to know if you can think of anyone who would want to hurt your daughter?'

Lorraine's lip trembled, until she bit it. With a shaking hand, she put her cup to her lips, sipped then sighed.

'Jane was loved by everyone. She was happy, carefree, always kind. I don't understand why anyone would hurt her.'

'When was the last time you saw your daughter?'

Mrs Nichols sucked in a shuddering breath, then let it go through pursed lips. Passing her tea to her husband, she closed her eyes and for a moment, Dawn thought she might break down. But the woman rallied.

'It was the Sunday before she disappeared. She was so excited when she showed me around our Newell Beach house. She'd spent a few weeks decorating the family room, which opens to the wide deck overlooking the water. There were sheer white curtains draped either side of the bifold glass doors and Indonesian statues dotted the decking.'

Lorraine's eyes glazed over, and Dawn gave her a moment.

'Do you know if she'd opened her studio to the public yet?'

'I'm not sure. I know she planned to run a few yoga sessions after she showed me around.'

'Do you know where she might have kept her guest list?'

'The Cairns Police looked but couldn't find a diary.' Lorraine glanced at her husband as she answered.

Mr Tenneson's tea was untouched. He placed it on the coffee table next to Ryan and huffed.

'We've been over all of this already Detective.'

'I'm sorry to have to ask again. I know it's frustrating, but the circumstances have changed. Jane was missing when the Cairns Police first searched. Now we could be looking for a killer Mr Tenneson. Everything, no matter how trivial could help us.'

Ryan drained his tea, then put the cup on the coffee table beside him as his eyes regarded Lorraine.

'Does she have any close friends we can talk to?'

'Tina is a good friend. She might know if Jane ran any classes. She's into all the health stuff too.'

Dawn pulled a notepad from her back pocket. 'Do you have a last name or contact information for Tina?'

It was weird to be back in long pants and even with cut off-sleeves on her tee, she was overheating in the humidity. Still, police detectives couldn't exactly get around in cargo shorts and tank tops. At least not if they wanted to be taken seriously by men like Tenneson.

'Tina Farrell. She lives at Newell Beach, a street back from the waterfront.'

Dawn scribbled down details in her own brand of shorthand.

'And how does your daughter know Tina?'

'They've known each other for years. We've been holidaying at Newell Beach since Jane was...' Her voice broke.

'Ten,' Tenneson interrupted, then reached for Lorraine's hand. The woman flinched.

Dawn glanced at Ryan whose sneer was a heartbeat away from a growl. What *was* their history?

'Where were you the day Jane went missing Mrs Nichols?'

'You can't.'

Ryan reached out and patted the woman's hand.

'It's just routine Lorraine.'

Dawn noted she didn't draw her hand away from Ryan's. One look at Tenneson told her he noticed the gesture.

Ryan let her hand go. Lorraine smiled, drew a slow breath and nodded.

'I got my hair done at Stephano's at nineish. That kept me busy for a few hours, then I caught up with Doreen Miller. Then I was home around three.'

Dawn jotted down details. 'Can anyone confirm you were home at three?'

Ryan glared at her, but she wasn't backing down. Everyone was a suspect until proven otherwise.

'Well Tyson got home around four, so I guess for the one hour, no, but Doreen will confirm what time I left Ricky's Restaurant.'

'Thanks for your time, Mrs Nichols, Mr Tenneson.' Dawn rose, slipping her notepad into her back pocket. 'If you can send me Doreen's contact information and can we ask you for the keys to access the Newell Beach property? We'd like to go over it again on our way back to Cooktown.'

'Cooktown?' Mr Tenneson rose, his eyebrows knitting together.

'I'm sorry. I thought we mentioned it. I'm based in Cooktown, assisting the Cairns police with this enquiry because Jane's body was found at the Keatings Lagoon Conservation Park.'

'What?' Tenneson was visibly flustered.

'Is that significant?'

Dawn waited and watched as Tenneson regained his composure.

'No.' He shook his head. 'Not at all.'

'Even though you opened the lagoon boardwalk?'

Tenneson's eyes narrowed.

'I know the place, yes. Of course.'

'But you don't know of anyone living in Cooktown who Jane would have been visiting?'

Tenneson drew his shoulders back.

'She disappeared from Newell Beach and left her dog behind. Why would she go to Cooktown without him?'

'So, there is no one you know in Cooktown who would want to hurt Jane?'

Silence hung a moment as Tenneson opened and closed his mouth. Finally, he shook himself.

'Of course not. Lorraine told you. Everyone loved Jane.'

Dawn waited, hoping silence would draw more out of the man, but he said nothing. There were more questions rolling around her head, but now wasn't the time.

'Can I ask you for the keys to the Newell Beach house please?'

Tenneson looked ready to object, but pressed his lips closed when Mrs Nichols rose from the sofa. She crossed the room to a side table and scribbled a number on a piece of notepaper.

'We use a pin-pad entry. Here's the code.'

Dawn met her in the foyer.

'Thanks for your time, Mrs Nichols and I am so very sorry for your loss.'

'Just find the bastard who did this Detective.'

Lorraine Nichols reached for Dawn's hand, shoved the paper into her palm and held her gaze.

'No matter who it is. They need to pay for killing my baby.'

The snarl on Lorraine's lips hit Dawn in the gut. *No matter who it is.* Did this woman know who killed her daughter? Was she unwilling to say anything in front of Tenneson? Or was it pure motherly instinct?

Chapter 10

Dawn gazed out over the blue ocean lapping at the shore as she waited for Ryan to unlock the Mustang. She hoped the vastness of the water would quell her emotions after delivering the death notice. It didn't.

She forced the burden aside, allowing her mind to mull over all the possible scenarios for why Jane Nichols was murdered and why she ended up in Cooktown. At this stage, they nearly all included Tyson Tenneson.

Something about the guy made her skin crawl, but if his wife backed up his alibi and the rest of it checked out, they were going to have to look for suspects and a motive elsewhere.

Still, the link between Keatings Lagoon and the MP couldn't be overlooked and as much as he said he didn't know anyone in Cooktown, Dawn was sure he did.

She slid into the passenger's seat.

'We'll need to check their alibis.'

Ryan was unusually quiet. No sarcastic quips, not even a grumble about Tenneson.

'I'll get Jamison and Reynolds onto it.'

She carried her monologue as Ryan fired up the engine.

'Are you going to tell me why Tenneson hates you so much? If Lorraine Nichols wasn't with him when you two had a fling, it shouldn't bother him.'

Dawn didn't ask about the age difference or the details of his affair. It was none of her business, but understanding Tenneson was her job. And getting some sense of who Mrs Nichols was, could be important.

The car revved as Ryan pulled away from the curb. The sour expression he barely held in check told her this was more than relationship stuff.

'Look. I get why you don't want to talk about the bedroom stuff.'

Ryan glared at her. She ignored him.

'But how on earth do you know these people? You're a cop. They are...' She scrambled for the right word.

'Socialites?' Ryan offered.

'Yes. Exactly.'

Dawn studied Ryan's profile as they entered the Captain Cook Highway roundabout and headed north once more.

'I checked you out before working with you Grave. Didn't you do the same to me?'

'Well no. Why would I? You were working on my sister's case and up until yesterday, I was a civilian in Queensland, out of my jurisdiction. Why? What would I find?'

The cloudy skies cast a glare through the windscreen. Dawn slipped her aviator sunglasses from her bag and popped them on top of her head, ready to put on. But she hesitated, trying to catch Ryan's gaze so he'd realise she wasn't giving up.

He glanced her way, huffed, then fixed his eyes on the road as he spoke.

'The age gap wasn't that much.'

She wondered why he thought the age was important but she followed his lead.

'How old were you?'

'Late twenties, Lorraine was early forties.'

Dawn let the silence hang. Ryan swallowed hard.

'She was between husbands. It was only one summer.'

A joke about toyboys and summer flings rolled around her head, but Ryan's expression told her now wasn't the right time to be funny.

'What happened?'

'It was over before it began.'

'The class difference?'

Ryan frowned at her, then shook his head.

'You really don't know do you?'

She sighed. 'Know what?'

'Let's interview this friend of Jane's and go through the holiday home with a fine-tooth comb.'

'Ryan. You can't change the subject like that.'

'Just Google me.'

'Google you?'

'There's a reason I get all the regional cases and it's not because of my clearance rate or local knowledge.'

'Can't you just *tell* me?'

'Look. All I'm going to say is, I have had a soft spot for Lorraine Nichols but it won't affect my investigation and I'm going to find who killed Jane. My past. Who I am and who I know has nothing to do with how well I do my job, even if the Queensland Police Service likes to keep me at arm's length.'

His body was rigid. The vein at his temple throbbed and Dawn could see this case was personal, but the Queensland Police keeping him at arm's length. What did that even mean?'

'Clint.'

She used his first name, knowing somehow this wasn't a work colleague kind of conversation. He glanced her way, then his eyes darted back to the road as they entered another enormous dual lane roundabout.

'You can tell me. Hell, you've seen my personal secrets bared open like a festering sore. What is it?'

Ryan's fingers gripped the steering wheel. His knuckles turned white as he sighed.

'I use my mother's maiden name. Ryan isn't my father's last name.'

Ryan kept his eyes on the road as he stretched his fingers over the steering wheel. Dawn waited, giving him space.

But when he said nothing, she pushed.

'Do I really need to Google you?' Her voice gentle.

Ryan sighed. His shoulders sagged. He licked his lips, bit down, then licked again.

'Tenneson is my older cousin.'

Ryan didn't make eye contact.

'You're related to that arsehole?'

'We were close buddies for years. Before he made it big in politics. We don't exactly see eye to eye these days.'

'You're a Tenneson? I might not have looked you up, but I researched *him*. Brisbane Grammar boy. UQ degree in economics and politics. Never worked a real day in his life.'

'That's him.'

'And what, you're the poor cousin?'

The apartment Ryan rented in Cooktown on his last case flashed before her eyes. The one with the view to die for balcony overlooking the Endeavour River. The one where she nearly joined him in his bed.

He said he put it on his Visa, and would get reimbursement, but Dawn knew the department never sprang for high-end accommodation. She knew he wasn't short of money. He'd offered to help out with the renovation, but not *that* kind of money.

Ryan said nothing.

'You're not a *poor* cousin at all. Are you?'

'Now you see why I get all the regional cases. My Chief, the department heads, they'll do whatever it takes to keep me out of the limelight.'

'And that's okay with you?'

'I solve cases. How the police media liaison officer chooses to release the findings to the press, is up to them.'

'And you're a Tenneson.'

Dawn tried not to gape as Ryan focussed on the next bend in the winding foreshore road back to Port Douglas and Newell Beach.

Ryan nodded to the phone still hovering in Dawn's hand.

'You better make that call to Reynolds and Jamison to chase up some alibis.'

Chapter 11

The road to Newell beach was flanked by rows and rows of towering sugar cane fields. Two teenage boys strolled down the right side of the road with bare feet, fishing poles and wide smiles, sparking memories Dawn buried years ago.

Growing up in Far North Queensland gave her a freedom she'd forgotten existed. Sunny afternoons fishing, swimming and hanging out were shattered when they found Tracey Warren's body floating in shallow water out at Archer Point.

As they drove past, the boys waved. Dawn envied the naivety of youth. Then shook the thought away. She was back in Cooktown. Back in the tropics with her sister and niece. There was still time to enjoy the freedom she left behind.

As they drew past the road to the boat ramp, Dawn gazed at the mixture of permanent living and holiday homes dotted along the foreshore.

A couple with two teenagers crossed the road, a large German Shepherd choking on the lead dragged the youngest boy along like an Antarctic husky.

Dawn grinned. Ryan kept his eyes focussed on the road. He'd barely said a word since explaining who he was. Dawn didn't try to make him talk. Her old boss in Adelaide was from money. He never spoke about his family either.

She suddenly realised she thought of Jack as her *old* boss. She planned to hang around Cooktown a while, catch up with Lisa and Abby, make sure her brother's case was reopened. But when did she decide not to return to her job with Adelaide Major Crimes?

She shoved the thought aside. For now, she needed to be thankful of her chance to connect with the only family she had left. As much as Ryan seemed to hate his family, at least most of them were still alive.

Ryan steered the Mustang toward a graded dirt track at the end of the main foreshore road. 'The house is down here.'

Dawn didn't bother to ask how her new partner knew where to find the beach house. He'd already explained he's spent a summer in Lorraine Nichols' bed.

'Your car isn't going to like the sandy track.'

Dawn pointed to the road ahead, where lumps of grey sand and uncut tufts of grass sprouted up in all directions.

'We'll park here. I need to show you where Jane went missing from anyway.'

'Jane. You sure you want to keep calling our victim by name?'

Ryan bit the inside of his lip.

'You're right. I need to keep this compartmentalised. Our victim disappeared from this stretch of Newell Beach. Not far from the family holiday home.'

'So are we sure she was snatched from the beach? The forensic techs didn't find any evidence of her going missing from the house?'

'Her dog was tied up to a bench. I'll show you.'

Ryan pulled the handbrake on and stepped from the vehicle. Dawn grabbed her handbag and slung it over her shoulder to follow.

Ryan's back disappeared into overgrown tropical rain forest as the clouds loomed dark and threateningly overhead.

Dawn lifted her sunglasses as she entered the tree line, allowing her vision to adjust to the dimness. A gentle breeze rustled the coconut palms that lined the beach, creating a crackling sound that echoed around them.

'Here is where the dog was found.'

Dawn turned in a small circle, taking in the surroundings. A concrete bench was set below Moreton Bay figs and mangrove trees. Torn palm fronds littered the understorey and the smell of rotting leaf litter blended with salty air to create an all too familiar scent.

'So did our victim tie the dog up? Or her attacker?'

'We don't know. There was no trace evidence on the dog. No DNA out of place.'

'Who found the dog?'

Dawn waited, while Ryan referred to case notes on his phone.

'The reception is crap here. I'll download the file if we can access the WIFI at the house.'

Ryan ducked under an overhanging branch and guided her through the trees onto the sand.

Dawn glanced up and down the long, flat expanse of wet sand. The tide was out, leaving acres of rippled seabed exposed. A few rocks dotted the area, but mostly, fine greyish-brown silt like sand covered hundreds of metres, as far as the eye could see.

A drop of rain touched her shoulder, then another.

'It's going to pour down any second.' Dawn pointed to the looming grey clouds. 'We should hurry up and get to the house.'

Ryan jogged up the beach.

'Follow me.'

Dawn watched his broad frame move with unexpected agility. She'd not jogged or done any type of fitness since returning to Queensland. Now, as she followed, her heartrate rose and sweat seeped from every pore.

'I'm out of shape. You'd think doing a reno would keep me fit.'

She huffed, as Ryan slowed in front of her to let her catch up.

'You look okay, but yeah, fitness takes weeks to get back, but only a couple to lose.'

Ryan wasn't gasping for air like her. His comfortable footfalls, even in dress shoes made her realise she needed to take better care of herself.

They reached a closely mowed lawn, scattered with palm trees towering over three storeys tall. A healthy collection of coconuts told her they'd not been trimmed lately. The wind kicked up a notch as rain began to fall consistently. A coconut cracked from the top of the tree, falling hard and bouncing a few metres away.

They jumped, then sprinted for the front deck area.

'Here.'

Dawn handed him the door code before dropping her hands to her thighs and willing her breathing to slow.

'You okay?'

'I'll live.'

Dawn glanced up as Ryan punched the code into the sliding door lock. Four beeps later, the light went green, and he slid the door sideways. Drawing the sheer curtains aside, he stopped. Dawn nearly slammed right into his back.

He lifted his left hand in a balled fist, his weapon already in his right.

She reached into her handbag for her gun.

'What's up?' she whispered.

Dawn's heartbeat thudded in her ears as Ryan slipped inside, leaving her tangled in reams of fabric. A few seconds later, Dawn followed him in, gun raised.

Books were scattered all over the room. Cushions were cut open. Yoga mats shredded. Even the artwork was torn from the walls, cut open and flung aside.

'Well I'm pretty certain the techs didn't make this much mess.'

'I'm pretty sure you're right,' Dawn agreed.

Chapter 12

Dawn followed Ryan as they crossed the large room, into a wide hallway. Ryan pointed left, then put three fingers up and counted them down one by one before stepping left into the next room.

'Police!'

Dawn followed a heartbeat later, going right.

'Police!'

Scanning the kitchen, Dawn noted the dark stone tops, white cupboards and timber floors were untouched, but as they rounded the benches, she found the floor covered in utensils and upturned jars of flour and rice.

One by one they cleared the rooms, finding bedding upended, side tables tossed, drawer contents splayed.

Ryan holstered his weapon and reached into his jacket pocket. Dawn wondered again how he managed to keep wearing a sportscoat when it was ninety eight percent humidity outside, but she was thankful he did when a pair of disposable gloves appeared in his hand.

Dawn accepted one glove and squeezed her right hand into it, flicking it over her sweaty wrist. 'I can't see any signs of a break in. I'll see if I can figure out how the intruder got in?'

Ryan retrieved his mobile and wandered back in the large room hunting for a signal.

'I'll ring the forensic team. Call out if you find anything.'

She was vaguely aware of him speaking with the forensic scientist from Friday morning's body dump, Tammy something, but focussed on the scene in front of her.

What could they have been looking for?

Money, drugs? Or maybe evidence relating to Jane's disappearance?

Drugs and organised crime were behind many of the murders Dawn worked on in the past, but there were plenty of other motives, like domestic violence and robbery. And then there were the truly gruesome serial killer cases. Dawn hoped Jane Nichols' murder wasn't one of those.

Dawn scanned a small desk between two bookcases that stretched floor to ceiling. The oak timber was real and held a small green porcelain pencil holder along with a pewter letter opener. A cord poked out of a round hole. Dawn followed it to a laptop charger, still plugged into the wall and switched on.

'Looks like a laptop could be missing,' she called over her shoulder, then laughed as Ryan loomed up alongside her.

'I've downloaded the earlier missing persons case file.'

'Any note about this missing laptop then?'

Dawn waited while Ryan scanned the file.

'Nothing noted, but that doesn't mean it wasn't missing then.'

'We'll need to see if they took any photos inside the house.'

Ryan scanned the file, his fingers flicking through photos, eyes squinting.

'Doesn't look like it.'

Dawn scanned the bookcases, almost empty now. The floor was strewn with paperbacks, magazines and hardback books on herbal medicine and anatomy.

A thought stuck Dawn. She turned to see Ryan who was frowning at the rear wall of oak panelling.

'Have they checked any cloud drive storage?'

Ryan glanced her way.

'I'll text Gleeson. She might have got the computer nerds to find out already.'

'This looks like someone was very keen to find something. What do you suppose they were looking for?'

'I told you last case we worked on. It's always about sex, love, power or money.'

'You know the family. Which is it this time?'

'All of the above.'

Dawn chuckled, but Ryan wasn't laughing.

This wasn't an ordinary case. Like the last time they worked together, this was deeply personal. No wonder Ryan wasn't on the case to begin with. She considered how long his boss would let her run the show. She was an out-of-town cop, reeled in by a Sergeant of a regional police station, to run a murder investigation linked to a prominent politician.

It was only a matter of time before the case was pulled out from under them. Either that, or the Cairns team was hoping she'd be a perfect scapegoat if they failed to find the killer.

'I'm going to call Reynolds. See if they have confirmed the parents' alibis.'

Dawn held her phone in the air, trying to find a signal as she wandered out onto the front deck. Water poured over the veranda gutters, but a small blue patch over the ocean promised it would clear soon enough.

Dawn leant against a glass fence separating the swimming pool from the main deck area. Two bars appeared on her screen. She dialled, scanning the concrete seating, spa, firepit and large umbrella which was folded to minimise damage during the wet season.

'Welcome to Cooktown police, this is Constable Reynolds speaking.'

'Ah. Just the girl I needed to speak with. It's Dawn. Have you confirmed our alibis yet?'

'Detective. Yes. Both Mr Tenneson and Mrs Nichols were where they said they were.'

'Who is Tenneson's PA?'

'A Julian Smythe.'

'Okay. Any other staff who used to work with our victim when she was at the MPs office?'

'There is a receptionist, named Mandy Lieberman, and a few volunteers who help out during campaign time.'

'Can we get a list of the volunteers? We'll do some interviews tomorrow and be back up your way by late afternoon.'

'Okay. You don't have a department email yet, or log on, so flick me a message with your email address so I can send you the list once I've compiled it.'

'Will do. Thanks Reynolds.'

'No problem Detective.'

Dawn tapped out a quick text, then slipped her phone into her pocket. If she stayed working as a Queensland Detective, she'd need to organise a new email address. Was she going to stay?

'Hey Grave. Check this out.'

Dawn spun round at the sound of Ryan's voice. Her stomach did a summersault and she wondered for a moment what Ryan would think if she stayed permanently. Shaking the thought away, she followed his voice back inside, crossed the polished timber floor and scanned the large room looking for him.

'Where are you?'

'In here.'

His voice echoed from behind a wall of storage cupboard doors. One on the far right sat slightly ajar. Dawn opened it to find Ryan's cheeky grin and a strobing kaleidoscope of colour on the walls.

'What the hell?'

'Looks like Jane was offering more than yoga at her retreats.'

'That or our Minister for Communities and Arts is into some freaky performing acts.'

Dawn circled the room, trying to decide where to look. Her stomach knotted, not because she was squeamish about S & M, but if Jane was a dominatrix, then there were a whole lot of unknown suspects they were going to have to try and fish out of thin air.

'Check this out.'

Ryan held a particularly nasty looking whip in his gloved hand and grinned.

'Put it down and leave it for the forensic team.'

Dawn slowly turned to take in the entire set up. Masks, a variety of ball gags, cuffs of varying types from regular to fluffy fur-lined, hung on display. An inversion table took up the centre of the room, a wooden chair with eyelets screwed into the arms and legs was tucked away to the side.

'We need to canvas the neighbours. See who has been coming and going from this place in the past few weeks.'

'Yes ma'am,' Ryan saluted. 'Just don't hurt me, please.'

'Did I miss something?'

Tammy's voice made Dawn jump.

'Nothing worth hanging out for.'

Dawn stepped to the side of the room to allow the forensic tech to enter. She was already decked out in disposable overalls, and shoe covers. Her goggles were pulled back on the top of her head and a surgical mask hung around her neck.

'You two need to get out of my crime scene.'

Dawn considered the forensic scientist a moment. She was nothing like the tech Dawn worked with in Adelaide. Penny was tall, likely six foot. Broad shouldered and walked like a farmer. Tammy was shorter, heavily built in a muscular fashion.

Penny's warped sense of humour was always a welcome relief when dealing with the dead, and so far, Tammy seemed to have a similar sardonic sense of humour.

Dawn waited for Ryan to leave, then turned to follow.

'Hey Detective.'

She turned back to Tammy.

'Looks like crime scenes are popping up around you like daffodils in spring.'

'Occupational hazard I'm afraid.'

'How's the big boy handling all this?' Tammy whispered and lifted her chin to the doorway as Ryan disappeared.

'Does everyone but me know about his connection to this case?'

The forensic tech shrugged.

'He's doing okay, all things considered. You got here quicker than I expected.'

'I was in the area when Ryan phoned it in. I was on my way when he texted about the missing computer and cloud storage.'

'Did you find anything yet?'

'Not yet, but the computer crew are doing their thing. Now let me do mine.'

'Keep me posted.'

'Will do.'

Dawn stepped back into daylight to find Ryan staring off into the distance. It was strange seeing the gruff cop so vulnerable, but this case must have been doing a number on his emotions.

Sure, he wasn't close to Lorraine Nichols anymore, but he was still related to Tyson Tenneson, despite not wanting to be.

'I've got Reynolds running the volunteers at Tenneson's office and doing a background check on his staff.'

'Something about all this feels personal.'

'What makes you say that?' Dawn was thinking the same thing.

'My gut,' Ryan waved dismissively. 'And before you say it, I know we need evidence, not gut feelings.'

'I'd trust your gut any day Ryan. The same way I'd trust mine and I think you might be right. This place isn't Tenneson's house. It isn't even in his name.'

'It wouldn't be. Lorraine's family have held this property for over forty years.'

'It looks pretty good for the age.'

'It's been renovated numerous times over the years. Got battered by cyclone Ita just last year. Storm surge inundated the place.'

'That explains the current condition and on trend decor.'

'Let's find our victim's best buddy in town and ask her about the hidden room.'

Ryan stuck his head inside the dominatrix dungeon.

'Gleeson. We're out of here. Got some interviews to do. You got uniform in tow?'

'Two minutes out.'

'Okay. We'll wait for them to rock up.'

'Thanks.'

Dawn's phone pinged. She opened an email attachment and scanned a list of names. One popped out immediately.

'You'll never guess who volunteers at Tenneson's office from time to time.' She didn't wait for a reply. 'Tina Farrell.'

Chapter 13

Ryan drove down the single lane, wet bitumen road. Although the rain had stopped, pools of water still flooded the deep roadside. It could take days for the water to drain away.

One side of the road opened to acres of sugar cane, rustling in the breeze. To Dawn's right, the street was lined with vacant blocks of land and homes of various vintages and state of repair.

'This place is only a minute's drive from the Nichols' beach house,' Dawn said.

'It makes sense. If Tina and Jane were good friends from years of holidaying here, they likely walked to one another's homes over the years.'

Ryan parked on the gravel driveway.

'Doesn't look like she's home.'

Dawn scanned the file Reynolds sent for a phone number.

'I'll try calling her. Make sure she's in. It's Saturday, she could easily be off with friends.'

Ryan put his hand on the door handle and waited.

'Do we have any work contact info?'

Dawn dialled the number. 'Reynolds didn't find anything.' She listened as the call rang out.

Hanging up, she slid her phone back into her pocket and opened the passenger side door.

Ryan followed her out.

'No luck?'

'No and no voice mail option. We're here. Might as well have a look around and try knocking.'

Dawn crossed the patchy lawn and stepped up the short staircase leading to a weather worn covered deck. She was barely on the landing before a deep bark echoed from beyond the door.

'Maybe she's in after all.'

Dawn knocked. The barking grew louder. Dawn heard footsteps from within.

'It's okay Rusty.'

The curtain on the side window flicked across to reveal a face. Dawn heard a chain rattle and the door unlock. Instead of opening wide to greet them, it opened a crack. The dog growled quietly behind the woman.

'What do you want?'

'I'm Detective Grave.' Dawn showed her new Queensland Police ID. 'This is Detective Ryan. We are here to talk about Jane Nichols' disappearance.

'I've given my statement. I wish I could do more.'

'Ms Farrell. I'm afraid we have some news, and we need to go over your statement again.'

The door didn't open wider.

'Can I see that ID again. And his?'

Wide eyes peered through the crack. The dog gave a quick bark of agreement with its owner.

'I'm sorry. Of course.'

Dawn held her ID up for proper scrutiny. Ryan did the same. They exchanged a look with one another. The woman was on edge.

'Just give me a second.'

The door closed. Dawn heard the chain rattle, then the door opened wider to reveal a narrow hallway lined with paintings.

'Ms Farrell. Can we come in? Is there somewhere we can talk?'

Dawn kept her tone calm. The dog growled. It wasn't unusual to find a pet so intent on protecting its owner, but

Dawn knew animals sensed emotions. This dog knew Tina was unsettled.

Tina held the dog's collar.

'It's okay Rusty.'

She stepped back, pulling the dog aside and waved her hand for them to enter.

'Hey boy. How's it going?' Ryan cooed. The dog's growl intensified.

'I'm sorry. He's not a fan of guys since…'

Tina stifled a sniffle and Dawn realised the dog wasn't hers. It was Jane's.

'I'm sure he's got good reason. Shall we find a seat? This news isn't going to be easy for you.'

Tina was anchored to the spot in the hallway, her eyes scrutinising Dawn's.

'She's dead isn't she?'

'Let's take a seat and we'll explain everything as best we can, hey.'

The woman nodded, turned and dragged the Labrador to the rear of the house. Dawn followed. Ryan kept his distance. If the dog didn't like guys, he knew better than to get too close.

The lounge room was small, neatly furnished with more art adorning the walls. A variety of styles from abstract to landscapes with some oils, but mostly watercolours and acrylics. They were all good, but Dawn was particularly attracted to the abstracts.

'Yours?'

She pointed to the artworks as Tina sat down and indicated for her to choose a seat.

'I dabble.'

'So what's the day job?'

'You said you had something to tell me about Jane? If she's dead, please just tell me.'

Dawn drew a slow breath. It was never easy telling someone that a person they cared about was never coming home again.

'I'm afraid Jane's body was recovered yesterday.'

'Oh my god. I knew it.'

Tina buried her head in her hands. Rusty whined and licked her arm, then her bare leg before dropping to his tummy and placing his head on his paws.

His dark brown eyes sulked up at Dawn.

Dawn gave the woman a moment before carrying on. They had a murder to solve, and it appeared Tina's life intersected Jane's in more than one way with possible connections to their case.

'I see you volunteered with Jane on Tenneson's election campaign.'

Tina's head flew up from her hands, her eyes wide, her chest heaving. For a moment Dawn thought the woman might lunge at her. Instead, she visibly collected herself, rolled her shoulders and drew a deep breath, puffing it out with effort.

Rusty sat back up, eyes alert, then a frown softened his stare as he studied Dawn, then Tina with confusion.

'I did. But only for the last campaign and never again.'

'I take it you don't like the guy.'

'That's an understatement.'

'Can I ask why?'

Tina reached over and scratched Rusty's ear. The dog cocked his head to one side and leant into the rub.

'Okay.' Dawn realised she wasn't going to get an answer to her question today. 'Can I ask if you knew Jane worked in the sex industry?'

Tina laughed, then rolled her lips at Dawn's confusion.

'She didn't.'

'Sorry? We have a forensic tech over at the beach house now, going through a sex dungeon that tells us otherwise. Was it run under the guise of a yoga retreat?'

'Jane wasn't a dominatrix. She was too soft and gooey on the inside to pull that off. She ran yoga classes for real.'

Dawn wanted to argue, but the woman looked sincere.

'Then maybe Jane was running the two businesses side by side. Charging one out under the same credit card system as the other, like a front to avoid detection.'

Tina sighed. Her shoulders slumped before she threw herself backward into the lounge chair.

Rusty lifted his ears, then relaxed.

'Jane ran a yoga retreat….'

Tina hesitated, like she was about to say more. Her eyes focussed on a painting in the corner of the room. Then she returned her attention to Dawn.

'I'm the dominatrix and yes, Jane put my customers through her books and paid me cash after tax.'

Dawn puzzled over the admission. Why the hesitation? It seemed like it could be true. She glanced at Ryan to take over and sat back to watch the woman.

'Do you think Jane's death is related to your work?'

Tina tongued her cheek, then sighed.

'I honestly don't know.'

Dawn frowned. Sometimes when people said *honestly*, that's exactly what they meant but something about Tina's words made the hair on Dawn's arms stand on end.

Ryan made notes, his eyes glancing at Tina as he spoke.

'We'll need a list of your clients.'

'Then you'll need a warrant.'

The earlier frail, heartbroken woman was gone now. The dominatrix had risen to the surface.

A warrant wasn't going to be easy. They needed to finish going over the victim's financials. Maybe they'd get lucky and find a merchant credit card charge to Tina's customers. Dawn tried a different tack.

'Can you think of anyone who might want to hurt Jane?'

'No. Jane was a beautiful person, inside and out. Soft, too soft, but no one would hurt her.'

The words seemed genuine. Spoken without hesitation. Yet Tina's eyes were pinched at the corners. Was it pain and grief Dawn was seeing?

'A boyfriend we don't know about?'

'No.'

'According to the missing person's report, Rusty was found on the beach, tied to a bench, right?'

'Yes.'

'Does he take to strangers well?'

The woman glanced at the soft brown eyes at her feet.

'He's a Labrador. They love everybody unless you try to hurt someone they love.'

'True.' Dawn considered if she had more questions, then glanced at Ryan who shrugged.

'Thanks for your time, Ms Farrell.' Dawn rose. 'If you think of anything, anything that might be useful even if it's only something trivial. Please let us know.'

Dawn indicated for Ryan to hand the woman a card. Tina frowned up at Ryan as she accepted it.

'How did she die?'

Rusty growled, making Ryan back away, hands raised. Dawn answered.

'We don't know yet. She's still being looked after by our pathology team.'

Dawn turned to leave.

'Where did they find her?'

Dawn turned back around. Ryan waited in the hall.

'She was discovered by a ranger at Keatings Lagoon up near Cooktown.'

'Cooktown?'

Tina's eyes grew wide but settled in a microsecond.

'Yes Cooktown. Is that significant in some way?'

'No.'

The answer was too quick. Not even a moment to consider it.

'Thanks for your time, Ms Farrell. We'll show ourselves out.'

Chapter 14

The stairs creaked as Dawn stepped onto the lawn. The swaying sugar cane and chattering birds were the only sounds she could hear as she opened the door and slid into Ryan's car as he started it. The throaty engine vibrated in her chest as her mind raced.

Ryan broke the silence.

'She knows something.'

'She does. But she's hard to read. One minute I'm certain I've got her pegged, then the next, I'm not sure. Her reaction to where the victim was found makes the place significant, but something doesn't sit right. We need to dig more, but first we need to interview the staff at Tenneson's office. See what they know about our Dominatrix and Yoga Instructor.

'And we need to interview Tenneson again. He must have known what the house was being used for.'

'No more than Mrs Nichols?' Dawn countered, waiting to see if he'd defend Lorraine Nichols or not.

Ryan put the car in reverse, swallowed hard, then turned to face her.

'Doesn't matter. It's Saturday anyway. The MP's office won't be open.'

'True. Maybe we should have a chat with the lead detective on the missing persons case first.'

'That should be interesting.'

The corners of Ryan's mouth curved but Dawn couldn't tell if he was smiling or sneering.

'Why? Do you know the detective well?'

'Cairns Major Crimes is a small team. Do you know everyone in the Adelaide unit?'

'I get it. You don't get along with the lead detective then?'

Ryan glanced over his shoulder as he backed out of the driveway.

'Oh, I wouldn't go that far.'

'Who's the lead anyway?' Dawn asked as the front window curtain flickered and Ryan shoved the car into drive.

Her instincts told her the sex dungeon and Tina were closely linked to their case, but what was the connection to Cooktown?

A sly grin crossed Ryan's lips.

'You'll find out.'

Dawn dreaded meeting the Cairns team. She'd waltzed in and taken their case right out from under them. An outsider. Someone they didn't know or trust. This wasn't going to be an easy meeting, but it was necessary.

'We need to chase up the pathologist. See if we have anything on a tox screen. I can't work out how the kidnapper got our victim from the beach, into a vehicle, all the way to Cooktown alive, then killed her out at Keatings Lagoon.'

'That's if you're right and they marched her out to her death.'

'There were no tire tracks from a wheelbarrow or bike to get the body out there.'

'Maybe she was dumped at the carpark and a croc stowed the remains under a log for a while?'

'She was missing for nearly a week before the body was found, so it's possible. But we have fibres from her clothing on the boardwalk observation hut. It must be where she went in.'

'True, but she still could have been dead by then.'

'That means two assailants.' Dawn chewed her lip. 'Let's get to the office, then the morgue, then hopefully we'll get some answers.'

'It's too late now to get from here to Cairns. It will be after hours by the time we get there.'

'So what next?'

'Let's book into accommodation in Port Douglas, enjoy a glass of wine and a meal and see what the night brings.'

'Meal, then bed.'

Ryan tongued his cheek to stop a grin.

'Sounds good to me.'

'Separate beds.'

'Of course. If you're sure?'

Dawn thought Ryan might wink any second, so she changed the subject.

'I know this car is fast, but you got to the crime scene quickly Friday morning. How is that? You didn't come into Cooktown on the police plane with the forensic team.'

Since finding her sister and taking long service leave, Dawn hadn't seen or heard from Ryan until last Wednesday, when out of the blue he called to check in on her.

'I was coming up to check on your house reno. Thought you might need a bit of muscle.'

'Michael is always around.'

Her sister's new boyfriend was helpful with lifting some of the heavier items, but for the most part, Dawn was managing the renovation bit by bit on her own. Unless you counted her six-year-old niece and her best mate Liam, but there was only so much a little kid could do and most of it, Dawn redid after Abby went to school.

It was a small price to pay to make up for not spending the first six years with her niece. Discovering she was an auntie was the last thing she expected when she went on the hunt to find her missing sister last month. But it was a very pleasant surprise.

'Yeah. But I didn't have much on. Thought I'd check in on your progress.'

'So you were on your way up when you got the call?'

'I didn't get reception until a few minutes outside Cooktown, but my chief knew I was up this way for the weekend, so he sent me out to follow up. I reckon if he'd known it was Jane's body, he might have thought better of it.'

'You haven't exactly explained why being related to Tenneson has you relegated to regional cases.'

'Money.'

'Money?'

'Yeah. My family has a lot of it and for some reason, no one wants to take a rich cop seriously.'

'I can't believe that.'

'They think I'm on a feel-good crusade or something. You know, looking after the little guy by finding the bad guys.'

'Maybe they don't want anything serious to happen to you. I get the impression it would be a PR nightmare to have a relative of the Tenneson family killed in the line of duty.'

'It doesn't matter the reason. I'm passed over for promotion. Given the small, low-profile cases and basically kept out of the media as much as possible.'

'Until now. How long before they rip this case out of our hands?'

'I don't know Grave. Your profile screams top rating PR. Young female detective, poached from SA. Your clearance rate is top notch. I think Sergeant Martin has the right idea and he cleared your temporary placement and ID without protest from the top dogs.'

'Great. Now I'll have everyone scrutinising the case and watching every step we make.'

'Happy to ride your coattails.'

Ryan glanced her way. The twinkle in his eyes was back.

Dawn studied his tight button-up shirt and the muscles beneath, reminding herself that she wasn't going to drink tonight. Ryan was attractive. There was no doubt they shared some chemistry, but she was only living in Cooktown temporarily and definitely not looking for a long-term relationship.

She knew Ryan wasn't either and a one-night stand would ruin their working relationship.

'Where are we staying? I've not even cleared an accommodation budget with the Sergeant.'

Dawn glanced around as they drove down the main road, lined with palm trees and framed by various resorts and caravan parks. A lush green golf course, with twin towers marking the entrance boasted its own exit from the roundabout where a signpost pointed toward the township of Port Douglas.

Holiday apartments lined either side as they turned left onto a congested road. Chairs and tables spilled out onto the walkway from eateries. Pedestrians strolled along the path, stopping to peer into shops.

'I know a spot, down by the harbour. Great sunsets, close to the restaurants.'

'Sounds expensive.'

'Nothing my Visa can't handle.'

'I bet.'

Dawn mulled over the idea of letting Ryan foot the bill for her accommodation, but decided it wasn't worth the fight.

'I think I might even be able to get the lead detective to call in and join us for dinner. We can quiz her about the case notes and see if anything we've discovered rings a bell.'

'Her?'

'Didn't I mention?'

Dawn could see Ryan knew full well he hadn't. He alluded to the fact Dawn might find meeting the lead detective on the missing persons case challenging, but something about his manner gave her the impression the reason was nothing to do with the case, or jurisdiction.

'Don't tell me. You slept with her too?'

His hand flattened over his chest as a curve crept across his lips.

'You think me that shallow?'

'Absolutely, but I'm not judging.'

How could she? Detective Clint Ryan was guilty of the exact same thing she was. Dawn knew too well about a life of one-night stands and corrosive relationships that didn't last long—one in particular was the reason she continually ignored Ryan's flirting.

Don't get close Grave.

She knew cops made shitty boyfriends and even crappier husbands. Something only experience could teach someone.

'You okay?' Ryan asked as he drove into the driveway of a three-storey home overlooking the marina.

Dawn sucked in a deep breath, set her shoulders back and smiled weakly.

'I'm fine. Let's invite this detective to dinner and see what we can find out.'

Chapter 15

The sun dipped beyond the horizon as streaks of pink, orange and purple illuminated the heavy clouds. Ryan slid the balcony door open. The light evening breeze lifted the curtain and blew it away from the doorway.

The detective was momentarily wrapped in sheer fabric, appearing with two glasses of white wine in hand.

'I thought you could use one of these while we wait for dinner.'

Ryan passed her a long-stemmed glass. She accepted it, despite her earlier promise not to drink.

Just one glass. She reminded herself.

But as the tang touched her tastebuds, she knew she wouldn't stop at one. Yet the night was early. They had a meeting with Detective Jade Parker and dinner to get through yet. She could moderate her intake and make sure she didn't make a fool of herself.

'What's the plan, with Parker? You know her. How should we go in?'

Dawn swallowed a sip of wine and immediately followed it with a second.

'This isn't an interrogation. Jade will be fine. She's going to be pissed we have the case now, but she'll get over it.'

'Because this case is linked to Cooktown, and we've got suspects in Cairns, we'll need a two-pronged approach on this one.'

Ryan turned to take in the view.

'True. What are you thinking?'

Dawn studied his profile in the fading light, then forced her mind back on the case.

'I'm thinking, I'll head back to Cooktown and investigate why Tina was stirred up about Cooktown and

Tenneson. His connection to Keatings Lagoon can't be ignored either. You and Parker can interview the staff at Tenneson's office on Monday and check their alibis. Ask them about Jane and Tina's work as a dominatrix. Maybe by then we'll have a cause of death and more to go on.'

Ryan swallowed a mouthful of his drink, swilled the glass thoughtfully, then turned to face Dawn.

'I'm coming back to Cooktown with you. Something about this case has me on edge. I'm not comfortable letting you go it alone in Cooktown.'

'You're not *letting* me do anything.'

Ryan shook his head. 'You know what I mean.' He checked his watch. 'Finish your wine. We've got to meet Parker.'

'I thought it was *Jade.*'

Ryan reached the sliding door and turned with a grin.

'You jealous?' He didn't wait for a reply.

Dawn followed him inside.

'Don't be ridiculous.'

She strode through from the balcony, across the living room to the long, white quartz counter and passed her empty glass to Ryan, who rinsed it and turned it upside down on the dish rack alongside his own.

He studied her as he wiped his hands on a towel.

'You know what it's like treading that fine line between work and socialising with co-workers outside the job.'

Dawn didn't actually know what that was like at all. She went out of her way not to socialise with coworkers, unless she counted Penny. The forensic tech from Adelaide was a great nightclub buddy.

She wanted to know more about Ryan's relationship with Parker, but why? She decided to change the subject.

'Where are we eating?'

Ryan finished drying his hands, studying her a moment before tossing the cloth on the bench and striding to the table by the stairwell.

'Let's get going. The restaurant is over the road at the marina.'

Ryan grabbed the room key, then jogged down the hardwood staircase. Dawn followed, admiring the light timber banister, matching floor and furniture in the beachside home.

She tried not to think about how much Ryan was spending to stay there. The location alone would be expensive. But this wasn't an apartment. It was a three storey, luxury home right across the road from the marina with breathtaking views of the water and surrounding hills.

As they stepped outside, humidity engulfed her. The earlier breeze was gone. The still air was thick with the scent of pending rain.

A lightning strike lit the sky as the first raindrop slapped her on the face.

'Did you bring an umbrella?'

'No. We better run.'

Ryan jogged across the road. Dawn right behind him, thankful she was still wearing her flats. As she thought about her shoes, she realised she wasn't exactly dressed for dining out. She was thankful the rain plastered her fuzzy hair down as she sprinted through the carpark toward the marina entrance.

A courtesy bus pulled up as they reached cover. Jovial tourists streamed out and bustled along the dimly lit walkway, past closed shops on either side.

Dawn rounded the corner as lightning flashed across the sky, illuminating the masts of the boats, floating at their marina berths. Timber decking echoed under foot, as the hum of chatter filled the busy restaurant.

'I hope you got an undercover seat,' Dawn asked as she noted the open-air seating along the front deck.

'There she is.'

Ryan strode past raised planters and the restaurant counter, into the enclosed dining area of the brewery. Dawn inhaled the scent of pizza and beer, which was instantly replaced with the aroma of jasmine and honeysuckle as a tall, thin, beautiful blonde woman levitated from her seat to greet them. Well to greet Ryan anyway.

'Clint. Glad you called.'

Parker's smile was delicate, seductive. Dawn frowned.

'You must be the infamous Detective Grave. I've heard so much about you.'

Dawn glanced at Ryan who shrugged to say it wasn't from him.

'Nice to meet you Detective.' Dawn held out her hand.

'Please, call me Jade. I like to keep it casual. It is Far North Queensland after all. Everything is pretty loose up this way.' Jade's handshake was firm.

'You're not from around here originally then?'

Jade sat down and waved for Dawn to join her.

'Sydney. Been in Cairns for five years now.'

Ryan scanned their faces a moment. Dawn noticed him relax.

'Can I grab drinks ladies?'

'I'll do the taster platter thanks Clint.'

Jade was quick to accept his offer. Dawn hesitated.

Ryan hovered. 'Another wine?'

Dawn procrastinated too long.

'I'll grab a bottle.'

She turned to protest, but he was gone. As he disappeared behind a planter filled with colours too bright to be real, the smile on Jade's face evaporated.

'Don't expect me to play nice just because you're sleeping with Clint.'

Dawn blinked a moment before the comment sunk in. 'What the hell!'

Parker leant forward over the table and drilled Dawn with her eyes.

'How else did you score this case out from under my team?'

Dawn mirrored the detective's position, leaning forward, hands flat on the table.

'I can assure you—I'm *not* sleeping with Ryan.'

Jade sat back and scoffed, then crossed her arms over her chest.

'Oh please. I see the way he gawks at you.'

Dawn ignored the comment. This wasn't about Ryan. This was about Dawn's ability to lead an investigation. She kept her tone calm and civil.

'I've been assigned this case off the back of my investigative ability and track record.'

Jade shook her head.

'Let's just say, I'm not one of your devotees.'

'Let's just say I don't exactly care. I'm in charge of this investigation whether you like it or not and as much as I enjoy having a cooperative team to work with, it wouldn't be the first time I've worked in a hostile environment.'

The women glared at one another, neither willing to give any ground. A bottle of wine appeared on the table. Dawn jumped. Ryan glanced from face to face. As Dawn looked back to Jade, she was surprised to see the woman's expression was once again all smiles.

Chapter 16

Ryan lifted the wine bottle from the ice bucket as another lightning bolt lit the sky. The clap of thunder came hard and fast, rippling through Dawn's body.

Was the detective annoyed about the case being ripped away from her, or her perceived notion about what was possibly going on with Ryan?

Jade's fake smile turned Dawn's way.

'So, what do you need to know?'

Dawn pursed her lips. How could the woman switch from outright hostile to butter wouldn't melt in her mouth, in the blink of an eye?

'Food first.' Ryan slipped menus around the table, seemingly oblivious to the tension between the two women, but when Dawn reached for the menu from his hand, he held it a few seconds too long.

She made eye contact. His expression asking if she was alright. She forced a smile. He pursed his lips, then let the menu go.

Dawn scanned it in silence. Her mind racing, her eyes seeing nothing. Her appetite was gone, but the wine was going to her head. She needed to eat.

'I'll grab the entrée scallops.'

She slid the menu back harder than intended. It careered across the table landing on the wooden deck beyond.

'I'm having a meat lovers pizza,' Ryan said.

'Of course you are,' Jade chuckled. It was forced, but they all ignored it.

'I'll have a pumpkin salad.'

Dawn wasn't surprised at the selection. The woman was wafer thin. Even her cheekbones were sharp.

Stop whining. She admonished herself.

The woman was probably a fine detective. But why the animosity? There was something personal underlying Detective Jade Parker's demeanour and Dawn's instincts were telling her it wasn't case related.

Dawn scooped up the menus, including the one still sitting on the floor.

'I'll order.'

'No. I've got this.' Ryan joined her.

'I'll expense it with Martin.'

She knew her tone was curt.

'I've got to grab our beers in any case.'

He nodded to the long timber bar where two taster platters of local brew were waiting. The four smaller glasses on each platter were various shades of ale. From dark, to light amber. The sight was alluring.

Dawn wasn't a big beer drinker, with all the tension and frustrated energy pumping through her body, she was sure she could have downed all four testers in less than thirty seconds.

She knew she was letting personal crap get in the way of her work. Pulling back her shoulders, she reset. She didn't know Jane Nichols. This wasn't like when her sister went missing. This wasn't like her brother's faked suicide. And she didn't give a crap what Parker thought of her.

'Okay. You win.'

She turned and plonked back down in her chair with a sigh.

Ryan leant in close to her ear. His warm breath made her stiffen.

'It wasn't a competition. Are you okay?'

He pulled back to study her.

She tried to keep the raging emotions from her face. Why was she so worked up? Glancing at the glass of wine, mesmerising in the soft brewery lighting, she realised why.

She'd been sober, not one glass of wine for nearly a month. One was never enough. It hadn't been for her father either. His drinking probably ruined her parents' marriage and sent her father to an early grave.

She waved him away.

'I'm good. Thanks Ryan.'

He opened his mouth, then closed it and stalked across the decking, dodging chairs on his way to the bar.

Dawn shoved her turmoil down deep so she could focus on work. Turning to Jade, she tried unsuccessfully not to look smug.

'I'm curious. How did your team miss the hidden sex dungeon at the Nichols' holiday home in Newell Beach anyway?'

'We weren't searching for a murderer. We were searching for a missing person.'

Jade reached for a coaster from the centre cutlery caddy and placed it under Dawn's perspiring glass without asking. She then extracted cutlery for everyone and placed a set in front of Dawn.

Was she suddenly trying to play nice, or was this a control issue?

'Still. A simple walk of the floor plan would have raised suspicion. Is there a reason you didn't take Jane Nichols' disappearance seriously?'

'We took it seriously. The scene was the beach not the house. The beach was where her dog was found. It's where a neighbour last saw her.'

'Which neighbour?'

'Some old biddy who lives on the foreshore there. Owns the bright purple house opposite the reserve where the Nichols' property entrance is.'

'Her statement wasn't in the file Ryan showed me.'.

'It should have been,' Jade huffed.

'Who has access to the file?'

'Me. Ryan. Rossi and Murib are all in Major Crimes in Cairns, but then anyone with database clearance could access the file.'

'So why would anyone tamper with your investigation? The witness only said she saw our victim on the day she died. Why remove the statement?'

'Apparently that's your problem now.'

Dawn was surprised Jade wasn't pouting. She stayed silent, letting the comment slide. Jade huffed again.

'I've got my copy. I'll send it to Ryan.'

Dawn opened her mouth to offer thanks as Ryan arrived and placed two platters on the table.

'What did I miss?'

He shoved one platter toward Jade, who reached for the first glass without consulting the description or the name of the beer sample.

'Parker was just going over why they missed our dominatrix's dungeon.'

'I bet that was a fun find.'

Jade's grin was mischievous but to Dawn's surprise, Ryan wasn't playing along with the inuendo.

She wondered over their history again but deleted the thought from her mind. She likely carried more baggage than the two of them put together.

Her mind recalled something Parker said a moment before.

'Did you say you have a Rossi on your team?'

Dawn waited but Jade was already sculling her second beer sample.

'Yeah.' Ryan answered. Dawn's flesh broke out in goosebumps as her stomach knotted.

'Is his first name Declan?'

Parker's eyes narrowed over the top of her almost empty beer glass.

'How did you know?'

Dawn suppressed the urge to vomit and tried to ignore the shudder running down her spine. It was nearly two decades ago now. It couldn't be him.

'Dawn. You okay?'

Ryan reached for her hand. She snatched it away. Lightning crackled across the sky. Thunder vibrated the roof as staff began bustling about, dropping café blinds along the western wall as a moist breeze picked up.

The soft rain from earlier grew heavy, hitting the tin sheeting like rapid fire. Thankfully a reply was impossible as the sound of pouring rain drowned out further conversation. Dawn fought the urge to jump up and run back to the apartment and hide.

It couldn't be him. How on earth was she going to lead this investigation if it were?

Chapter 17

Dawn flung the toilet door open with a thud. The panic attack came from nowhere. She'd been fine for over a month. Drawing quick breaths, she hung her head over the bathroom basin and turned the tap on.

Scooping up water, she patted her flushed cheeks and studied her reflection in the mirror.

'Get your shit together girl!'

She spoke to the person looking back at her.

A thump on the bathroom door made her jump.

'You alright in there Grave?'

'I'm fine. Be out in a sec.'

What was she going to tell Ryan? And what about Detective Parker? She'd made an utter fool of herself in front of a colleague. Great first impression of a tough cop, up to the job of leading the investigation.

How was she going to walk back out there and act like nothing ever happened?

'You've got five minutes or I'm coming in after you.'

'I said I'm fine Ryan. Just cramps.'

Playing the female card was unfair, but it was all she could think of in the moment. Would he believe it?

Maybe.

She flushed the loo, even though she didn't need to go. Then pressed the silver dryer button and waved her hands through the warm air. The bathroom was small, tiled to the ceiling, with moisture beading on the ceiling from the humidity outside.

The heat from the dryer was only making it worse. Sighing, she turned and opened the bathroom door, right into Ryan's worried expression.

'You haven't got cramps.'

Well, it was worth a try. She thought.

'I'll explain later. Not here. Not with *her*.'

Ryan glanced from her to Parker sitting at the table, well into her last beer sample, and back.

'I thought you were getting along fine.'

'You'd think so wouldn't you.'

Dawn didn't wait for a reply. Crossing the restaurant, she wound her way through the chairs and plonked down on the seat she'd occupied before.

'Sorry about that. Now where were we?'

Parker frowned, glanced at Ryan as he sat back down and opened her mouth to speak, but closed when the waitress arrived with their food.

'Meat lover's pizza?' the waitress asked.

Ryan raised his hand as he sat.

'That's me.'

Dawn saw the entrée plate in the woman's hand.

'I'm the scallops.'

Ryan filled her glass and she suddenly wished she'd ordered something more substantial.

'That makes you the pumpkin salad,' the waitress smiled. Parker plastered a polite grin on her lips. Dawn nearly scoffed aloud as the waitress left the table.

Ryan grabbed a piece of pizza and shoved half the slice in his mouth, but his eyes were watching Dawn closely. Questioningly.

She'd have given anything to be able to go back to the apartment and forget any of this happened, but she also needed to know if Rossi was involved in the case. If he was, he might have taken the details from the file when he found out she was looking after the case.

'What's your history with Rossi then?'

Parker's salad was untouched.

Dawn filled her mouth to avoid answering immediately. The scallop was tasteless. She chewed excessively as she considered brushing off the question. But there was no point. Sooner or later, they'd discover the truth.

But how much detail did she need to share?

'He's just an ex.'

'What!'

Parker and Ryan exclaimed in unison. Dawn put another scallop into her mouth.

Ryan dropped his half-eaten piece of pizza on the plate. 'You and Rossi?'

Parker picked up her fork and smiled. 'Great.' She waved her loaded fork at Ryan. 'You and he can exchange notes.' She finally shoved food into her gob and pointed her empty fork victoriously at Ryan.

'Shut it, Parker.'

'Touchy,' she mumbled over a mouthful.

'It's not noteworthy. Can we get back to the case?' Dawn didn't wait for a protest. 'Did you find any receipts from our victim's yoga business? A credit card machine maybe?'

'What business?'

Parker wasn't shovelling food into her face anymore.

'Jane Nichols was a yoga teacher, but her friend, Tina, said she was putting her own dominatrix work through Jane's card machine, and on her books.'

'News to us, but you know we didn't know about the dungeon. We didn't go deep into her financials, but there were no recent withdrawals from her everyday accounts and nothing significant popped out on her Visa card statements in the days before her disappearance either.'

'Let's take a look at her banking again. Since we now know she was found in Cooktown, there might be a receipt for accommodation you missed.'

'Go for it. I'll get it sent to Ryan's email, but we didn't miss anything.'

Parker shovelled another forkful into her mouth. The fake smile waned, and a scowl creased her brow. She was getting edgy.

'So you didn't find a boyfriend? No social media stuff worth noting?'

'Nothing like that. We were thorough. Jane Nichols was missing, and she was high profile, but we couldn't find any evidence to suggest foul play was involved.'

'Except her dog was tied up and abandoned on the beach.' Ryan's tone was critical.

Parker rolled her eyes.

'Yes, but that led us to believe she'd gone for a swim and possibly drowned.'

'Were her clothes found on the beach?' Dawn asked as Ryan started refilling her glass.

For a minute, she was confused, having not recalled drinking the last one. Was it the tension of finding out about Declan or maybe it was Parker breathing down her neck. Either way, she waved her hand to stop him from topping it up fully.

'I've not eaten enough to keep drinking.'

'Then order something decent. Or do you want a piece of this?'

Ryan waved at his almost empty pizza plate.

'Are you sure you two aren't sleeping together?'

Parker's grin was back.

'Just tell us if you found her clothes.'

'No, we didn't, but why would we? She lived a few metres away.'

'Then why take her dog with her? That's pretty lame, even for you Parker. Tenneson must have been putting the pressure on. Why didn't you send divers out if you thought she'd drowned?' Ryan's expression was tight.

'Because Tenneson wasn't putting any pressure on us. In fact, he didn't want us to search the house at first. But since the house isn't his, it's his wife's, we got the go ahead anyway.'

Dawn and Ryan exchanged a look. The same question passed between them, but it was Dawn who asked.

'So why didn't Tenneson want the house searched?'

'Give the girl a kewpie doll.'

Parker's smile was gone, replaced by the sneer Dawn saw earlier.

Dawn rose, placed her hands palm down on the table one by one and leant forward. Her stomach was churning—not because Tenneson didn't want the house searched. Parker continued to sneer. Dawn held her gaze.

'This is a murder investigation Parker, which *I'm* leading. I want your team up bright and early in the morning. Briefing is at 7.00, sharp!'

Without another word, she turned and strode from the restaurant, vaguely aware of Ryan scrambling to follow.

Chapter 18

Dawn waited outside the apartment feeling like a complete idiot after she realised the keycard was in Ryan's pocket.

Why did Parker piss her off so much? And why did she care?

As Ryan drew up behind her, she realised the answer to her question. Parker accusing her of sleeping with him to get on the case made her blood boil. But it shouldn't have. She'd learnt long ago to let the rubbish and mudslinging from her coworkers slide. Reacting never got her anywhere.

Years on the job taught her not to throw her weight around. It only annoyed her male colleagues. But she'd rarely experienced this kind of animosity from a female co-worker. Was Parker jealous? And was her own reaction a case of protesting too much? Was she letting her partner get too close?

A hand touched her shoulder. She jumped.

'You okay?'

Dawn sighed, turning to face Ryan.

'I shouldn't have lost it.'

'Which time?' Ryan's lip curled into a grin, softening his words.

'What's Parker's story?'

Ryan stepped forward, opened the door and held it. Dawn noticed he'd taken the time to retrieve the wine bottle, still half full.

She didn't need alcohol. She needed a good night's sleep and a chance to get her head straight, but the question in Ryan's eyes told her he wanted an explanation, at least about Rossi.

'Parker is a lot like you.' Ryan closed the door.

Dawn started up the stairs.

'I don't think so. That nice as pie act was just that. The moment you left the table the devil came out.'

Ryan's laugh followed her up the staircase. Dawn turned toward the window when she reached the top, to see the harbour lights glimmering through the sheer curtains and floor to ceiling glass. Another bolt of lightning cracked across the sky, threatening a fresh downpour.

'Parker's done it hard. She's fought her way to where she is. Like you, she doesn't suffer fools gladly. I think she was testing you.'

Dawn contemplated Ryan's remark as another fork of lightning broke across the sky, followed immediately by rolling thunder. Despite the windows being closed, moisture hung in the air, weighing down on her.

'Then I think I failed miserably.'

Ryan stepped up behind her, his warm hands touching her shoulders as he turned her to face him. She avoided eye contact like a child in trouble—embarrassed and lacking in confidence.

'I don't think so.'

He lifted her chin.

'You held your ground. Took charge. Told her to suck it up and get her shit together.'

Dawn looked into his clear blue eyes and for a moment she thought he might kiss her. As he released her chin and stepped away, she quelled her disappointment.

Maybe I am getting too close.

He strolled to the kitchen, retrieved the glasses from the drying rack and poured them a glass of wine each.

'Now tell me about Rossi.'

Dawn accepted the overly full glass despite her inner voice warning her she was in no state to drink. Another glass and she might find herself on a roll, unable to stop. Like her father, Dawn didn't have an off switch. Too many times she'd woken up unable to recall the night before.

Ryan led her to the plush modular lounge, but instead of sitting, he drew the curtains back and dimmed the lights. The lightning seemed to answer the call, striking the sky with vengeance.

As he opened the front doors, hot heavy air filled the apartment. Dawn's heart ached with the weight. The first few years of her adult life were a complete mess. Was she going to share her history with Rossi?

Ryan broke the tension.

'I've worked with Rossi for years. He's a right dick, so I get why you might not think much of him—even why he's your ex, but he *is* a good cop.'

Dawn sipped her wine, trying to work out where to start. She'd not even told Lisa about Rossi. Composing herself, she decided to keep it vague. Ryan was a work colleague and nothing more.

'Declan was in my brother Fraser's grade. When mum disappeared, I went off the rails big time. Declan Rossi was there, not always in a good way.'

Dawn sipped her wine hoping to leave it there, but Ryan wasn't appeased.

'So you had a teenage fling with him. That doesn't explain why you went white and ran to the loo like you were going to throw up.'

Adjusting her position on the lounge, she sat silently, willing him to drop the subject. The sky lit up, as thunder rumbled overhead. Her body shuddered in response. She wouldn't tell him everything. She couldn't—if she started, she might not be able to stop herself.

But she'd give him enough.

'When I left town, it was with Declan. I didn't have wheels. He did. When Fraser died, he said he'd take me away—take care of me.'

'I can't see you needing to be taken care of.'

Dawn shook her head, drawing a slow breath. Ryan waited with gentle eyes.

'You didn't know me then. You know about Fairweather.' She didn't wait for Ryan to nod. Sucking in air, she rushed on. 'After his touchy-feely episode, I was messed up, but then mum disappeared without a trace. Dad started drinking even more heavily and I was left running the household—making sure Lisa got to school and did her homework and then Fraser died.'

Dawn's heartbeat sounded in her ears as oxygen refused to fill her lungs. A crack of thunder made her gasp. Raindrops the size of dollar coins pinged against the outdoor furniture and balcony tiles.

She continued to hyperventilate. Ryan squeezed her hand.

'Just breathe Dawn.' He shuffled closer.

She shook her hand to say *no*, then pointed to the window where raindrops landed on the timber floor.

'I'm fine.' She didn't want him to hold her or give her any reason to lose control. 'Get the doors.' She waved him away and placed her head between her knees, willing herself to control her breathing.

A moment later, she glanced up to see Ryan shielding his face from the rain as he pulled the doors closed. A childish giggle escaped her lips.

'Glad I could entertain you.' Ryan rejoined her on the lounge and collected his wine glass. 'You don't have to go on. What happened between you and Rossi is none of my business. I shouldn't have asked.'

Dawn drained her wine. Ryan reached for the bottle and refilled it. She didn't protest. With each mouthful, the pain in her chest ebbed away.

'It's okay. You were going to find out soon enough. I worked in a bar on the Gold Coast while Declan decided to join the police force. A joke really, because when we were in Cooktown, it was Declan who got me into so much trouble with Constable Martin.'

'The sergeant.'

'He is now, but Ross is the one who set me straight. He didn't press charges when I got caught with the spray can Declan gave me.'

Another crack of lightning lit the sky. Dawn let it drag her away a moment as she tried to build up the courage to say what needed to be said.

'When Declan was near the end of his police training, we got married.'

'Married!' Ryan failed to keep the surprise from his voice.

Dawn sighed.

'A mistake. Declan got a job on the Gold Coast, working mostly nights around Surfers Paradise clubs and bars. He was dealing with his own crap back then. I'm sure he's sorted himself out since.'

Ryan looked ready to ask more about Rossi, but his question surprised Dawn.

'So why did you leave?'

'He might have left me.'

'Not likely.'

Dawn bit her cheek as she considered how the truth would affect Ryan's working relationship with Rossi in the future. He didn't need to know why she left.

'We grew apart.'

He opened his mouth to ask for more but stopped himself. Dawn could see in his eyes he wasn't buying her story. Not after her loo dash. But Ryan had the good sense to realise she wasn't going to tell him everything today.

'And you moved to Adelaide.'

'Not straight away. I joined the police in Queensland but transferred to SA after basic training.' She was going to say to get away from Rossi but stopped herself. 'The rest is history as they say.'

She forced a smile to her lips, watching as Ryan sucked his teeth.

Dawn was relieved when he changed the subject to work.

'What's your take on Tenneson not wanting Parker's team to search the house?'

'He knew the dungeon was there.'

'That's my take too. We'll call back in to see Tenneson tomorrow.'

'If he knows about Tina's work, then he might be willing to share his knowledge on her clientele or convince Tina to.'

'That's if he isn't involved in Jane's death.'

'I don't see why he'd want her dead.' Dawn drained her wine and rose. 'There is a reason our victim was in Cooktown, willingly or not. And if we can find out why, we might be able to find her killer.'

Ryan joined her at the sink.

'You going to be okay working with Rossi?'

'I'm a big girl. History is history.'

'He won't be happy you're leading this case.'

'No, but he'll live with it, or I'll take him off it.'

She smiled on the inside and out. She wasn't nineteen anymore. She wasn't afraid of Declan Rossi, or his

108

connections. Right now, all she was thinking was how he better have cleaned up his act or she'd rip his career out from under him.

Chapter 19

The wide, tree-lined street bustled with early morning traffic. Ryan slowed, turning left, he steered his Mustang toward the underground parking entrance. As they entered, Dawn glanced up at the Courthouse and the adjacent modern glass-fronted building which housed the Cairns Police Headquarters.

Her stomach tightened as Ryan guided his vehicle around the high roofed parking area. They passed well-lit parking spots, clearly labelled for high priority police vehicles. A row of white four-wheel drives lined the left, while a variety of darker sedans, with chequered police stripes filled various spots around the structure.

Ryan nodded toward an unmarked vehicle as he parked in a restricted spot.

'That's Rossi's car.' His tone was informative, but Dawn read his worried expression.

'I'm fine Ryan.'

Ryan's eyes studied her as they stepped out of the Mustang. It seemed Ryan knew she was holding back the full story about Rossi. Her new partner's instincts were good and she wondered how long she could keep him in the dark.

Ryan hovered, chewing his cheek like he wasn't sure what to say. Finally, he waved toward a brightly illuminated stairwell but didn't move.

'He'll be a dick.'

Dawn kept her expression calm, even though her stomach was rolling like she might vomit any second. Maybe Ryan could read her better than she wanted him to.

'I know.'

Ryan nodded, then led the way. Two sets of stainless-steel lift doors flanked the stairwell. Dawn suspected the stairs bypassed the reception area. She was only too happy to keep her head down and get on with the morning briefing.

The stairs doubled back, then opened out into a wide hallway, leading past an open office area, lined with more private offices, likely used by senior staff. Laughing and voices echoed down the hallway from an open door. Dawn could hear Parker's melodic tones, then Rossi's voice broke through. Her stomach tightened.

Ryan stopped a few steps away from the briefing room. 'You good?'

Dawn nodded and strode past him, catching the smirk on his lips. Voices stopped as she entered.

'Morning everyone. I'm Detective Grave. Thanks for meeting so early.'

She drew her shoulders back and made her way to the front of the room where a blank whiteboard waited. Picking up the black marker-pen, she drew a line down the middle of the board.

'Parker and Rossi I know. Ryan of course. Let's get the last few intros sorted and we can find a killer.'

Rossi's eyebrows were high. Dawn scanned Parker's face to find a vicious grin lurking.

She didn't warn him?

Dawn let the thought fester a moment, but Ryan interrupted with introductions.

'This is Detective Murib.' Ryan pointed to a man with dark olive skin, bushy black eyebrows and a long, thin, crooked nose. A wide smile split his moustache and beard-framed lips.

'Pleased to meet you Detective.' He rose from his seat, hand outstretched.

'You too Detective.'

Dawn shook his hand and nodded for him to return to his chair. Scanning the room, her eyes fell on a young constable with ginger hair. He scrambled from his seat with wide eyes. Dawn noticed his pressed uniform, polished shoes and gloss black belt.

'This is Constable Jed Craig,' Ryan offered, then introduced two more constables.

Dawn nodded, exchanged pleasantries then drew a slow breath.

'Okay team. I'm sorry to butt into this investigation, but the body found at Cooktown on Friday has been confirmed as your missing person Jane Nichols, so we are working this as a joint investigation.'

Murmurs rolled around the room. She soldiered on knowing her next statement was likely to elicit objections.

'I've been given lead on this by Queensland Police.'

Rossi found his voice. 'But you're SAPOL!'

Dawn was surprised he knew she'd taken a job with the South Australian Police Force. The thought he might have kept tabs on her after she left unnerved her. She told herself it was probably just cop shop talk.

'That's correct Rossi, however I'm on leave and been temporarily contracted to Queensland Police.'

Dawn turned to the whiteboard, attempting to move on.

'Why are you in charge?' Rossi rose from the chair, his tone taking on a hint of malice she was only too familiar with.

Dawn watched Parker roll her lips to supress a snigger.

'Not your call Rossi.' Ryan pushed off the desk and crossed to stand in front of her ex.

Dawn shook her head and opened her mouth to interrupt but didn't get the chance.

'Sit your arses down both of you.'

A broad man in uniform entered the room. Dawn noted his sergeant stripes.

'Sergeant,' she nodded.

'Grave. Have to say I'm not impressed we're not taking lead on this, but the Nichols family doesn't care who finds out who killed their daughter. Let's get on with it. It's your case—for now.'

Was that a threat?

'I'm just here to oversee station procedure and make sure we get a fair crack at it.'

Dawn nodded, turned back to the small group of faces in front of her, avoiding Rossi's steely gaze, but not missing Parker's smirk.

Smoothing her features, her eyes found Ryan's. His face was calm. He didn't say a word, but an unseen energy passed from him to her. She drew herself up.

'Okay. We don't have a postmortem report yet, but the forensic tech found yellow fibres, matching our victim's clothing, on the boardwalk hut overlooking the water. There were no signs of a struggle, so either our victim was carried to the dump site, unlikely considering the terrain, or she walked out, was killed, then dumped off the boardwalk into the water.'

Dawn wrote at the top of the whiteboard in block letters.

WHY COOKTOWN?

'So far, we've not found any connection between our victim and Cooktown. We did find a dominatrix dungeon in her family holiday home. Ryan and I'll be talking to Tenneson today because we believe he knew about the hidden room but told you nothing.

'We'll also follow up with the victim's closest friend, Tina Farrell who lives in Newell Beach, along with a Mrs Lundstrom, who apparently doesn't miss anything. Then we'll head to Cooktown to find a connection.

'I'd like Rossi and Parker to follow up with Tenneson's staff. Ask about Tina Farrell's relationship with Tenneson, and our victim. Find out where they all were the afternoon our victim disappeared.'

Dawn didn't mention how Mrs Lundstrom's information went missing from Ryan's file notes, but as her eyes fell on Rossi, she couldn't help but wonder if he'd pulled the information because he knew she was on the case. But his surprise when she entered said otherwise.

'What do you want me to do?' Murib's eyes were eager.

At least someone seemed pleased to do their job and not give Dawn a hard time.

'I'd like you to run a background check on Tina Farrell. She's holding information back. She claims it was her dominatrix dungeon at the beach house. She said Jane Nichols was putting her clients through as yoga clients to cover the paper trail and maintain anonymity.

Parker said you have our victim's financials. Dive a little deeper and see if you can find a merchant account for Jane Nichols' yoga business or a bank account she could have been running her clients through.

See if you can find a connection to Cooktown while you are there. Clients from there. Any reason she'd go willingly to Cooktown.'

Rossi interrupted.

'But her dog was left behind. Surely she'd have taken her dog with her to Cooktown if she went willingly?'

Rossi wasn't saying anything she and Ryan hadn't already debated.

'We agree. But something isn't adding up. I can't explain exactly why, but even though the crime scene didn't look like our primary scene, I think it was. There were no drag marks.'

Ryan's phone pinged. Dawn carried on as he began scrolling.

'The track was narrow and rough. Unless the guy was built like the Terminator, I can't see how he could have carried our victim all the way to the hut on his own.'

'Maybe he wasn't alone?' Ryan offered, eyes still on the screen.

'What?'

Dawn waited as Ryan continued to read.

'Gleeson has emailed the tox screen. Our victim had large amounts of cocaine in her system?'

Dawn frowned.

'Large like an OD?'

Ryan put his phone away.

'Let's go find out. Coroner has her on the table now.'

Dawn scanned the room.

'Okay, you know where we are at. Ryan and I'll be back in Cooktown tonight. Parker, Rossi, text me with any updates as soon as you check out the alibis and Murib, anything of interest, let me know or pass the information on to Constable Reynolds at Cooktown if you can't get a hold of me.'

The station sergeant mustered the constables from the room. Dawn realised she didn't have his name but brushed the thought aside.

'Sergeant.' The man turned. 'Can you pass my mobile on to the team?'

He nodded, his face sour like he'd sucked a lemon. Dawn shrugged it off and watched the room empty, all except Rossi who waved at Parker to head out alone.

Ryan joined her, cleaning the whiteboard.

'The team will have a board going in the Major Crimes office.'

'No worries.'

Dawn turned to leave but was halted by Rossi standing between her and the door. His expression was hard to read.

Ryan cleared his throat behind her.

'Can I borrow you a minute?'

Rossi's eyes were on Ryan, not her. But there was no doubt it was Dawn he wanted to speak with.

Dawn turned to Ryan. 'I'll meet you outside in a sec.' She nodded to the door.

Ryan's eyes scanned hers, then Rossi and back. A frown creased his brow.

She patted his shoulder. 'I've got this.'

'I'll be right outside.'

Was that a warning for Rossi or supposed to comfort her?

Ryan closed the briefing room door, but Dawn was sure he'd have an ear to it to make sure a fight didn't break out.

Dawn crossed her arms over her chest. 'Rossi?'

'What's with you and Ryan?'

Dawn ignored the question.

'What do you want?'

Dawn's heart thudded in her chest as he pursed his lips, glanced over his shoulder at the closed door, then drew a breath.

'Dawn. Don't be like that.'

'I'm here for one reason Rossi. To find a killer. The last time I saw you, you were up to your eyeballs in bikie gangs and drugs.'

It wasn't technically the last time she saw him, but she didn't want to relive her last night with him right now. Swallowing hard, she pressed on before she lost her nerve. 'I didn't expect to see you here and I'll be keeping a professional eye on you, so let's keep things formal.'

Rossi stepped forward. She stepped back as memories flooded back.

'I'm sorry.' He reached for her arm.

She snatched it from his reach.

'Too late Rossi. I hope you've changed, but maybe you haven't. We have a cocaine connection now. That seems pretty convenient to me.'

Rossi opened his mouth, frowned, closed it shaking his head.

'And Mrs Lundstrom's details were missing from Ryan's file. Why is that?'

'That's got nothing to do with me.'

'All I can say Rossi is it better not have.'

She shoved him aside with a flat hand on his chest and opened the briefing room door to find Ryan right behind it.

'Let's go.'

Chapter 20

Ryan followed her down the stairs into the undercover parking area.

'You okay?'

Dawn turned on him, nostrils flaring.

'Will you stop asking me that? I don't want to share my corrosive relationships with you right now! We have a murder to solve. Where's the morgue?'

She strode across the carpark, stopped outside his Mustang and tapped her foot, wishing she'd just said *fine*.

Now Ryan was aware how working with Rossi was getting to her. After all these years she should be fine. She wasn't a broken-hearted teen anymore. She was a confident and accomplished police detective, in control of her life.

Ryan studied her over the car roof. Even in the florescent lighting, she could see him holding back more questions.

'Don't ask. I'm not telling you anymore.'

Dawn tried the door, but it was still locked. Glaring over the car, she waited.

'The coroner's office and forensic pathology are next door in the Magistrates' building.'

She saw him resist the urge to grin.

'Of course they are,' she huffed.

'I've texted Gleeson. She'll meet us at the morgue where Greg will be conducting the autopsy.

'Great. Let's go.' She waved her hand for him to lead the way. 'Any idea who might have deleted our little old lady's report from the file before it was sent to you?'

Ryan crossed the carpark. Dawn followed.

'No idea. Is that what you asked Rossi?'

Dawn considered if this was Ryan trying to get her to reiterate her conversation, but decided it was a safe question to answer.

'I did. He said he didn't know anything about it. I'm inclined to believe him. I don't think he knew I was on the case, judging from Parker's gloating when I turned up. Unless she had reason to keep the information from you?'

Ryan pressed a button on the lift.

'I can't think of a reason. We're not close. Don't move in the same circles, but we get along fine, usually.'

There was a tone in Ryan's voice telling her he was re-evaluating his relationship with Rossi by the minute.

'Did Gleeson say there were any signs our victim was an addict?'

'The text was brief. Let's see if Greg can shed some light.'

The doors opened on the lift. Ryan stepped in and pressed the button for the basement as Dawn joined him. The lift jolted, then dropped a floor at lightning speed. The doors opened to a wide, white corridor straight ahead, with passageways to the left and right. Double doors blocked the entrance in either direction.

This wasn't Dawn's first morgue visit. Hospitals seemed like cosy apartment buildings in comparison. Her last visit to a morgue was to identify a body she thought might be Lisa's.

It was found in the same area as her sister's abandoned car. A heart wrenching moment—to be relieved someone else was dead and your loved one was safe felt wrong on so many levels.

At least this visit wasn't regarding a family member. She'd certainly experienced her fair share of those.

White walls glistened and the pungent smell of bleach permeated the air as Ryan led her down the end of the centre corridor to a reception desk.

Tammy Gleeson leant over the counter, chatting with a staff member. She glanced up as they arrived. Smiling, she waved them over.

'Hey team. Let's get this show on the road.'

She turned and began walking, not bothering to check if anyone was following. The receptionist held out a clipboard, her expression nonchalant. Ryan signed, then Dawn as Tammy pressed a green button on the wall and two doors whooshed open automatically.

A wave of cold air swept toward them. It was a shock given the outside temperature, but Dawn knew another level of chill would greet them once they entered the autopsy suite.

The white vinyl-clad walls gave way to a light blue-grey colour as another set of automatic doors flew open. To the left and right of the hallway were two autopsy suites, clearly marked by signs on the faux wooden doors. She guessed the touch of timber was supposed to warm the space.

It failed miserably.

Tammy pressed the button and the two doors swung inwards. Stainless steel, bright lights and wall to wall vinyl engulfed them on arrival.

'Ah Detectives.'

Doctor Mayfield's smiling eyes glanced their way for a split second, then focussed back on removing Jane Nichols' vital organs.

'Morning Greg.'

Ryan crossed the room. Dawn hesitated a moment but followed, ignoring the knot in her stomach and the goosebumps all over her skin.

'I believe we have a cause of death, unless we find more toxicology to the contrary.'

Greg didn't look up but waved a bloody glove for them to come closer.

'See here?'

Dawn and Ryan peered where he indicated. The flesh was white and pasty but a scattering of purple and blue indicated bruising.

Dawn shifted her gaze from the body to the doctor's face.

'You said you thought she was strangled from the petechial haemorrhaging in the eyes. Does this confirm it then?'

'Toxicology says she was high as a kite, but yes, cause of death wasn't an overdose. She was strangled. There is bruising here, a fracture in the hyoid bone and the petechial haemorrhaging, plus I found traces of what appears to be fibres embedded in a wound here.'

He pointed to the side of the victim's neck, but it was an unrecognisable mash of sinew and muscle tissue.

'I think your killer expected the crocodiles in the lagoon to dispose of the evidence. Gleeson here will be able to give you more once she's finished examining the fibres I collected earlier.'

'Done!' Tammy grinned at the doctor's wide eyes.

'You out to impress someone?' Greg teased. Tammy blushed.

'Just doing my job,' Tammy assured everyone. 'The fibre is bright green nylon, not sure what it's from yet. Find me a sample and I'll be able to match it, but it's too broad to point you in any specific direction for now.'

'Not helpful then?'

Ryan returned his gaze to the remains under Doctor Mayfield's scalpel. Dawn noticed Tammy waiting on Dawn's response. She nodded, then smiled encouragingly, but wondered over the attention.

Was it a mentoring thing?

Dawn was likely ten years older than the forensic tech. Maybe that was it. She shoved the thought aside and watched as Doctor Mayfield studied their victim's hands and fingernails.

'Did you find any trace under her nails?' Dawn asked when Ryan didn't. Her partner seemed distracted. It was expected considering his relationship with Mrs Nichols and his association with Jane.

'No signs of a struggle. No defensive wounds, but we did get some trace from under her nails earlier.' Doctor Mayfield didn't look up.

Tammy answered for him.

'No DNA to test though I'm afraid. I still need to run a trace on her clothing. I'll let you know if anything odd pops up there.'

Doctor Mayfield waved a bloodied glove in dismissal.

'And I'll do the same when I'm finished with her.'

'Thanks Doctor Mayfield.'

Dawn turned to leave.

'I said call me Greg.'

Dawn noticed his smiling eyes again and tried to ignore the flutter in her stomach. Ryan rallied from his funk.

'Always the charmer. Watch this one.' He hoicked a thumb at the doctor, whose eyes twinkled in agreement.

'Oh I will,' Dawn joked as she led the way from the autopsy suite.

Ryan hurried after her, changing the subject.

'Time for another stop off at Tenneson's place then?'

'Sounds like a plan to me.'

Dawn didn't look back.

Ryan trailed behind her to the lift in silence. When he didn't speak inside the lift, Dawn wondered over it, but said nothing.

He seemed more distracted than expected.

As the lift doors opened and they stepped out, he put his hand on her arm. She stopped, frowning at his earnest expression.

'I wasn't joking. Greg is a player.'

'Aren't we all?' Dawn strode across the carpark toward the Mustang. She sensed Ryan's eyes on her back, but she shook the sensation away. They were heading back to Cooktown, so it was a pointless comment to make. So why did he make it?

As much as she fancied a quick fling with the doctor, other things were on her mind right now. Someone dosed their victim up on cocaine and strangled her. Now, even more than before, Dawn was sure of two things.

Jane Nichols was alive when she went out to Keatings Lagoon and…she knew her killer.

Chapter 21

Dawn dialled the Tenneson home as Ryan turned the key on the Mustang. The thump of the motor gave her tingles, in a good way. She always liked muscle cars.

It said a lot about how she managed to find the most drop-kick boyfriends over the years. As the phone rang, she studied Ryan.

Was he a bad boy?

Mrs Nichols' voice drew her from her thoughts.

'Mrs Nichols. Very sorry to disturb you but we have a few more questions for Mr Tenneson. Is he home?'

'No. He's off at golf.'

The woman's tone said she wasn't too pleased about it either.

'Okay. Where will we find him playing?'

'He'll be at the Moon course.'

Dawn wasn't familiar with the area. She glanced at Ryan as she repeated the name.

'The Moon course?'

He nodded he knew it.

'Thanks for your time, Mrs Nichols.'

'You found out anything?'

The desperation in the woman's voice hammered into Dawn's chest.

It was a pain Dawn was familiar with. Nightmares—sleepless nights—constant tightness in your gut, tying it in knots. A tension that radiated around your entire body and knew no outlet.

Dawn had tried them all. Sex, alcohol, boxing, running, swimming like she did as a kid. Nothing relieved the anxiety.

'We have some leads Mrs Nichols. Whoever did this will pay for it.' Dawn was about to hang up, then thought about the tension between the woman and her husband yesterday. 'Mrs Nichols, have you thought of anything that might help us?'

She considered asking about the hidden room.

'A diary, or notebook. Maybe Jane left something with you that might be helpful?'

Silence filled the space.

'It's alright Mrs Nichols. You have Detective Ryan's number if you think of anything.'

Dawn pulled the phone from her ear, ready to end the call.

'Detective.'

Dawn placed the phone on speaker.

'Yes Mrs Nichols.'

They waited. Dawn rolled her lips with anticipation.

'You'll find Tyson on the eighteenth hole by now.'

Dawn glanced at Ryan who looked as confused as she was. There was something Mrs Nichols wanted to share but decided not to. The way she snatched her hand away from Tenneson's the day before. There was something going on. She'd see if Reynolds found anything dirty on the guy.

'Thank you Mrs Nichols. We'll be in touch.'

Dawn ended the call and turned to Ryan.

'What do you think she's hiding?'

'Nothing good. Tenneson and she didn't exactly look lovey dovey in their living room.'

'You noticed that too?'

'Yep.'

'Did she tell you anything when you were alone with her?'

Dawn didn't say how *lovey dovey* they looked when she came in, but maybe she was reading too much into it.

'Let's get to the course and see what he has to say about Tina Farrell and the dungeon at the beach house.'

'I'll chase Reynolds up and let her know the Cairns unit will follow up Tenneson's staff alibis, Tina's background and the financials for our victim's yoga business. So she can focus on Tenneson's background check. We still don't have an alibi for Tina Farrell.'

'You think the friend is involved?'

'Don't you? She pulled the search warrant card pretty quickly and it was her dungeon hidden behind the walls.'

Ryan turned into a narrow tree-lined driveway with a view over the harbour and ocean.

'I agree our prime suspects right now are Tenneson and Farrell, but what's the motive?' He glanced at her.

'And what's the Cooktown connection?' Dawn added as the vehicle slowed in front of a low-set clubhouse. It looked more like a caravan park office than a fancy golf course bar and restaurant.

'He plays golf here? I had him pegged for a prestigious club in an opulent, mansion clubhouse with marble floors and manicured greens.

'This course is cheap, and the view is pretty spectacular from the fairway.'

Dawn unclipped her seatbelt and opened the door.

'Talking from experience?'

Ryan did the same, slamming his door and ignoring her comment.

'The eighteenth hole is over here.'

Not waiting for her reply, he locked the car with the key fob and started walking around the side of the sprawling building.

Shade sails hung over an outdoor eating area, complete with Ikea grade outdoor chairs and tables. A family sat at a table with what smelled like bacon and egg rolls. A small terrier sat drooling at the little girl's feet.

'They allow dogs at the golf course?'

'It's a casual course. Sprawls out along the beach and into the hills.'

'Why would a local MP come here to play?'

'Only one reason I can think of.'

Ryan stopped as he rounded the corner. Dawn drew up alongside. Ahead of them, Tenneson pulled his own clubs and chatted with two men dressed in cargo shorts and polo tops, printed with indigenous artwork. One was built like a New Zealand rugby player, the other wore a scraggly goatee flecked with carrot red highlights.

'Detectives.' Tenneson drew up on the concrete, wiping a smile from his features and replacing it with an earnest expression.

'Minister. Can we have a word?' Ryan's tone wasn't polite.

A sneer crossed Tenneson's lips, but he smoothed it instantly. His two companions frowned as they scanned from Dawn to Ryan.

Dawn stepped forward, suddenly curious about Tenneson's friends.

'Aren't you going to introduce your friends?'

'No.' Tenneson waved a discreet dismissal toward his friends, before striding past Dawn and Ryan. 'Let's find a place to talk out of the sun.'

Tenneson wore long sleeves and a cap, making Dawn sure the sun wasn't the issue. His friends watched with curiosity. Dawn slipped her phone from her pocket as she followed the Minister to the covered area behind the clubhouse. As she reached the corner, she turned, phone in hand and snapped a quick photo.

The men turned away, too late. She was sure she snapped a decent shot to run through the database. The printed shirts and dress shorts weren't fooling her. Their skin was light, which in itself didn't exclude them from Indigenous heritage, but the tattoos on the bigger man's arms reminded her of something she'd seen years ago. Back when Rossi worked on the Gold Coast.

She joined Ryan as he continued his questioning.

'What do you know about Tina Farrell's business operating out of the Newell Beach house?'

'Business? No idea what you mean.'

Ryan splayed his feet and crossed his arms.

'You trying to tell me you didn't know about the dominatrix dungeon hidden behind the yoga room cupboards?'

Tyson Tenneson chewed his bottom lip, then lied.

'I assure you I have no idea what you're on about.'

'Spoken like a true politician. Lying comes naturally to you, doesn't it?'

'Don't make this personal Clint.'

Dawn cleared her throat and stepped forward, touching Ryan's arm gently.

'Minister, the Cairns detective in charge of Jane's disappearance said you were fervently against a search of the Newell Beach property. I'm wondering why?'

Tenneson sighed, stopped glaring at Ryan and turned to make eye contact with Dawn.

'Jane went missing from the beach. I didn't see any point.'

It was Dawn's turn to press a few buttons.

'Especially when you had your own little playroom. I can see why you wouldn't want anyone finding it. Bad luck for you we did. Who commissioned the renovations after cyclone Ita?'

'We are done Detectives. Any further questions can go via my office or lawyer. Your choice.'

'I'm sure your wife will be overjoyed at your cooperation with our investigation.'

Dawn suppressed a grin as Tenneson squirmed.

'You're barking up the wrong tree.' Tenneson pointed his finger at Dawn. 'I looked you up Detective. Budding career in Adelaide. A stone's throw away from a promotion. Made me wonder what brought you to Queensland and I did a little digging.'

Dawn held her phone up.

'I'm doing a little digging of my own Minister. I have a few photos I'll be running through the police database. Those friends of yours looked awfully familiar.'

Dawn flicked to the photo of the two men and showed it to Ryan who grinned as he deliberately took his time zooming in on the photo. He passed the phone back and Dawn turned it to Tenneson.

'The guy on the left, with the tattoos, I'm sure I've seen him in a mug shot.'

'Keep fishing Detectives. Like I said, you're off track by miles. I didn't hurt Jane.'

'Maybe not, but someone you know,' Dawn tapped the photo, 'maybe one of these two, could easily have given the order. We are diving into your campaign contributions as we speak Minister. If there is even a whiff of impropriety, we'll find it.'

'My lawyer is Jim McDowell. Don't contact me again.'

Tenneson turned and stormed away, clubs jostling and rattling along behind him.

Ryan watched him retreat, then turned to Dawn with a wide grin.

'I think we hit a nerve.'

Chapter 22

Dawn mulled over various scenarios as Ryan drove the Mustang too fast along the winding road north to Port Douglas. Dark clouds rolled in over the ocean, making it grey and uninviting.

Even if it were sunny and clear, this time of year in northern Queensland was stinger and croc season. Most people were too cautious to swim in the ocean unless it was inside a netted beach or out in the crystal-clear waters of the Great Barrier Reef with stinger suits. As inviting as the water temperature was, for most, the risk was too high.

Dawn dragged her eyes from the ocean to Ryan as a thought popped into her head.

'Someone took Mrs Lundstrom's details out of the diary. Is there anyone new in the department? Someone you don't know, don't trust one hundred percent?'

'No one I can think of with connections that link with cocaine or prostitution.'

'Tina Farrell isn't exactly a prostitute, Ryan. We put her occupation in the sex industry basket, but being a dominatrix isn't about the sex. Even if she were having sex for money, she doesn't strike me as the kind of woman to be in someone's stable.'

Ryan glanced her way, but his eyes snapped back to the road as a low moving caravan came into view.

'What makes you say that?'

'She's confident. Quick to call the warrant card too.'

'I've seen plenty of tough women who fold when faced with a dominant guy.'

A shudder ran down Dawn's spine. Was she one of those women? Ryan must have seen something in her expression. He changed the subject.

'The only newbie on the missing persons case would be Constable Craig, but you saw him. Freckles, red hair, shy smile. Butter wouldn't melt in the poor kid's mouth.'

'Someone kept that information out. Let's see what the Cairns team finds when they check the alibis for Tenneson's employees. Hopefully Murib finds something in Tina or Jane's financials.' She slipped her mobile from her pocket. 'I'll text Reynolds the photo of Tenneson's goons and see what pops up. I think it might pay to ask Sergeant Martin to run a check on Constable Craig and maybe Rossi while he's at it.'

'You don't trust your old hubby?'

Ryan was fishing.

'Martin knows Rossi from his teenage years. I think he'll be happy to run a check. When Rossi worked in Surfers Paradise, he was very chummy with a few bar owners with links to bikies.'

Ryan pulled out next to the caravan, hit the pedal to the floor and whizzed past. Dawn's heart stopped beating a moment as Ryan took his eyes off the road and glared her way.

'What are you saying?'

'Watch the bloody road.' She pointed then tried not to hyperventilate. 'I'm not saying anything. I don't think Rossi pulled the old lady's information from the file. And a lot has changed in nearly twenty years, but still…'

'You think he was dirty?'

'I honestly don't know Ryan. But as soon as we found out cocaine was involved in Jane's murder, my ears were twitching.'

Ryan grinned.

'I didn't notice.'

'Ha ha. Funny. You know what I mean.'

'Send the text. I doubt he has any record, or he wouldn't have made detective, but no harm in doing our due diligence.'

'There is if Rossi finds out.'

Dawn's fingers tapped buttons as Ryan drove the car down the esplanade at Newell Beach and stopped outside the purple beach house. Dawn bit her lip as she hit send.

Ryan pulled the keys from the ignition and opened his door. 'We better make sure he doesn't find out then.'

Dawn opened her door. Ryan rounded the bonnet and met her on the white stone path leading to the raised undercover deck and front door.

'Let's see what little old Mrs Lundstrom has to say that's so important it needed to come out of the file.'

'This should be interesting.' Dawn led the way down the path.

The white crushed rock was bordered by lush cordylines in every colour imaginable. Bright magenta leaves were overshadowed by lengthy flower spikes, dotted with white and pink petals.

The green carpet of lawn was closely mowed and flawless. Even the front deck was recently stained. Dawn was suddenly aware of the enormity of work involved in bringing her family homestead up to this pristine standard.

She waved her hand as she mounted the steps.

'I wonder how she keeps up with all this.'

The sound of yapping erupted from beyond the door as soon as Dawn spoke.

Ryan puffed out his cheeks.

'Another dog!'

'Not a dog person then?'

'More of a cat guy.'

Dawn's eyebrow rose, but on the inside she smiled.

'Me too.'

The door opened a crack before Dawn could knock. She flipped her ID open and turned it to the door.

'Mrs Lundstrom. I'm Detective Dawn Grave and this is Detective Clint Ryan.'

Eyes peered out. The small dog growled from between the older woman's feet. Dawn resisted a chuckle. The little chihuahua was hardly a threat to anyone, but it was certainly a great warning signal.

'Can I see that ID closer luv?' The woman adjusted the position of her multi-focal glasses.

Dawn reached forward, noticing the bright purple frames. The very same shade as the house.

'Of course,' she smiled.

'What's this about? Is it about Jane?'

'Actually, yes Mrs Lundstrom. Can we come in?'

'No.'

The tone was indignant.

'Alright then. We've found Jane Nichols Mrs Lundstrom, but unfortunately, she's deceased. We understand you see most of the traffic coming and going from the Nichols' beach house.'

'Dead? How?'

'We are yet to determine her cause of death Mrs Lundstrom. You sure we can't come in?'

'I'm sure.'

The dog continued yapping. Dawn fought the pounding in her head and tried to hide her frustration. The woman's caution was understandable given the news.

'Did you see anything strange around Wednesday October 7th?'

'I see everything, every day. Like I told that young officer.'

133

Ryan scanned the updated notes he'd received from Parker, then glanced at Dawn, the micro shake of his head told her they didn't have the officer's name.

'Which officer would that be?'

'I don't know his name. Tall, ginger hair with a pimple face or was he freckle faced?'

Mrs Lundstrom held her chin, the door wider now. The dog finally quiet.

The description was obviously Craig, but why didn't he lodge the woman's statement? An oversight maybe?

'Okay Mrs Lundstrom. What did you tell the officer?'

'I didn't tell him anything luv.'

Dawn frowned and opened her mouth to ask a question, but the woman carried on.

'I gave him my diary, with everything in it. Don't you people talk to each other?'

'We are liaising Mrs Lundstrom, but I'm with Cooktown police, not Cairns.'

'Cooktown?'

'Yes. That's where Ms Nichols was found.'

'Good grief. That's miles away. But it makes sense.'

Dawn exchanged a look with Ryan.

'How so?'

The door opened widely. Dawn noted the walls covered in family photos. A tan and white chihuahua lay on a hallway chair, by the phone, head on paws, dark eyes now bored.

'A few days before Jane went missing, I spotted a very flash looking car going into the Nichols' place.'

'Did you get a registration number?'

The woman pursed her lips and shook her head with irritation, then eyed Ryan like Dawn had a screw loose.

He licked his lips. She resisted the urge to kick him in the shins.

'Isn't that what I just said luv?'

It was Dawn's turn to shake with confusion.

'Sorry Mrs Lundstrom. I don't follow you.'

'That's why I knew the car was from Cooktown.'

Dawn waited. She was obviously missing something. A quick glance at Ryan said he was none the wiser.

'The number plate. It had a slogan on it, and it was one of those fancy ones. You know the ones that people pay thousands of dollars extra a year to have on their car. Bloody stupid waste of money if you ask me. If they've got that much money they should feed the poor and house the homeless or something …it's just …'

'Sorry to interrupt Mrs Lundstrom,' she hid the lie, 'but what was the registration number?'

The woman scratched her chin, then pinched at the grey hairs poking in odd directions.

'I don't know if I can remember. Ask that young pup of a cop. It was all in the diary.'

Dawn drew a slow, frustrated breath. Just as she was about to give up and give Constable Craig a grilling, a thought popped into her head.

'Will do Mrs Lundstrom, but you said you knew the plate was from Cooktown. How so?'

'There was a picture behind it. And it said Cooktown at the bottom with some fancy slogan about a river and Far North Queensland.'

'And it had a custom number too?'

'It did.'

'Thanks for your time, Mrs Lundstrom. You've been a great help.'

Dawn's mind was racing. She hurried to leave, but the old woman interrupted her.

'Don't you want to know who else was around when the young Nichols girl went missing?'

Dawn turned back to see the woman standing with her arms across her chest.

'Of course Mrs Lundstrom. I thought that was all you could recall.'

The woman's finger whipped into the air and waggled with vigour.

'No. That's all you asked about missy.'

Dawn wanted to correct the woman with *Detective*, but pressed her lips together, composed herself then continued.

'Please go on.'

'That Tina girl. From over the way.' The woman waved behind her. 'She took the dog for a walk the same morning. I know they said all over the news it was Jane who tied the dog up before she went missing, but I told that nice young police man how I saw Tina walking the dog that morning.'

'Tina Farrell, Jane's friend.'

'Yes. That's her. She comes and goes from their place all the time.' The hand was waving again, this time down the road leading to the Nichols' holiday home.

'Any other cars visit often?'

The woman tutted.

'It's all in my diary.'

'Did you recognise anyone?'

Dawn fought to keep her tone civil.

'The Minister of course.'

Ryan interrupted Dawn's next question.

'Does Mrs Nichols come out often?'

'Not anymore. Not since the yoga studio thingy started.'

Ryan frowned. Dawn asked the next question.

'About the yoga studio Mrs Lundstrom. Were all the visitors in your diary?'

'Yes. Of course. I do the gardening every day and I'm with Neighbourhood Watch.' She pointed to the sign on the corner of her street and the esplanade. 'I keep a close eye out. We are out in the middle of nowhere here and hoons come screaming down the road all the time. That's what the diary is for.'

'Thanks again for your time Mrs Lundstrom. We'll be in touch if we have any more questions. Can I leave a card for you?'

She glanced to Ryan who rummaged in his front pocket for a card. As he handed it over, the old woman frowned at him.

'I think I've seen *you* here before…'

Ryan didn't let her finish.

'Not for a very long time Mrs Lundstrom.'

The woman's smile told Dawn she knew the exact day, time and circumstance of Ryan's hot and heavy summer with Lorraine Nichols.

Chapter 23

Tina Farrell's house was quiet, curtains drawn, no car in the driveway. Much the same as the day before. Barking erupted as Dawn stepped onto the porch. The sound echoed around the yard, not from behind the door.

The urgency in the dog's bark made her skin tingle. Dawn glanced at Ryan, whose expression was tense as he pointed to the left side of the yard. She nodded and followed as he leapt effortlessly from the porch deck and stalked past the front of the house, hand on his weapon. Stopping, he stuck his head around the corner and ducked back.

'It's clear,' he whispered.

Stepping around, he hugged the side of the building as the dog's barking intensified. The deep tone was threatening enough, but as Ryan rounded the back corner into the yard, the animal snarled at the end of the lead.

'It's okay boy.' Ryan held his left hand up. The dog continued to growl. 'We're here to help.'

Ryan drew his weapon, nodding toward the wide-open door on the rear landing. Dawn drew her purse-sized Derringer, reminding herself she needed to get a police issue weapon. The dog snarled as Dawn mounted the first step.

'Ms Farrell? It's detective Grave. Are you okay?'

There was no response. Dawn glanced over her shoulder to find Ryan following right behind her. She stopped at the top of the stairs.

'Tina. Are you in there?'

Still no response. Dawn turned and lifted three fingers for Ryan to see. He nodded he understood as she counted them down, one by one.

When the last finger dropped, they entered. Dawn going right, gun drawn.

'Police! Hands in the air!' Dawn yelled into the vacant living area. Pointing over the barrel of her tiny pistol, she indicated she was going to enter the room to the right. Ryan shook his head and stepped forward.

'That peashooter won't stop anyone in a hurry,' he whispered and she didn't protest.

They continued to clear each room, finding no one home, nothing out of place. Finally, they returned to the rear deck. The dog's barking was hoarse and half-hearted now.

'The poor bugger has probably been at it half the day.'

Ryan jumped from the landing.

'Be careful. He doesn't look any friendlier than he did when we got here.'

The Labrador was tied up on a chain next to the garage with the side door open so he could find shelter. The scene didn't look out of place, but where was Tina? And why was the back door of the house left wide open?

Dawn watched Ryan fill a water bucket by the back tap and cross the unkempt lawn toward a shed.

'It's okay boy. We'll find her. Been having a bad trot lately hey mate.'

Ryan placed the bucket at the animal's feet. The animal rose from its haunches, sniffed the bucket—eyeing Ryan with obvious scepticism.

'I'll call Parker,' Dawn offered as Ryan's phone rang.

As soon as he straightened and collected his phone from his pocket, the dog buried its head in the bucket and drank deeply.

'No need. This is Tammy now.'

He put the call on speaker as Dawn joined him.

'Hey Gleeson.'

'Hey yourself. The tech team have gotten back to me about the cloud storage and missing computer.'

'Great. You can tell me when you get here?'

'Get where?'

'We have another missing person.'

'Shit. Who?'

'Jane Nichols' best friend.'

'Send the address. I'm on my way.'

Ryan ended the call and shoved his phone in his back pocket. She could see sweat marks under his arms and down his back and was sure her shirt looked the same. The weather was growing more humid as the clouds formed over the green hills beyond Newell Beach.

She pointed to the darkening sky.

'It's going to bucket down soon.'

Ryan patted the dog's head. To Dawn's surprise, the Labrador let him.

'Let's take a look around before forensics get here. Inside will be fine, but we might lose any evidence out here when it rains.'

Ryan's phone rang again as they retraced their steps back to the house, trying not to disturb the scene.

'Yeah. Gleeson is on the way.'

The person on the end of the call spoke but Ryan didn't put it on speaker. Dawn was left wondering who he was speaking to.

'I need you to check the evidence and find me the diary Constable Craig got from the old lady here at Newell Beach. Not sure why he didn't mention it at the briefing this morning.'

Another unheard reply, but Ryan's body went rigid, and Dawn's stomach responded to his sudden change of demeanour with a knot of tension.

'What do you mean "*what diary*"? The old lady here gave Craig a diary of every car and person coming and going from the Nichols' beach house. And it wasn't Jane she saw walking the dog, it was Farrell. Apparently, she's with Neighbourhood Watch and takes the role very seriously.'

Ryan listened a moment.

'You better find him and get that diary from evidence.'

More unheard conversation. Dawn wanted to make Ryan put the phone on speaker, but his expression was so intense, there was no way she could get his attention.

'What do you mean?' Ryan nodded to whatever the caller said. 'You better.'

As he ended the call, Dawn thought he might throw the phone, not pocket it. His nostrils flared a moment as he composed himself.

'Craig never logged the diary.'

'An oversight?'

'I don't think so.'

'I'll call Reynolds and see if they found anything on him.'

'You do that. I'll canvas the neighbours and find out how long the dog's been barking and if they saw anyone here.'

The dog whined as though he knew Ryan was talking about him. They turned to see his dark brown eyes peering sadly over his paws, eyebrows creased. Did the dog know something was wrong? Dawn wanted to reassure him, but she couldn't. Her gut was saying the same thing. Tina was missing. The only question was...did she go willingly?

Chapter 24

The phone call to Reynolds rang out. Dawn sighed, typed a text and joined Ryan at the neighbour's home. As she stepped up onto the front porch, her phone buzzed. She turned away from the door and answered.

'Reynolds. We've encountered a complication.' The phone line echoed. Dawn scanned the screen to see if the poor reception was her or Reynolds.

'Sorry Detective, reception isn't great at the moment.' A rumbling sound echoed down the line. 'Give me a second.'

The muffled sound of rubbing fabric, footsteps and more thunder eventually gave way to quiet.

'Okay. Got you. What's up?'

'Tina Farrell has disappeared, and some evidence has gone missing. Constable Craig either mismanaged it, or he's deliberately left it out of the evidence log and storeroom. Did you find anything on him?'

'I ran a check like you asked. Couldn't find any sealed juvenile records, his police career is short, but spotless and nothing jumped out in his personal life except… I was about to call you after I ran his social media accounts.'

'What did you find?'

'Constable Craig isn't very careful with his privacy settings.'

Dawn wanted Reynolds to hurry up and explain but held her tongue.

'He's allowed friends of his friends to share his posts and you'll never guess what I found.'

'Don't have time for guessing games Reynolds.'

'Sorry. You're right. A recent photo he was tagged in came up and it's got Tina Farrell in it.'

'Email me a copy. Anything on the photo I sent?'

'Nothing popped out in our outstanding warrants. I wish we had fancy software, but we don't, so I'll be going through known felon records to see if I can recognise either of them.'

'What about the tattoos? Anything distinguishing?'

'Damn. I should have thought of that. I'll see if we can enhance the photo and get back to you.'

'Thanks Reynolds. Good job on the social media stuff.'

'Thanks Detective.'

Dawn ended the call and turned to see Ryan moving on to the next house. She jogged to catch up.

'Anything?' she asked as she jumped the low flower bed between neighbouring properties.

'Not yet. You?'

'Reynolds hasn't found any warrants for the two guys at the golf club, but she's found a photo linking Craig to Farrell.'

Her phone pinged as if in response. She opened her email account and downloaded the picture. A group of five people huddled on the deck of the Newell Beach house, drinks in hand. A firepit cast eerie shadows over the faces, but three popped out instantly.

'Check this out.'

Dawn turned the phone to show Ryan the photo. He squinted.

'Both our victims with Craig. Does Reynolds know who the other two are?'

'No. No idea yet. Maybe we need to call Parker. I'll send you this pic and the one of the two guys with Tenneson. Her team might have better luck than Reynolds finding their identities.'

'Good idea.'

Ryan was about to make the call when a marked police vehicle, followed by a white van and a grey sedan entered the street.

'Looks like back up is here. You go sort them out. I'll call Parker.'

Ryan's hand hovered over the screen but stopped as the vehicles pulled up outside Tina Farrell's house and Parker stepped out of the grey sedan. Rossi opened the driver's side door a moment later.

Dawn bit her cheek. Then told herself to toughen up and be professional. This was about Tina and Jane, not about her history with her ex.

'Parker. Rossi.' Ryan crossed the neighbour's lawn and met the detectives. Dawn followed, not wanting to throw her weight about again.

'Ryan.' Parker glanced past her new partner and nodded to Dawn. 'Grave. Looks like missing persons cases are following you around.'

'I think these are more likely linked to your station than me, Parker.' The quip was out of her mouth before she could stop herself.

She spent the first few years as a cop learning to let snide remarks slide by. Biting only ever riled up the guys she worked with and ended up hurting her in the long run. Why was Detective Parker able to hit a nerve so easily?

'What Grave meant to say is we were just about to call your station in.' Ryan nodded at her. 'Show Parker the photos.'

Dawn retrieved her mobile phone, opened the file and turned the photo to Parker. 'This is Constable Craig, tagged on social media by a friend. And this is' Dawn pointed.

'Tina Farrell and Jane Nichols.' Parker beat her to it. 'What the…' She turned to Rossi. 'Craig knows our victim

144

and,' she glanced at the house, 'this one too. Run a check on him,' she ordered.

'Already done. When I found out about the missing evidence, I asked one of my team in Cooktown to run him. She's the officer who found this.'

Dawn fully expected Parker to lose her cool, but the woman only huffed.

'Find anything else?'

'No. Clean as, but while we were interviewing Tenneson about the hidden room, we noted two undesirables with him.' Dawn flicked through her phone for the photo she took earlier, then turned it to Parker.

'They were dressed in Indigenous tops, maybe trying to pass themselves off as members of his volunteer team. Something about them didn't look right. Do you know either of these guys?'

Parker studied the picture with a deep frown. Finally, she shook her head and looked at Rossi who rounded the vehicle and joined her.

Dawn turned the phone to show him the picture. His eyes studied hers a moment too long.

Ryan stepped alongside her.

'Recognise either of them?' His tone was sharp.

Rossi scanned the screen. The corner of his eye twitched. She knew that tell well.

'What is it?'

Rossi bit his bottom lip.

'I don't recognise them, but that tattoo is affiliated.'

Dawn turned the photo back and zoomed in.

'How the hell can you tell from that distance?'

'I just can.'

Rossi turned toward the house where Tammy was already donning shoe covers and overalls.

'Need any help Gleeson?' he called out and strode across the lawn. Dawn's stomach screamed at her to keep the guy off the scene. His history came rolling back at her.

'We've got this Rossi.'

She turned to Parker, who was studying her carefully.

'Can you two find Craig? He's mixed up in this somehow. Gleeson will know soon enough if there's any sign Tina Farrell was taken against her will.'

Rossi was halfway across the lawn now.

'But you said she left the dog. That sounds like she left in a hurry.'

Dawn hurried after Rossi, thinking fast. She didn't want him anywhere near this case, but her power to stop him entering the scene was limited.

'It's not her dog and if she's running, it could be because she knew more than she was telling me.'

She grabbed Rossi's arm harder than intended and changed the subject.

'Tell me about the tattoo.'

Her mind was racing. If Rossi was linked to Jane's death, why mention the tattoo? Maybe he was aware she'd find out soon enough and it was his way of covering his arse.

Was she thinking too hard? Did she seriously believe Rossi would be mixed up in Jane Nichols' murder?

Dawn tensed as Rossi ignored her question and mounted the front deck. Ryan's voice made her turn.

'Parker. I think it's better if you and Rossi track Craig down. He knows you. Trusts you.'

Parker and Ryan exchanged looks. She waved a hand at Rossi who'd stopped at the top of the stairs.

'Come on Rossi. Let's find Craig. The last thing we need is an internal investigation in our department.'

Rossi chewed his lip a moment, then shrugged like he really didn't care, but something in his eyes told Dawn he did. Was it because he was involved? Or because Dawn ordered him to stand down?

'Let us know if you find him,'

Dawn stared as Rossi passed her.

Her ex-husband's hand flew to his brow in a mock salute.

'Yes Ma'am.'

Parker grinned. Dawn sighed.

As the grey sedan motor started, and the car drove down the road, Ryan leant in close.

'You think he's involved?'

Dawn drew a slow breath, carefully considering her answer.

'Believe me. He's capable of it. But I bloody hope not.'

Chapter 25

Dawn pulled a pair of gloves from her back pocket, finally getting back into the swing of things after renovating the house and working on her own time schedule. It was strange being back on the job, but as Tammy handed her a pair of shoe covers, she realised how much she'd missed it.

They entered the home through the small hallway lined with artwork. Dawn noted the paintings were undisturbed. On entering the living area, she found nothing was out of place. The cushions weren't disturbed, the curtains were neatly drawn, and nothing was left out of place on the coffee table.

She turned slowly within the space. Ryan glanced her way, his expression likely mirroring hers.

'No sign of a struggle.'

He nodded agreement.

'Let's check the bedrooms.'

Ryan returned to the hallway. Dawn followed as he entered the first bedroom on his right.

'This looks like the main.' He pointed to the queen bed, matching bedsides and a dressing table lined with cosmetics.

More artwork adorned the walls. Mostly abstract, with soft colours and pastel highlights. Dawn reached an antique freestanding wardrobe. It reminded her of the one in the bedroom she used to share with Lisa.

The gloss white, Queen Anne legs and carved doors were out of date, but quaint. As she opened the door, the scent of camphor laurel brought memories flooding back.

Her mother swore the wood species kept silverfish and other pests from damaging the clothing. Thinking of her mother made her smile a moment, until sadness swept through her. She wondered if they'd ever find her mother's remains.

She helped the search team for the first few weeks after they found out her mother wasn't missing, she was murdered. But Archer Point was a vast area of tropical forest and inaccessible hills. Even with a cadaver dog, they failed to find anything.

At least the man responsible was behind bars. Her brother's staged suicide and murder were unrelated and remained unsolved. For once, she wished Lisa would bug her with scenarios and far-fetched ideas about what happened to Fraser.

But since she'd agreed to stay in Cooktown with Lisa and Abby, her sister seemed to have finally put Fraser's death to rest. It was now Dawn who was doing everything she could to push for new evidence in the otherwise stone-cold case.

'Check this out.'

Ryan's voice dragged her from her thoughts. Turning, she saw him standing by the dressing table, a black electrical cable in his hand.

She crossed the room and took the end of the cord in her gloved hand.

'Is that what I think it is?'

'Yep. Same brand laptop charger we found in Jane Nichols' place.'

'Do you think it's the same computer or did they have the same model?'

Ryan pulled the dresser away from the wall to unplug the charger.

'Either way, you've gotta wonder where these computers keep disappearing to.'

Ryan's phoned rang in his pocket. He retrieved it, checking the screen with a frown.

'Who is it?'

'No idea.'

He put the phone on speaker as he answered. 'Detective Ryan.'

'Detective.'

Dawn recognised Mrs Lundstrom's voice. Ryan's eyebrow rose.

'Mrs Lundstrom. What can we do for you?'

'It's what I can do for you Detective. After you left, I had a thought.'

Ryan rolled his eyes. Dawn stifled a chuckle.

'I might have given that police officer my old diary, but I started a new one.'

Dawn wondered why a new diary was relevant, but then a thought struck her. She leaned forward, suddenly holding her breath for Mrs Lundstrom's nosey neighbour news.

'You know how I told you Tina took Rusty for a walk, then everyone went crazy looking for Jane ...' Mrs Lundstrom didn't wait for a reply. 'Well, I saw a car the same day, it was the same one I saw a few days later. Not the one with the Cooktown plate. I recorded the number again, in my new diary.'

Dawn glanced at Ryan.

'You still there?'

'Yes, go on Mrs Lundstrom.'

'I didn't think of it earlier, when you came by because the car didn't drive down the beach house driveway. It parked in the dirt carpark out front, but I wrote down the registration number after I saw the driver.'

'What was the registration number Mrs Lundstrom?' Ryan asked. Dawn pulled her notepad from her back pocket. As Mrs Lundstrom read it out, Dawn scribbled the details down.

'What made you concerned about that particular car Mrs Lundstrom?' she asked.

'Because when the driver got out, his mate joined him and they just looked sketchy, if you know what I mean.'

Dawn couldn't believe they might finally have a break in the case. At least a solid lead. She leant over the phone so Mrs Lundstrom could hear her clearly.

'Sketchy in what way?'

'Rough blokes. The kind you don't want to bring home to mum.'

'If I send you a photo, could you identify them?'

'Sure. One had a big tattoo down his right arm. Looked like he should have been driving a Harley, not a car. The other was scrawnier.'

'After they parked, where did they go Mrs Lundstrom?'

Dawn could hear the woman's smile over the phone.

'They walked right down the driveway to the Nichols' beach house.'

'Thanks Mrs Lundstrom. I'll send you a photo now. Is this mobile number okay?'

'Yes Luv. Fine. Did you find my old diary? I would like it back you know.'

'We'll be in touch Mrs Lundstrom.'

Ryan ended the call. Dawn tapped out the mobile Mrs Lundstrom called from and sent the photo over. Less than a minute later, a thumbs up emoji appeared on her screen.

'It's them.'

'Nice. Now we need an ID.'

Dawn dialled a number.

'The registration number should help.' The call connected. 'Reynolds. Run me a registration thanks.'

'Sure. Shoot.'

Dawn gave out the number as Ryan left the bedroom and checked the remaining rooms. A whistle brought her attention back to Reynolds.

'What?'

'The car is registered to Tenneson's office.'

'Thanks Reynolds.'

Dawn ended the call and rushed from the room, colliding with Ryan as he exited the room across the hall. Ryan's hands reached out to steady her, his arm held her at the waist tightly. Neither of them spoke a moment.

The sound of someone clearing their throat made them separate. Tammy grinned at them from the end of the hallway. Before she could say anything, Dawn jumped in.

'The thugs Mrs Lundstrom saw were driving one of Tenneson's cars. Time to get a search warrant for all his financials.'

Ryan put his hands in the pockets of his pants self-consciously as Tammy shuffled past them in the hallway.

'We should get one for Tina Farrell and Constable Craig while we are at it.' He sounded all business as the forensic tech made her way to the front door, waving her hand over her head.

'I need you two to take a look at this.'

Dawn glanced at Ryan who turned to follow Tammy down the gravel driveway to the single garage where the dog was still tied up.

She opened the main, barn-like doors with a creak to reveal a white sedan. 'Looks like she didn't drive herself.'

'Is it registered to Tina Farrell?' Dawn asked as she entered the shed to glance in the windows.

'Your department I'm afraid.' Tammy tapped the window with a gloved hand. 'Do you want me to process this too?'

Dawn spotted two empty water bottles, an energy drink bottle, a glass kombucha bottle and an empty chip bag. It seemed odd considering Tina's house was tidy. Why was her car messy with rubbish left inside?

She tried the door, which opened. Turning to Tammy, she nodded.

'Yep. If Tina Farrell didn't take her car, then we have to assume she hasn't left willingly. We need to process everything.

'Will do.'

Ryan waited for Dawn to reach him.

'We done?'

'I think so, for now anyway.'

Tammy began walking with them toward her van.

'You didn't ask about the laptop.'

Ryan turned to face the tech.

'Looks like we might have two missing laptops, but you're right. What did you find?'

'The forensic computer technicians have found a cloud account under Tina Farrell's email address, but they need a warrant to gain access and up until now, we didn't have probable cause.'

Dawn started typing an email on her phone. 'We might have some luck now she's missing.' She nodded for Tammy to go on.

'We did get a bit of luck though. The cloud account was last accessed in Cooktown at 7.13 a.m. the day before Jane Nichols went missing.'

Dawn stopped typing and glanced up.

'Cooktown again.'

'Ryan stalked to his car, keys already in hand.

'Looks like you were right Grave. There is a Cooktown link.'

Dawn followed.

'Yes, but that doesn't put Jane in Cooktown, only Tina. No wonder she went pale when we said Jane died there.'

'Ah. Hang about guys.'

They turned toward Tammy.

'If you are both leaving, should we get the uniforms to call Council to come and get the dog?'

The Labrador chose that moment to howl.

'Do you need to process him?' Dawn asked.

'I've checked him over. There's no blood. His teeth are clean. He's not tried to bite anyone, and I didn't find any fibres on him.'

Dawn drew her phone from her pocket.

'I'll call Council.'

Ryan put his hand on hers.

'We know his name now. Rusty. Maybe we should take him to Lorraine. He *is* Jane's dog after all.'

Dawn wondered if Ryan was looking for another excuse to see Lorraine or if he might have warmed to the animal. As she followed him back toward the shed, she decided it was probably the latter.

The Labrador sat up high on his haunches, eyes bright, tongue lolling, as though he knew they were contemplating taking him with them.

As Ryan approached, the dog pranced on the spot. Had he forgotten about Jane and Tina already? Maybe, but she hadn't. Why was Jane in Cooktown? It seemed Tina was there too. Did she have anything to do with her friend's murder, or was she a victim too?

The open back door, and the car being left in the shed gave the impression Tina didn't leave willingly. All Dawn could think about was how the next call she received could easily be to attend another murder scene.

She hoped it wasn't.

Chapter 26

Rusty struggled for balance in the back seat as Ryan steered the Mustang back down the James Cook Highway. Dawn was beginning to know each and every turn by heart.

Ryan glanced over.

'We can kill two birds with one stone.'

'We aren't going to get a warrant before we get to Tenneson today.'

'We'll drop the dog off and then maybe, if Tenneson is there and we tell him what we know. He might cave.'

Dawn shook her head.

'You know that's a bad idea. If we tip him off, he'll delete or burn anything incriminating before we can get a warrant.'

Dawn gripped her seat as Ryan overtook a slow-moving van before turning to catch her gaze.

'Tenneson isn't an idiot. He's not leaving a trail behind for us to find. But if those thugs killed Jane, he might be afraid of them. He might be willing to turn on them for protection. If not for him, maybe for Lorraine.'

Dawn was silent a moment as Ryan overtook yet another car. Rusty panted in the backseat, seemingly as eager as Ryan to get to wherever they were going. She could have sworn the golden-haired Labrador was smiling.

'He didn't look the slightest bit afraid of those guys. None of this makes any sense. I'm going to make a call.' Dawn held her phone up to make sure the signal was decent, then dialled.

The call connected quicker than she expected.

'Detective Grave. Nice to hear from you.'

The smooth, deep voice on the end made her smile. Ryan gave her a strange look, no doubt wondering what she was grinning about.

'Greg. Glad I caught you.'

Ryan rolled his eyes.

'Just wondering if you confirmed a time of death. I know it must have been hard considering the decay.'

'Actually, I was going to call you, about the case.' The latter was added as an afterthought. 'You say the victim went missing last Friday afternoon, right?'

'That's what our timeline indicates, although no one actually saw Jane on Friday and we believe she might have left the beach house a day or two before.'

'Our entomologist found evidence to suggest your victim could have died at least a few days earlier than Friday the 9th.'

'How so?'

'It appears the body didn't submerge straight away. Maybe the killer didn't weigh it down because they thought a croc would take it quickly, but there are a few factors that give us a window of twenty-four to forty-eight hours before the victim was reported missing.'

'Really helpful info. Thanks Greg.'

'You're welcome, Detective.'

Dawn was about to end the call when Greg spoke.

'Any chance we can grab a drink while you're still in town?'

Dawn was thrown by the invitation. Greg flirted with her on scene, but she thought it was part of his persona.

'I'm actually heading back to Cooktown this afternoon Greg, so maybe we can catch up next time I'm in town.'

'Absolutely.'

The pathologist ended the call. Dawn stared at the screen a moment, then put her phone away.

'Greg has evidence to suggest our victim died up to two days before she was reported missing.'

Ryan turned left at the Palm Cove roundabout and slowed to navigate the narrower street.

'That makes finding the owner of the Cooktown vehicle, priority number one. Has Reynolds found anything yet?'

'Not yet. I'll chase her up and we can help when we get there later today, but didn't Mrs Lundstrom say Tina took Rusty for a walk the day before Jane went missing? If Jane was already dead, why was the dog with Tina? And how did Rusty end up tied to a park bench Friday? Did Tina know where Jane was all along? We know she wasn't telling us everything. And now she's missing. Is she running? Or has she been taken?'

Ryan pulled up outside Lorraine's house, switched off the motor and turned to Dawn.

'Her car wasn't missing. We know she knows Constable Craig. Maybe she's not missing, but with him. He could have picked her up.'

Dawn grabbed her phone and started texting.

'We need to see if Parker has managed to track him down. If not, we need a BOLO out on his car.'

Ryan opened the door. 'Text Reynolds while you're at it.' He was barely out before Rusty leapt over the leather trim and bounded from the vehicle.

Dawn cringed as the dog's claws scraped the seats, but Ryan didn't seem to notice. Maybe he wasn't a cat person after all.

She reached for the lead from the backseat.

'You better…'

She didn't get a chance to finish her sentence. Rusty was panting at the front gate obediently before she could hand Ryan the lead.

'At least he's well trained.' Ryan slammed his door.

Dawn stepped out and joined them at the gate as Ryan rang the call button.

'Yes?'

'Lorraine. It's Clint. I've got Rusty here.'

'What?'

'Just open up and I'll explain.'

Dawn studied her partner. The corners of his eyes were pinched. Nothing about this case was easy for him. Was he still in love with Lorraine? The whole situation made her think of the Rod Stewart song *Maggie May*.

Mrs Nichols was close to twenty years older than him, but she could see how the woman would have found the young Clint Ryan attractive. With his broad shoulders, flirty smile and arrogant gait. He was still pleasing to the eye.

The buzz of the gate snapped her from her daydream. Rusty bounded into the yard like a puppy chasing butterflies. Dawn stifled a chuckle.

The door opened before they reached it. Rusty burst past Lorraine, tail wagging, ears alert. As she watched the Labrador sniff and search his way around the house, she realised he was looking for Jane.

'Oh my!' Lorraine's hand flew to her lips as tears spilled down her cheeks.

'Rusty!' Ryan ordered. The dog ignored him.

Instead, Rusty sat back on his haunches and growled in front of the door Tenneson came out of on their last visit. The sound sent a chill down Dawn's spine.

'Rusty?' Ryan's question did nothing to gain the dog's attention.

'Where is Mr Tenneson today?' Dawn asked. Mrs Nichols turned at her question, but she said nothing. 'Is that his home office?'

Silence greeted her second question. Ryan glanced her way, then approached the dog who was now lying outside the wide, timber office door.

'Is he in there?' Ryan put his hand on the door.

'No.' Lorraine finally found her voice. 'He's at work.'

'On a Sunday?' Dawn asked.

'Apparently something urgent came up.'

Dawn's phone rang before she could ask another question. Ryan opened the office door as Dawn answered the call.

'Dawn. It's Rossi.'

She forced herself not to say the first words that came to mind. He was her subordinate on this case. He was bound to call her if he found something.

'What's up?' She was surprised at the casual tone in her voice.

'You know how I recognised that tattoo.' He didn't wait for a reply. 'I was pretty sure I knew which gang he was affiliated with. I ran the mug shots. The big guy is Ralph Payne, or better known as Wolf, the other guy is a novice.'

'A novice. Never good news.'

Ryan glanced her way. Dawn was aware he hadn't asked for permission to enter Tenneson's office. The house was Lorraine's, and she wasn't putting up a fight, but still, they needed an invitation.

'Can you hold a second Rossi.' She put her hand over the phone, not waiting for his reply. 'Mrs Nichols. Is it okay if Detective Ryan takes a look around the office? It seems Rusty has picked up a scent.'

The woman glanced from her to Ryan. The expression on her partner's face was sympathetic, almost pleading.

'Yes. Go ahead,' she agreed and Ryan stepped through the doorway, Rusty hot on his heels.

'Rossi. Sorry about that. I've just found out the two guys in the photo were parked up outside the beach house after our victim disappeared. We have an eyewitness. The car they were driving was registered to ...'

Dawn glanced at Mrs Nichols' who seemed to be watching what Ryan was doing, but she reconsidered her words in any case.

'A person of interest. I'll send you and Parker the details. I'm betting the novice was ransacking the beach house as part of his initiation. There must have been something the gang were looking for.

'Or, the novice was cutting his teeth on his first kill. These bikie gangs don't mess around. Some members can make their way into the gang because they are tough and have connections, but skinny, runty little scrags like this one—they need a kill to make the cut.'

'Maybe, but Greg has widened our time-of-death window, so the suspect pool has also widened. I'll send you the details. In the meantime, see what you can dig up and if you can find them, pay them a visit.'

Dawn shifted the phone from her ear, ready to end the call, but heard Rossi say something.

'What was that?' She strained to focus as her eyes were fixed on Ryan scoping out Tenneson's office.

'Dawn. I'm sorry.'

This time she heard, but hung up without a word. The last thing she needed to hear right now was Declan Rossi's apology. The night she packed her bags and finally left, played like a bad movie in her head. Instinctively, she rubbed her face, the sting returning like it was only yesterday.

No, he wasn't going to be able to say sorry and just be forgiven.

'Grave. You need to see this.'

Dawn shook her head, trying to clear the memory as Ryan's voice found her. Placing her phone in her back pocket, she entered the Minister's study, scanning the walls and finding Ryan standing over a gigantic modern Australian-ash desk.

A drawer was open. Dawn hoped Ryan didn't force it open without a warrant, but as she focussed on Mrs Nichols, she saw a key in the woman's hand.

A half-covered stack of paintings leaning against the wall behind the desk caught her eye a moment, but her partner drew her attention as he lifted a photo in his freshly gloved hand and turned it so she could see.

The gasp left her lips before she could stop herself.

'We shouldn't have any issues getting a warrant now.'

'Well, if that photo doesn't seal the deal, this one should do the trick.'

Ryan lifted another photo and turned it to Dawn to reveal the Minister in tight leather hotpants, a ball gag in his mouth and tied down to the inversion table from the dungeon.

'That's something you can't unsee,' she shivered.

Chapter 27

Rusty panted from the back seat. Ryan fell into the driver's seat and slammed the door without putting his key in the ignition.

Dawn hurriedly typed out a text message to Reynolds and the Sergeant with an update and to ask for copies of footage from traffic cameras on all roads leading out of Port Douglas to Cooktown from the Wednesday evening before their victim disappeared right through to when she was found.

She suggested they check CCTV footage from truck stops and out of the way fuel stations along the route too.

A thumbs up from Reynolds told her the message was received.

Ryan dialled Parker as Dawn sent an email to update her and Rossi with Greg's findings and to request an officer visit Mrs Lundstrom for an official eyewitness statement.

Turning, she studied Ryan's expression as he growled down the phone.

'What do you mean the warrant was denied? Try again! I'll email you the photos, but Tenneson has been visiting Tina Farrell, who's now missing, and the man's been seen hanging out with known bikie thugs. The same guys who were seen entering the Nichols' beach house after she was reported missing. They could be our murderers, or they could have taken evidence to protect Tenneson.'

It didn't surprise Dawn the warrant was denied. The MP wasn't only a prominent politician, he was linked to one of the wealthiest families in the area. But they had more evidence linking him now.

'No, we've not found the old biddy's diary, but she's ready to give a statement and she has her *new* diary with the registration number recorded. Grave sent you an update. Try again.' A pause. 'Of course I want a BOLO on his bloody car!'

Ryan ended the call and for a moment Dawn thought he might throw the phone. Rusty whined and dropped his chin on the detective's shoulder. Ryan patted the Labrador's head reflexively.

'It's okay boy. We've got you.'

He glanced at Dawn and waited while she hit send on a final text to Murib, requesting a follow up on Jane Nichols' financials, along with Tina Farrell's and Constable Craig's.

Ryan appeared concerned.

'Are you sure Lisa is going to be okay taking Rusty in?'

'Lisa will be fine, and Abby loves animals,' Dawn assured him. 'Are we searching Tenneson's office?'

'No go. Parker said the warrant was denied and Sarge isn't prepared to use the affair to try again. Apparently, an affair wasn't a reason to kill his own stepdaughter.'

'What about blackmail?'

'You really think Jane was blackmailing him?' Dawn sighed.

'I don't know. Maybe. But now the dominatrix is missing and what about his association with known bikies?'

'All circumstantial apparently.'

'Then we need to head to Cooktown and follow up the vehicle seen at the Nichols' place the day before she was likely killed. It's the only lead we have. Rossi is chasing up the two bikies who were seen here. He's got names.'

Ryan started the car and pulled away from the curb with his foot flat to the floor. The motor roared. Rusty shook with excitement and Dawn struggled to get her seatbelt on.

'What's the hurry?'

'We need to check on the old biddy on the way to Cooktown. She's our only witness to those bikers and the

Cooktown plates and without her diary, we only have her word.'

'You think someone might try to silence her?'

'I think the Cairns station might have a leak. If Craig is up to something, he could have friends on the inside tipping him off, or...'

Dawn waited, but when Ryan didn't explain further, she studied his features. Something in his eyes told her what he was thinking.

'I know I said Rossi could be dirty, but he's the one who ID'd the bikers, including the novice who might well be our killer.'

Ryan said nothing as he pulled onto the James Cook Highway heading north. Dawn watched him chew his lip, knowing he wanted to say more.

'Don't get pissed with me but I did a little digging.'

Her stomach knotted as she hoped he didn't dig too deeply.

'It was a long time ago. Ancient history.'

'I know, but I thought you might want to know what I found.'

Dawn didn't answer. She was too busy telling herself Ryan couldn't have uncovered the truth or he wouldn't be so calm.

He took her silence as permission to go on.

'I have friends in low places, and it turns out Rossi was working a legitimate gig. Sanctioned by the Feds. AFP wanted it to look real, so they asked him to go under-cover, as himself, a cop on the take. It worked. He got inside one of the biggest organised crime families on the Goldie.'

'It consumed him.'

'I have no doubt.' Silence filled the car until Ryan spoke her name. 'Dawn.' His words were softly spoken. He waited for her to turn to him. 'Even though he's clean now, he doesn't deserve you back…'

'Don't worry, I'm not planning on going back to him, but I can see where you're going. Maybe I should forgive him?'

Ryan glanced her way as they left the town limits and drove the well-worn winding road back to Port Douglas.

'Only for your sake, not his.'

If he knew everything, would he still say that?

****

The next forty-five minutes were spent in silence as Dawn tried to put the pieces of this case together and distract herself from thinking about those early years, being married to Rossi.

They escaped Cooktown together, young and filled with hope after finally breaking free of the oppression and pain she grew up with. But she was barely eighteen when they got married and only a few years older when she left him.

The first slap stung. Her face tingled like it happened yesterday. She rubbed her cheek, recalling the pain surging through her body as he slammed her into the bedframe—eyes wild, pupils dilated.

He never told her he was working a case. For her, it was all real. Hard up for money, she took a job in a local bar. At first, he worked nights so he could see her, but when the bar turned out to be bikie affiliated, Declan became a regular and got caught up in the life—or so she thought.

Working with bikies required a certain personality. He could have been weak and desperate, but they knew if he were, the bikies would use Dawn as leverage.

She wasn't sure if the AFP realised he was in over his head, or he was working with them all along. Now she couldn't help wondering if things could have gone differently.

Shaking her head, she told herself it was unlikely.

Organised crime and the life he led brought out the bully in Rossi. There was no doubt he likely justified what he did in his own mind a hundred times.

Now he was a good detective, from all accounts. And he was begging her to forgive him. A knot tightened in her gut. She quelled it. Ryan glanced across as he pulled up outside the purple beach house overlooking the ocean.

Mrs Lundstrom glanced up from the front deck, squinting, then rose. Dawn noted there was no sign of a Mr Lundstrom and she couldn't help wondering again how the older woman managed to maintain the lawn, and the lush garden beds.

But she'd already told Dawn every waking moment was spent tending her lovely garden, which was why she knew who came and went from the Nichols' house. A right old busy body. They were a police officer's best and worst friend, all wrapped in one.

Dawn undid her belt and stepped out before Ryan could ask again if she was okay. What Rossi did wasn't in the report filed at the hospital. She'd refused all the tests offered and given an abridged version of the night's events.

She couldn't risk telling her partner the whole story. There was no way she could know how he would react. Besides, it wasn't his burden to bear.

'Mrs Lundstrom.' Dawn approached, being careful to stick to the defined pathway.

The woman dropped her weeding fork into a pocket on the front of her floral gardening apron before shoving her gloved hands on her hips.

'Detective. Did you find my diary?'

Dawn smiled at the woman's direct tone.

'Not yet, but we will.'

'What are you here for then? I told ya all I know.'

'We've had a few developments, and we were wondering if you might have someone you could stay with for a few days.'

'I'm not going anywhere Luv. Been living in this old house for forty-eight years. They'll be carrying me out in a box.'

Ryan stepped around the bonnet of his Mustang and joined Dawn.

'You've been a wonderful help in our investigation Mrs Lundstrom.' He laid on the charm, including the dimpled smile he could muster at a moment's notice.

'You can cut that charm now Mister. I'm still not going anywhere.'

Dawn grinned as Ryan drew himself up, ready to argue, but she interrupted.

'Mrs Lundstrom.' She stepped forward. The woman stepped back suspiciously. Dawn held her hands up, palms facing the woman in surrender. 'We won't force you to do anything you don't want to.'

'Damn right you won't.'

'To be honest, this isn't about you.' Dawn decided to shift gears. 'You could stay right where you are, in the line of fire if it were up to me, but with your diary missing, you're our key witness. You see it turns out whoever killed Jane, could have taken Tina Farrell too and we suspect it could be one of the people you saw here last Thursday.'

Mrs Lundstrom removed one gardening glove, then the other.

'But didn't Jane go missing Friday?'

Dawn's heartrate kicked up a notch as she realised she might have to give out information she shouldn't be sharing with anyone outside her investigative team. But this lady wasn't missing a beat, despite her advanced years.

'As I said, there's been a development. A few actually. There is a good chance someone might know you spoke to the police and witnessed the comings and goings of a possible murderer. We'd like you to find a safe place to stay.'

The woman screwed up her mouth, opened it to say something, then shook her head.

'I'll be fine here.'

She began putting her gardening gloves back on.

Dawn wondered over the woman's response, then a thought struck her. She lived alone. Was in her seventies. Spent her days gardening and watching the neighbourhood.

'Mrs Lundstrom. If you don't have somewhere. I have a spare room at my place, but it is in Cooktown.'

The woman's eyes brightened. Ryan coughed. Dawn had no idea why until she realised they now had to babysit an old woman, her dog and a stray, but not before taking the three-hour drive to Cooktown, in what was essentially a two door sportscar with a rear seat the size of a suitcase.

Chapter 28

Ryan's expression said, "*what the hell were you thinking*", as he opened the tiny boot to stow Mrs Lundstrom's larger than expected overnight bag.

Dawn shrugged. What was she supposed to do? Leave the woman a sitting duck? It was Ryan who was worried about her. Neither of them was willing to put her life on the line.

They didn't have a spare room either. Although Abby had two beds in her room, Dawn wasn't willing to expose her niece to a stranger. It was going to be Dawn who abandoned her bed and bunk in with her niece for the night.

But she didn't exactly have a choice. Ryan said it himself. Leaving Mrs Lundstrom alone, unguarded, was dangerous and they were short-staffed enough. Dawn wasn't comfortable leaving the old woman's safety to a constable she didn't know. Especially if they had some sort of leak at the local station.

Dawn opened the door and helped Mrs Lundstrom in. Ryan tied Rusty on a shorter lead to one side of the tiny rear seat. As Mrs Lundstrom buckled her belt, Dawn passed the yapping Chihuahua onto her lap. Rusty dropped to his belly and plopped his head on his paws calmly, despite the low growl from the tiny animal.

'Shush Greta. Where are your manners?' She patted her little companion, then rubbed behind Rusty's ears. For a moment, Dawn could have sworn the Labrador grinned slyly.

'Do you seriously think someone might hurt me? I don't like leaving my garden unattended.'

'I wouldn't ask if I didn't think the threat was real Mrs Lundstrom. But I'm sure we'll have this sorted in no time.' Dawn assured her as she slipped into the front seat and buckled her own belt. Ryan's expression said he bloody well hoped so, but she wasn't sure what his issue was. It wasn't his sister she was going to have to clear this with. She only hoped Lisa would understand.

'You honestly think I saw a killer?

The woman's earlier bravado was fading.

'We think so Mrs Lundstrom.'

'Bella.'

Dawn turned to view the rear seat. 'Sorry?'

'Bella. You should call me Bella. This Mrs Lundstrom stuff sounds too stuffy if I'm going to be staying with you. And we should call past the supermarket on the way. I'll be doing the cooking, and do you have a garden I can tend?'

Dawn licked her lips. Lisa did the cooking. She wasn't sure how her sister was going to take any of this. The subject of food made Dawn's stomach grumble.

'Have you had lunch?'

Bella's tone was disapproving.

Dawn didn't answer. She'd not even had much of a breakfast. Her stomach protested loudly.

'Young man,' Dawn grinned, Ryan rolled his eyes, 'you need to get some food into the detective here before she fades away.'

'Yes ma'am.'

Ryan drove into a service station.

'Don't you ma'am me and not here. Up the road a bit. I know a spot.'

They drove on. Dawn's phone pinged in her pocket as Bella pointed out a fresh fruit stall on the side of the road. Dawn wasn't a big fruit eater, but she wasn't about to complain. Even a banana now would do the job of staving off her hunger pangs.

She retrieved her phone as Ryan pulled over and obediently helped Bella from the rear seat. Rusty whined. Greta growled.

There was a chuckle in Dawn's voice as she answered.

'Detective Grave speaking.'

'Detective. It's Reynolds. We got a hit on some CCTV footage.'

Dawn pulled her notepad from her top pocket.

'Who? Where?'

'There's a service station, off the main road. Trucks use it quite a bit and they have excellent coffee.'

'Where Reynolds?'

'Lakeland, off Foyster Drive, opposite the caravan park.'

'Got it. Who did you find?'

'We've got two hits. Tina Farrell's vehicle on Thursday morning, not sure if she was coming or going from Cooktown. Then Constable Craig's early this morning.'

'How did you find that? Does the station have monitored CCTV?'

'No. I called around. Gave a description of the vehicles along with Farrell and Craig. The owner thought he remembered Farrell. So he went back through the CCTV for me. He's a lovely guy.'

'Great work Reynolds.'

'Ah Detective?'

'Yes?

'Are you heading back to Cooktown yet?'

'Yes. We'll call into Lakeland on the way.'

There was a silence, then Dawn heard Reynolds take a deep breath.

'What is it Reynolds?'

'It might be nothing, but I've been through our victim's financials. I found her merchant services account and other than a few charges, there isn't much going into the yoga business.'

'So Farrell lied about using our victim's account for her clients then?'

'Looks like it. But I found something else?'

'What?

'One of the charges to Jane Nichols' yoga studio was quite large so I ran a search on the credit card holding and it comes up with a Cooktown address.'

Dawn could hear Reynolds typing on her keyboard. 'I did a search on the owner of the address, and he has customised Cooktown number plates.'

'Well done, Reynolds. Get all the info together but don't interview anyone. Got it? Not until I'm back.'

'Of course, but can I come with you? I'd really like to see this one through.'

There was a tone to Reynold's voice Dawn knew only too well. It sounded like her over fifteen years ago.

'You got it Reynolds. But can you do me a favour first?'

'Sure. What do you need?'

'I need you to call my sister for me.'

Dawn outlined her plan to escape Lisa's wrath. The old Queenslander was full to the brim already, and now she was bringing home an extra. But it was the two dogs Dawn was really concerned about. She knew how she'd feel if the roles were reversed.

Lisa was going to be more fuming.

Chapter 29

Ryan's Mustang scraped its belly as he navigated the narrow, rough track. Trees crowded the entrance to her family home. A month ago, she would have given anything to be somewhere else, but today, as the two-storey building, with worn and faded paintwork came into view, her heart skipped a beat.

Her niece waved from the balcony before leaping to the stairs—her blonde ringlets flying behind her like the golden Labrador's ears when Ryan let his window down moments earlier. The dog drooled on his shoulder as he leant over to stick his head out the opening. The little girl squealed when she spotted the dog's head, tongue lolling, lips smiling.

'Auntie Dawn. It's Auntie Dawn Mummy and she's got a *dog*!'

That was one of Dawn's questions answered. Abby didn't seem the least bit upset she was bringing a dog home.

Wait until she sees the chihuahua, Dawn thought.

Now to see what the six-year-old thought of the cranky old woman they tore from her home a few hours earlier.

Abby hopped from one foot to the other as Ryan stepped out of the vehicle. Rusty leapt over the seat and out the door, running a wild circle around the car before returning to Abby, tail wagging, hips with it.

'For the love of…' Lisa appeared on the balcony, wiping her hands with a dish cloth. Ranger Michael two steps behind her as usual.

Dawn waved.

'I'll explain. Did Reynolds call you?'

Lisa handed the towel to Michael and started down the stairs.

'She did, but she mentioned a guest, not a dog.'

Dawn flipped her seat over and held her hands out to accept Greta from Mrs Lundstrom.

'What, two dogs!'

Dawn cringed, then put the dog on the ground, turning to assist Mrs Lundstrom from the back seat. The task proved more difficult than expected. After three hours cramped in the backseat, the old woman's legs weren't too steady. Ryan climbed back into the car and slid the seat as far forward as possible. Dawn levered the woman out with a grunt.

Bella scowled at Dawn before smoothing her floral dress down and turning to face Abby and Lisa with an expression Dawn hadn't seen yet. The woman's eyes twinkled, her lips curved at the edges and the first words out of her mouth nearly floored Dawn.

'I'm so grateful you offered your lovely house.'

Lisa turned back to the wall of replaced cladding Dawn was yet to paint, then returned her gaze to Dawn, a question in her eyes.

Dawn started the introductions.

'Mrs Lundstrom…'

'I told you Luv.' She waved her hand dismissively at Dawn, then turned her attention to Lisa. 'Call me Bella.' Reaching out, she clasped Lisa's hand in both of hers and squeezed. Then half bent over toward Abby 'And what's your name sweetheart?'

Dawn was sure the old lady would have dropped to her haunches to speak with Abby if it weren't for the cramped ride in Ryan's car.

'My name's Abby and this is my mummy and up there is,' Abby leant closer, mouth behind her hand, 'is her boyfriend.' She whispered in the way six-year-old girls do.

Dawn glanced up to see Michael chuckling, no doubt pleased Abby was accepting him into her life.

'Well dinner is nearly ready. Why don't you all freshen up? I'm so sorry about the stairs Bella.' Lisa held her hand out to assist the woman.

Bella waved it away with a smile.

'That's fine Luv. I'm old, not decrepit. Still spritely enough to make it up a few stairs.'

Lisa hovered, arms at the ready as the older woman mounted the first step. Dawn quietly gave herself a pat on the back for having mended each and every one of those damn treads or Mrs Lundstrom would have fallen on her arse with the first one.

No one else seemed to notice her handy work.

Ryan followed her with Bella's bag as Abby led Rusty and Greta to a bowl of water, then gave Rusty the grand tour of the understorey workshop and storage area.

Dawn doubted the dog was planning on staying downstairs, but where the dogs slept was Lisa's call, not hers. The old Queenslander might officially be theirs, left to them when her father died, but it was Lisa who stayed in Cooktown and had lived there all her life.

Dawn met Lisa at the top of the stairs as Michael guided Bella inside.

'Give her my bed. We won't stay. I've got a case on the go and the team is waiting for us at the station.'

'You still have to eat.'

'We picked up some fruit on the way.'

'But I've got news I wanted to tell you about. Come and eat.'

'News?'

Dawn's stomach tensed. Something in her sister's eyes said the news might be a shock.

'Don't tell me you're pregnant.'

Her sister slapped her arm lightly.

'Dawn!'

Ryan returned to the deck after dropping off the bag. A frown joined his eyebrows.

'You ready?' he asked.

Dawn waved him to the car.

'Give me a second. I'll be down.'

She watched Ryan a moment, then turned to Lisa.

'If you're not pregnant, what's so urgent?'

Lisa's chest rose more than once as she composed herself. Dawn could see the thoughts running through her sister's mind.

'It's about Fraser's case.'

Dawn swallowed but said nothing. The case had been under investigation for nearly a month now, but even if they reopened it, there was very little evidence to go on after all these years.

'What's up?' Dawn could hear the nerves in her voice.

'The Coronial Inquest on his exhumation is in.'

All Dawn could think of was why no one had mentioned it to her. Surely Sergeant Martin knew about it.

As if reading her thoughts, Lisa carried on explaining.

'They rang me at lunchtime. I was finishing up early so I could get Abby from school while you were working.'

'Lisa, just tell me. What did they find?'

'I don't understand all the guff, but the coroner officially re-opened the case.'

'Did she tell you under what grounds?'

Lisa shook her head.

'Don't worry. I'll find out.' She gripped her sister's forearm.

'Auntie Dawn. Come on. It's dinner time.' Abby appeared from behind them. Obviously unaware of the gravity of the adult conversation happening under her nose.

'It's okay Abby. Auntie Dawn has to get to work. We'll save her and Clint something to eat.' Lisa took her daughter's hand and guided her inside.

As she closed the door, she caught Dawn's eye. Her sister's expression reflected the feelings rolling around Dawn's stomach. They'd waited all their adult life to make everyone believe the truth they'd known all along.

Fraser *didn't* kill himself.

Chapter 30

Dawn slipped into the front seat, her mind numb, her body working on autopilot.

'Are you okay? Ryan studied her expression, hand on the keys in the ignition.

She contemplated off-loading to her new partner how she was feeling about Lisa's news, but now wasn't the time. He'd find out soon enough.

'All good. Let's get to the station. Reynolds said she's found a link between Jane Nichols and a local with a Cooktown custom number plate.'

Ryan reversed the car without another word, but his eyes flicked back to her as soon as they turned from her driveway onto the road.

'You can stay with me tonight.'

Dawn balked.

'I mean, if the old lady and the dogs and the kid are all too much for you. There's a spare room in the apartment.'

Dawn recalled the view from the balcony and the kiss she never should have let happen.

'Is that the same one you stayed in last time?' Her voice was too casual, even to her own ears.

'Yep. I heard you offer your bed to the old biddy.'

'Call her Bella. I think she'll kick you in the shins if you don't. Did you see how she turned on the charm with Abby?'

'And she said *I* was putting on the charm.'

Ryan parked outside the station. Dawn scanned the looming dark clouds through the windscreen.

'We better make a run for it.' She pointed to the sky as she slammed the Mustang door, slung her bag across her body and sprinted for the station entrance without waiting for a reply.

She sensed Ryan behind her as she pushed the glass door open. The foyer was empty. Behind the reception desk sat an officer she didn't recognise.

'Can I help you?'

'Detectives Grave and Ryan.' She patted her pants for her ID, but Ryan's appeared before she retrieved hers.

'Oh. Sorry. We've not met.' The officer rounded the counter, hand outstretched. 'I'm Constable Brett Chung.' His eyes smiled with his lips.

'Pleased to meet you, Chung. You're new?' Dawn accepted his hand. Ryan followed.

'Just transferred from Darwin.'

'So the sticky summer isn't a shock?'

'No Ma'am.'

'Call me Detective or Dawn. I'm not your boss or your mother.' She smiled to take the edge from her words.

Was she irritated about being surrounded by so many young constables? Apart from the sergeant and the senior constable, Dawn was beginning to believe she was the oldest member of staff. It wasn't a comforting thought.

The young officer grinned. Returning to the counter, he buzzed them through to the rear. 'Sergeant is expecting you. He said to go straight through to his office.'

'Will do.' Dawn opened the hallway door. 'Thanks Chung.'

'Pleased to meet you Detective.'

Dawn stepped through. Ryan right behind.

'He was flirting.'

Dawn ignored him as she knocked on the first door to the right in the hallway.

'I noticed.'

179

The door opened, preventing Ryan from going on about Dawn encouraging him.

'Grave, Ryan. Get in here.' Sergeant Martin held the door and stepped aside. 'I've been holding Reynolds back all afternoon and I'm running out of excuses.'

Dawn smiled. 'I told her she could come with me when I conduct the interview.'

Sergeant Martin opened the door on the other side of his office and led them through to the team office beyond. A murder board was front and centre, next to his office door. Reynolds and Jamison glanced up from their desks as she and Ryan entered. Dawn glanced around for the Senior Constable, but he wasn't in the room.

The sergeant waved at a photo on the board.

'I bet Reynolds didn't tell you who the suspect is?'

'No.' Dawn turned to study it.

'This is Les Richardson, a prominent art dealer from Sydney.'

Dawn approached the board.

'And he lives in Cooktown?' She tried not to sound surprised.

'Part time. Yes. Flies into the local airport in his own private plane. Keeps his Aston Martin garaged and fuelled nearby, ready and waiting for the flick of his fingers.'

'You sound jealous.' Dawn leant against Reynolds' desk.

The sergeant put his finger and thumb together and opened a gap.

'Just a tad.'

'So you want me to tread lightly?'

'If it's not too much to ask.'

'Good luck with that,' Ryan chuckled.

Dawn scowled. Then turned back to the Sergeant.

'He's only a person of interest at the moment and judging by what you just said, he might not even have been in the car when it visited the Nichols' beach house.'

'Exactly.' The sergeant returned to the doorway leading to his office. 'Reynolds, get your skates on.'

The young constable hopped to her feet and shimmied around her desk.

'Ready when you are Detective.'

Dawn glanced at Ryan.

'You still riding shotgun?'

'You bet.'

'Then we better take a police cruiser because I don't think Reynolds' legs are going to squeeze into the back of your muscle car.'

Ryan scrutinised Reynolds' height, then glanced at Jamison who was over a foot taller than Dawn.

'Reynolds maybe. Jamison, no way.'

Jamison screwed up his nose.

'Very funny.'

Reynolds crossed the room, plucked a set of keys off the keyring near the senior constable's desk and turned with a broad grin on her face.

'I need to grab my utility vest and sign my weapon out. I'll meet you out front.'

'Where's the senior?' Dawn resisted the temptation to refer to him as Constable Constable. The guy didn't exactly like her at the best of times. Now wasn't the time to make fun of his last name.

Reynolds started down the hallway leading to the locker room. Jamison glanced up from his desk to answer her question.

'No idea. He got a call earlier today. Seemed a bit rattled and took off shortly afterwards without a word.'

Dawn was about to ask more questions, but Sergeant Martin's door opened. The pensive expression he wore set Dawn on edge.

'Dawn. Can I see you a minute?'

'Sure.' She entered, Ryan behind her, until the sergeant put his hand on her partner's chest.

'This is private mate. Dawn can loop you in.'

Ryan frowned as Dawn realised this was about Lisa's news. Turning, she touched his arm. 'I think I know what it's about. I'll tell you later.' He didn't back out of the office. 'I promise.'

Ryan's nostrils flared, then he nodded and backed out of the doorway. As Dawn closed the door, she noted the concern in his eyes.

Taking a steadying breath, she reminded herself her long service leave would be up in six weeks. She was only staying until Fraser's case was reopened and the house was liveable.

But something in Ryan's eyes, and the vision of Abby standing on the veranda, frantically waving to her *Auntie Dawn* stabbed at her heart.

The Sergeant flicked the venetian blinds closed, shutting out any prying eyes, then turned to Dawn.

'Dawn. The Coroner's Office phoned a few minutes ago. Her findings are in and she's reopening the investigation into Fraser's death.'

The sergeant rounded his desk. Dawn pulled a chair out and sat on the edge.

'Lisa told me before I came down.'

'Dawn I'm so sorry. If we stuffed this up back then, it's on me.'

'No. It's on the sergeant at the time and the detectives who didn't do their due diligence.'

Sergeant Martin leant over his desk, hand outstretched like he was trying to reach Dawn.

'Still. You came to me. You told me about your suspicions.'

Dawn slumped back in the chair.

'I've been telling everyone for years. So has Lisa.' She waved her hand. 'I don't really hold anyone responsible Ross.' She used his first name, hoping to make it less formal. 'Just Fraser's killer. I'm relieved we'll get a run at the case now.'

The sergeant slid back in his chair, his shoulders hunched and for the first time since returning to Cooktown, Dawn noticed the grey at his temples.

'That's the thing Dawn.'

Her stomach knotted.

'What?'

'Coroner's directed Queensland Police to ensure you stay *out* of the investigation.'

She jumped to her feet.

'What?'

'And the Senior too.'

That must have been why he stormed out earlier. She began pacing.

'Just because I'm related to the victim and the Senior is connected through the suicide letter, the one we know Fraser *didn't* write remember, doesn't mean we can't be impartial and do our jobs.' Dawn's voice sounded high pitched, even to her own ears.

A shadow hovered outside the sergeant's window. Ryan must have heard her elevated voice.

Sergeant Martin rose, rounded the desk and sat on it facing Dawn.

'We know Fraser didn't kill Tracey, but her name was in the suicide note. The Senior is Tracey's uncle, and you know he became a cop because of Tracey's murder. Queensland Police, my bosses, yours now, aren't open to negotiation on this. Dawn…'

He used her name hoping she'd look at him, but she couldn't. She was too angry to think.

'Dawn. I'm sorry. It's out of my hands.'

She swore under her breath. For two decades all she wanted was to clear her brother's name and find his killer. If it wasn't for last month's case where Tracey Warren's murderer was finally found and locked up, the local cops would still be none the wiser.

Now she was going to have to sit on the sidelines and watch another mismanaged investigation into Fraser's death.

'But…' His tone gave Dawn a shred of hope. 'I think I managed to get someone we can trust into the investigation.' The sergeant smiled.

Dawn's heart jumped along with her stomach.

'Who?'

A knock on the sergeant's door startled her.

Sergeant Martin pointed to the door.

'Come in Ryan.'

Ryan stepped in and opened his mouth, but the sergeant interrupted him.

'Did you get a call from the coroner's office?'

A grin split his lips.

'I certainly did.'

Dawn almost leapt at her new partner. She couldn't exactly say why, but Ryan was the one person she knew she could trust with this investigation. Now this tied them together on so many levels.

'So rack off you two.' The sergeant waved his hand toward the open doorway. 'Ryan, we'll go over the case notes tomorrow morning early. For now, get over to Mr Richardson's place. Reynolds has the address.'

Dawn turned, a mix of excitement and apprehension hit her like a double-shot cocktail.

'And Grave,' she turned back at the tone in the sergeant's voice, 'remember, prominent art dealer. Play nice.'

Chapter 31

Reynolds drove the police Landcruiser while Dawn got her bearings. Ryan didn't appear happy with the backseat but knew better than to complain.

As the constable turned the vehicle onto a dirt track a few hundred metres from the lookout, Dawn frowned.

'I didn't know anyone lived out this way. Thought it was National Park.'

Reynolds kept her eyes on the smooth track. Gumtrees, remnant mango trees full of fruit and tropical vines and undergrowth closed in around them as the track turned into a sandy single lane road.

'Most of it is, but this acreage is privately owned.'

The vehicle lurched. Ryan grunted as his head hit the roof despite the seatbelt.

'Lucky we *didn't* bring my Mustang.'

'Not far now.'

Reynolds grinned in the rearview mirror as Ryan rubbed his head.

Dawn gaped as an expansive estate come into view, but it was nothing compared to the fabulous view of the ocean.

A large two-storey octagonal building sat amongst gumtrees and palms. Walkways covered in iron roofs and paved with decking stretched out like octopus' arms, leading to Fijian style bungalows complete with thatched roof and timber-louvre windows.

'Is this a resort?' Dawn asked.

'I don't think so. Richardson is a multi, multi-millionaire from all accounts.'

'From art?' Ryan's tone matched Dawn's scepticism.

No one got *this* rich from art.

Reynolds steered the police vehicle around a central garden of palms and brightly coloured pots overflowing with Cooktown Orchids.

As they drew to a stop, a man wearing a white sarong and hat appeared on the veranda. For a moment Dawn thought it might be Richardson, but the dark complexion and oriental features weren't what she was expecting.

When he stepped up to open the door, she knew he wasn't the owner.

He tipped his head as Dawn stepped out.

'Officers, Mr Richardson be expecting you.'

His accent was faintly familiar. Malaysian or Indonesian, Dawn couldn't be sure. But his slight frame and short stature were consistent with either.

She glanced at Ryan who stepped out the back seat waving the man's hand away as he attempted to close the door behind him.

'Follow me.' The man stepped away without waiting to see if they followed. He spoke with his back toward them. 'How I introduce you.'

'We'll make the introductions if you don't mind.' Dawn kept her tone neutral, but clear.

The man stopped outside a pair of timber-framed double glass doors and smiled knowingly.

'As you wish.' He opened the right door and held it for them to enter. Reynolds scurried up to join them, slipping inside as the manservant closed the door. He studied her with squinting eyes.

'She's with us.' Dawn waved Reynolds forward.

'As you wish.'

The tone didn't sound anything like a diligent butler or personal assistant. On the contrary, Dawn struggled to ignore the slight mocking.

He gestured for them to follow him down the hall. As he turned and gave them his back once more, Dawn glanced at Ryan who shrugged like it was normal behaviour. For him it might be. Being related to the Tenneson family and growing up with money was a far cry from her background.

All the pomp and ceremony seemed out of place in Cooktown. Dawn wondered why the man would set up his holiday home here, when there were so many popular places like Coffs Harbour, Byron Bay, Noosa or Port Douglas to choose from.

Modern artwork adorned the walls—out of place considering the tropical Fijian style décor.

They passed closed doors either side of the hallway and Dawn wondered over the design. Most opulent homes opened immediately into a huge living space, but this was different. The ambience of the wide passage gave a museum vibe, while the side rooms made her think of a Japanese bath house.

The assistant stopped at the end and waited for them to catch up.

'You sure I no announce you?'

Dawn opened her mouth with a quick retort on her lips, but Ryan interrupted.

'This isn't a royal gala mate. You were advised we were coming, so we'll make our own introductions.'

'As you wish.' He propelled the heavy timber doors, entered and almost bowed. Dawn stifled a laugh. 'Sir. The police are here, and they give me no names.'

The man sitting on a wide daybed waved his hand in the air dismissively.

'It's fine Ketut. Grab some refreshments.'

Dawn interrupted.

'That won't be necessary Mr Richardson. We won't take up too much of your time.'

'Nonsense.' He waved his hand to send his servant on his way. 'Ketut.'

At least Dawn knew his nationality now. Ketut was an Indonesian name for the fourth born son and she wasn't aware of its use in Malaysia.

'I'm Detective Grave, this is Detective Ryan and I understand you spoke with Constable Reynolds earlier.'

'Lovely to put a face to the name.'

The man's hazel eyes sparkled at Reynolds. The young officer glanced at her feet as her cheeks blushed. Mr Richardson then turned his gaze on Dawn, and she noted the gold flecks in his eyes.

Her focus was drawn from his eyes to his bare chest. She guessed his age, mid-fifties, but his physique said otherwise. His body was taut and tanned, his chest smooth and oiled.

Ryan cleared his throat. Dawn's eyes returned to Richardson's.

'We won't take up too much of your time. Just a few questions about your relationship with Jane Nichols.'

'The dead girl. Sad to hear.'

It was a strange way to describe a victim, but Dawn carried on.

'You've heard about the murder then?'

'Murder?' Richardson's hand landed on that bare bronze chest. 'I thought it was an accident.'

'She went missing from Newell Beach and ended up at the Keatings Lagoon. We are fairly certain foul play is involved.'

'Of course. Of course.' He finally sat forward on the daybed. 'What makes you think I knew the girl?'

There it was. Dawn supressed a smile.

'Your car was seen entering the Nichols' family holiday home in Newell Beach the day before Jane went missing. Thursday before last.'

'Ah. Yes. Ketut would have been driving.'

Of course he was, Dawn thought but said nothing. Instead, she waited. Suspects often spoke into silence if given the chance.

Dawn saw Reynolds open her mouth to speak. She cleared her throat and glared at the inexperienced officer. Reynolds rolled her lips and dropped her eyes back to her feet.

'And why was Ketut at the beach house?'

The corners of Richardson's mouth curved and Dawn's skin tingled, but the expression was gone in a heartbeat.

'I was hosting a yoga retreat for some of my clients. She was running the retreat.'

'Artists or buyers?'

Dawn thought about Tina. About how her car had been seen on CCTV footage at the service station inside their death window.

'Both.'

'Did Tina Farrell attend?'

'As a matter of fact, she did. How did you know?'

Dawn shrugged.

'We'll need a list of all your guests Mr Richardson.'

'I'm afraid you'll need a court order before I can share my guest list Detective. Some of my clients are very prominent businesspeople and they value their privacy.'

Dawn tongued her cheek as she considered how to get the list without jumping through hoops and waiting for a warrant.

It was Ryan who spoke into the silence.

'We could do that and get a warrant to search the premises while we are here.'

Dawn glanced at Ryan. The slightest grin hovered on his lips. Reynolds on the other hand wore a cheshire-cat smile.

'That won't be necessary.' Richardson waved as Ketut returned with a tray of glasses and a platter of sliced fruit.

'Ketut. Get a list of the yoga retreat guests for these lovely detectives.' He rose and stretched with an exaggerated yawn. 'If you don't mind. I'll be taking a quick dip now.' He untied his loose-fitting yoga pants and Dawn suppressed an audible laugh.

Reynold gasped, then gaped.

The eccentric art dealer strutted to a wall of glass, slid it aside and strolled to the edge of a crystal blue pool surrounded by sandstone pavers and overgrown potted ferns.

He stopped at the edge, toes dangling, then turned. 'You're welcome to finish the refreshments while you wait.' Then he dove into the pool.

Ryan swore under his breath.

Chapter 32

Ryan dragged his door closed with a thud.

'Pompous arse.'

Dawn eased her seatbelt out and grinned.

'Nice arse it was too,' Reynolds snorted as she turned the key and the motor fired up.

'At least we got a list of his guests,' she offered as she steered the car from the smooth driveway back to the rugged track.

'You and Jamison go over those names when we get back. I want a statement from each of them explaining exactly when and where they last saw our victim and if they noticed Tina Farrell at the event.'

'You got it Detective.'

'And we need a background check on Richardson. No one makes *that* sort of money dealing in art.'

'Unless it's the stolen kind,' Ryan offered.

'An angle worth investigating. He certainly didn't want us pulling a search warrant.' Dawn glanced over her shoulder. 'Nice call by the way.'

'Thought it might do the trick.'

Dawn focussed out the windscreen as the bushland gave way to old Queenslander homes and lush tropical gardens.

'So, we know Jane was here Thursday. Ketut picked her up to run the yoga clinic, explaining the charges on our victim's merchant account. Our window for her death is wider now, so it's possible Jane didn't run the clinic or if she did, she might not have been there long before she was killed.'

'So our suspect pool is now widened to everyone on this list.' Ryan held up the piece of paper Ketut gave them.

'That's assuming everyone who attended was added to the list.' Dawn glanced back at Ryan. 'We should also check out Ketut. But it won't be easy without his last name.'

Ryan leant forward and stopped as his seatbelt grabbed.

'Rich arseholes like Richardson claim everything they can on tax. My bet is Ketut is on the payroll. Shouldn't be too hard to track through the taxation office.'

'That's providing he's not illegal.'

'Good thing I got a photo of him then.' Reynolds focussed on the road as Dawn and Ryan glanced her way. She noticed them staring. 'What? No one pays any attention to a police officer when there are two detectives in the room.'

'Is that why you went to ask a question?'

Dawn was ready to reprimand the young constable, but she planned to do it in private. Now, as she watched the woman suppress a grin, she had to admire the distraction.

Dawn patted Reynolds on the shoulder. 'Well done, Reynolds. We'll run him through immigration when we get back to the station.'

Ryan flopped back in his seat.

'I'm wondering why an art dealer sets up a holiday home in Cooktown.'

'I was wondering the same thing. And what's the *real* connection between him and Jane Nichols? Did Tina recommend her friend for the yoga retreat? And if so, why didn't Tina mention where our victim actually went missing from. And Rusty ...'

Dawn couldn't get the dog out of her head.

Ryan's voice dragged her from theorising further.

'We won't know unless we track her down. We know Tina Farrell and Constable Craig are friends. And where does Jane Nichols fit in? Are they all more than friends? This could be a love triangle gone bad.'

Reynolds parked outside the station as another torrent of rain began to fall.

'Does it matter? They are both missing.' She switched off the motor and the windows began to fog up instantly.

'According to Parker, so is Tenneson.' Dawn searched the vehicle for an umbrella, suddenly wishing she'd grabbed her coat before they left. She'd forgotten how the tropics could dish out volatile weather. One minute it was sunny and steamy, the next it was grey and pouring.

'There's wet weather coats in the back.' Reynolds pointed and Ryan turned to peer over the back seats.

'When did Tenneson go missing?'

Ryan's voice was muffled as he pulled two dark blue rain jackets from the back and handed them to Dawn and Reynolds.

'Don't know exactly but it seems Parker decided to see if Tenneson was where he said he was.' Dawn was surprised the detective went out of her way to follow up. Maybe she needed to try to start fresh with the woman.

'Good on her. But if Tenneson is gone, maybe he's Richardson's link to Jane? Was the art dealer on the campaign donor list? Ryan reached back for another coat coming up empty.

Reynolds shimmied into the coat, then turned to Ryan. 'Not that I noticed.'

'We need to go over this inside.' Dawn flipped the hood over her head. 'Let's grab some food. Looks like it's going to be a long night of checking out witness statements.'

'We've still got the CCTV footage from the Lakeland service station to go through,' Ryan offered as he rose to his knees to peer over the seat.

Dawn glanced at Reynolds. 'Good job on the distraction. I thought you were going to put your foot in it for a second.'

The young constable blushed. 'I nearly did, but when Richardson stopped looking at me, I saw Ketut coming back with the tray and he seemed distracted. I snapped a shot.'

'I'm glad you were honest with me Reynolds. You've got great potential, but you've got a lot to learn. Still. That photo could be exactly what we need.'

Dawn turned and opened the door, not wanting to embarrass the constable or force her to say anything. As she bolted through the pouring rain, feet splashing water in the air with every step, she recalled her first few years on the police force and how she wished she'd had a female detective to help her along the way.

Back then, women were rare and those who made it to detective were tough, hardworking, unforgiving women. Even when Dawn came up through the ranks, it was a difficult slog most of the way.

Now, if she could give a helping hand to talented officers like Reynolds and the young Constable Williams she met in Coober Pedy, then she would.

Female officer quotas were one thing. Getting the right people into the right job was another thing altogether.

She flung the station door open. Ryan arrived a fraction of a second behind her, dripping wet. Water ran from his fingers as he flicked his arms in front of him. A puddle at his feet formed on the lino floor. The new officer Chung shook his head in mild disgust.

'What! There were only two bloody coats in the car and there's nowhere outside to drip dry.'

Dawn wanted to laugh, but Ryan's face was crestfallen. Reynolds drew up behind Dawn.

'Follow me. We've got a tack room for all this stuff.'
Ryan rolled his eyes.

'Alright for you two. What am I going to do? Stick my head under the toilet hand dryers?' No one replied as he trudged along toward the door. Chung waved them through with a wicked smile.

Dawn stopped in the doorway.

'I know this isn't exactly your job, but can you order a load of pizzas for the team? I have no idea what everyone eats, but we've got a ton of paperwork to sift through and it's going to keep everyone here late.'

'No problem. I'll dial it up now.' Chung waved her on.

Dawn's stomach growled as she followed Ryan and Reynolds down the hall and into a locker room. As she peeled her soaking wet jacket off, all she could think about was where Tina Farrell could be and was she in danger, or involved in her friend's murder.

Things weren't adding up and every time she tried to make them, Tina's statement—the dog walk—the dog being tied up at the beach a day after Jane left with Ketut… Nothing was making sense.

Chapter 33

The smell of pizza lingered in the office. Dawn rose, stretched and crossed the room to the boxes laid out on the senior constable's desk. It seemed the right spot for them, considering the man hadn't returned to work since he got the call about Fraser's case.

The fact annoyed her to no end. They were short staffed, with a load of legwork that needed to be done and the one man who could help her organise the constables was missing.

She opened the first carton to find a vegetarian pizza, but decided she ate enough vegetarian at Lisa's place. Her sister never ate meat and while Dawn respected her sister's choice, she was a carnivore through and through.

As she opened the meat lover's box, her stomach made the decision for her. Reaching for the last piece, she turned to find Ryan hovering at her shoulder.

'Did you want this one?' She held the piece of pizza out. He shook his head, but something in his eyes made her stop and study him. 'What's up?'

'Nothing.' He brushed past her to make his selection. 'Have we got Tina and Craig's financials back yet?'

'No. I'll chase them up.' Dawn studied Ryan's back a moment, before crossing the room and drawing up alongside Jamison. She still didn't have a Queensland Police log-on, so she delegated the task.

'I'll see what's happening.' Jamison typed with unexpected proficiency. It was a vast difference from Ryan's hunt and peck method, but these kids were cops of a different era.

Touch typing was likely a prerequisite with the amount of computer-based work, data entry, surveillance and email trails they were required to follow.

At thirty-eight, she knew she was still young, but in that moment, she felt like a dinosaur. She wondered how her boss back in Adelaide managed in times like this. He, along with most of the team were in their late forties, early fifties and would have seen the massive changes in technology from the late eighties to the present day.

Now, in twenty fifteen, she could hold a computer in the palm of her hand, with a larger RAM and hard-drive capacity than Jack likely used at his Pulteney Grammar private school.

Jamison's voice dragged her from her daydream.

'Here. Tina Farrell's records are in. But we are still waiting for Constable Craig's.' He tapped the screen. 'Do you want me to print out what we've got?'

'Yes thanks.'

Dawn waited as the laser printer fired up across the room.

'How are we going with those witness statements?'

Jamison glanced up from his computer.

'Most aren't picking up. The few we've spoken to don't recall seeing Jane after the first yoga class of the day.'

'That's strange. If it was a yoga retreat, surely, they expected more classes?'

'You'd think so.' Ryan spoke through a half-full mouth. 'Unless it was more about art and less about yoga.' His eyebrows wiggled.

'Stolen art you mean?' Dawn frowned, trying to read his expression.

'I was thinking acrobatic art. You know. Swingers party or something. You saw all those rooms set up in the house.' He took another bite of his pizza.

'You would go there.' Dawn turned back to Jamison who wore a smile.

'Find their addresses, sort them into locations and get the local police to go door knocking. Including you two if any of them live locally.'

'On it.' Jamison started typing.

'Detective.' Dawn turned to Reynolds' voice as she collected the first print out.

'Yes?'

'I just got off the phone with Detective Parker in Cairns. She wanted to let you know there's still no sign of Tenneson. They've checked with his electoral office staff. No one has seen him since you and Detective Ryan interviewed him at the golf course.'

'Damn.'

'And there's something else.' Reynolds waved for Dawn to come over. Ryan stuffed the last bite of his pizza in his mouth and joined her.

'This is Richardson's background. I've double checked and can't find anything linking him to the Minister, but Ketut.' The young officer brought up a photo on the screen, wiggling the computer cursor over it with obvious excitement.

Dawn focussed on where the little blinking arrow pointed and smiled. At least some pieces were starting to come together.

Ryan grunted and slipped his phone from his jacket pocket.

'We need to call the AFP. Maybe the feds have some more info on him.'

'Or maybe we have someone closer to home who can help.' Dawn knew who she needed to call. A shame it was the last person she wanted to speak to right now.

Too much history. Too many memories. Dawn shut her eyes but knew it wouldn't wash away the past.

'We aren't dealing with a Columbian crime syndicate, or even Triads. This is closer to home.'

She turned to see Ryan's expression. A mixture of confusion and concern.

'You call the AFP. I'll call Rossi.'

Chapter 34

Dawn's stomach churned as she tapped her ex-husband's number into her phone. A number she'd been blissfully unaware of for nearly twenty years. When she moved to Adelaide, she wasn't only escaping her messed up family life in Cooktown.

She was running away from one of the worst decisions she'd ever made. As she thought about Declan, a tiny piece of her heart ached for how he used to make her feel. Those days after her mother disappeared, when she was lonely, angry, abandoned.

He'd been there for her.

She held her breath as the call connected.

'Dawn.'

His voice hadn't changed. It stirred in places she'd locked and thrown away the key to years ago. Ryan glanced her way as she opened her mouth to speak. His eyes drilled into hers with unasked questions.

He wanted to know if she was okay. She couldn't answer him. She simply didn't know.

She smiled and turned away so he couldn't overhear her conversation while he waited on hold with the AFP.

'Rossi. We need some intel, and you seem like the quickest option.' She knew her tone was curt. It needed to be. There was absolutely no way she wanted to open an old wound like the one Rossi left her with.

'Ah.' He hesitated but recovered quickly. 'What's up?'

'We've got a local here with an Indonesian manservant who seems off. We've run his face through immigration, and it popped. Ryan is on the phone to AFP now, but I think this could be linked to drugs.'

'And you think old habits die hard.'

'You said it Rossi, not me.'

She heard him huff on the other end of the line. A stab of guilt swept over her, but it was quickly followed by a vivid memory of pain. She forced herself to stay the course.

'You went off the rails Rossi.' She hurried away from Reynolds and Jamison. Leaving Ryan still on hold. 'If anyone has connections in the drug game, it's you. You found those bikie mug shots quick enough.'

'I recognised the tattoo and knew where to look. It was a lucky break. That life was a long time ago Dawn. I can't say sorry often enough, but I gave it away when you left.'

'Don't mind if I don't believe you Rossi. Why didn't you tell me you were on the job?'

She shook herself. Why on earth did she ask that question? She didn't want to know. She wanted to forget.

A creaking door and the sound of water told her Rossi was trying to find a quiet place.

'I should have told you, but I wasn't allowed to. It's in the past Dawn. I admit I got addicted to the life. As soon as the investigation wound up, I quit the stuff, cleaned up and I've been straight ever since.'

A toilet flushing snapped her back to reality.

Focus on your work Grave!

'I'm sending you a photo. Take a look. Run it past your old pals and see what you can find out. He's not even supposed to be in the country so I'm expecting our lead here will dry up very quickly. He'll be on the move if he gets the slightest idea, we know who he is. We need to move fast Rossi.'

There was a moment of silence.

'I don't have any pals, not ones I'd risk showing a photo of an Indonesian drug connection to, but I'll do some digging.'

'That's all I can ask.'

Dawn pulled the phone from her ear to end the call, but stopped when she heard his voice call her name once more.

'What?'

'I know it doesn't mean much now. But I was out of it. I had to have been to do what I did and make you leave.'

'The photo is on the way Rossi.'

Dawn ended the call, her hand shaking, her heart racing. It didn't matter if he was telling the truth. She'd lived through his addiction. He was in deep, too deep. There was no doubt he immersed himself in the life. Prostitutes, bikie chicks, heroin. During his time undercover, he'd learnt to take what he wanted, by force if necessary.

She didn't want his apology. Her past was what made her who she was now. A dead-beat swim coach. A drunken father. A wife beating husband. They fuelled her drive and made her good at her job.

She was no one's victim. She pulled her shoulders back as a hand landed lightly on her shoulder. Spinning, she nearly elbowed Ryan in the cheek, but stopped a few inches short.

Ryan stepped away with wide, questioning eyes. Every fibre of her body was taut. Relaxing the muscles of her face, she rolled her shoulders and let the memories abate with her tension.

'What did AFP say?'

'You first.'

'Rossi knows a few people. He'll see if Ketut has connections with the drugs found in our victim.'

'AFP are aware of Ketut. They have an open investigation into drugs coming via Indonesia into Darwin and Far North Queensland.'

'Cooktown is an easy port. Deep water access. There have been drugs found off the coast here before. Did they say if Richardson is involved?'

'They haven't found a link.'

Dawn made her way back to the laser printer she'd abandoned mid print.

'That's not an answer.' Collecting up the financials, she scanned as she spoke. 'We need to keep digging with Richardson.'

'AFP told us to back off.'

'Of course they did. But murder trumps the war on drugs. We lost years ago. Time to sign the bloody treaty and legalise the shit. Maybe then Jane Nichols would still be alive.'

'We don't know her death is linked to drugs.'

'We don't, but it's a damn good lead.' She opened her mouth to continue her rant, but something caught her eye. 'Look at this.'

Ryan appeared at her side, peering where her finger pointed.

'Whose records are those?'

'Tina Farrell's. We don't have Craig's yet.'

'What am I looking at?'

'If Tina came up here from Cooktown, and she stopped at the service station in Lakeland, where is the fuel charge?' Dawn tapped the dates on the credit card statement. 'It's a week ago. This is up to date.'

'She used someone else's card, or someone else was with her?'

'That or she paid cash.' Dawn scanned her watch. It was after 7.00. They weren't going to get a hold of anyone this time of night.

'Reynolds. Jamison. Time to head home. I'd like you here at 7 a.m. sharp. Jamison. Follow up on Craig's credit card and banking records. Put a little pressure on the bank if you must. Go over Farrell's cash account statements and see if she withdrew any cash before leaving Newell Beach. And get those witness details out to the various stations to follow up.'

Dawn crossed the room and began stacking up pizza boxes from the Senior's desk. If he decided to turn up for work tomorrow, the last thing he'd want to see was a mess on his desk.

'What do you want me to do?' Reynolds stacked papers on her desk.

'Scan the CCTV footage to see if anyone was with Tina Farrell on the Thursday she came up for Richardson's art retreat. It looks like it's likely the day our victim died.'

'You got it Detective.'

Dawn tossed the cardboard boxes in the bin and headed for the door. She needed water, and rest. Her heart was pounding, her vision narrowing. She was on the verge of a panic attack, and she had no idea why.

She took another step, then her legs refused to move. Falling toward the Senior's desk, she flattened her hands on the table and sucked in air while desperately trying to keep her balance.

'Dawn. What's up? What's going on? You've been out of sorts all day.' Ryan touched her arm. She snatched it away.

'I'm fine.' She sucked air through her nostrils and forced each breath out slowly between pursed lips. 'I just need to get home, check on Mrs Lundstrom and get some rest. I'm running on empty.'

'The offer still stands.' Dawn gave him a side-eye. 'In the spare room. I promise.' He lifted his hands, but she focussed on his blue eyes.

He was worried about her. She tossed up her options. Peace and quiet at Ryan's and the possibility he'd want her to explain why she was off. Or the mad house of Lisa's place.

With Abby and the dogs and Cherry the cat and Mrs
Lundstrom.

Sighing. She straightened.

'No night caps. No chats. Just a shower and sleep.'

'Deal.'

For once, he didn't make a wise crack. For the first time
ever, she felt safe accepting his offer.

Chapter 35

The rain eased as Ryan pressed a button on his console, opening the double garage under the apartment he'd rented. Parking the Mustang inside, he turned the motor off, but didn't move to get out straight away.

Dawn's mind raced. She had her go-bag in the back of his car—a weird thought filled her mind about whether she had another pair of knickers in it or not.

Shaking the idea away, she turned to open the passenger's side door, but stopped as Ryan's hand settled on her knee.

She closed her eyes, willing him to let go so she could get out, have her shower and hope the day would disappear into more pleasant dreams.

'You don't have to talk, but if you decide to, I'm here Dawn. Listening. No strings.' Ryan removed his hand, opened his door and stepped out, rounded the back, opened the boot and retrieved their bags.

She joined him and climbed the flight of stairs from the polished concrete to the first floor of the apartment.

'Cuppa?'

Ryan always offered alcohol. Always seemed to have an ulterior motive.

'I'm having a hot chocolate, and I've got marshmallows.' An impish grin split his lips.

'Shower first, then yes. Thanks. I could do with something to settle my brain.'

'Take your time.' He waved casually on his way to the kitchen, but as Dawn turned, bag in hand to head to the bathroom, she knew his eyes followed her.

He wanted to know more. She desperately needed to keep this part of her past to herself.

Opening the bathroom door, she was greeted with ceiling high polished stone walls, brushed chrome tapware, double sinks and a thick shower-screen making the room appear larger than it was.

Plush white towels hung on the railing, touching them gave her a homely, safe feeling. As she slipped her clothes off, she could smell her own sweat. Her underwear was damp from perspiration.

She cranked the hot water tap up full, before turning to study her reflection in the mirror. Her hair needed cutting. The short style grew curly when it was in need of a cut and with the humidity, it was frizzed up and unruly. Shaking away all thought, she adjusted the shower temperature and stepped in.

The hot water seemed wrong given the humidity and outside temperature, but something about the steam rising, mirrors fogging and hot water hitting her scalp let her escape.

She imagined herself in a day spa sauna, whiling away the stress of her day. Slipping to the bottom of the shower, she sat, water running down her face, mixing with tears she didn't know she was shedding.

Her insides were throbbing like a festering sore, putrid, red and waiting to explode. She slowly rose, reaching for the tap, her hand shaking. It wasn't adrenalin, fear or anxiety causing the tremors. She wanted a drink, desperately.

'Declan,' she whispered, then shook her head. 'Rossi.'

He was the last person she ever expected to see in her life again. Her emotions were confused every time she heard his voice or saw his face.

No. She told herself. *Take control. You're not a victim.*

She focussed on her breathing as she soaped up her body and massaged her neck. Her hands slid along her arms as she imagined Ryan's fingers kneading her neck—his lips kissing her shoulders. Forcing the image away, she focussed on finishing her shower, telling herself it was a cup of chocolate then a good night's sleep. That's what she needed. Nothing else.

She wasn't going to swap one addiction for another.

No alcohol. No sex. No dependency. She scolded herself.

Drying and dressing, she took the towel with her into the living room, drying her hair as she entered. The sweet smell of chocolate guided her to the breakfast bar, where Ryan was dropping marshmallows into cups, overflowing with hot chocolate.

The curtains were drawn on the balcony windows. Ryan nodded toward them, she turned to see a fork of lightning split the sky.

'Beautiful isn't it?' He handed her the drink.

'Spectacular.' She sipped the froth, savouring the sweetness. 'It's one of the things I missed most about living up here.'

Ryan rounded the kitchen bar and sat on the chrome stool next to her.

'You planning to stay?'

She sipped another mouthful, not knowing the answer to his question.

'I don't know yet. Abby is fantastic. I can't believe I missed her first six years. And Lisa…' Dawn stopped as her heart ached, and her eyes burned.

'You missed her.' Ryan's words were tender.

Dawn sniffed, drew her shoulders back and blew out a slow, controlled breath.

'More than I thought possible.'

Ryan sipped his drink, then leant his elbows back on the counter and watched another lightning strike. Dawn did the same. The silence was pleasant, but then Dawn's mind started playing out scenarios.

What if she told Ryan? Would he try to retaliate? How much could she share?

She sipped her chocolate. Ryan drained his, rose and went to the sink to wash the cup.

'Time to hit the hay. I'll see you in the morning.' He placed his mug on the drainer and turned.

Dawn wasn't sure when she moved, but she found her hand on his arm as he stepped away from the sink.

'He beat me. Then he took what he wanted without permission. So I left.'

The words spilled out without emotion. She couldn't stop them. His arms wrapped around her like her father's used to, back before her mum left and life was good.

She knew it was stupid, but that firm hold was something she thought no longer existed.

Ryan didn't rant. He didn't threaten to kill Rossi. Or make him pay. He simply rubbed her back and spoke soft words into her hair she couldn't even understand.

Later, as she snuggled into clean sheets, she recalled his words as clear as a bell.

You're so strong Dawn. You can do anything. You can overcome everything.

Chapter 36

Dawn's phone pinged as she entered the kitchen. The smell of toast made her stomach grumble.

'Don't know what you have on it, but we've got peanut butter, jam, Vegemite.' Ryan's tone was casual. No hint of last night's offload.

'Vegemite is good. Any coffee?'

'Sorry. Out of beans, but we can grab one from the coffee shop near the Sovereign Hotel.'

'Finding your way around then.'

Ryan shrugged. Dawn pulled her phone from her pocket.

'Ah. Jamison's got Constable Craig's financials.' She tapped out a message to say they were on their way in.

A reply came back.

See email.

Dawn frowned, opened her email account to find an attachment. Craig's credit card statement was attached with three amounts circled.

'Check this out.'

Ryan rounded the bench and leant over Dawn. The fresh smell of his cologne filled her nostrils.

'What?'

'Here,' she pointed. 'This is a charge on Craig's credit card for the fuel on Thursday 8th, then there's the charge yesterday, and…'

'Damn, what are we waiting for?' Ryan reached for his toast.

Dawn buttered hers, added Vegemite and scurried to follow him down the stairs to the garage.

Ten minutes later, he parked the Mustang in front of the Sovereign Hotel.

For once, Dawn was thankful they weren't in a marked police car. The last thing they wanted was for Constable Craig to take off again.

Dawn retrieved her pocket pistol from her bag and shoved it into the back of her pants knowing it would show in her pants' pocket.

'You really should get a service weapon issued.' Ryan suggested as he slipped his jacket on over his shoulder holster.

'Then I'd have to wear a big bulky jacket like you, to hide it.'

He eyed her back with an eyebrow raised.

'It's not exactly invisible under your shirt you know.'

'It is from in front. And today, that'll do.' She stepped out, smoothed her shirt down and closed the car door.

Ryan joined her as they jogged up the steps to the motel office entrance.

'I still think you should get a service weapon.'

'I haven't had time. I'll get one. I promise.' She didn't wait for a reply. She opened the glass door and a wave of cool air rushed out.

Dawn approached the counter, flipped her ID open as Ryan did the same. 'I'm Detective Grave. This is Detective Ryan. You have someone here registered under the surname of Craig or Farrell.'

The receptionist was in her fifties. Her brown eyes studied Dawn's a moment before she realised this wasn't a question, and answering wasn't an option.

She tapped keys on her computer. 'I'll check.' She wriggled the mouse, then tapped some more. 'Yes. A Mr and Mrs.'

Dawn glanced at Ryan. His eyebrows lifted. Were they actually married? How could they have missed that?

'That's them. What room are they in?'

'I don't know if I'm supposed to share private information without a warrant.'

Dawn smiled, a story developing in her head as she opened her mouth to speak.

'Craig is one of us. He's with the Cairns police department and we can't reach him on his phone. We need to get him back to work. There's been a major incident.'

The woman glanced at Ryan, who nodded with a worried expression, telling the woman the incident was indeed major.

She leant forward and whispered.

'It's not terrorism, is it?'

'I'm afraid we aren't at liberty to discuss that, but Constable Craig is required back on duty. We didn't want to have to interrupt his honeymoon.'

'Oh I knew they were newlyweds. That ring, and the smile on their faces was just…you know…'

Dawn didn't, but she smiled and nodded.

'They are in room 21, but I'd definitely knock if I were you. I think they were going to stay in, naked, for the entire week.' The woman winked.

'Of course.' Dawn assured the woman knowing full well they were more likely to kick the door in than knock.

'Down the hall, turn right, up the stairs and along the balcony. It's about midway along.'

Dawn strode away, but stopped as Ryan tapped the counter and smiled.

'Thanks for your help.' The little dimple on his chin sprung to life.

Dawn rolled her eyes. It was the same charming smile he put on for Shaz and the mystery book club members at the Cooktown library. The same one he used for the school receptionist. She wondered if it was the same innocent smile he used when Lorraine Nichols and he spent a summer of debauchery together.

'*Snap out of it!*' She grumbled to herself. Ryan could smile at and sleep with whomever he wanted. It was none of her business.

'Let's go,' she called and turned to follow the receptionist's instructions. Ryan hurried up behind her.

'It doesn't hurt to be polite you know.'

'She's too old for you.'

'I don't know. I'm kind of partial to older women.'

Ryan's tone said he was enjoying the conversation way too much.

'So I've noticed.'

Dawn avoided eye contact as she mounted the stairs two at a time. Ryan caught up quickly.

'What's the plan. Knock and enter? Kick it in?'

'We don't have probable cause to kick it in. He's away from work without an explanation. That's hardly illegal and the receptionist told us they were perfectly cosy when they checked in, so he's not kidnapped Tina, or vice versa.'

'I don't know. Craig might be persuaded to play along with the right incentive.'

They reached the top of the stairs and Dawn rounded on her partner.

'Are you saying a guy would play along with a kidnapper to give her what she wants in the hopes of getting lucky?'

'That's not what I said. I said *he* might have been under duress, not Tina. She is the dominatrix after all.'

'But they checked in with wedding rings and played happy husband and wife. I don't think so.'

'Come on then. I want to know if our local boy is in on all this or just a stupid dumb twit with a crush on a dominatrix.'

Chapter 37

Dawn spotted a cleaning cart on the balcony and pointed. Ryan nodded he understood. Passing room number 21, they stopped outside a room, door wide open.

'Excuse me.'

A young woman in shorts and tank top jumped at the sound of Dawn's voice.

'Sorry. Didn't mean to startle you.' She flipped her ID open as the woman removed earphones. 'I was wondering if you can knock on number 21 and see if they'll open the door for you?'

Dawn was expecting an argument, but the tall, slim woman flipped her ponytail, yanked off her rubber gloves and tossed them on the cart.

'Sure.' She started walking toward the door.

'Ah, maybe take your cart with you,' Ryan suggested with a back handed wave. She frowned.

'We have reason to believe a woman is being held inside against her will. We'd like a distraction,' he carried on explaining.

The lie slipped from his lips so easily Dawn was left wondering what else Ryan might not have told her about Lorraine Nichols or his connection with this case and the Tenneson family.

The woman didn't baulk, instead, she waved Ryan out the way of her trolley and began shoving it along the balcony toward the room. Dawn hurried past her, ducked under the window and flattened herself against the wall, hoping Craig wouldn't see her if he snuck a peek from the window.

Retrieving her gun, she nodded to Ryan as the cleaner stopped outside the door, banging her fist with enough force to make Dawn cringe.

'Housekeeping!'

Dawn flattened herself. Ryan did the same on the left side of the doorway. For a moment, Dawn thought no one was in, but the rattle of a door handle and security chain caught her attention.

'Can't you see the….' Craig's hand waved over the *Do Not Disturb* sign hanging on the doorknob.

Dawn grabbed the cleaner and pulled her away from the doorway as Ryan hip and shouldered the door wide open.

'Police!'

'What the!'

'Hands where I can see them,' Dawn yelled as she joined Ryan, gun drawn.

The constable stumbled back, hands shot to his ears, eyes wide.

'What's!'

'Where's Farrell, Craig?'

'What the hell…'

Ryan stepped forward. Dawn kept Craig in her sights as Ryan grabbed the constable's hands and dragged them behind his back.

As soon as he was secure, she scanned the room. The bathroom door was open, the mirror fogged up, moisture dripping from the walls.

Warily, with her back to the wall, she approached the room and eased toward the open doorway. Stopping, she listened, hearing nothing over Ryan wrestling the constable into handcuffs.

'Tina. You need to come out.' Dawn held her breath.

Another moment passed without a rustle or the sounds of breathing. She needed to enter, but Tina could be armed. The woman's role in her friend's disappearance, and subsequent murder still wasn't clear. She could walk right into the line of fire.

Taking a breath, she ducked, shoved the door open and rounded into the room in one quick motion. The door thudded against the wall with enough force to make the shower screen wobble. Dawn aimed the barrel of her gun at empty space.

'Clear!' she called, before shoving her gun back into the band of her pants and turning to find Ryan steering constable Craig toward the bathroom.

'Where is Farrell?' she demanded.

'Gone!'

'Where?'

'I can't say.'

Ryan shoved the young officer against the wall, yanking his restrained arms up behind his back hard enough to make the guy's shoulder crack.

'You're up to your neck in this Craig. Come clean now or you'll be facing murder charges. Accessory after the fact at the very least.'

Dawn patted Ryan's hand. He let the tension off a little as Craig groaned.

'Look Constable,' she adopted a smoother, calmer tone, 'we know Tina was in Cooktown when Jane Nichols was teaching at a yoga retreat. We also know Tina took Jane's dog for a walk *after* the retreat and knew Jane didn't go missing, at least not from Newell Beach.'

Craig's face was still firmly pressed against the bathroom wall. Dawn bent so he could see her face. 'Tell us what's going on. We need to know her side of the story.'

'I don't know anything. I'm just doing a friend a favour.'

Dawn changed tacks as Ryan turned their suspect around to face her.

'The receptionist said you were married. Are you?'

The silence said it all. Dawn knew how to make Tina and Craig talk now. Ryan's grin said he was thinking what she was thinking.

'Mate, Tina could be in really big trouble. We know this is related to organised crime in some way.' Craig's eyes widened for a microsecond, but he recovered quickly.

Was he as stupid as he was making out to be? Dawn couldn't be sure, but this was her only avenue of enquiry until they found a witness from the retreat.

'We are still putting all the pieces together, but we don't have a lot of time. The guys responsible are getting ready to bug out and Tina could be in trouble if they think she knows anything.'

Dawn put on her best worried expression, hoping the constable would buy her sincerity. But in truth, she was genuinely concerned. The photos of Tina with Tenneson suggested one thing, but the way the house was left, even if she left with Craig willingly, gave her serious concerns about Tina's safety.

'We know Tina was either covering for Jane or someone else.' Dawn waited. Craig shook his head. 'We know about her dominatrix work.' His eyes met hers. 'Is that why you kept the old lady's diary, with the comings and goings of her clients?'

He shook his head. She carried on, hiding her frustration at his lack of cooperation.

'You left Tina's house in a hurry. We know thugs turned over the beach house after Jane's body was found. What were they looking for? The diary?'

Craig's shoulders began to sag. A woman cleared her throat at the doorway and Dawn forgot all about the cleaner.

But as she turned, the cleaner appeared to be waiting for the popcorn to arrive.

The woman standing with her hands on her hips with a scowl was the receptionist.

'I don't know what the hell is going on here *Detectives,* but I'll be having a word with Sergeant Martin about this mess.'

She waved her hand around the room. Dawn followed the hand, failing to see an issue. The room was spotless, except for a lamp on the floor, still intact.

'They said he had a girl in here against her will Mrs P., I wouldn't have let them in otherwise.' The cleaner leant against the door frame, waiting for the fallout.

'She didn't let us in, he did.' Ryan shoved his prisoner forward.

'Are the cuffs really necessary? Am I under arrest?' Craig whined.

'You're a flight risk.' Ryan shoved him past the two women who stepped back, frowning as he passed.

Dawn scanned the scene one more time. The bathroom door handle might have put a hole in the wall, but the glass screen and mirror were undamaged. Craig didn't exactly put up a fight.

'I'm very sorry about the mess and the Cooktown station will reimburse you if anything is broken, but I'm certain *nothing* is.'

'You better hope not young lady.'

Dawn rushed after Ryan as a grin split her lips.

Young lady indeed! She could live with that.

Chapter 38

Dawn studied Craig from behind the one-way mirror. As a cop, Craig knew she'd be standing there. He glanced up and watched the glass as if to agree with her.

She turned to Ryan.

'What's your take on this?'

'I don't know. He's not the sharpest tool in the shed, but he kept the old lady's …'

'Bella's.'

Ryan sighed.

'Bella's diary. Did he do it because Tina told him to? Or of his own accord? Or for someone else entirely? Richardson maybe?'

'We've not found a connection between him and Richardson.' Dawn turned and opened the adjoining room door. 'Let's ask him where it is. We'll start there.'

Ryan followed.

'Sounds like a plan.'

Sergeant Martin met them in the hallway. Dawn's hand hovered on the interview room door.

'He's asked for a union rep. He won't say anything until they arrive.' Martin's expression reflected Dawn's frustration.

'Can we still question him?'

Martin nodded to the closed door.

'You're welcome to try.'

Dawn began to formulate a plan in her head. Although Craig and Tina were now married, he didn't seem concerned she could be in any danger. Was he worried enough about his job? Would he talk to save his career? It was the only leverage she had right now.

Opening the door, she was met with cold air pumping into the small room. Dawn resisted the urge to shiver as she pulled out a chair and sat. Ryan joined her, sitting next to the recording equipment.

Harsh lighting made the young constable appear pale, but Dawn wasn't going to be soft on the man. She spoke as she shuffled papers on the table.

'How you going mate? Need a drink before we get started?'

Craig scanned Dawn's face as she kept the friendly smile plastered in place. His eyes darted to Ryan, still wearing the same scowl from earlier.

Craig slowly shook his head.

'I'm fine. But I need to get out because Tina will be coming back to the motel room soon and if I'm not there, she'll get...' He seemed to be searching for the right word.

'Scared?' Dawn supplied.

'Yeah. Scared.'

Dawn let silence hang a moment. Then asked the question niggling at her subconscious over the past few days.

'Scared of who, Constable? Who are you running from?'

Dawn wasn't sure if it was her instincts, or her heart telling her Tina wasn't involved in her friend's murder. Maybe it was wishful thinking.

Constable Craig wiped his unrestrained hands on his pants as his legs jostled beneath the table.

'I just need to go.'

Dawn inched forward, waggling her finger for the constable to lean in, as though she were about to share a big secret.

'I need Mrs Lundstrom's diary first mate.'

Craig's brow lifted. Did he really think they wouldn't find out?

'I know you failed to submit it into evidence at the Cairns' station. Your boss knows too.'

Craig's eyes landed on Ryan who nodded in agreement.

'You're in deep shit mate. There isn't any easy way out of this.' Ryan's tone was dramatic.

Craig's eyes darted to the door.

'You *could* wait for your Union rep.' Dawn sat back in her chair and folded her arms across her chest. 'And I'd fully understand why you'd do that, but...'

Craig's eyes found hers—brow furrowed. She could see he was waiting for the *but*. Was he ready to talk to her?

'If you talk to us now. If you give us the diary...' She put her elbows on the table and eased forward in her chair. 'You could keep your job.' She glanced at Ryan with pursed lips. 'Maybe some disciplinary action. A course on procedure. That kind of thing.'

Silence greeted her. She waited, her heart thudding in her chest despite her calm exterior. They needed the diary.

The constable's mouth opened and closed. He shook his head, then opened his mouth again. Nothing came out. Dawn waited as he chewed the inside of his mouth and sucked air in through his nostrils.

'The diary. You want the diary?'

Dawn resisted the urge to slap the idiot. What a stupid question. Was he stalling for his rep? She nodded.

'And we need Tina Farrell's whereabouts.'

Silence hung a moment and for a second Dawn thought he'd keep quiet.

'You'll find them together.'

Dawn glanced at Ryan who stifled a grin. She turned back to Craig.

'And where might that be?'

'She took the car. I don't know where she was going, but the diary is in the car with her.'

Dawn fought the urge to grunt out loud, but restrained herself with the knowledge that Cooktown wasn't a big place.

There weren't too many places Tina could go where the car wouldn't be seen or a local wouldn't recognise her from a description.

Dawn knew better than anyone—everyone knew everyone in a small town.

She jumped up. The constable flew back in his chair.

'I want a full statement from you Craig. We know you are friends with Tina Farrell and our victim. Something you should have disclosed up front. You know you shouldn't have been on this case. Did you stay quiet so you could make sure Tina wasn't implicated? Or are you covering for someone else?'

Dawn grabbed a pad and pen and slammed them down in front of the constable. He visibly cringed, then relaxed.

'Who did you put your career on the line for?'

He gaped at her a moment. Then his eyes seemed to clear.

'I didn't take the diary for Tina.'

Dawn frowned, caught Ryan doing the same, then turned back to Craig.

'Then who the hell managed to convince you to keep evidence from being logged?'

The constable bit his lip, then pulled them together like he suddenly realised he'd said too much.

'I'd like my union rep now thanks.'

Dawn slapped her palms flat on the table and glared at the young police officer.

'If you are covering for a murderer Craig, all deals are off the table.'

Craig crossed his arms, sat back and pressed his lips so hard together he looked like a child refusing medicine.

'Tina used your credit card to buy fuel on her way to Cooktown.' The constable's face twitched. 'Were you in the car with her Constable?'

Confusion crossed Craig's face. He shook his head, more to himself than to anyone in the room.

'Can I speak with my union rep, *please.*'

Dawn shoved the pad toward Craig. 'One chance mate. That's all you get.' She turned and stormed from the interview room, vaguely aware of Ryan recording an end note to the interview before joining her.

Thoughts jumbled around her head. Who the hell was he covering for if it wasn't Tina? As the door closed on the interview room, Dawn rounded on Ryan.

'We need to find out who else this kid knows.'

'You got that right.' Ryan followed Dawn down the hall and around the corner into the office.

Reynolds snapped to attention as soon as she saw them. 'Detectives!'

Dawn sat on the corner of the closest desk.

'What you got Reynolds?'

'I did a bit more digging, and you'll never guess what I found.'

'You're right.' Dawn struggled to keep her tone calm. Reynolds frowned.

'About what?'

'I'm not guessing Reynolds.'

'Sorry.' Reynolds bit her lip. Jamison sniggered. Ryan cleared his throat, reminding Dawn she might need to brush up on her interpersonal skills.

'Sorry Reynolds. Go on.'

'I did a dig into the companies who contribute to the MP's campaign, and it took a lot of scrounging but one of the companies is a trust. It seemed weird so I found out who the overarching company was and who the directors are and....

Dawn spun her finger in circles. 'The point Reynolds.'

'Yes. Sorry. The director is Richardson.'

'The art dealer Richardson?'

'The very same.'

Dawn turned to Ryan who was grinning.

'Looks like we need to pay the art dealer another visit.'

Ryan nodded toward Reynolds. Dawn understood the hint. She shouldn't have needed it, but she was off her game on this case.

'Good work Reynolds. Now I need you to keep digging into Craig. I want to know who else he could be protecting. If it isn't Tina Farrell, who would he steal evidence for?'

Reynolds spun so fast her ponytail nearly slapped her face.

'On it.'

Chapter 39

Another downpour greeted Dawn as she opened the front door of the station. Water cascaded from the gutterless roofline.

She glanced at Ryan.

'Make a run for it?'

He nodded, rummaged in his pocket for the key fob and pressed the button. As they bolted through the pouring rain, the Mustang indicators flashed.

Even Dawn's fingertips were dripping wet as she pulled the passenger door closed, chest heaving, shoes soaked.

'Refreshing,' Ryan grinned.

'Hardly. But criminals don't seem to care if the weather isn't perfect.' She pulled her seatbelt on. 'Let's go find out more about Richardson's connection to Tenneson and see if either of them knows Craig.'

Ryan flicked his lights on and backed from the curb with caution. Heavy rain obscured his view as the deep roadside drains began to run like a creek bed.

He shifted into *drive* and proceeded warily down the main road, turning up Hogg Street and winding his way up the hill toward the Richardson estate.

'Has the team finished checking in with all the yoga retreat visitors?' Ryan asked.

'Not yet. Most weren't local, but Jamison and Reynolds are trying to reach the ones who are. Someone must have seen our victim leave the premises the day she died. If they didn't, then it's very possible she died on the estate.'

'I can't see it. What's Richardson's motive?'

'Maybe Ketut and the drug connection.'

'You think Jane found out about the drugs?'

'She was dosed up with cocaine which is an expensive drug and not what you'd expect a yoga instructor to be into. Dope maybe, but cocaine, not so much. It's more the drug of choice for professionals and those with high pressure jobs. Richardson is in the prime position to reach that market. Maybe she stumbled onto something at the retreat?'

Ryan glanced her way.

'Still. It's a big leap to murder.'

A flash of colour in the dim daylight and sheeting rain caught Dawn's eye. As her head snapped around, Ryan did the same. Leaning on the horn, he narrowly avoided a silver sedan travelling at speed down the centre of the narrow road.

'What the hell!' Ryan muttered as he steered his car through a rutted roadside, back onto the bitumen.

Dawn watched the car disappear in the vehicle's side mirror.

'That looked like an Aston Martin to me.'

'What do you want to do? Follow it, or see if Richardson is still at the estate?'

Dawn deliberated a moment too long. Ryan hit the brakes hard, pulled the handbrake like a stunt car driver and spun the vehicle on the spot.

'Call it in,' he ordered as he flicked on the hidden lights on the Mustang's grill. A siren blared.

Dawn gripped the handle above the window to steady herself as the car fishtailed and sped forward. She fumbled for her phone, adrenalin making her fingers clumsy and uncoordinated as she searched for the number she wanted and dialled.

'This isn't the city, Ryan. We can't control a high-speed chase in Cooktown, in this weather and if Richardson *is* driving, we could kill our main lead.'

Ryan flicked the automatic shift down two gears. The wheels spun.

'Just call it in. I can handle this Grave.'

Dawn opened her mouth to tell him she was already on the phone as the call connected.

'Reynolds. We've spotted Richardson's car speeding away from his place. We are in pursuit. Get a couple of patrol cars out and we'll keep you updated.'

'Was Richardson driving?'

'No idea. Visibility is shit in this rain, but even if he isn't, we can leave him for now. We need to find whoever is driving the Aston. They could be running, but either way, they might have answers.'

'You got it. Current location?'

'Heading South, turning on to Boundary Street. You have the vehicle details?'

Ryan steered around a corner. Dawn grabbed the handle above the window, trying to lean into the turn.

'Hold the line Detective. Sergeant Martin has Jamison and Chung heading out the door now, and yes, he knows the car. Everyone does.'

Dawn stiffened as her eyes scanned through the windscreen, desperately looking for vehicles that might not have seen their lights in the rain.

Ryan eased on the brakes. Dawn held her breath as they slid sideways through the town's busiest intersection, taking the Charlotte Road exit. A flash of brake light in the distance revealed the Aston Martin taking the racecourse bend and gaining distance.

Ryan slipped the car back a gear once more.

'I think he's heading for the airport,' Dawn offered as she put her phone on speaker. 'Reynolds. We are on the airport road, heading past the racecourse. Have any flight plans been lodged for Richardson's jet?'

'I'll check. If they have, I'll ask them to stall.'

'That's all we can ask without a warrant.'

'Chung should be right behind you.'

Ryan glanced in his rear-view mirror.

'I see him.'

Dawn's heart pumped so hard she could hear the rush of blood inside her head.

'Reynolds. Any luck on the flights?'

'I'm checking as fast as I can.'

The rain pelted down on the windscreen. The vehicle's wipers were on full speed, but sheets of water continued to obscure the view.

'We need to slow down Ryan.'

Her partner ignored her as the bright blue townlet sign for Marton whizzed by.

'You don't know these roads well enough.'

Her hands were clammy now, but as she glanced at Ryan, she could see there was no give in him. The Mustang hugged the road like a race car.

'Got it!' Dawn jumped as Reynold's voice squealed over the phone line. 'There is a flight plan booked from Cooktown to Port Moresby in New Guinea.'

'It must be Richardson behind the wheel,' Dawn guessed.

'Not necessarily. What about Ketut?' Ryan kept his eyes focussed. 'He might know we are on to him.'

'What I'd like to know is, do they have Tina in the vehicle with them and if they do, why would they take her out of the country?'

'Maybe they aren't.' Ryan's statement hung in the air as Dawn tried not to think about Tina already being dead like her friend.

'Reynolds. Get Jamison to head to Richardson's place. With Chung in pursuit, we've got this.'

'On it.'

Dawn watched Chung's flashing lights in the side mirror as Ryan drove as fast as possible in the pelting rain. The Endeavour River bridge was barely visible.

'Slow down. The airport turn off is just after the bridge.'

'I know.' Ryan was focussed, determined. He didn't touch the brakes even as the vehicle aquaplaned through a low section of water running over the road.

Dawn gripped her seat. Taillights flashed ahead, then spinning headlights and more taillights shone through the driving rain.

'What the hell!'

Dawn involuntarily wiped the screen with her hand, knowing in the back of her mind it would do nothing to clear the view through the heavy downpour.

Time slowed as the wipers squealed on the glass before a headlight beam veered skyward. Dawn braced a fraction of a second before Ryan slammed the brakes on.

His evasive driving experience took over as he eased back on the brakes and the ABS kicked in. The vehicle steadied with a shudder.

'They've gone off the bridge!' Her stomach knotted.

The Mustang idled to a stop, Chung pulling up alongside them. Reynolds' voice echoed from the footwell.

'You guys, okay?'

Dawn rummaged at her feet and retrieved the phone. Gasping she croaked out a reply.

'We're good Reynolds. Get an ambulance and State Emergency crew out here. Looks like the vehicle has gone into the river.'

'Better get a croc hunter out too,' Ryan grinned. 'Or we might be minus a suspect or two.'

Chapter 40

Chung appeared at the passenger's side of the Mustang before Dawn could open the door.

He held a navy, long thin raincoat out.

'Here you go Detective.'

'You're a godsend mate.' She struggled into the sticky material, already wet from rain, then clumsily slammed the car door.

Ryan stepped out into the torrential rain.

'Hey. Where's mine?'

'Sorry mate. Only had one spare. Ladies first.'

'Hang on a minute. I thought this was the age of equality.'

Chung grinned from under his wide brimmed hat as water cascaded around him like a waterfall.

'Let's just say chivalry isn't entirely dead yet.'

Dawn strode toward the bridge, ignoring the water all over the road, soaking into her shoes.

'Stop blabbering you two. We need to check the vehicle.'

Chung glanced her way, then scurried up behind her.

'Good luck with that Detective. The Endeavour is pretty deep here and I'm not jumping in after anyone. It's wet season and the crocs are mobile this time of year. Not to mention the stingers are hatching out.'

Dawn puffed out her cheeks and glanced at Ryan to see him turning around and striding back to the Mustang.

'Where are you going?' she called into the sheeting rain.

'I'm getting back in the car until the rain stops or Emergency Services arrive.'

Chung nodded agreement.

'Probably a good call Detective.'

Dawn ignored him. She needed to at least check for survivors. She sensed Chung following her as she reached the bridge railing. Rain cascaded over the road gutters, pouring into the river below.

'You better get out some cones and reflectors. No one in their right mind will be out driving around in this, but best to be cautious.'

He waved a casual scout-like salute.

'You got it Detective.'

She peered over the railing of the bridge, scanning the water below. A large croc slid from the muddy bank, into the water and effortlessly circled the vehicle, upside down in the water below.

She stepped back, considering the railing height and wondered how the vehicle cleared the bridge. There was no doubt they were travelling at speed, but the crash scene investigators would have their work cut out for them figuring this one out.

Her eyes settled on the mangled wreck below. There was something not quite right about the scene. Pacing, she waited impatiently for the SES to arrive. At least the rain was easing up, but a waterfall continued to run down the nearby embankment and over the bridge.

Her phone buzzed in her pocket. She answered without looking at the caller ID.

'This is Detective Grave.'

'Detective. It's Reynolds. I've received a call back from one of the people who was at the yoga retreat, and they say they saw our victim.'

'Finally. Someone with a bit of good news.'

'Yes. Sort of.'

'What do you mean?'

'Well, according to this witness, Jane Nichols conducted the first class of the morning which started at 6 a.m. Then, while the witness was having breakfast, she noticed a car pull up in the driveway. She said she saw Jane Nichols hop in.'

'Did she get a licence plate?'

'No. She didn't think anything of it, but when Jane didn't return, she told Mr Richardson about it.'

'Damn him.'

'I'm here at the retreat now with Jamison.'

There was a tone to Reynolds voice that made Dawn's stomach churn.

'And.'

'And it's deserted. No one is here.'

Dawn glanced down at the broken wreck below. Water poured over the vehicle as the river flowed out to sea. Another crocodile slid into the water.

'Probably because they were all in the car which ran off the road.'

'Maybe. We've managed to get a search warrant on the grounds. This was the last place our victim was seen.'

'Good work Reynolds. I'll finish up here and meet you there shortly. There isn't much we can do here and if they are all in the wreck, there won't be any plane taking off to New Guinea.'

Dawn hung up, resisting the urge to lean on the railing and hang over for a closer look. The crash scene team wouldn't want anything disturbed.

As she turned to leave, the car dislodged and rolled over. It wasn't unusual when a vehicle crashed into the water. Air pockets could cause the vehicle to shift. But as the car rolled, Dawn gasped.

She opened her mouth to call Ryan, but a groan to her left made her turn. Lying in the mud, almost invisible in the sheeting rain was a figure, struggling to rise.

'Flaming hell!' The figure slipped in the riverbank mud as water flowed down the slope. 'What the …'

Dawn sprinted toward the roadside, arms waving.

'Ryan. Chung!' She slapped the side of the Mustang as she whizzed by. 'Chung, we have a survivor and it's not any of our suspects.

Chung followed her waving hand with his eyes.

'Where the hell is the ambulance?' The sound of sirens in the distance answered her question. 'Chung, stay with this guy and get a statement as soon as the paramedics are done.'

The constable slid down the embankment as Ryan opened his door and half stepped out.

'What's …'

'Get back in. Start the car!'

Ryan didn't hesitate.

Dawn flung the door open, jumped into the seat ignoring her seat belt and the dripping raincoat.

'It's not an Aston in the river. They ran someone else off the road.'

Ryan shoved the Mustang into drive. The wheels slipped on the wet bitumen as the V6 lunged into action.

'The plane?' Ryan questioned as the seatbelt alarms pinged in irritation.

'Reynold's already told the staff to delay any take offs, but we can't ground a plane without a warrant. This bad weather should buy us some time.'

'Let's hope so.'

Dawn finally reached for her seatbelt, followed by her weapon.

'What tipped them off? This was a planned flight. Were they running?'

'The big question is who was running?'

Chapter 41

The rain eased to the occasional drop as Ryan pulled up outside the Cooktown airport, tyres squealing.

Dawn threw her seatbelt off and jumped from the vehicle. Stopping as she surveyed the deserted, empty runway. The only sound she could hear was the persistent drip of raindrops from the rooftop and the cacophony of croaking frogs growing louder by the second.

Ryan joined her, gawking at the quiet structure as steam rose from the tarmac.

'We missed them.'

Dawn shook her head.

'No way they got clearance to take off in this heavy rain.'

She shoved her gun into the small of her back and retrieved her ID from her pocket as she sprinted across the green grass to the tiny terminal building. The raised board structure was smaller than most homes in Cooktown. She and Ryan bypassed the disability ramp and slipped under the railing onto the veranda.

Passing two old church pews, they entered to find more recycled church seating, a wall of tourism brochures and a high, wide desk with a fan buzzing. Beside the desk sat a woman in a high-vis vest, head down, reading an electronic book, toes tapping to an unheard tune.

Dawn cleared her throat. The woman didn't move. Ryan approached, reached over the desk and flipped his ID open in front of the book. The woman leapt from her chair.

'Oh shit!' She grabbed her chest and dragged her earbuds from her ears. 'You gave me a bloody heart attack.' She scanned her surroundings—suddenly aware Dawn was also holding up her ID.

'We requested all planes be delayed. Has anything taken off in the last hour?' Dawn waited for the woman to nod at the ID before putting it away.

'Ah, nah. All flights were delayed by the weather in any case. I'm waiting for the Cairns plane now, but other than that, nothing. There was a private jet scheduled to land, but the pilot was rerouted when the bad weather hit.'

'Any idea where they landed?'

Dawn hoped it wasn't close enough for Richardson or Ketut to drive to.

'Nah. Sorry. Not my department.'

Ryan turned in a slow circle.

'Is airport security anywhere handy?'

The woman chuckled.

'Ah, other than the refuelling crew, I'm it. Chief cook and bottle washer as they say.' Her hands were on her hips as she spun in her own circle. 'Ground crew, security, check in clerk, luggage police.' She pointed to a set of scales that reminded Dawn of the old general store she visited as a kid.

Ryan stepped toward the exit. 'Can we take a look around?'

Dawn followed Ryan out onto the veranda, the woman two steps behind.

'Ah. The Cairns plane should be landing soon, so you'll need to stay off the tarmac.'

'Thanks, we'll find our way around.' Dawn smiled.

They jumped from the veranda and jogged toward the solitary gate leading to the runway.

'Ah.' She called from the veranda. 'You two can't go through the gate with a plane landing!'

Dawn waved the comment away without turning.

'It's not a freeway out there. We'll be fine,' she called back.

Ryan eased the unlocked gate open and grinned.

Cooktown was a small regional airport, where light planes came and went from very few destinations, and not often. The fact the gate wasn't secured didn't surprise them. Maybe the drugs theory had merit after all. It was the perfect place to import cocaine undetected. No sniffer dogs. No radar or x-ray equipment.

They peered down the runway. There were no aircraft hangars to hide a vehicle or jet in. Fuel tanks were the only intrusion on the otherwise vacant area.

Ryan turned to face her.

'There's nothing out here. Not even a parked-up plane and nowhere to hide a vehicle.'

Dawn drew her mobile phone from her pocket and began dialling.

'If Richardson's jet was rerouted, we should find out where to. Ketut or Richardson could be on the way to intercept it now.'

'They lost the element of surprise. They won't get out of the country so easily.'

'I don't know.' Dawn listened as the call rang. 'Security isn't exactly on the ball in these small airports.'

She waved her hand toward the gate to illustrate her point.

'True.'

Dawn's call connected.

'Sergeant. It's Dawn.'

'Yep. Got that.' The Sergeant was all business.

'I'm on my way to the Richardson house shortly but wanted to update you. Richardson's plane was rerouted for the weather. Can you find out where and make sure whoever was planning to be on that plane doesn't get out of the country?'

'Will do Detective. One thing before you go.'

'Yep.'

'Craig's union rep has arrived, and after a little discussion, says the kid's ready to give us an update.'

Dawn grinned. Ryan raised an eyebrow at her. She lifted a finger to indicate she'd fill him in shortly.

'Has he finally gotten worried about Tina being missing?'

'Better than that. We got a vehicle make from the witness who saw our victim get into a car and leave the yoga retreat.'

'Really. Tina's?'

'You got it. We've also managed to get access to Tina Farrell's cloud. The forensic techs are downloading everything as we speak.'

'Did Craig give you any indication of what they were into?'

'Craig doesn't strike me as that smart. Maybe Tina Farrell has been dragging him along by his you know whats.'

'I'll check in with Reynolds and Jamison at Richardson's, then join you at the station to interview Craig.'

'You got it Detective.' Dawn could hear a smile in his voice.

'Thanks Sergeant. For getting me back on the job.'

'You're welcome, Dawn. I know you're a good cop and I know good cops aren't settled by doing house renovations. It was purely self-serving, I promise.'

'See you soon.' Dawn ended the call.

'What's up?' Ryan's expression was optimistic.

'Nothing concrete yet but looks like Craig and Tina were up to something together.'

'My money is on blackmail. We found the cameras in the dungeon. Then the photos with Tenneson under Farrell's whip.'

'Stop grinning.' She admonished him as her phone rang. She checked the ID.

'It's Rossi.'

Ryan chewed his lip as Dawn answered the call. She knew what he was thinking. She only hoped he was as calm when he saw Rossi next, as he was last night.

'Grave. What you got Rossi?'

'Trouble!' Dawn could hear tension in Rossi's tone. 'I got some intel on Ketut and it's all bad.'

Dawn waved Ryan toward their car. He opened the runway gate and waited for her to pass through before letting it clang behind them.

'He's connected to drugs. No surprise there though, what's so bad?'

'He's not a drug runner Dawn.' Rossi's use of her name was disconcerting for more than one reason. The sound of it on his lips brought back memories, both good and bad. She always did have a thing for the bad boys.

'What Rossi? Spit it out.'

'He's a cleaner.'

'Shit!'

Ryan pressed the key fob to unlock his car but stopped with a creased brow, his hand hovering on the door handle.

'Exactly.'

'So, is he here to get rid of Tina and Craig?'

'Or Tenneson. He's still missing.'

'The only connection we have with Tenneson so far is the photos of him with Tina in an uncompromising position and the fact Richardson is paying money into his campaign budget.'

'That's not all we have now. We've been handling Tenneson's disappearance our end and Parker got an idea all this might not be drug related, well not directly.'

Dawn waved at Ryan, then opened the passenger's side door and slid inside. Ryan got in and put his belt on. She covered the phone speaker with her hand.

'Let's get to Richardson's place I'll explain in a second.'

'You there, Dawn?'

'Here Rossi. Get to the point. We've got a warrant on Richardson's place to act on now.'

'Okay. Maybe you don't follow politics, but I saw something in the papers the other day that got me thinking.'

Dawn listened as Ryan started the car.

'Tenneson was set to block a bill to legalise medicinal marijuana, but he seemed to be backing off.'

'You think Richardson was putting pressure on Tenneson to vote against legalising medicinal marijuana and when he softened, they what—blackmailed him?'

'It's a theory.'

'Not a terrible one. The question is, was Tina a willing participant and how did it all lead to Jane Nichols' death?'

Dawn thought about Rusty being taken for a walk again. Pieces were starting to make sense but there were now more unanswered questions than before.

'Thanks Rossi. Keep looking for Tenneson. We need to know what's going on. Our victim, the photos of him with Tina Farrell. He could be the key.'

'Will do. But Dawn ...'

'Not now Rossi.' She knew what he was going to say. She didn't want to hear it. Too little, too late.

She ended the call and turned to Ryan as he guided the Mustang back onto the road to Cooktown.

'Tenneson is either in on all this, or, he's another victim.'

'I take it, he's still missing.'

'He is. The photos of Tenneson with Farrell suggest blackmail. We need to get a hold of his financials, Tina's too. But I don't see his vote on medical marijuana being that big of a deal.'

'I agree. It's only dope.'

'And he's affiliated with a party who love privatising *everything*. He'd have benefactors on both sides of this argument. Richardson might want to keep dope illegal, so he doesn't mess up the soft entry to heavier drugs, but the pharmaceutical companies are likely lobbying for the legalisation bill to pass.'

'Bout time I say.'

'I don't disagree, but murder puts Richardson's whole operation at risk. Rossi just told me Ketut is a cleaner, so maybe they decided our victim was too much of a risk or...'

'They used Jane as leverage to get Tenneson to change his vote and something went wrong.' Ryan finished her thought.

'It's possible, but still too many questions and not enough answers. Let's search Richardson's place and see if we can piece this together.'

'Rossi and Parker got any idea where Tenneson could have gotten to?'

Dawn shook her head. 'Nothing yet. Would Lorraine know?'

Ryan shrugged. 'Maybe. I can make a call.'

'I think it's worth a shot. After we finish at Richardson's, we can interview Craig. Maybe Ketut's occupation can prove Tina is in serious trouble. Hopefully then we can figure out where he and Tina fit into all of this.'

'That's assuming they are both innocent in the murder.'

Ryan's words rolled around Dawn's head. It wasn't a new thought. The more she considered Rusty being left tied up on the beach to lead authorities in the wrong direction about where and when Jane disappeared, the more she considered the woman knew a lot more than she was telling anyone.

The back door being left open, and the dog abandoned, pointed to a hurried exit from town, but why come to Cooktown? They had the diary. They knew who was coming and going from the Nichols' beach house. They could have brought the evidence to the police.

They needed to find Tina to get some answers. Was she the ringleader, a co-conspirator or another victim? And was she still alive?

Chapter 42

Dawn sat on the corner of Reynolds' desk, staring at the murder board as the constable's fingers typed out a report.

Searching Richardson's place was a complete waste of time. It wasn't only deserted— it was clean as a hospital surgical suite. Literally. Other than Richardson's prints on the front door handle, it was wiped down and bleached clean.

If it was where Jane Nichols died, there was no sign of it left behind. But as Dawn mulled over the information on the board, she was surer than ever that Jane died out at Keatings Lagoon. Sometime between leaving the yoga retreat and Friday night, she was strangled and thrown over the edge of the observation hut into croc-infested waters.

It was amazing her body surfaced at all.

Dawn's stomach grumbled. She'd missed lunch and it was getting late. Glancing at her watch, she realised the time. Still, they needed to interview Craig before anyone was going home. Tina was missing, Jane was dead, Craig was in custody, but there was no sign of Richardson or Ketut and Tenneson was in the wind.

Sighing, Dawn rose and turned into Ryan's chest.

'Whoa up!' He pulled his arms wide, a coffee cup in each hand. 'You look like you need coffee before we quiz the constable, and his rep is off grabbing him dinner.'

Dawn reached for the cup Ryan held out. 'How nice.' She sipped her drink. 'At least some of us get to eat.'

A noise over Ryan's shoulder made Dawn stop, cup on her lips ready for another mouthful.

'Auntie Dawn! Where have you been all day?' Blonde ringlets bounced as Abby raced across the room.

Dawn passed her coffee to Ryan who took it obligingly as Dawn dropped down to intercept the little girl running at full speed.

'Abby. What on earth are you doing here?' Dawn swept the girl into a hug and plonked her on her left hip.

The answer came around the hallway corner.

'Sorry, but I know you won't have eaten, and Bella insisted we should find you and feed you.'

Dawn glanced past Lisa as she entered the team office to find Mrs Lundstrom carrying a basket over her arm.

'You didn't…'

Dawn's protest was sharply interrupted.

'Yes she did.' Bella waggled a finger.

Abby squeezed her arms around Dawn's neck as Lisa leant in with a one arm hug.

'Yes, we did and not because Bella said so. You look shocking.'

Dawn lowered Abby to the ground.

'You say the nicest things.'

Her tone was soft, like Lisa's hug. Too many years had gone by without the touch of her sister, or home cooked meals or…

Bella placed the basket on Reynolds' desk. The young constable vacated her seat and cleared paperwork away without protest.

'Don't go anywhere young lady. We have plenty for everyone.'

Reynolds halted her retreat, her eyes landing on the basket. Jamison grinned sheepishly from behind his desk. Dawn could hardly blame them. It was a hectic day. None of the team stopped for lunch and bags of potato chips and coffee only went so far to stave off hunger.

Bella opened the lid on the cane basket and peered inside like Santa into a Christmas sack.

'We've got egg and bacon pie. It's easy to eat, even cold and cupcakes that Abby helped me make—didn't you dear girl.'

Mrs Lundstrom smiled at Dawn's niece, who grinned back happily as she used Reynolds' seat to climb onto the desk. She sat, hand out, ready to distribute the goodies.

Dawn's heart ached that her parents weren't alive to see their granddaughter. There were no grandparents in Abby's life because the little girl's father's family were estranged. She wasn't sure if it was fear of rejection by Lisa or embarrassment over their son being convicted of sexual assault and rape of a minor.

Maybe they didn't even know Abby existed. Did it matter? Would Lisa want them to know?

Bella held up a piece of pie in a serviette. Ryan didn't waste a moment, sweeping it up without a thought. Jamison was next, followed by Reynolds. The sergeant's door opened and before long, the entire team was huddled around Reynolds' desk as Abby handed out pie, cupcakes, cans of drink, smiles and cheerful chatter.

'Here.' Bella passed a piece to Dawn who was holding back, taking in the moment.

'Thanks.' Dawn accepted the pie, biting into it with a moan. 'That's delicious.' Her words were muffled through her mouthful of food.

'What's that up there?' Bella strode toward the murder board with spritely steps.

'Ah. That's not really…'

'Who's he?' Bella placed her finger on a photo of Richardson.

'You really aren't supposed…' Dawn placed her pie on the closest desk and attempted to turn the board around.

'I've seen him before.'

Dawn stopped. Ryan turned, a mouthful of food and his pie held ready to refill. Sergeant Martin cleared his throat.

'Where?' Dawn asked.

'Who is he?' Bella frowned as she drew closer, eyes squinting.

'It doesn't matter who he is Mrs Lundstrom.'

'Bella.'

'Bella, where did you see him?'

'At the park, outside the beach house. You know, the dirt bit.'

'When Bella? When did you see this man?'

Bella rubbed her chin like she was massaging whiskers. 'It was last Wednesday, maybe Thursday.'

'Was he alone?'

'No. He drove up in the fancy car I saw the next day, you know the one that drove into the Nichols' beach house, so it must have been before Thursday.'

Dawn resisted the urge to hurry the old woman along.

'Anyway, he was with Tina. I thought it was very strange. They were arguing about something, then the man snatched something out of her hand, got in his car and drove away. It's all in my diary. Haven't you read it?'

'No Mrs Lundstrom. Not yet.' Dawn didn't bother explaining. 'Is Craig's rep back from fetching his dinner yet?'

Sergeant Martin swallowed his mouthful and placed the remainder of his pie on the corner of Reynolds' desk.

'Let's go and see.'

Ryan shoved the last of his pie in his mouth, reached for a can of cola, grabbed Dawn's unfinished coffee and followed.

Dawn waited for Ryan in the hallway.

'Time to put the constable under some pressure.'

Ryan cracked the top of his can.

'You got that right.'

Chapter 43

The interview room was stuffy. The heavy rain left moisture hanging in the room despite the air-conditioning. A stocky man rose as they entered, hand outstretched. Craig remained seated, a piece of pizza inches from his lips, his wide eyes peering over the top.

'Don't get up Craig.' Dawn didn't hide her sarcasm.

'I'm Dean Stanford. I'll be sitting in on your interview.'

Dawn shook the man's hand. Ryan did the same as Dawn dragged a chair out and sat.

'You've had time to consult with your client.' She crossed her arms and leant forward to lean her elbows on the table.

'Yes. Thank you.'

'Then maybe the constable is ready to explain why he withheld evidence from a murder investigation and where Tina Farrell can be found?'

'I think you'll find this whole thing is just a mix up. A lack of communication on the constable's part, maybe.'

'I doubt it. We asked straight up questions before you arrived, and your constable here offered very little except to say he didn't have the diary we were chasing anymore.'

Dawn glanced at Ryan who nodded for her to go on.

'We'd like to know who asked the constable to withhold the diary that held the comings and goings of anyone and everyone from the Nichols' beach house in the days leading up to the disappearance and subsequent murder of Jane Nichols. That diary quite literally could hold the identity of a murderer.'

Dawn knew she was being dramatic, but she wanted the police union rep to understand how much trouble Constable Craig was in.

'My client has explained to me that this was a misunderstanding.'

Ryan slapped the table.

'Not buying it. Craig kept the diary secret. Didn't hand it in to evidence immediately and now tells us it is in his car, which is missing, along with Tina Farrell. We still only have his word she's unharmed.'

Craig stopped eating at the mention of his wife.

Dawn realised he was young and hungry, but was he simply not smart or was he faking disinterest in the interview?

'Look Craig. Tina is in over her head. We've come from Richardson's place. It's empty. Cleaned out. We know his manservant has strong connections with organised crime and the drug trade, so it stands to reason Richardson does too.'

Dawn focussed on Craig who seemed more interested in what was on his pizza than what Dawn was saying. She needed to make him realise his new wife could be in danger.

'Craig.' He made momentary eye contact. 'Tina knows Richardson well enough to know about the drugs. We've spoken to a witness who said they saw Tina arguing with Richardson. They picked his photo from a line up.'

It wasn't strictly true, but close enough. She pressed on, hoping to convey a sense of urgency.

'It's possible Jane Nichols' death is related to the drug trade and Tina probably knows Richardson was involved. We know someone asked her to take Rusty for a walk the day after Jane was already dead. She's in this up to her eyeballs mate. She could be in real danger. You need to tell us what you know.'

Craig glanced at his rep more casually than Dawn would have liked. The constable's eyes then landed on Ryan, who sneered.

'Would you really let the girl get killed to save your career?'

Craig finally put the pizza down and waved his hands in front of his chest.

'I don't know anything. I got the diary, from the old lady, after she said she'd seen Tina arguing with someone.'

'You told us you took the diary for someone else. Are you saying you lied?'

The constable glanced at his rep, who nodded for him to tell the truth.

'Tina didn't know. I told her after.'

Dawn checked her temper.

'Has Tina been involved in blackmailing Tenneson? Is that what Richardson had her doing?'

It was their only working theory, but Dawn still wasn't sure how blackmailing an MP could turn to murder unless it was an accident and people like Ketut and Richardson didn't make those sorts of mistakes. Amateurs did, but not cleaners and drug dealers.

Dawn thought about Tina's opinion of Tenneson, and a thread of information niggled at the back her mind. Craig's voice made her drop the thought.

'I don't know exactly. I know she needs money. Her mum's house is gonna be repossessed by the bank if she doesn't pay the debt down real soon.'

Dawn turned to the one-way mirror, knowing the sergeant was listening in. She needed to check out Tina's home. Was the mortgage overdrawn? How had they missed it when checking Tina's financials?

'So Tina needed money and she asked you to keep the diary?'

'No. I just knew she was in trouble, and I didn't want it to get worse. I had no idea any of this might be linked to Jane Nichols' murder.'

The union rep rolled his eyes, sighed and tapped the desk with his flat palm.

'I think we are done here Detectives. Constable Craig has admitted to misconduct, and we'll be requesting disciplinary action as it is his first offence and of a rather stressful nature involving his new wife. I'll be recommending he take stress leave while he awaits the verdict.'

Dawn rose, leant forward with her hands on the table, and fixed her eyes on the union rep.

'We'll be keeping Constable Craig here a little while longer. We've heard nothing to prove he isn't a co-conspirator in Jane Nichols' murder, and he's withheld information relating to the blackmail of a federal member of parliament.'

The rep rose, leant in and mirrored Dawn's position.

'He doesn't need proof Detective, you do.'

Dawn sighed for the benefit of the Police Union rep. She knew they had nothing but circumstantial evidence on their murder case and professional misconduct. She also knew that letting Craig go too easily wouldn't have the desired effect.

'You can go Craig, but I'm warning you, if you have anything to do with this, we'll find out. And if you know where Tina is, you better tell her to get her arse in here and explain herself. Before Richardson catches up with her.'

Or one of Tenneson's gang affiliated friends. She kept the thought to herself.

Maybe they were chasing the wrong drug connection. Maybe Tenneson's thugs killed Jane and when he found out, he took off into hiding.

Dawn turned to Ryan, nodded, then strode for the door, hoping Ryan would take her lead and finish off what she started.

Letting him go wasn't part of the plan, but when they realised they didn't have enough evidence to hold him, Dawn decided to use him as bait to lure Tina out of hiding.

She knew Ryan well enough to know he'd catch on. At least she hoped she did.

Ryan slid his chair back and eased over the desk as Dawn reached the door.

'Detective Grave is spot on mate. Withholding evidence in a murder investigation is serious stuff, but accessory to murder is another story altogether. You need to find your wife so she can back up your story.'

Ryan joined Dawn in the hallway and closed the interview room door. Reynolds scooted around the corner and skidded to a halt.

'Tina Farrell inherited the house from her mum and Craig is right, it *was* mortgaged up the hilt and the bank *was* knocking on the door to foreclose.'

Dawn turned to Ryan.

'It must be bad. New legislation has made it very difficult for banks to foreclose on homeowners.'

Dawn suddenly clicked to what Reynolds said moments before and turned to find the young woman grinning widely.

'*Was*?'

'Yep. *Was*. 50K was just paid off the loan. It covered the entire balance. That's why we didn't see it in the financials. It's no longer a current loan.'

Ryan scoffed.

'And she paid it off just like that.'

She strode toward the team office area. 'Good work Reynolds.'

As she rounded the corner, she found her family gone. The sounds of laughter and Abby's chatter were a memory, replaced by typing keys, ringing phones and emptiness.

Why didn't she stay and finish dinner with her family? Craig could have waited. Because Tina Farrell could be in danger, that's why.

She chewed her lip as she studied the murder board. Ryan drew up alongside, a can of cola in one hand, an unopened lemonade in the other.

'We need a tail on Craig.' Dawn glanced around the team room. 'Is the Sergeant around?'

'He is.' Sergeant Martin came down the hallway. 'I've organised Craig's personal effects. He'll be on his way out any minute. Why? What do you need?'

'I need Craig tailed and I've got work for these three.' She waved her arm at Jamison, Chung and Reynolds—a sense of pride and connection made her chest tighten as she considered all three young constables as *her* team.

'Sure. I'll make it happen. What are you expecting?'

Dawn studied the murder board. The photo of their victim's mauled body made her chest tighten. None of this was coming together. Every thread they pulled unravelled, but then stopped and tied itself off in a knot.

'Not sure yet. Tina Farrell picking him up might be too much to hope for, but…'

'I'll get someone onto it.'

The sergeant disappeared through his office.

Ryan passed Dawn a can of lemonade.

'Do you think it will do the trick?' he whispered.

'I don't know, but thanks for playing along. I think Tina Farrell is genuinely into this thing, well over her head. If Craig knows anything, he'll know how to contact her. Let's hope his union rep encourages it.'

'He'd be mad not to. Incompetence as opposed to interfering in a murder investigation and withholding evidence. It's a no-brainer.'

Dawn cracked the can open and took a sip.

'Fingers crossed you're right.'

Chapter 44

Ryan rummaged through the picnic basket left on Reynolds' desk. Chung grinned and joined him as they retrieved a cupcake each.

Dawn couldn't find her appetite. Her half-eaten egg and bacon pie sat discarded on a paper serviette. The bizarre thought of how Bella managed to make her vegetarian sister cook meat in her house provided a much-needed distraction.

But it didn't last long. Turning, she shook her head at Chung and Ryan scoffing the pink iced cupcakes with smiles wider than kids in a candy shop.

'You done?' Dawn crossed her arms.

'Why?' Ryan spoke through a full mouth, then swallowed. 'We got somewhere to be?'

'I guess not. Maybe I should go home and try to catch a few hours' sleep?'

'In that madhouse?'

Dawn opened her mouth to argue, but Ryan was right. Abby would still be awake and Bella was staying in her room and Michael might well have been staying over with Lisa. She wasn't up to bunking with a six-year-old.

Ryan's phone buzzed in his pocket. He rummaged around with one hand, the other occupied with another half-eaten cup cake.

Dawn suppressed a smile as he managed to slide the bar across to answer with his frosting covered thumb.

'Detective Ryan.' His eyes glanced up at Dawn. Her senses were alert. 'Yes, she's here.' He held the phone out and mouthed one word.

Tina!

She sucked in a breath and punched the air with excitement.

'Detective Grave speaking.' She kept her tone calm.

'I've got the diary,' Tina's voice quavered.

'Tina. I know you're scared. You need to come in and explain.'

Silence hung. Dawn strained to hear any background noise over the phone. Anything to give her an idea of where Tina was calling from. When Tina remained silent, Dawn pushed.

'It's not looking good for you, Tina. We know you took Rusty and left him at the beach after Jane was already dead. And we are waiting on your phone records because your car was seen picking Jane up from the retreat.'

Dawn could almost hear the wheels turning in Tina's silence. She jumped when the woman spoke.

'It's not what you think. I didn't kill Jane.'

'Come in and we can talk it over. Maybe you have an alibi.'

'I…' Tina stopped herself from saying more.

Dawn needed to keep her speaking.

'I believe you. I know you wouldn't hurt Jane, but whoever killed her could be looking for you. You could be in danger Tina.'

Tina laughed, a hollow, sad sound.

'We'll keep you safe,' Dawn promised.

'No one can keep me safe, and they'll just get away with it, like they always do.'

Dawn's mind was racing. Was she talking about Ketut and Richardson, or was this the guys who trashed the beach house?

'Not if you testify. We can keep you safe.'

'So you said. But I don't think you can. I know who killed Jane and it wasn't me. I was at the retreat with a local hippy chick who works at the clinic here.'

Dawn's mind flew to her sister's receptionist, and she couldn't help wondering why Emily wasn't on the guest list they had.

'Pretty green eyes and dreadlocks?'

'That's her,' Tina sighed. 'I thought I knew who killed Jane, but … now … now I'm sure.'

'You're being cryptic Tina. Come into the station. Tell us what is going on. Give us the diary. Let us put the pieces together. I know you like playing role games, but this isn't a game. These guys are dangerous.'

'You don't need to tell me that Detective. I was just trying to make ends meet. How did it all go so wrong?'

Dawn could hear the tears in Tina's words. There was so much sadness and pain. She opened her mouth to speak, but Tina interrupted. Her tone now firm, demanding. The dominatrix was back.

'Meet me out at Keatings Lagoon tomorrow at daybreak.'

'That sounds very clandestine Tina. Just come in and unravel this puzzle. We'll confirm your alibi, and we'll find the murderer.'

'You want a murderer? Then be at the Lagoon at daybreak.'

Dawn closed her eyes, aware nothing she could say would change Tina's mind.

'Okay. We'll be there.'

'Not we, you need to come alone. If they see a bunch of cops, it will all be over.'

'I can't come alone Tina.' Ryan's body tensed. She put her hand up to keep him quiet. 'Who are they Tina?'

'If you want Jane's killer, you'll come alone.'

The line went dead.

'Damn!' Dawn nearly tossed the phone at Ryan. 'Stupid girl.'

'What? Where does she want to meet you? You can't go alone.'

'She is planning something silly. Did Lorraine tell you where to find Tenneson? We *need* to find him. This is all linked and we need to know who the key players are, before Tina ends up dead.'

'Dawn. You're not contemplating going to meet her alone. This could be a set up.'

'Keatings Lagoon. Why there? Jane, the Lagoon, this is linked to Tenneson. Did they kill Jane and dump her there as a message for him?'

'You're not listening to me.'

Dawn rounded on her new partner.

'I am listening. I'm trying to figure this all out so we can put a stop to it before Tina gets killed or I need to stick my neck out. If you haven't called Lorraine yet, Call her!'

She tossed his phone back.

'I'm going to the ladies.'

Without another word, she stormed down the hallway, past the passage leading to the interview rooms and exit and on to the toilets. The door slammed hard against the door stop as she flung it open.

She crossed the grey tiled floor to the basin and braced herself with both hands. Staring into the mirror she asked herself.

What am I missing?

Reaching out, she turned the cold tap on and washed her face, trying to rinse away a day of sweat. The tropical heat was getting to her, making her wonder if she should pack up and head back to Adelaide—to the cooler winters and oven baked summers.

Then an image of Abby's curly hair and Lisa's soft smile made her shake her head. Sergeant Martin gave her a job. Fraser's case was finally reopened. She couldn't leave now. But this case was rattling her foundations. A young woman was dead, and the evidence so far said her friend was involved in her murder, but something bigger was behind it.

A bang on the door made her jump.

'Grave. They've found Tenneson.'

Ryan's voice was muffled through the fireproof door.

'Be there in a sec. Get the team organised.'

'You got it.'

Dawn glanced up into the mirror and laughed at her mousy brown frizz. The short style, overdue for a cut, now looked like something out of an 80's movie. Running the cold tap once more, she damped it down, ran her fingers through and smoothed out the spikey pieces over her ears.

Ryan was outside the door, one foot up against the wall. He sprang forward and joined her brisk march down the hallway.

'He's been hiding out in a cabin out in the lake area of the Atherton Tablelands.'

'You got a hold of Lorraine quickly.'

'I called her yesterday.'

'Sorry for barking at you.' She tried to ignore the guilt.

Ryan shrugged—his expression relaxed.

She refocussed. 'Tenneson was running scared then?'

'Sounds like it. Parker's team downloaded Tina's cloud documents—copy is on the file. Apparently, there were photos of Tenneson, as expected, along with two members of the Senate in rather compromising positions.' Ryan grinned.

Dawn ignored the inuendo.

'So we are still thinking this is about changes to drug laws?'

'Don't think. Know. Tenneson says they tried to blackmail him with photos of him with Tina, but when that didn't work …'

'They took Jane.'

'The two thugs with him weren't friends. They were there to pressure him. When we arrived, they took off, giving Tenneson an opening to get out of Dodge.'

'Coward.'

'I'm guessing that's what Lorraine is going to say when she finds out he let Jane die.'

Dawn returned to the main team room to find Reynolds, Jamison and Chung waiting. Sergeant Martin entered from his office with a grim expression.

'Okay everyone. Do we have eyes on Craig?'

Sergeant Martin cleared his throat. 'Yeah. Nah. Seems our boy gave us the slip.'

Dawn held her breath and began counting. Losing her cool wasn't fair on anyone, but she definitely didn't want to rant at the station sergeant.

'Alright.' She nodded to herself, then clapped her hands like a basketball coach urging her team on.

'I assume Ryan has updated you all.' Heads nodded. 'Let's get this sorted then. I've got to meet Tina…' Dawn glanced at her watch. 'In less than twelve hours, and we've got a lot to organise before then.'

'You can't meet her alone,' Ryan said again.

'I don't plan to, but she needs to think I am. She said that if *they* see cops, they'll bolt.'

'So, she's expecting company.' Ryan sat on the corner of Jamison's desk.

'If I read between the lines right, she's planning a trap of some sort.'

'What do you mean?'

'She's using herself as bait. She told me she knew who killed Jane. She also said they would get away with it like they always do.' Dawn approached the murder board. 'So if it isn't Tina, who is it? Let's go over what we've got.'

Sergeant Martin stepped forward with a photo.

'Crash team confirmed registration on the car in the Endeavour River wasn't the Aston and not of any interest.' He stuck a photo of the wreck on the board.

'How's the old guy who got run off the road?'

'Doing okay. Wasn't wearing a seatbelt, which is usually a bad thing, but in this case, he was thrown from the vehicle. Apparently, the stupid old bastard had the side window open because his car windscreen was fogging up. Got on the wrong side of the road and ended up going over the embankment trying to avoid the Aston.'

'So why was Ketut driving at such a pace?' Dawn glanced around the room for input.

'Someone tipped him off?' Ryan offered.

'That's my guess. But who? Tina and Craig came back to Cooktown in a hurry. Left the dog behind and forgot to close the back door. Why did they come back?'

'To find out who killed her friend?' Reynolds suggested.

'Or to tip Richardson off?' Ryan added.

'She could have done that by phone.' Dawn scanned the faces in front of her. 'Where are Farrell and Craig's phone records?'

'I've got them.' Chung waved a print-out in his hand.

'Go over them. Find any numbers of interest. We need to know if Jane called Tina. If Tina or Craig called Richardson.'

'On it.' Chung began separating the paperwork.

Reynolds held her hand out to him. 'I'll grab Craig's.'

Chung agreed and handed them over as Dawn joined Ryan against Jamison's desk. Leaning in, she whispered, 'Tina was more than afraid on the phone, she was heartbroken. I could feel her sadness in every word. She doesn't believe we can hold whoever killed Jane. She gave me the impression she was going to sort this out herself.'

'But she called you.'

'Exactly. She called me. Why?'

'Because she trusts you.' Ryan patted her shoulder. 'And so do I. You've got this Dawn.'

Chapter 45

Dawn finished a phone call, hung up, then crossed the room to the murder board.

'Okay everyone, listen up. We've got leads all over the place and not a lot of things are lining up.'

She pulled the top from a whiteboard marker and tapped next to a picture of Tina. 'I've confirmed Tina's alibi for the time her vehicle was seen collecting Jane from the yoga retreat.'

She marked the details on the timeline.

'And Emily also told me the retreat had a strict no devices policy. So we aren't likely to get any photographic evidence of who was driving Farrell's car.'

Ryan stepped forward, plucked the marker from her hand and circled the picture of Tenneson.

'Parker has confirmed Tenneson is claiming he was being blackmailed. When Jane disappeared, he assumed it was related to the medicinal marijuana bill. But if Richardson and Ketut wanted him to vote in their favour and influence the two senators in the other photos we found, then why kill her?'

Silence greeted the question.

Dawn waved her hands like a conductor. 'Come on people. Let's hear your ideas. No matter how stupid. We need to nut this out.'

Jamison put up his hand up like he was in school.

'To prove they mean business.'

'No. Good idea, but no. They lost their leverage when Jane died. While they had her, they had him by the balls.'

Reynolds rounded her desk and lowered her butt to the edge, finger on her chin.

'Our victim didn't know she was being held. She left the yoga retreat willingly in Tina's car. We have a witness.'

Dawn retrieved the whiteboard marker from Ryan who smiled like he enjoyed the game. Shaking her head, she scribbled on the board.

'Exactly. So either she found out she was in trouble and panicked or this isn't related to Richardson and any drug legislation.'

The drug link felt like a weak motive for murder all along. But as Dawn put a question mark next to Richardson's photo, she wondered again what the motive could be.

Ryan's voice drew her from her thoughts.

'We know Tina was at the retreat, and we have an alibi confirming it, so if she wasn't the driver, who was?'

Dawn nodded, then added a question mark next to Tina's car with the word *DRIVER*.

Dawn turned to eager faces. Reynolds got her attention with a wave.

'So why did Tenneson run and hide?

Dawn added the question next to Tenneson's name on the board.

'Good question. We're still missing something. Tenneson wasn't scared of those guys at the golf course, and if they tossed the Newell Beach place as we suspect, then Tenneson might have given them the code. There were no signs of forced entry, and they could have been looking for Tenneson's videos.'

Everyone remained silent as Dawn paced.

'We need to go over all the evidence so far. Reynolds and Chung, finish with those phone records. We don't have Mrs Lundstrom's diary, but I don't see organised crime risking their entire operation on bribing or blackmailing a politician over legalising marijuana. Let alone killing Tenneson's stepdaughter to make a point.'

Chung pointed to the whiteboard.

'But the dominatrix videos and photos found on Tina Farrell's cloud storage.'

Dawn chewed the end of the marker pen, her eyes scanning the murder board for answers that weren't coming.

'Chase up the evidence. We've got a few hours. We know Craig's credit card was used both times Tina filled up with fuel.' Dawn turned to Reynolds. 'Did you finish checking out the CCTV footage?'

'No, sorry. We've been a bit busy.'

'It's okay. Get onto it now.' Dawn tossed the whiteboard marker back where it came from. 'Let's go everyone. We need to know who all the players are before I walk into the unknown tomorrow morning.'

Activity erupted around her. Dawn didn't move. Ryan stepped up alongside her.

'What are you thinking?'

'I don't know. Something doesn't feel right.' She turned to Chung. 'Can you run something for me? Check what Craig was doing October 8th and 9th. Tina used his card, but maybe.'

'Sure.' Chung clicked keys on his keyboard.

'You think he was with her?' Ryan whispered.

Dawn shrugged. 'He could be our driver, but what's his motive?'

'Ah.' The tone of Reynolds' voice made Dawn turn.

'What?' She glanced at Reynolds' expression.

'I can't believe I didn't check this earlier.' The young officer was mortified.

'What have you found?' Dawn crossed to Reynolds' desk.

'I'm so sorry,' Reynolds said.

'It's okay Reynolds. We've all been busy. What have you found?'

'Check this out.'

Dawn and Ryan rounded Reynolds' desk from either side. Leaning in, they watched as the young constable rewound the footage.

'This is the counter, where the driver paid, except...' Reynolds brought up another recording in the corner. 'This is the driver in the car.'

'Which day was this?'

Ryan pointed to the screen.

'It's Tina's car, not Craig's.'

'So it was the day *before* the retreat.' Dawn strode to the whiteboard, ripping the lid from the marker pen on the way.

'That little bastard. He's been playing us for fools.' Ryan was ready to punch something. 'Withholding the diary. He said he was covering for Tina, but he was with her when she went to the yoga retreat. He could have picked Jane up and killed her.'

'Yes, but the question is still the same. Why?'

'I don't know, but Craig is in it up to his eyeballs.'

'Er, Detective.' Dawn turned to Chung's voice and waited. 'I've checked Constable Craig's roster and he was off work the 7th, 8th and 9th October.'

'So he didn't just drop Farrell off and head home.' Dawn turned to Reynolds. 'How are the phone records going?'

'Craig made a few calls to unlisted mobiles over the past few days. It will take us a few days to trace them and only if they're not pay as you go.'

'Okay, check Farrell's records.'

'Done.' Chung waved a piece of paper. 'A call was made from Richardson's landline to Tina Farrell's mobile at 7.18 a.m. on Thursday the 8th. I checked, and it came from the extension number assigned to our victim's room.'

'That's not long before Jane was seen getting into Tina's car. And it's five minutes after Tina Farrell's cloud account was accessed in Cooktown.'

'Farrell didn't have her mobile on her.' Ryan stated the obvious.

Dawn blew out a breath, trying to let her frustration go. 'No, it looks like Craig did and we just let him go?'

Ryan nodded. 'Do you think he killed her?'

'Tina said something on the phone. This isn't word for word, but something about thinking she knew who killed Jane, but now *knowing* who it was. I told her about her car Ryan.'

Ryan chewed his lip. 'I don't like this one bit, Grave. Tina might be using herself as bait, but it sounds a lot like you could end up a sitting duck.'

'I don't know what she's planning, but I don't think she wants me dead.'

'She could just as easily be in it with Craig. I don't trust her.'

'Neither do I, but the only way to find out what she knows is to meet her out there. We'll be ready.' She glanced at her watch. There were three more hours until sunrise. 'Let's go over our plan team. Let's bring them in.'

Chapter 46

Dawn parked next to Craig's vehicle, wondering how the guy slipped away from his tail and if Tina was with him, would she be safe? She was confident Craig didn't know they were aware he picked Jane up from the retreat.

As she stepped out, a mosquito buzzed around her head. She swore under her breath, berating herself for not lathering up with bug repellent.

Moisture formed on her face, attracting more insects. The air was still as mist rose from the warm ground and floated like mid-city fog. As she stepped from the gravel carpark, onto a narrow trail, wet grass soaked her boots.

She swatted a mozzie with one hand, the other inside her coat pocket on the butt of her pistol. Not the little pocket one she carried all week. As a precaution, she signed out a police issue Glock 22.

Dawn debated over her assumption that Tina was luring her friend's killer out into the open. Ryan was right. Tina could easily be setting a trap for her, but killing one cop wouldn't stop the investigation.

Still, no matter how hard she tried, she couldn't discern a motive for killing Jane. Tenneson was guilty of being a career politician, likely with his finger in a lot of pies. There was no doubt Richardson and Ketut were involved in organised crime and there was a link with Tenneson, but that was for the AFP's organised crime unit to deal with.

Tina owed money and it was now paid off, so she might be guilty of blackmail, but murdering her friend didn't make any sense.

Still, she'd seen people kill their closest friend or family member for love and money. All Dawn knew was Tina was at the retreat when Jane left. There was nothing to say she didn't leave later and meet up with Craig and kill her friend.

The sound of the bush coming to life was all Dawn could hear. Frogs croaked. Kookaburras greeted the rising sun and the undergrowth rustled with the sound of small creatures scurrying away. Dawn shivered at the thought some might be snakes.

The quiet calm was broken with a shrill scream.

Dawn was running before she could get a sense of where the sound came from. Fighting the urge to call out Tina's name, Dawn struggled on through the narrow track. Wispy branches scratched her cheeks. Tall grass threatened to trip her. She bounded over a fallen tree into a clearing and slid to a halt.

'What are you talking about?'

Dawn barely recognised the male voice over the thudding of her heart. She scanned the two people in front of her. Struggling together. A gun twisting and turning between them.

Dawn drew her gun.

'Stop. Both of you. Put the gun down.'

Craig's eyes darted to Dawn for a split second before refocussing back on Tina. His brow creased.

Tina's eyes were wild, unfocussed. But for a moment, her gaze locked on Dawn.

'*He* killed Jane.'

'I didn't...'

Dawn's left hand rose. Craig closed his mouth and let go of the gun. Finally, his police training kicked into gear.

Maybe he was smarter than she thought. He kept the diary a secret and was likely driving when Jane was picked up from the yoga retreat, but did that make him a killer? They still didn't have proof.

Tina drew back with the weapon still in her hands. Her face contorted, the gun shaking in her grip. Craig threw his hands up in front of his face.

'Put… the… gun… down… Tina.

'I can't. He'll get away with it. They always get away with it.'

Dawn's pulse rushed in her ears. It didn't matter if Craig was guilty of killing Jane or not. He was unarmed and backing down.

'Tina. We'll sort this out at the station. Put the gun down.'

The woman's eyes focussed on Dawn's fleetingly. Dawn knew she needed to act, *now*. But shooting Tina wasn't an option.

A rustle to the right surprised Dawn. A glint of sunlight flared obscuring her view. Craig called out. Tina screamed. Dawn rushed in, then froze.

Ketut held Tina hard to his chest, knife in hand. She wondered if it was Ketut Tina wanted to lure out all this time, but then why fight over the gun with Craig?

Craig twitched. Dawn held her hand up, eyes scanning the young constable, then Tina. Everyone froze a moment. Dawn tried to collect her thoughts.

Ketut's voice broke the silence.

'Toss your gun on the ground or I cut her throat.'

Dawn lifted her arms wide, then lowered the gun to the leaf-littered ground, her eyes not leaving Ketut's.

'I don't understand why you killed Jane. Was it an accident?'

Ketut chuckled… deep, throaty. Dawn shivered.

'Kick your gun away Detective.'

Dawn did as he instructed.

'And your backup.'

She opened her jacket to reveal her sleeveless tee-shirt. No shoulder holster or weapon belt.

'I'm not carrying a spare.'

The chuckle sounded again, doing nothing to ease the tension in Dawn's neck. He tapped the blade against Tina's chest, the tip inches from her carotid artery. Dawn's blood ran cold. One slip and the woman would bleed to death.

Tina's eyes were on the ground, her body shaking. Was it rage or fear? Dawn couldn't be sure.

'Okay.' Dawn kept her left hand in the air, then cautiously reached down to her ankle, removing her pocket pistol. She hesitated, considering if she could get off a shot, but Tina was in the line of fire.

As if knowing what Dawn was thinking, Tina lifted her head and defiantly made eye contact.

'Don't let them get away with it.'

Dawn shook her head.

'I'm not going to risk your life, Tina.'

'I'm not worth saving. Jane's death is all my fault.'

'I don't think so Tina.'

Dawn's eyes drifted to Craig whose expression was more calculated than she remembered. Was he a killer? Was he one of the *they* Tina spoke of? Did he lure Jane to her death?

Taking a slow breath, she gauged where her team would be. Ryan would be chafing at the bit to move in, but Dawn wanted all the cards on the table before she showed her hand. Carefully, she tossed the Derringer in the opposite direction to the Glock.

Craig's eyes followed it warily, then snapped to hers.

Was she making a mistake trusting the cop in him? If he was an innocent patsy, he'd back her up. If he wasn't…she hoped her team was ready.

'Where's Richardson? How long have you been doing his dirty work?' Dawn drew the cleaner's attention.

Ketut grinned. His white teeth bright against his darkened skin.

'No talking.' Ketut stepped aside, dragging Tina with him toward Dawn's gun. 'Start walking.' He nodded for her to lead the way down the narrow track.

She noticed him crouch down, dragging Tina with him, to pick up her Glock as she stepped over a log and started in the direction he pointed. She heard Craig fall in behind her as tall trees gave way to spindly paperbarks along the water's edge.

'Is this what you did with Jane, marched her out here to her death?'

Dawn needed to stall. She knew Ryan wasn't far away, but there was no way anyone could get a shot off while Ketut held Tina so close. For the first time in months, she wished Senior Constable was around. Sergeant Martin said he was good with a long-range rifle.

She only hoped Ryan was better.

'I'm sorry. This isn't how I planned it.' Tina's voice quavered from behind Dawn.

Dawn turned to see tears streaming down the woman's face. Ketut was wiry and thin, but strong. His arm held the knife tight over Tina's chest, the blade so close, one slip would end the woman's life.

The Indonesian made eye contact. She glared.

'You won't get away with this Ketut.'

She saw him smile and wave her gun in his left hand, then tap the blade on Tina's chest.

'Detective Ryan!' Ketut's words sent a chill down Dawn's back. 'I know you're out there. Make a move and your girlfriend dies first.'

'What's the plan? I don't get it Ketut. You're going to kill me first? Or Tina? Then what about the constable here? As soon as you fire on me, Detective Ryan will shoot you. You know that. Right!'

Soft footfalls and crushed leaves from behind were her only answer. Sneaking a peek back over her shoulder, she noted Ketut's grim expression.

He knew he was going to die.

She wondered what would make a man so loyal he'd die to stop a witness from revealing secrets. Because the more she thought about it, the more she realised Tina held all the secrets.

She thought about Lisa and Abby and how she was finally reconnecting with them. She couldn't help worrying what Lisa would do if she were killed. There wasn't anything she wouldn't risk protecting her sister and niece.

In that moment, she realised why Ketut might casually accept his fate and risk death. He had one job. Kill any witnesses. He was the cleaner!

She spun around, hands in the air. Ketut stiffened.

'They've got your family, haven't they?'

His eyes widened, then his brow furrowed.

'I can help,' Dawn promised.

'You can't help them. They are in Indonesia.'

Dawn held her hands up higher, stopped and turned completely to face the assassin. Craig frowned and stepped aside, allowing Dawn to focus on Ketut.

'Please. Trust me. We can do this. We can make a statement, saying you died trying to kill us. They won't hurt your family if you're dead.'

'He...' Ketut's knife hand loosened.

Dawn could see him wavering and pressed on.

'Ketut. Put the weapons down. Let's stop and talk about options. You always have options.'

A twig cracked to her left. Dawn spun, expecting Ryan.

'Don't shoot him Ryan.'

Dawn was frozen, eyes on her Derringer in Craig's hands.

'Don't shoot him Craig.'

The young constable ignored Dawn and took aim.

'After everything I've done for you. This is how you repay me?

'Don't Craig. You'll kill them both,' Dawn screamed.

'Two bad eggs in one shot.'

'You bastard.' Tina lunged forward, pulling Ketut off balance. A shot rang out, missing both of them.

All Dawn could think was,

Where is Ryan?

Chapter 47

Ketut's face creased with confusion. Dawn saw Craig realign his weapon toward Tina. The Glock Ketut was holding was now on the ground, halfway between her and Tina. The decision was made before she contemplated it.

Turning, she threw herself toward Craig. His weapon turned her way as her feet left the ground. The last thing she heard was Ryan's voice, growling.

'Stay down or I'll blow your head off. Hands where I can see them.'

She wasn't sure who he was talking to as her body collided with Craig's legs. He crumpled beneath her, his weapon firing past her head. Pain exploded in her ear.

Resisting the urge to grab her head, she wrestled the young constable, crawling up his legs to his torso as he punched her away. One of his legs broke free, his boot glanced her cheek.

Dawn punched at his back, hoping to find his kidney or soft tissue and not bone. A whoosh of air told her she found her target.

Reynolds' voice rung out loud and clear.

'Stay where you are! Don't move Craig.'

The constable didn't stop wriggling. Dawn's eyes found Ryan's as he cuffed Ketut. She thumped Craig in the back once more, but it was Ryan's boot that stopped all movement. Dawn held tight a moment, to be sure Craig was still before rolling to her back in the musty smelling, mulch covered ground.

Her heart raced. Her ears rung and her chest burned from the lack of oxygen. She closed her eyes.

'You bastard.'

Dawn opened her eyes again to see Tina step up and kick Craig in the side. He wouldn't have felt it. Dawn heard the crack, when Ryan's boot collected the constable's jaw. The paperwork was going to be a nightmare, but he wasn't waking up any time soon.

'How could you!' Tina dropped to her knees, sobbing.

Dawn rolled over and crawled to her hands and knees. Rocking there, she struggled for air. Ryan dropped next to her his hand held out to help her up. She was tempted to refuse, but as she glanced into his eyes, he smiled, somehow knowing what she was thinking.

'I know you can manage, but…'

She slapped her hand into his and struggled to her feet as Reynolds crouched down next to Tina and wrapped an arm around her shoulder. It would have been a tender moment, but Dawn knew it wasn't going to last.

As she dusted the leaf matter from her pants, she saw Reynolds help Tina to her feet, turn her and press the cuffs into place around her wrists.

Tina might not have killed her friend, but she kept too much to herself for too long. They needed to interview her, and she'd likely face charges.

The thought saddened Dawn. Tina was left to her own devices too young and did whatever it took to survive. Something Dawn understood all too well.

But the more she thought about where Tina set up her business, the more she was sure Tenneson was involved.

Her mind drifted to Rossi, their marriage and how it ended. He was like her back then. They were both young, alone and incredibly stupid.

Did he deserve another chance?

Ryan patted her shoulder as they entered the carpark.

'You okay? All in one piece?'

'All good. Thanks Ryan.'

Ryan nodded toward the police van.

'Let's get them back to the station. I think Craig is going to need an ambulance, I'll wait around for it.'

Dawn hobbled toward the rising sun.

'It's going to be a long day.'

Ryan reached her car and opened her door.

'Any word on where Richardson is?'

Dawn slipped into the driver's seat.

'Not yet. We've got his photo with every agency. His passport has been flagged.'

She rummaged for keys in her pocket, then slipped them into the ignition. Every muscle ached but not as much as losing a suspect. She glanced up at Ryan who was hanging over the car.

'Let's hope he doesn't have a dozen of them.' She reached for the door. 'See you at the station.'

Ryan didn't move away, his eyes held hers a moment before he stepped back.

'See you at the station.'

Chapter 48

The murder board blurred into a mass of colour and alphabet soup. Dawn needed sleep. Lots of it. But they still didn't have enough evidence to charge anyone with Jane's murder.

As her eyes scanned the photos of the beach house, she puzzled over motive again.

Turning, she spotted Ryan chatting to Reynolds. The young constable flicked her ponytail over one shoulder and giggled.

Dawn liked the ponytail better than the severe bun the woman wore on the first day they met, but as she watched Reynolds' eyes flutter, she fought feelings she couldn't quite explain.

Ryan glanced her way. The smile on his lips disappeared. He nodded, patted Reynolds in a 'Good job mate' kind of way and crossed the room to Dawn.

'What's up?'

Dawn turned back to the murder board and pointed at it as she chewed her lip.

'I'm not seeing a motive for Jane's death anywhere on here.'

'Tenneson. The vote.'

'No. Not buying it. Tina thinks Craig did it. What's his connection to Tenneson and Richardson? Besides, you don't kill someone close to an MP and expect them to cooperate. No. This is personal. Someone took Jane out to the Lagoon. They wanted it to be there because Tenneson would either understand the message or be implicated.'

'The drug legislation still makes sense.'

Dawn didn't respond. Part of her wanted to wrap the case up. They could put together a string of charges to ensure all three of their suspects went to prison for years, but nothing that proved murder. Nothing that would bring closure for Lorraine Nichols.

As her eyes studied the photos of the beach house, the beach where Jane was thought to have gone missing. Rusty tied to the bench. The laptop cord and no laptop.

'The laptop!'

Dawn spun around, seeking out someone who could chase up leads.

'Laptop?' She heard Ryan repeat but ignored him.

'Reynolds. Did you find a laptop at the retreat?'

'Ah.' The young constable's fingers were tapping her keyboard. 'I didn't see one, but I'll check the evidence log. Why?'

'Just a hunch, but our victim and Tina Farrell owned the same model laptop, or at least their cords were the same make and model.'

Reynolds glanced up with pursed lips.

'Nothing on the scene. We still don't have the diary Craig kept out of evidence either.'

'Excellent. I think I can figure out why Jane Nichols called Tina's mobile and why Craig picked our victim up. Now we need to prove who murdered her.'

Dawn crossed the room to stand beside Chung. The young officer glanced up at her.

'Get the techs to chase the IP address of the last person who accessed Tina's cloud account. Time and date too if they can get it.'

Ryan joined her at Chung's desk, his brow creased.

'Don't we need to interview Tina?'

'Not yet. We could interview Craig, but he's still in surgery thanks to a broken jaw.'

Ryan puffed up his chest ready to defend his actions, but Dawn pressed on. 'So that leaves Ketut. I think I can convince him to turn on Richardson.'

'Drugs and corruption aren't our brief. We want a murderer and Tina says it's Craig.'

'Do you believe every woman who smiles at you Ryan?' Dawn pushed off Chung's desk.

'You said you thought she was innocent. I'm the one who said she couldn't be trusted.'

Ryan followed, finger pointing to her, then his chest and back again.

'We need evidence.' Dawn strode toward the interview rooms. 'We talk to Ketut, then hand him over to AFP. I know someone I can contact there.'

'Then we talk to Craig?' Ryan asked.

Dawn didn't respond. Instead, she turned back to see Chung, Jamison and Reynolds all focussed on her retreating back.

Reynolds wore a grin. Chung was frowning and Jamison's mouth hung open like a side-show clown game.

'Someone track down the owner of those mobile phone numbers on Craig's account.'

Reynolds started typing.

'On it.'

Jamison's fingers flashed, along with his grin.

'Let's bet on who gets there first.'

'No contest.' Chung pointed to the printer already humming across the room.

Dawn crossed the room, snapped up the paper, ran her finger down the numbers, times and dates with names alongside. Nothing of interest popped out at her.

'Nice work Chung. Now I need tower locations on the calls from pay as you go numbers.' She glanced at Jamison.

'You can sort that because Chung still needs to follow up the IP info.' She turned to Chung. 'I need it in the next hour.'

Chung gave her his usual, casual scout salute.

Grinning, she turned to Reynolds. 'Get me Tenneson's bank records. Every account he owns.'

'What am I looking for?'

'I reckon you'll know it when you see it. But focus on the accounts in his name, not joint. If my hunch is right, what we are looking for will be in accounts only he operates. Make sure to include his campaign accounts.'

Dawn was desperate to find a motive. They now knew who picked up their victim from the retreat, but they were still hunting down evidence to nail her killer. And something in her gut told her Tenneson and the dump site were the link, but the connection was just outside her reach.

Ryan lent in close.

'Do you want to let me in on the secret?'

'It's only a hunch for now.'

Chapter 49

The wiry Indonesian sat, arms crossed, face stern. Dawn dragged out her chair and sat, fidgeting with a manila folder. Ryan joined her, pressed a button to begin the recording before leaning back, mirroring Ketut's position.

Dawn opened the folder, studying it without seeing it. There was not much they knew about Ketut. Only that he was illegally in the country, a known fixer for drug smuggling operations and a friend of Richardson's.

Dawn glanced up from the folder.

'State your name for the recording.'

Ketut said nothing. Dawn smiled.

'Okay. Ketut. We'll pass you straight on to the AFP. The federal police will do one of two things—deport you back to your employers and we know what they'll do, or, hold you for information in relation to drug trafficking, people smuggling and whatever else your employers are up to.'

Dawn waited. His eyes remained focussed on a spot on the table in front of them. Not the folder. Not his hands or his lap or Ryan. Just an invisible, insignificant spot.

'But you have an option. One that might be favourable.' Still no eye contact. 'Do you like Australia?'

His eyes met hers.

'If I could organise a visa, for you and your family, would you tell me what I need to know?'

'You can't.' The words were barely audible. 'They have my family.'

'You said that, but your country has a very strong stance on drugs. If you tell us what we need to know about Jane Nichols' murder, we can raid your employers and find your family.'

Ketut laughed.

'You live in fairytale.'

Dawn sighed. He was probably right. His family could be anywhere. Possibly not even still in Indonesia.

'Look. I get this isn't ideal. You're right. I can't promise you anything, but I have friends in the AFP. I can pull a few strings. Like I said, maybe we can notify Indonesian authorities and tell them you died here. Maybe then your employers will let your family go.'

'Too many maybes.'

'I know you didn't kill Jane Nichols.'

Ketut's eyebrows rose.

She knew she couldn't get an official statement from Ketut, but she wanted to confirm her theory. Ketut was good at hiding his emotions—most of the time. But she could read people. Their body language, twitches, tells.

'Tina was working with Richardson, wasn't she?'

Ketut pressed his lips together.

That was a yes. A good test question she already knew the answer to.

'Did you find the laptop Jane Nichols left behind?'

A twitch.

'The one with all the blackmail photos on it that Richardson used to coerce politicians to do his bidding.'

A knock on the door made her jump.

Reynolds stuck her head in.

'An immigration lawyer just rocked up to see Mr Ketut here.'

Dawn frowned. Ketut didn't request a lawyer. How on earth did anyone even know he was arrested? As she glanced back to Ketut, she noted the curve of his lip.

Richardson!

Of course he'd want Ketut out from under our scrutiny as fast as possible.

Dawn rose. 'Show them in. I think we have what we need.'

Ryan mumbled something into the recording and followed her out.

A short Asian woman brushed past them. Dawn paid no attention as her eyes fell on the interview room across the hallway.

'We need proof. I can't go in there and interview Tina until we are sure.'

'Sure of what?'

Jamison rounded the corner waving a piece of paper. 'Got it!'

'Got what?' Ryan asked.

'50k, taken from his campaign budget. Spoke with his PA and no one knows what it was for.'

'The exact amount paid off Tina's loan. It insinuates blackmail, but it's not enough.' Dawn mumbled, turning to Ryan. 'We need Craig's statement.'

'He's still unconscious. I thought he killed Jane.'

'Look, I think Tina was blackmailing Tenneson and Jane found out. I think they swapped laptops. But I need proof.'

She turned to Jamison.

'Has anyone traced that IP info yet? We know when the cloud was accessed in Cooktown. I need to know who had the laptop at the time.'

'Chung is still on it.'

'Tell him to hurry up.'

Jamison ducked away cautiously.

'On it.'

Her frustration was obviously evident to everyone.

'All of this doesn't tell us *how* Jane got cocaine into her system.' Dawn pulled her phone from her pocket and dialled. The call connected after one ring.

'Nice of you to call Dawn.'

The doctor's light tone made her smile. Ryan frowned.

'Greg. Sorry to bother you. Have you finished the Nichols' autopsy report yet?'

'Actually, it was done a few hours ago. I uploaded the report.'

'Oh sorry to bother you.'

'Not at all. Can I save you time? What did you need to know?'

'Any idea how the cocaine was administered?'

'Ah, that was tricky. No way to see if there were any needle marks due to the condition of the body, but organs and overall health of the victim didn't indicate she was a regular drug user. Neither did hair samples.'

Dawn waited. Knowing pathologists loved to expand on their findings, and air their knowledge.

'We did find her stomach contents intact, amazingly. She drank kombucha before she died, and tests confirm it was likely laced with cocaine.'

'Thanks Greg. That's exactly what I needed to hear.'

'Ah.' She heard him start to say more but hung up before he could continue.

Turning to Ryan she grinned.

'What?'

'Cocaine was administered in a drink.'

'Okay, so why are you smiling?'

Dawn strode down the hallway to the team room as memories of their search of Tina's house came into her mind.

'Because I think I know when, how and who.'

Rounding the corner, she spotted Reynolds typing in front of her computer. Chung was still busy searching for IP information and Jamison was gone.

She wondered if maybe she'd upset him but brushed it off. He was a big guy and a few frustrated words from her shouldn't be enough to worry him.

'Reynolds. Ring Tammy Gleeson and ask her for a report on what was found in Tina Farrell's car. Ask her to pay special attention to a bottle of kombucha I saw there. We are looking for any traces of narcotics.'

Reynolds picked up the desk phone and dialled.

'Sure.'

Dawn turned, then stopped. She got Reynolds' attention with the wave of her hand. 'And interrupt me as soon as you get the result.'

'Will do.'

Dawn carried on down the hallway. Ryan scurried up alongside.

'What are you thinking?'

'I'm thinking it's time to interview a possible murderer.'

'You think Tina did it now? But she's got an alibi.'

'She has an alibi for when Jane was picked up. Everything else points to her. I hope she left the evidence we need to prove it.'

Chapter 50

Dawn put her hand on the interview room door handle and turned to Ryan.

'Without solid evidence, we've got nothing. Tina isn't stupid. You've seen her file.'

Ryan nodded.

'Single mum. Tough childhood. Left on her own when her mum died.'

'With a huge mortgage to pay by the look of it and no real employment.'

'You think she'd kill her closest friend?'

'I think she believed she had no choice.'

'But where does Craig fit in all this?'

'I don't know yet.' Dawn turned the handle. 'Follow my lead.'

Ryan grinned.

'Always.'

Dawn rolled her eyes as she opened the interview room door.

Tina glanced up, doe-eyed and teary. For a second Dawn wavered, then reminded herself that the woman was a born actress.

Dawn slid out a chair and plonked down with exaggerated tiredness.

'I think you chose the wrong profession Tina.'

The woman's eyes opened even wider, then her brows furrowed as though she were genuinely confused.

'Sorry?'

She kept her voice quiet, gentle. Dawn nearly laughed. She was a dominatrix. Her job was to play the part of a powerful woman. But did that make her a strong woman?

'You fooled me. Totally. For a while.'

Tina seemed to register something in Dawn's words. Sitting back, she lost the doe eyes. The corners of her mouth curved as she sat back in the plastic chair and folded her hands in her lap.

'I don't know what you mean Detective and I'd like to go home soon. This has been a very troubling ordeal. Losing Jane…'

'You can drop the act Tina. We've traced a few things down that make it very clear Tenneson was being blackmailed with images of you and him in your dominatrix dungeon.'

Tina laughed. Dawn's skin crawled.

'I have no idea what you're talking about.'

Dawn carried on as though Tina hadn't spoken, but in the back of her mind she was still piecing the evidence together. A picture popped into her head of artwork in Tenneson's home office. The style, the colours. Was it Tina's handy work?

It was obvious Tina was connected to Richardson. That gave her access to the narcotic which drugged Jane. But something was niggling at her.

'To begin with, I thought Richardson was taking advantage of you. Maybe you didn't know he'd set up recording equipment in your dungeon, but then I realised how unlikely that was.'

Tina's expression turned into a sneer.

'I'd like a lawyer now please.' Her tone was calm, polite even.

'Of course. That's your right, but don't you want to know what we know?'

'I don't care what you know. Whatever you think you know, is wrong. I told you Jed killed Jane. It's up to you to figure out the rest. I've not done anything wrong, and this is shaping up to be a complete stitch up. I knew this would happen. This is exactly why I didn't want to come in. I'd like my lawyer now.'

'Do you have one you'd like us to call? Or do you need a court appointed one?'

Dawn knew Tina didn't have money to spare, at least not money she wanted to spend on a defence lawyer. But would Richardson bail her out? A thought hit her. Richardson was a card worth playing.

'I could call Richardson and ask him if he knows a good lawyer?'

Tina's face contorted. Dawn had found her leverage.

'Once he finds out you've been arrested, he's going to be keen to keep you silent.'

Tina fidgeted. The plastic chair creaked. She licked her lips as she considered the implications. Ketut risked his own life to kill her. What would Richardson or one of his goons do once Tina was released on bail?

'But of course you can have a lawyer.'

Dawn rose. Tina's eyes met hers. A knock on the door broke the staring contest.

Ryan slid his chair under the desk and opened the door, holding it for Dawn. Reynolds met them in the hallway, a huge grin plastered on her face.

'Craig is awake.'

Ryan started down the hallway.

'Great. Let's get his statement.'

Reynolds tapped his arm.

'Hang on. We got the search results from Tina's car.'

Dawn's heart thudded. This could be all they need.

'And.'

'They found traces of cocaine in the empty bottle of kombucha. They've sent it off to get DNA sampling.'
Reynolds waited.

'Finally. Evidence to prove Craig or Farrell killed our victim.'

Ryan sighed. 'But which one did it?'

No one liked the idea of a cop killing anyone.

'Craig said something, out at the Lagoon. He said, "*after everything I've done for you.*" Does that mean he killed Jane for Tina, or he picked Jane up so Tina could kill her later? It was Tina who took Rusty for a walk and made it look like Jane was never in Cooktown.'

Ryan shook his head, a frown creasing his brow.

'But who set up the Newell Beach house? Who made it easy for Tina to blackmail politicians? Someone paid for all the recording equipment and Tina was broke.'

Dawn turned to Reynolds.

'Has the architect gotten back to you yet?' She shook her head. 'Get him on the phone or send Parker and Rossi out to see him. Ryan's right. We need to tie up all the loose ends. I'm thinking blackmail, but Tina's reaction in there a minute ago makes me wonder.'

'Will do Detective, but we've also confirmed the IP address you asked about. Chung found the cloud was accessed via a private hotspot in Cooktown.'

Dawn waited. Reynolds smiled.

'It was Jane Nichols' private phone.' Chung smiled.

'Perfect. Finally, some evidence to back up the theory. The laptops get swapped by accident. Jane finds the blackmail images, maybe even drug related information on Tina's computer. She phones Tina's mobile but gets Craig. Craig comes out and picks her up. She tells him what she's found. Did he know?'

Ryan scoffed. 'What, that his new wife was a dominatrix playing with politicians?'

'We need to finish interviewing Tina.'

'Hang on.' Ryan's voice made Dawn stop.

'What?'

'You still think she did it?'

'I don't know. But the cocaine came from somewhere and we can't tie Craig to Richardson. Only Tina.'

'But why the Lagoon?'

'I don't know.' Frustration edged into Dawn's muscles. 'Maybe it was convenient. No cameras. No witnesses. Or maybe it was a statement. One Tenneson wasn't going to miss. I'm not sure Tina liked the man very much. Call Parker. Ask her to get Tenneson to confirm he was being blackmailed for money, as well as his vote. Warn him that his wife might be interested in knowing the truth if he isn't willing to cooperate.'

Reynolds pointed to her chest.

'Me?'

'Yes, you. And call Tina Farrell a lawyer. She's going to need one.'

Ryan scowled.

'Lorraine deserves the truth either way.'

'Nothing stopping you explaining later,' Dawn grinned.

Ryan shook his head in admonishment but the grin on his lips said he liked how she thought.

'Let's go deliver the bad news to our friend and see what happens. Guilty or not guilty.' Dawn twisted the door handle.

'That is the question.' Ryan finished the sentence.

Chapter 51

Dawn entered to find Tina, hunched over, head in hands staring at a spot on the desk as though the weight of the world sat on her shoulders. Something about the woman's expression made everything Dawn was preparing to say slip away.

The dominatrix looked tired, worn and defeated—usually a good thing for a cop. But Dawn's mind was racing. Was this another act, or had she read the evidence wrong?

The kombucha bottle in the car, the cloud storage full of compromising photos and the money indicating blackmail all pointed to Tina trying to keep her life secret. And if she was innocent, why wasn't she talking and why keep the diary hidden?

Dawn approached the interview desk and waited for Tina to make eye contact. When the woman didn't, she chose a new course of action.

'We've called you a lawyer Tina. You don't need to talk to me now, but I wanted you to know we found evidence in your car to prove Jane was drugged with cocaine in a bottle of kombucha. DNA sampling should prove your friend drank from the bottle.'

Tina swallowed but kept her eyes on the same spot. 'Just get on with it. I told you on the phone that they always get away with it.'

Dawn dragged a chair out from the table and sat, resisting the urge to grab the woman's hands and plead.

'Who are *they* Tina?'

Tina sighed. 'Men. They are all the same.'

Dawn glanced up at Ryan and nodded toward the chair alongside her and the recording equipment.

Her partner frowned but flicked the record button on and dragged his chair in with a squeal as he sat. Dawn screwed up her nose with annoyance. Ryan shrugged. Dawn ignored him and focussed on her suspect.

Studying her a moment, she sighed.

'Tina, is this another act? You've been evasive, and uncooperative. Your behaviour is exactly what I'd expect from a killer trying to side-track a murder investigation. Why else would you keep quiet when you know more about your best friend's murder?'

'You wanted the truth, but it won't do a damn thing. Even that diary Jed took doesn't prove anything.' Dawn waited, letting Tina digest her choices. The woman sucked in a breath. 'I thought he was different. I really did, but...'

Dawn opened her mouth to fill the silence, but a gentle grip on her thigh from Ryan made her stop. Scanning his face, she saw him lift an eyebrow in the silence.

Turning back, Dawn resisted the urge to tell Tina what they knew. Everyone was lying to them. Craig kept the diary under wraps. Richardson didn't report Jane missing from his yoga retreat. Tina took Rusty for a walk and left him tied to a park bench. Tenneson didn't want the beach house searched and ran off, claiming he was in danger from the thugs he was chummy with at the golf club.

Dawn was so lost in her muddled thoughts she jumped when Tina broke her silence.

'I didn't kill Jane.'

Dawn resisted the urge to say *that's what every murderer says*.

'I realised Jane and I switched laptops when I got home after the retreat. I knew she was missing, and I was worried she found out about the drugs.'

A thought struck Dawn and she couldn't keep quiet any longer. Tina was going in circles, and she needed answers.

'You said you wouldn't say anything without a lawyer when we first interviewed you.'

'Richardson told me to take Rusty for a walk and make it look like Jane disappeared a day later. He wanted to avoid the attention. When you said her body was found in Cooktown.' She didn't need to say more. Dawn read between the lines. Tina grew up tough and self-preservation was instinctive.

'I told you on the phone about Jane being picked up in your car after the morning yoga session. That's why we searched the car and found the tainted drink.'

Tina puffed out a breath and nodded, her eyes on her hands.

'It made sense as soon as you said that on the phone. I thought Richardson killed Jane, but when you said that… I can't believe I missed it.'

'Missed what?'

'You know I was at the retreat without my phone when Jane got in my car.'

'Yes, but Jane could have been killed later. When you met Craig out at Keatings Lagoon.'

Tina lifted her head and fixed her hazel eyes on Dawn. They glistened with unshed tears.

'I was with dozens of people during the art exhibition after breakfast. I didn't leave the retreat until Jed picked me up. I told you, I didn't kill Jane.'

'But you know who did.'

Another sigh.

'It doesn't matter. I've got no proof.'

'How does the blackmail fit in?'

'I've never blackmailed money or favour out of Tenneson. It's him you should be charging. He is a dirty old…'

A knock on the door made Dawn turn as a crack appeared.

'What is it Reynolds?'

'We've got a DNA match on the water bottle.'

'Excellent.' Dawn rose.

'And a partial fingerprint.' Reynolds continued.

Dawn turned back to Tina who lifted her hands in surrender. 'I can tell you who killed Jane. But it's up to you to find the evidence to prove it. Like I said, they always get off.'

'We also have the information on the architect,' Reynolds offered.

Dawn was beginning to understand why Tina's paintings were in Tenneson's office, but she needed Tina to explain.

Dawn waved Reynolds from the room. 'I'll be out in a second Reynolds. Good job.'

When Reynolds closed the door, Dawn turned toward Tina.

'You need to stop going in circles Tina. I'll get the proof, but you need to give me a name. If you weren't involved in blackmailing Tenneson, how did you get 50k of his money?'

Technically it wasn't Tenneson's money, but Dawn wasn't about to reveal that.

'He bought some of my paintings to make it legitimate, but it was payment for services rendered. He's been screwing with me for years, literally.'

Dawn nodded, understanding the underlying inuendo. Tina was only in her early twenties. Ryan appeared to be even less impressed as he fidgeted by her side. He might not like Tenneson, but he was related to the man.

'If you didn't kill Jane, then that leaves …'

'Jed.' Tina's tone was flat.

'But why?'

'I don't know.'

Dawn started to piece things together. Jane Nichols tells Constable Craig she found photos of Tina having sex with Tenneson, right under his nose. But why kill Jane? Surely, he'd want to kill Tina?

'How did he get the cocaine? Was he in Richardson's employ?'

Tina laughed.

'No. Tenneson's.'

Dawn shook the shell-shock away.

'What's Tenneson's connection to drugs?'

Tina remained silent. She tried another question.

'You're saying Craig took the diary for Tenneson?'

Tina shrugged. 'Possibly?'

'If he worked for Tenneson, and found out about your relationship...'

'It wasn't a relationship. It was a business. I recorded the sessions and gave them to Tenneson. I had no idea what he was using them for, but I kept my own copies on the laptop, which Jane got by accident.'

'If you weren't blackmailing Tenneson, then why did he have photos in his locked desk drawer?'

Tina shrugged and pursed her lips. 'He was a dirty bastard. When my mum died, he came over, a lot. Maybe he liked to keep a souvenir when I wasn't in his reach?'

'So why the videos with the two senators?'

'Nothing to do with me. Tenneson has been working with Richardson and I'm sure the senators aren't the only people they blackmailed. I've had a lot of clients over the years.'

'Where's your laptop?'

'I wish I knew, but everything is in the cloud.'

Dawn nodded, knowing they'd already accessed the information, but they needed more than Tina's testimony to put someone like Tenneson behind bars. They still hadn't found her client list. She shook the thought away and forced her mind back on the murder. Organised crime wasn't her job.

But a little voice in her head told her protecting women like Tina was. She silenced it.

'Why would Jed kill Jane out at Keatings Lagoon?'

Tina puffed out her cheeks.

'Jed's been on Tenneson's payroll forever. That's how we hooked up again. We went our separate ways after school, but he moved back after joining the police force. He knew I was in deep, and we had plans to get out once the house was paid off, but if Jane found the photos and showed him.'

Tina shook her head.

'Poor Jane. She probably thought she could trust Jed when he answered my phone. He's a cop after all.'

'That doesn't explain Keatings Lagoon.'

'You'll have to ask him. Maybe when he saw those photos, he wanted to frame Tenneson. Or it could just be a coincidence. He might not have known Tenneson was connected to the Lagoon. Jed's not the brightest guy.'

Ryan chuckled.

'An understatement. He's still cuffed to a hospital bed, so maybe it's time we asked him what he was thinking.'

Ryan slid his chair back. Dawn wanted to ask so many questions about Tenneson but for now, they needed to arrest a killer—if they could find the evidence they needed.

'We'll keep you here for your own protection Ms Farrell. I'd seriously think about turning over all you know about Richardson and Tenneson's involvement in this drug operation.'

Tina glanced up as Dawn slid her chair under the desk. There was something in the woman's eyes telling Dawn hell would freeze over before she turned on Richardson.

Tenneson on the other hand—maybe there was a slim chance they had enough to put him behind bars for grooming a minor and setting up an illegal sex business.

But like Tina said, money and contacts often protected guys like Tenneson. But Constable Craig wasn't a brain surgeon. If he had links to Richardson, and was now guilty of murder, maybe he'd roll on Tenneson and Richardson. Maybe!

Chapter 52

The room bustled with bodies as everyone collated evidence. Dawn scribbled on the whiteboard while the printer produced a copy of the report confirming Constable Craig handled the tainted kombucha bottle.

It was only a partial print. He must have thought he'd wiped the bottle down, but not thoroughly enough.

Her phone pinged in her pocket. She retrieved it and read the message.

Dinner at ours.
Bella has cooked up a storm.
Bring Clint.

Dawn smiled, put her phone away and clapped her hands like a school mistress. All eyes fell on her.

'Right. Chung. Send Parker the details she'll need for Tenneson's arrest. We can't link him to Richardson and drugs, but the architect from the Newell Beach property has confirmed he was the one who designed the hidden room. A search of his bank records should show the camera equipment, or the tradesmen he paid to set it all up, but if not, the equipment serial numbers should do the job.'

'On it now Detective.'

Dawn sorted out papers on the Senior Constable's desk, not feeling guilty about taking over his space since he'd failed turn up for work yesterday, or today.

'Tina's testimony should be enough, but I think his wife might have a thing or two to say about Tenneson grooming Tina when she was a minor. Something about her body language told me Tina wasn't the only one.' She glanced at Ryan who nodded. 'Get Parker to reinterview Mrs Nichols.'

Chung nodded, already picking up the desk phone.

Dawn rolled her chair under the desk, and despite her lack of sleep, a lightness filled her spirit. Deep down she was relieved Tina wasn't involved in the murder of her friend.

But the systematic abuse of a young woman riled her more than she could contain. Maybe it was her own history which fuelled the rage, but Tina's comment about *them* always winning, or getting away with it, hit a raw place in Dawn's heart.

'Reynolds, is Jamison still at the hospital with Craig?'

'Yep. He's not left him alone since he regained consciousness.'

'Great job everyone.' Dawn collected her new police issue weapon from the safe and slipped it into the shoulder holster. The weight of the weapon was comforting.

Ryan grinned.

'It suits you.'

She slipped her thin linen jacket over the top and led the way from the office.

'Don't get used to it. I've got a house to renovate and a job to get back to in Adelaide.'

Ryan mumbled something incoherent, but she was on her way out the door, her mind on Craig.

She waved the paperwork in her hand as Ryan pressed the unlock button on his Mustang.

'I've printed the report confirming Craig's partial was on the bottle. Nothing like forensic evidence to get a suspect talking.'

Ryan shook his head as he slid into the driver's seat.

'The kid was dumb to think we wouldn't notice the missing diary, but not thoroughly wiping his prints is beyond stupid.'

Dawn clipped her seatbelt on.

'Not throwing it away was stupid, unless he hoped to frame Tina.'

Ryan shook his head and smiled.

'If he did, he didn't know she had a solid alibi.'

Dawn laughed.

'Yeah. Not the brightest. Let's hope he's stupid enough to bury Richardson.'

The hospital was only two streets back from the police station. Ryan parked out front and locked the car as they entered the emergency department. Dawn flashed her badge and was waved down the hallway, past the triage rooms and into the wards.

A nurse on the duty desk glanced up. Dawn showed her ID again.

'Detective. Your boy is down the end of the hallway in an isolated ward to the left.'

'Thanks.' Dawn stepped away from the counter and waited for Ryan to draw alongside before strolling down the hallway and turning left.

Jamison lingered in the hallway, laughing with a dark-haired woman with full lips and sparkling brown eyes.

He was so intent on his conversation, he failed to see them approaching. Dawn cleared her throat.

'Ah, Detective. Ah.'

'Jamison, how's our suspect doing?' Dawn smiled at the nurse.

'I'll catch you later Sam.' The nurse touched the tall officer's arm. He blushed.

'Yeah. Sure Kristy.'

Dawn realised she didn't know Jamison's first name. Sam. It suited him. She watched him smile at the retreating nurse, then cleared her throat again.

'Ah. Yeah. Suspect. He's awake, just been served dinner.'

'I don't need a running commentary *Sam*,' Dawn teased.

'Sorry Detective.'

'Just messing with you Constable. Good job and sorry about being such a tough boss the last few days.'

'No. You're not. A tough boss, that is.' Jamison pushed the door open as he spoke. 'Not, *not* sorry.' Jamison stumbled.

'I know what you mean Jamison. Hang out here.'

'Will do.'

Dawn entered the room, Ryan a few steps behind her. Constable Craig was finishing off his food, through a straw. His broken jaw was wired shut. Red and purple bruises were forming right up to his eyes. Interviewing him when he couldn't speak was going to be very difficult.

'Constable Craig,' Ryan scoffed.

'Don't you mean *former* Constable.'

'Sorry Detective. You are correct.' Dawn tipped her invisible hat at Ryan. 'Jed Craig, you are being arrested for the murder of Jane Nichols…you have…' Loud voices in the hallway made her stop and turn.

Jamison's voice was clear 'You can't go in there.'

Another male voice, then another.

'Oh. Yeah. I don't know …' Jamison hesitated.

The door opened, Ryan crossed the room to intercept the intrusion, but it wasn't a nurse or doctor forcing their way into Craig's hospital room.

Ryan's gun was in his hands before Dawn could react. Two muscle bound guys with tattoos all the way up their arms and around their necks loomed in the doorway. Both wore jeans, white tee-shirts and carried pistols strapped around their waist and tied to the bottom of their thigh.

'Put your hands up,' Ryan yelled.

The door opened, hitting one of the men in the back. Jamison stumbled in.

'Wait up Ryan.' Dawn yelled and waved her hand to halt her partner. 'They're AFP.'

Ryan threw her a look but didn't lower his weapon. The shorter of the men lifted his hands in the air.

'Sorry. We called ahead to the station but missed you, so came straight here.'

'What the hell are you doing here Anderson?' Dawn glanced at Craig and sighed when she saw the stupid grin on his face.

It seemed he wasn't as dumb as she thought he was. At least not when it came to saving his own skin.

'Will someone tell me what the hell is going on?' Ryan lowered his weapon but didn't holster it.

'Your boy over here is coming with us.' Anderson's kiwi accent brought back memories that curled Dawn's toes. His eyes met hers. 'Do you want to tell your man what's what?'

'He's not my …' She shook her head. Anderson hadn't meant what she thought. He grinned. Ryan frowned.

'How did you find out we were arresting him?'

'Union rep contacted us yesterday. Said we needed to come grab him before you did.'

Dawn turned on Craig. 'You little …' She sighed. 'You told your rep you murdered our victim and let us run around … and you kicked me …'

'We'll preview your evidence, but Richardson is our target and we've been given authority to make a deal.'

Dawn opened her mouth, closed it and threw her arms in the air.

'He murdered an MP's stepdaughter.' She pulled out Tenneson's name because it suited her. She failed to tell them the very same MP was likely going to jail very soon.

'He can bury an entire drug operation.' Anderson crossed the room and uncuffed Craig's wrist from the side rail before opening the cabinet alongside the bed and pulling out a bag of clothing.

Craig swung his legs over the edge of the bed. Dawn rounded on him and shoved him back down.

'The war on drugs is a waste of time. Someone else will step up and replace Richardson. But this guy *murdered* a young woman. We still don't know why. Her mother deserves closure. She was only twenty-four, with her whole life ahead of her.'

Anderson grabbed Craig by the arm and hoisted him out of bed and shoved the bag of clothes into his chest.

'I'm not taking you anywhere in that.' He eyed Craig's hospital gown. 'Put on some pants.'

Dawn's earlier good mood evaporated.

'You can't take him Anderson.' She started toward the AFP officer, but Ryan's hand landed lightly on her shoulder.

'Let it go Dawn. He's caught. We've done our job.'

Craig pulled on his shorts, ripped off his gown and shoved on a shirt before Anderson turned him around and pressed the loose cuff onto his bare wrist.

'Listen to your man there Grave,' Anderson smirked.

This time he was insinuating they were a couple, not merely work partners.

'You really are a bastard you know.'

'Just doing my job Grave.' Anderson marched Craig out of the room.

Dawn gaped at his back, reminding herself why she didn't date cops.

Chapter 53

The large kitchen bustled with activity. Abby sat on the worn wooden table licking a bowl of chocolate cake batter that was plastered from ear to ear along with her grin.

Lisa handed Dawn a glass of white wine.

'Here. Take this and get out the way. It's chaos in here.'

Lisa's cheeks were flushed. Michael and Clint were on the balcony, talking in hushed voices. Dawn shook herself as she internally referred to her partner by his first name. It's what Lisa always called him.

But Dawn chose to keep the man at arm's length, for good reason. The position with the Queensland Police was temporary—to stop the boredom while she renovated the family home.

Dawn crossed the kitchen toward the door leading to the balcony. Lisa put a gentle hand on her arm and nodded in the direction of Abby and Bella.

'I hope you don't mind. I've asked her to stay with us.'

Dawn was speechless. The idea of Abby having a grandmother figure was good, but confronting.

Not trusting her words, she said nothing and smiled. Lisa let her arm go and Dawn rushed to open the screen door and escape to the balcony before she said something she would regret.

Ryan spotted her, holding his hand up to interrupt Michael.

'Dawn. You okay. You look like you're about to throw up?'

Michael laughed.

'We've seen that out here before. Pretty spectacular.'

Dawn suppressed the memory of hurling her guts up over the balcony. It wasn't a memory worth reliving.

She sipped her wine and shook her head, reminding herself that one was her limit. Especially after Lisa's news. Did she have a say? Probably not. This old Queenslander was Lisa's forever home. It was Dawn who left and took twenty years to come back. It wasn't her place to dictate who lived there … but Bella?

Turning to Michael, she leant in close. Ryan hovered.

'Did you know Lisa invited Bella to stay? Where is she going to sleep? My room still?'

'I've still got a room,' Ryan offered.

'You rent the place. How is that going to work when you go back to Cairns?'

'Well, actually I bought the place.'

Dawn gawked. Then shook her head.

'Of course you did.'

Michael started laughing. Dawn glared at him.

'What's so funny?'

'Your face. Honestly. You've spent so long alone. You don't understand the value of family.'

Dawn frowned, glanced at Ryan for support, and got none.

'He's right you know.'

'For crying out loud!'

Michael patted her shoulder.

'It's only for a few weeks. She's a lonely old lady who virtually witnessed a murder. Give her a break.'

The screen door creaked. Lisa appeared with a wide smile.

'Michael. Can I borrow you a minute?'

'Sure.' He stepped away and disappeared inside.

Dawn rubbed her hands over her face.

'You look tired.' Ryan's tone was gentle.

She shrugged.

'I am, but this is good.' She waved her hand toward the kitchen where a hum of activity filtered through the screen door.

'Any word from AFP?'

'Fortunately. Yes. At least we can give Lorraine some closure.' Ryan clinked his beer bottle with her wine glass. 'Craig got the cocaine from Richardson. I don't think he realised what the idiot planned to do with it. AFP are still digging, but Tenneson might face a few more charges before the investigation is over, but I digress.'

She swilled her wine, trying to make it last.

'Do you need a refill.'

'No.' She shook her head. Her relationship with alcohol was a conversation for another day. 'Craig took Jane to the Lagoon because of its convenience. He had no idea Tenneson opened it. He was simply looking for a secluded site, close to the road and not far from town. The marshy, deep, croc-infested waters were just there.'

'He really isn't a bright spark.'

'Bright enough to get his rep to call AFP in.'

'We don't know he thought of that.'

'True.' She sipped another tiny mouthful.

'Did they find the green cord?'

'It was a lanyard from the retreat. Jane would have already had it around her neck.'

'So she went with him willingly, like you said.'

Dawn shrugged and drained her glass.

'He was a cop. She trusted him.'

Ryan sculled the last of his beer.

'Did he say why he killed her?'

'Not for Tenneson, or Richardson. He said he did it to protect Tina.'

'The dumb shit. He killed her best friend. Her only friend.'

'Yep. Apparently, he did it to prevent Jane from confronting her stepfather and ruining Tina's business arrangement with the politician. You were right. It's always sex, love, power or money. Seems this time, it was love.'

Ryan shook his head as the screen door creaked, then slammed against the wall. Abby flew onto the balcony, chocolate cake batter still on her lips.

'Mummy says it's dinner time and we're celebrating.'

Dawn glanced at Ryan who shrugged.

Abby rushed forward and grabbed Dawn's free hand.

'Come on. You get the best seat.'

Dawn glanced over her shoulder, her eyes meeting Ryan's before Abby hauled her inside.

'What are we celebrating Abby?'

'Bella is selling her house and giving us the money to finish the renovations. We can put a new room on for her and finish the new kitchen and you'll have that thingy bathroom you wanted and...'

Dawn didn't hear the rest of Abby's prattling. Her head was spinning. Just over a month ago she was living alone in Adelaide. Working crazy hours. No social life. Few friends except work acquaintances and now...here she was in Cooktown.

A place she swore she'd never return to, and living with her sister in the house that haunted her childhood.

'Here.' Abby pulled Dawn down into the seat at the head of the table. 'You sit here and you, Detective.' Abby reached for Ryan's hand and dragged him to Dawn's left. 'Sit here and you.' Abby helped Mrs Lundstrom into a chair at Dawn's right. 'Sit right here and make plans with Auntie Dawn.'

Abby stepped back with hands on hips, a wide grin and sparkling eyes like she'd created a masterpiece.

Dawn sighed. Ryan leant over.

'The spare room offer still stands.'

Dawn was about to take him up on the offer, but a cold hand touched hers. She turned to see Mrs Lundstrom's shy smile. For a second, Dawn wondered if it was the same expression which convinced Lisa to let the woman stay, but as Bella squeezed her hand, she understood what had occurred.

'Thanks for letting me stay Luv. I know it isn't what you planned.'

'What about your house, and garden and your family? I saw all the photos on your walls.'

Bella was silent a moment. The bustle of plates and cutlery faded into nothing as Dawn watched the older woman swallow hard.

'They are gone Luv.'

Dawn was about to ask more, but Bella plastered a grin on her lips.

'Besides, if you go back to Adelaide, you know I'll be here to look after them this way.'

Ryan leant across Dawn with a mouth already full of mashed potato.

'She's not going back to Adelaide Mrs Lundstrom.'

Bella waggled her finger at Ryan.

'I told you to call me Bella and that's fabulous news.'

Dawn glanced at the two people either side of her, one then the other and sighed.

'Do I get any say in any of this?'

The answer didn't come from Clint or Bella alone. Every voice in the room echoed the word.

'No!'

Dawn gaped, then grinned.

'In that case. Where the heck am I sleeping tonight?'

****

Thanks for reading! I hope you enjoyed *Grave Intent.* I'd love to see your review at your favourite online bookstore.

Grave Mistake - Book 3 in the *Dawn Grave* series, will be available from all good bookstores in late January 2025. Or you can preorder via my website at www.fionatarr.com

If you would like to learn more about me or my writing, you can follow me on Facebook or Instagram, or visit my website www.fionatarr.com.

If you are looking for something to read while you wait for the next instalment in the *Dawn Grave* Crime Series, you might like to consider my *Opal Fields* Series.

Join Constable Jenny Williams as she searches for her missing cousin in *Her Buried Bones*. Book 1 in this bestselling Australian Crime series set in a remote mining town.

‹

Printed in Great Britain
by Amazon

52183975R00180